# swimming inside the sun

## David Zweig

SECOND GUESS MEDIA / NEW YORK

Copyright © by David Zweig 2009
Various forms of this book are Copyright by David Zweig 2006, 2007, 2008

Library of Congress Control Number: 2009904849

ISBN: 978-0-615-29750-7

Published by Second Guess Media
www.secondguessmedia.com

Book design by J.J. McGowan
Some interior illustrations by Aaron Meshon

The following people helped bring this book to life.
An eternal thanks to:

Readers: David Yoo, Nick Fowler, Nellie Kurtzman, Ron Carlivati. Graphics Gurus:
J.J. McGowan, Shoba Seric, Aaron Meshon, Ayako Otoshi, Jason Bodner, Marc Levitt.
Hard drive support: Susan Zweig. All around everything: Doreen Bucher.

I got static in my head
the reflected sound of everything

Elliott Smith,
*Tomorrow Tomorrow*

# swimming inside the sun

I am not here. I know it seems like I'm here. But I am not.

I am puttering around my apartment in slippers and yesterday's boxers and t-shirt. The place is so warm the bottom of its lone window is fogged. I crack it open then lean over, swiveling my head up and down and side to side in the stream of frigid air. I put my lips in the crack and breathe, entertained watching my breath outside. I try to remain still, nervous I'll inadvertently kiss the soot-covered windowsill. I pull back carefully like I'm removing a bone from the guy in *Operation*.

It's sometime in the afternoon, the exact hour really doesn't matter. I pick up a fresh package of post-it notes off the coffee table and unwrap it, maniacally crinkling the cellophane wrapper before throwing it to the floor. The new pad of yellow squares is like an asthmatic's inhaler to me, even if it's not always needed I'm relieved to have it near. And what the hell, I wasn't planning on writing, I was just opening the pack for something to do, but now that it's in my hands, words, ideas, theories are frantically emerging in my head like code running across a computer screen. I start scribbling. There's not enough space for me to write comfortably at the table. I shove the dusty 4-track out of the way setting off a tectonic shift of magazines and notes and the plate from last night's burrito. A *Victoria's Secret* catalogue that was accidentally put in my mailbox but I kept anyway and—this is kind of embarrassing—an essay contrasting Adorno and Baudrillard that I printed-out off the web, all ten numbing pages of it, spill to the floor. I keep a peripheral eye on the 4-track as part of it now is hanging over the edge. I make a mental note to move that damn thing off the table already; I don't know why it's here, I haven't recorded anything in months. It's as much of a farce being out in the open as that guitar propped in the corner.

But let's pull back a little:
See the edges of the screen now in view, then the seats, as we keep

pulling back, appearing row by row. Until we see me. There I am, in the theater, about twenty rows back, watching me on the screen in my apartment. It's a good-sized screen in one of those newish, plush, suburban-style theaters that are nearly everywhere in the city these days. I mourn the closing of any art-house joint, quirky seats, poor sightlines and all, but reluctantly, I admit it: like the sensible dad trading in his roadster for the minivan, I prefer the comfort of this charmless place. But I'm getting distracted. What's important is this is what I mean by I am not here. I mean, I am here in the theater, not there in the apartment. But I really am there, in the apartment. This distance, separation, the third-person watching of myself—I am sick, it's an illness, bad wiring, faulty current, perhaps it's chemical, they think everything's chemical these days. But maybe it's not. Maybe it's a gift. Not a gift one wants necessarily but nevertheless, a sort of superpower like x-ray vision only not cool like that.

So there I am, up on the screen. I'm sitting on the couch hunched over the table, my head down, intently scrawling away. It's awfully awkward seeing myself, especially alone (as in alone on the screen). And even though no on else is in the theater to see this, there's something so vulnerable about it; it's still creepy feeling there is a voyeur watching you even if the voyeur is yourself. And there's an awareness of yourself you think you want to have, until you are presented with the evidence. It's like hearing your voice on someone's machine. *I really sound like that?*

Up on the screen I see me turning my head spying the 4-track anxiously. Seeing it hang over the edge gives me the same unease as standing on one of those dinky balconies that jut off the facade of high-rise apartment towers. But if it hasn't fallen by now, I reason, it won't fall.

The separation spells have been happening for so long I don't even remember when this all started. And it used to be just once in a while but these days—ever since I got dropped, that's when it really began to pick up—it seems as though it's happening at some point every day, and maybe even all the time on some low-grade level. Sometimes I can't even tell if it's on or off. I'm left stranded in a dimensional jetlag, conscious life reduced to a woozy fusion of two worlds, the purity of the Now sullied by a vague sense of awareness, self-consciousness, ever-present like a TV station's ghosted logo forever in the bottom corner of the screen.

And, so, as I am watching myself hunched over the table, starting on a fifth little square of yellow paper, writing with a fervor and hand-cramp not reached since the days of Mr. Saliventi's twelfth-grade history tests (all-essay obviously), I try to remind myself that there is a world where there is only one POV, one angle through which life is experienced, *the* angle, where the brain only registers *Now*.

Without perceiving the transition, I've come back to that world. The screen having dissolved with the same unconscious trajectory as falling asleep. I am no longer aware of the film, I am simply inside it, and I am once again wholly present, here.

It is now sometime later in the day. I have left the theater. I have left my head. I have left my apartment!

I'm walking down Lower Fifth Avenue and it's bracingly cold. My face hurts from the wind but as usual I forgot my scarf so I must suffer. But this bitterness outside makes me feel good. Feel good because it's the bite, that slap in the face, that proverbial pinch that makes me feel alive. Glorious discomfort. (But discomfort nonetheless, so) I keep adjusting the collar on my pea coat that is now turned up to protect my scarfless neck. The coat is old and the collar keeps flopping down, so for the past three blocks I've been holding it up with my right hand, the pain in which is now quickly progressing to a raw numbness. My other hand however is toasty warm, resting in a loose fist in a pocket. This doesn't seem fair at all to my right hand.

I imagine my hands are different people and the right hand/person is terribly suffering; he's a Con-Ed guy working on the gas lines in the street in the dead of winter, even his insulated Timberlands and Carhart jumpsuit are not enough to battle hours of manual labor in the cold. At the same time, the privileged left hand/person is a beautiful coed taking a nap on her (perhaps inappropriately) adoring professor's requisite leather couch in his cozily heated office as a gentle snow falls on the pastoral quad of the main campus outside his third floor leaded paned window.

I could even things out and switch hands but if poor Righty is going to be representing the utility company workers he's going to have to put in his time and suffer some more. After all, those guys are out there all day! I feel like I need to write something down on a note but I don't have any post-its in my pocket so I'll have to remember it for when I get home. But I'm not going to talk about the notes and all that stuff now. Perhaps we're already getting sidetracked a bit too much from the action and I don't want to lose you, so we'll just get to all that stuff later. Ok, so . . .

As I cross 10th Street going south, I see my wife approaching all bundled up, her scarf, eight miles long, billowed around her neck, like a giant cradle for her head. From underneath a gray knit hat hangs a curtain of sleek dark-brown hair that disappears behind her back. She notices my stare and returns a stone-faced glance revealing nothing except that she must have some interest in me on some level, otherwise she wouldn't even have looked. My wife's face looks strong but sad, sweet even. She wears an expression indeterminable between solemn longing and mere fleeting interest—This look I receive on the streets so often from them, my passing wives of New York City, betrays only what I allow myself to believe.

We hold each other's eyes as we approach and she even turns a little as we pass but she does not break stride and after one more step, she abruptly turns her head back forward and our moment is gone. And she is gone, down the street and from my life. What did her look mean?

*I am lonely too. Come get me, please! Don't let me slip away!*

My steps slow. If I run I'll catch her, she can't be more than a block away.

I rehearse the line in my head, "Excuse me, I don't mean to frighten you but it seemed like you and I shared something there for a moment." But:

I keep walking. Because I know that nothing is ever as good as that moment. Because in that glance is everything I could ever want and dream. Because in that moment there is no future and there is no past. Because in that moment I am unencumbered by reality and left to the beauty of the unknown. And everything remains perfect when it is unknown. But still . . .

I have so many wives out there on the street. If only we could just tell each other . . . Inside me something smolders with such vehemence I see ambers under my skin. I stop abruptly and turn around. I think I see her head amidst the other walkers but I'm not sure. At this distance they all appear just a bobbing, impressionist marble of grays and browns. I turn back around and amble on. Then, with head ducked to the wind, I quicken my pace. There will be another. There always is.

I

Andrea Leibman lived upstairs from me. I was attracted to her in that way that we are attracted to certain women we always see, like the ones in school or in an office—by default. Newness always excites but strangely there's something about familiarity too that can make some women appealing. Maybe it's that they're easier subjects for a lazy mind in search of fantasy. I've never been one to jerk off to images of models or movie-stars, their beauty and celebrity, their very distance, prevents me from ever buying into the fantasy. But with Andrea, someone whose comings and goings I had witnessed for upwards of four years, making the leap one day from small talk in the stairwell to sweaty, naked, impulsive sex in one of our apartments—while basically absurd in a porno-movie-plot-twist way—still held plausibility. That it technically was possible with her seemed to be enough.

Early one evening I was leaving the building when I saw her in the lobby getting her mail.

"Hey Andrea," I called to her back. She had on a black t-shirt and neon pink pencil skirt. The color combo reminded me of a black-light poster.

"Hi Dan." She gave a quick, almost not-even-a-glance my way as she closed her mailbox with one hand and read the top envelope from the stack of mail held in her other hand. Andrea was always pleasant to me whenever we saw each other in the building or occasionally passed each other on the street, but I always felt there was a thinly veiled aloofness underneath, that when she was talking with me she knew she was better than me and she knew that I knew that.

"So. What are you up to these days? I haven't seen you in a while."

"I haven't been around. I just got back from Myanmar."

"Cool." Where the fuck was Myanmar? "What were you doing there?"

"Backpacking around. Just . . . absorbing." It always seemed like she was either on the way to or from the airport, meeting with people in LA or going hiking in some trendy exotic place like Laos or Tibet. Never mind that my trekking fantasies never could get beyond picturing myself with the runs in South America or demented with oxygen depletion on the side of some mountain in Nepal, I still was jealous of her adventures. It felt like I hadn't left New York in ages. "What's going on with you? How's the music?" she said with a strange inflection, like she was trying to zing me. Or was I just imagining the inflection? I knew she thought I was one of those guys who just likes to *say* he's a musician so he can sound cool, perhaps as much to himself as to everyone else, but behind all the motions—the erratic shows, the failed albums—is just a guy working crappy jobs, destined for nowhere.

"Going well." I flashed a big smile.

"Great," she said raising an eyebrow. What did *that* mean? "Well, I'll let you get going," she said tapping the edges of the envelopes into her palm.

"Yeah. Just heading out for a bite. I think it's time for Burritoville."

"Ooh," she dragged out the "ooh," pursing her lips, bending the note down, "Burritoville. Not my thing."

"Oh come on. It's Mexellent," I said and headed toward the vestibule.

As I pulled the door she called to me, "I'm having a party tonight, if you want to stop by."

"Thanks. Not sure what I'm doing," I lied, "but maybe I'll swing by."

"Great." She was backpedaling toward the stairs now. "So I'll see you later."

"You know they have a neon sign," I said, leaning against the door, my voice suddenly sounding different from inside the vestibule.

"Who?"

"Burritoville. They have a sign that says Mexellent . . . I'm just saying . . . it was their joke not mine."

"Oh."

"You know . . . I didn't want you to think . . . it's not my word," I clarified.

"Oh," she said again and disappeared into the stairwell.

The TV from the girl's apartment next door is blaring at geriatric listener levels. God, I'm so sick of hearing her damn TV on all the time! And being annoyed with her for blasting her TV means that inevitably I get mad at myself because it reminds me that I'm home all the time to hear it. She's watching a sit-com because there's a glaringly fake explosion of laughter every few seconds with almost metronomic regularity. She just switched from what clearly is her favorite show because I hear it nightly, *America's Funniest Home Videos*. It must be in syndication on some stratospheric advanced cable channel. (I hope—that it would be on a major network or that she owns DVDs of the show is too overwhelming to contemplate). Worse than the studio audience is its soundtrack of onomatopoeia: the *boing!* of an uncoiled spring when a man gets hit in the balls; the *whoooo—ooo—ooop* of the slide whistle accompanying a child slipping and falling on a patch of ice; and the punishingly hackneyed, Schaudenfraude-signaling sound of the twentieth century, the *whah, whah, whah* descending notes of a plunger-muffled horn following just about any unfortunate moment, (which on *AFHV* means basically any physical accident). These sounds night after night, blast into my life as if she had a nail-gun and was firing three-inch bolts through our adjoining two-inch sheetrock wall. Whenever we see each other in the hallway there's a part of me that's always a little shocked she doesn't have a look of embarrassment on her face, knowing that I know what's going on in that apartment of hers. *I know you watch* America's Funniest Home Videos *on a regular basis. What do you have to say for yourself?* But she always seems fine, happy even.

There's another burst of laughter. I get close to the wall trying to discern what the hell she's watching now. The only thing more irritating than hearing someone else's music or TV is hearing it but not being able to tell what it is.

*"Joey!"* "Heh, heh, sorry Rachel." Studio laughter.

"Dayna!" I pound on the wall. "Enough already!"

She thumps back, presumably with her foot because the wall shook.

I wasn't in the mood to listen to music but clearly it was a volume war now. I popped in a Tool CD and turned it up until the floor rumbled with every hit of the kick-drum (which in Tool's music with all its time signature and tempo changes, I hoped would sound through the wall like the world was coming to an end). Alone in my room, protected from embarrassment, I ran around doing all sorts of clichéd heavy metal rock-god moves, leaning over head-banging in synch with the riffs wishing my shaggy hair were longer, air-guitaring it with legs splayed and cock forward, the works. The moves felt so natural, so tied to the music. It's a shame they basically come off as cartoonish these days—overused on stages in the 70s, and debased in the 80s in hair-band videos choreographed to the extent of a Fosse production—now they're only performed in ironic mockery. 'Cause man, the pure head-bang, and I don't mean nodding your head, I mean legs bent and braced shoulder-width and your whole torso swinging up and down with the beat—it's as close as modern man can get to the spirituality of a Native American drum dance. Alvin Ailey step aside, this is the real shit.

Emboldened by the primal yet complex fury of Tool I spent near an hour prowling about my small apartment rocking-out. Even when I got tired of the more aerobic maneuvers, I was always at minimum bobbing my head with jutted chin as I absent-mindedly tried on different outfits. Like jocks going through a heavy-metal psyche-up ritual listening to *Welcome to the Jungle* in their locker-room before a big game, I do my own rock routine before having to socialize.

I settled on jeans, a wide, black leather belt, and white undershirt, a look that has become my uniform as of late, going for that whole I'm-too-actualized-to-care-about-being-fashionable-but-I-secretly-want-you-to-know-I-do-care thing. The shirt fit tightly over my four-times-a-week push-ups-enhanced frame (they really work!) but not so tight as to be trendily indie-rock-small.

Despite my aversion to these sorts of forced-chatter events, flattered by the invite, I was excited to go to Andrea's. But as I stepped out of my apartment and was locking the door a feeling swept through me that I'm embarrassed to even tell you about. I fretted that simply showing up at Andrea's automatically would make me appear not that cool to, or at least not above, anyone there. If I really were cool I'd be somewhere else cooler, doing something else cooler, not there. (Sadly, even the psychic benefits of a metal fest are no match for my dementia).

I decided the best way to handle this was to slip in to any conversation that I was *just dropping by from downstairs.* Translation: *I'm here but I didn't make a special trip to be here (like you). I'm just doing Andrea a favor, being a nice neighbor.*

As I walked down the hall away from my apartment, I slightly nodded to myself, satisfied with my cool-ratifying schpiel. I felt exhausted before I even left my floor but pausing at the door to the stairwell, with a long exhale, I mustered up the nerve to travel the two flights up to Andrea's studio.

I stood in front of her door and listened to the languorous beats of early trip hop muddled with the low, unified rumble of urbane, idle chit-chat. It sounded like there were enough people inside that I decided against knocking and just turned the knob and went in. A few people near the door turned their heads then quickly went back to their conversations when they determined I wasn't anyone of interest. I remained there, my back to the door surveying the room for a moment. Fifteen, maybe twenty people were scattered in small groups. Andrea's bed was flipped up against the wall and her coffee table was pushed into a corner to create some semblance of open space. New York apartment party. It occurred to me at that moment what I should have considered earlier but didn't—aside from Andrea, I didn't know one person there. I'd just as soon become a wallflower than awkwardly approach strangers in conversation at a party. If I'm one-on-one somewhere, like a store or an elevator, I can talk to anyone if the mood strikes me; you might be surprised to know that I'm actually quite friendly in those circumstances, perhaps because nothing is expected or required. But being at a party, where mingling is requisite, I have problems.

I made a beeline to the kitchen to get myself a drink. Not so much so I could quickly loosen up with some alcohol but just so I had something to do, for at least two minutes. Andrea was in the kitchen holding a cosmo or some other pink drink that girls* tend to favor. She was talking with two other girls, neither of whom warranted anxious interest.

Despite the small crowd, no, because it was a small crowd, I felt ill at ease. There was nowhere to disappear. I smiled at Andrea and opened the fridge looking for a beer. I stared at the couple rows of Heinekens and Brooklyn Lagers stacked horizontally on each other, my head halfway inside the open door. *Hmm, this is starting to feel good, my head buried in here. I don't have to talk to anyone. Ok, if I could just stare into this refrigerator for the next hour I'll be fine. People will simply assume I'm a very discerning beer drinker having trouble making up my mind.* I started scanning the contents on the door, a half-used ketchup bottle, various fancy mustards, a raspberry jelly on the middle rack, pretending to be contemplating what beer I wanted thinking I could emit that vibe via ESP or something in case anyone was watching. I strangely felt like a voyeur looking at all her used

---

* Apologia/Explanation on usage: I'm using the word "girls" here knowing that it's a loaded synonym to toss around for "women." But our language has a serious shortcoming in that there is no female equivalent of *guy*, (other than *gal* which no one uses anymore). So, regardless of your politics and/or level of semantic militancy, I hope you can accept this usage moving forward.

condiments. Knowing that Andrea actually uses A1 Sauce, (What, is she grilling steaks in her studio apartment?), and leaves a pile of mini duck sauce packages from takeout Chinese wedged in the butter compartment somehow felt as personal as seeing her underwear drawer. These were her private quirks and preferences, the type of stuff only a boyfriend or a family member would know, on display, maybe not as guarded as lingerie but no less personal. I took a quick breath, grabbed a Heineken and left the safety of the chilled womb.

When you're at a party and the host is the only person you know and you're not all that close to or comfortable with the host, you must fight every urge in your body to be clingy. Don't talk to her at all except to say a quick hello and thank you on the way out. Definitely don't budge in on some conversation she's having, certainly with people she'd rather be talking to than you.

I turned to Andrea and the two women. "Hey, I'm Dan."

She looked hotter than her normal self. She's one of those girls who tend toward the non-high maintenance look. No makeup, no uber-girly or trendy clothes. So, it was surprising to see her lips glistening with lip-gloss and with a low-cut top revealing a bit of her 34-Bs (educated guess). Her black curly hair usually up in some sort of bun-with-a-chopstick thing, was now down and free, luscious squid ink fusilli falling just beyond her shoulders. It was very thick and shiny but looked like I could still run my fingers right through it. She must have used a lot of conditioner.

"Hi; Julie," one of them said to me disinterested, then took a sip of her drink. She had on that sparkly eye shadow that girls wear at night but she put a little too much on or maybe the color was wrong. It made me think of a pre-teen experimenting with her older sister's makeup kit.

The other friend gave me a pregnant stare, that kind of one-second hesitation where you just know someone is checking you out. Since she was about to speak to me she thought she could get away with it, playing it off as if either she was being careful not to jump on Julie's words, or simply as an inattentive pause. But she and I both knew what was happening in that second. She wasn't very attractive—her skin was pale in that mid-winter, sickly kind of way as if she were under a fluorescent light, she had long, entangled hair like a stretched-out brillo pad, and a forgettable face; but just the same, I was glad to have my ego padded by her attention. I felt bad for her and saddened that she was eyeing me, basically pleading for me to be interested in her. The world is cruel. I broke eye contact and glanced down. She was wearing a tight red t-shirt with a faded silkscreen promoting the (likely non-existent) *East Owensville High Badminton Team Undefeated '84-'85* that accentuated her chest, and while hardly redeeming enough, was still kind of sexy and cute in a sporty, hipster sort of way.

"Are you friends with Paul Collins and Amy Ganz?" she finally says.

"Yeah, how do you . . . ?"

"I thought I recognized you! We were both at their party last year, on July Fourth." She hadn't been giving me the "eye" after all; it was only a look of recognition, not desire. Cue the horn player: *whah, whah, whah.*

"Oh, yeah . . . right! Sure. I remember you." I have no recollection of her.

"You must be friends with Paul, right?"

"College."

"Me too. With Amy."

I barely knew Paul at Rutgers and I hadn't spoken to or seen him since school until we randomly were at the same bar one night. In that strange rush of seeing someone from another part of your life even if you weren't close, we got all chummy for an hour at one in the morning and he invited me to the party he was having a week later on the 4th. We hadn't talked since. It's always struck me a bit fraudulent the way everyone uses the word "friend" so loosely. But with a touch of self-loathing, I decided it wasn't worth the effort of correcting myself, declaring my mere acquaintanceship with the guy.

and sloppiness, and consequently perhaps more so with myself for being with her; I find her only passably attractive and yet I of course will continue to move forward with her. I will go as far as she will let me. Because this is what I have always done with girls, whether I like them or not. And with a girl like her it's not even lust, it's a sort of involuntary mechanics, a following through on an inevitability, as if I have no choice in the matter. The things we do with strangers all for some petty and fleeting physical contact and a nugatory boost to our ego.

In our suck-face, we've migrated a few feet in from the door. Standing in the middle of the room, lit by just the sickly, flickering glow of the TV, we undress each other. We start out sloppy, both of us tripping on our pants' legs and her head getting stuck in the collar of her shirt. But I unhook her bra with ease and it slides off her shoulders and down her arms with a grace that doesn't befit the occasion. I place my hands on her hips, slip them underneath her panties and glide them down to mid thigh where they get stuck for a moment until she closes her stance and they drop to the floor silently with a swift indifference to their royal importance. (When you've spent a disproportionate amount of your waking [and non-waking] hours over the course of your life thinking about girls and specifically, what lies underneath their skirts and pants and sweaters, there's something still a little exciting and almost profane in seeing their underwear nonchalantly on the floor. I still half-expect panties to be treated in some reverent manner like Crown Royal whisky, each pair sold in its own purple velvet bag). She quickly grabs my boxers and yanks them down.

So there we are, two strangers standing stark naked except for our socks. I'm not attracted enough to her to get near her sweaty-drunk-girl feet so I start taking off my own socks and am relieved when she follows suit with hers. Perhaps if you are not willing to take someone's socks off you shouldn't be having sex with them. I sigh internally which seems to have the opposite effect of the mild catharsis one gets from a real sigh;

something that should have been expelled from my body is left inside. It's unnerving to me, like when I'm around one of those people who suppress their sneezes. You just know it can't be good for you.

She's not overweight but she's soft. One of those not-quite-fat yet still flabby people. I can't decide if she used to be heavy and after losing the pounds her skin never quite rebounded or if she used to be thin and this is the downward spiral of someone hitting her mid twenties who doesn't eat well and doesn't work out. Shit, maybe it's all just genetics. I instinctively feel sorry for her, the way I often do with any girl whose body is less than prime, imagining the insecurity she must endure. Growing up with two older sisters, who despite being fairly pretty and having boyfriends for large portions of their junior and senior years respectively, constantly fretted over their looks and their weight—(with Jennifer, the younger of the two developing an eating disorder that led initially to shouting matches with my parents and ended in worried talks in hushed tones and a two week stay at the Rogueford Center, a "troubled teens" clinic)—has indelibly marked my perception of how women view themselves. But this girl tonight seems so at ease with herself, not self-conscious, that I conclude she simply must not care. She had no coyness when we disrobed, there are no nerves as we stand here, even when she stood at the door, though there was her giggle, it was more playful than bashful. Good for her, I think. What wonderful self-confidence! But then I think perhaps she *should* feel self-conscious about her weight. She's in her twenties, there's no excuse for her to let her body fall apart at this age. *Learn how to eat right! Get in shape! Get some self respect and take care of your body!* Unless of course it *is* genetics and not her fault, I remind myself, and start to feel sorry for her again. . . . *Cut it out Daniel! Just focus, please.*

I can feel a little bit of a paunch pressed against me as we embrace. I grab two handfuls of ass. She has the body type that would have been celebrated, lusted after in Classical times or fawned over in a Renaissance painting. It's quite unfortunate for her type of woman in America today. Because there is something intrinsically sexy, *womanly*, about a woman with some squish. I'm not talking overly Rubenesque, I just mean someone with some shape. Thin girls look good in clothes but it's the ones with some squish that *feel* good underneath you. I'm instantly hard and pressing up against her crotch. I can feel her getting wet. I gently pull back and lead her over to the bed. Without hesitation, she climbs on and lays on her back.

I straddle her on my knees. My dick sticking out like a flagpole off the Plaza Hotel, so hard and straight it hurts. I reach over to my nightstand, pull open the drawer and fumble around for the supplies. My hand struggles over various papers and objects. *Passport. Notebook. What's this? Nope; torn out Billboard article,* "Bryter Layter Dropped by Warners." *Ahh, here it is, the slick wrapper I'm looking for.* I pull it out, tear it open and suit up. There's something almost appealing about the routine of putting on protection. Rather than diving right in to sex, it forces a sort of ceremonial importance to the occasion.


4:53 a.m. She's snoring. Disgust in myself and her is only mildly tempered by the satisfaction of adding another contemptible name on my metastasizing list of picayune female conquests. I can't smell her breath but it looks like it stinks; her chapped lips and her alcohol mouth, slightly open, no doubt filled with pasty saliva. Although I haven't looked, this is the type of girl who bites her fingernails, who wears pilly cotton underwear, who feels or at least looks ungainly and wrong in a dress and heels. She probably went through a phase in college where she struggled with the decision to shave her armpits. The anti-girly girl: her thick mess of hair, her schlumpy jeans and unisex t-shirt, her unselfconsciously un-modern body. Even her hair down below, as I noticed just before I slipped it in, was left *au-naturel*, a rare find among all the landing strips and putting-greens favored by New York City women these days.

I find myself lamenting that in place of this ruffian there isn't a Pilates-toned sweetie with delicate wrists and slender limbs, snuggled under my comforter, peacefully engaged in a Beatlesque Golden Slumber. Her pumice-buffed feet ever so slightly grazing my leg. I feel guilty of course for thinking this. (Aren't I cooler than that? Am I just a tool of advertising and media, buying into unhealthy standards imposed by a sick culture, blah blah blah?) This girl, Amy's friend, whose name I forgot upon hearing it, or did she not tell me?, seemed so uninhibited (or maybe just unaware? No, she must be aware of her self). As I stare at her laying there, I'm embittered by a rotten jealousy of her for being so free, so unselfconscious, or even worse, aware but un-self-hating. I then chide myself for feeling this way and for not being more attracted to her. *I should find this beautiful, this is what a woman is supposed to look like.* My shame and envy rise in waves with each new grunted inhalation she takes though her nose and spoilt open mouth.

So much time goes by where nothing happens. Days and days, months of the same basic shit. And yet here it is, this night that God* has thrown me. All the girls, they're like markers along the time-line, breaks in the bludgeoning monotony of my life. Without these reference points it would all just wash together.

7:03 a.m. I wake up to the sight of her sitting up in bed, her back to me as she gazes at the brick wall of the building ten feet away in the alley out the window.

"That was the first time I've done that in a long time," she says.

"Really?" I say with a little more surprise than I intended.

"No," she says through laughter, "that came out wrong. I mean you were the first *guy* I've been with since . . . since, like, high school. I had a boyfriend then but I've only been seeing women since college."

Ohh. I always *thought* there was something vaguely man-indifferent

---

* I don't believe in God in any sort of religious sense but I often use the word as a catch-all rather than saying "the universe" or "fate" or any other term that signifies unknown forces.

about Andrea. Nothing specific, just an air I suppose. Not to jump to any conclusions but this would sort of explain that. I wonder if these two used to (or still do?) hook up. Neither of them are one of those city butch lesbians, with the boy's underwear sticking out above their jeans. It always seems like one of the two in a lesbian couple is the "man." So maybe they didn't . . . wait a minute; she's not a lesbian, she was just with me. What, was I an experiment or something? Ahh, who cares. It's still a marker on the time-line, it just has an asterisk next to it.

"Oh. Well, I hope I did my gender proud. Did I bring you back to the good side?" Shit. Am I being funny, or rude?

"It was nice. It was good."

By 7:11 she's out the door. I get up, take a piss, then crawl back in bed avoiding her side and fall back asleep.

• • •

I'm pacing around my apartment. Just finished a bowl of cereal, took a shit, splashed water on my face, ran wet fingers through dirty hair, and now I'm left with myself, no job, no impetus, no plan. Another day in stink-city, New York in August, garbage roasting in a concrete oven. Despite the day facing me, though, I should feel better than I do, at least temporarily. After all, as of a few minutes ago, I am a pound or two lighter, a small victory of gastrointestinal function.

You know there's a separate brain in your gut—really—not an actual compressed, noodle-ball like in your head, but all the nerves, chemicals, receptors, they're all there. That's why when you're nervous you have butterflies in your stomach not in your head. Your gut-brain knows you better than you know you. It's all fight-or-flight stuff carried over from our cavemen days still lingering in our DNA. Here's the strange part: when you're in fight-or-flight mode at the maximum level, when you're not just nervous but *terrified*, rather than being tense, every muscle in your body taut, ready to spring you into action or retreat, an opposite reaction takes effect, and the GI muscles go slack to protect you. Basically the worst scenario you can be in if you receive some sort of trauma is if you have food or waste in your system because it could contaminate your body if your GI tract is punctured or damaged enough. That's why people piss or shit themselves when they're terrified—it's your gut-brain emptying-out your system, preparing you, just in case. The problem for me is I live my life in a near-perpetual state somewhere just below terror, meaning I'm at the highest possible level of tension without ever going over, without getting that release.

My system's wound tighter than the head on a piccolo snare. Unless I down a heaping bowl of bran in the morning, food turns to cement somewhere along the way in my plumbing. In the beginning—when was that . . . two, three years ago?—one bowl of bran was enough to get things moving but after a few months I noticed that I kept increasing the amount in the bowl, then it was upped to a bowl and a half, then two bowls. My system was building tolerance, like they warn on the nose-spray bottles, *frequent or excessive use may cause symptoms to worsen.* There should have been a warning on the box! It's the dirty secret of cereal industry. Or maybe it's just me. Has there been a study? They must have done a study on this.

Up until a few months ago, for years I'd been having my cereal every morning with soy milk. (Don't get me started on why I don't use cow's milk, that's a whole other story). Today though I'm having it with *rice* milk because . . . well:

here I am shuffling around my apartment, a morning film of perspiration percolating through the dried glaze of last night's sweat, a congealed crust recipe of nonoxynol-9, cum, and vaj juice looking like the frosted topping on an apple crumble tangled in my pubic hair, and depression or is it aim-lessness or is it ennui hanging heavy in the August air like the fetid fumes still dissipating from the bathroom. There is such a dearth of movement/action/

drama in my life that perhaps it was inevitable, knowing that energy is neither created nor destroyed, some sort of focal balancing would take hold, that since there is no movement *externally* then all that unused energy must go somewhere. And that "somewhere" is my head. And the particularly cruel part about all this is that even though I am in a terrible rush to get out of wherever this place is that I am, in betrayal I behave as if all I have is time, the hours and days stretching on and on like some epic never-ending film that I was bored with after the first ten minutes.

And for me, with all this time comes the luxury, the burden, the responsibility even, of worry. And how can it not? How can I not stew in guilt over decisions I've been forced to make or that I avoided—should I have handled things differently with Ash, could I have prevented any of it from happening?; should I not have bought those Rod Lavers with the blue accents, the heels of which I'm staring at sticking out from under yesterday's t-shirt on the floor, because I didn't really *need* them, I already have Lavers in green, I just *wanted* new shoes, am I just a tool of the consumption-crazed society, a shopping zombie whose actions have consequences even if I don't see them, directly, right there, in front of me, like the eleven-year-old girl in China working in the factory twelve hours a day (but on the other hand, yes, I know, maybe that's still better than the way she had it before when her family had even *less* money but still . . . ), all the fuel used to get the shoes on some container ship across an ocean then on a truck across the country, the leather—who knows how that cow was treated right before his death, and perhaps all those resources human, animal, environmental could have been used for something more worthwhile, something bettering the world, what that is I do not know but still . . . , but on the other hand, I don't really buy that much stuff and my green Rod Lavers were pretty damn filthy and were starting to fray and the treads on the bottoms were wearing down and isn't variety important, a healthy part of human nature, and besides, I'm aware that there are problems with consumption and this lifestyle of disposable goods and that's a start, isn't it?, I'm actually thinking about it, which is better than most, that means something, right? but no, if I'm aware and thinking about it but still doing it anyway then I'm even worse than the people too lazy or selfish to even consider it when they buy a new pair of shoes; paper or motherfucking plastic—either way, I'm fucked, we're all fucked; continually worry about everything out of my control—terrorists, hurricanes, and illness, oh the fear(!) of illness and even death when these days we know so much about how our bodies work? Because, sure, the more we learn the more cures we have, new medicines, procedures, treatments but I can't help but focus on the fact that the more we learn the more we know what can go wrong. And so much can go wrong! That's why today with my cereal I'm having rice milk instead of soy milk. Because I've become afraid they're going to come out with some study that says too much soy may give you cancer or gall stones or *something*. I'm pretty sure I saw that as a headline on the cover of *Mother Jones* one day when I was loitering around the magazine racks in Tower Video. There always seems to be these studies coming out saying that too much of this or too much of that ("this" and "that" half the time being things we were told were good for us just the year before) gives you cancer. So, out of prudence/fear (pick one), I'm making a concerted effort to spread my diet out, not too much of any one thing, including the seemingly "good" things. I must diversify. Now I alternate between boxes of rice and soy milk to hedge my bets. I'm not going to be one of the schmucks caught off guard when the soy study comes out!

BUT every once in a while, the dumpy Key Food near me has a sale on this one brand of soy milk, so I go crazy stocking up on it, buying five or six boxes and leave the pricier rice milk on the shelves. The problem is I then get sick from the anxiety of exclusively having soy milk every day for three or four weeks in a row as I use up my bargain stash. With each spoonful I can feel little cancer cells in their infancy being given the fuel to grow. *More soy! More soy!* They're calling out. If only they had been combated with the power of rice milk! But no, I had to save sixty cents per container. So, due to my frugality, for a month after each sale, I suffer through breakfast lamenting every spoonful of soggy, carcinogenic, soy-soaked bran I put in my mouth.

As I take a drink of water I mark on the chart on the fridge that it's my fifth day of Poland Spring, which means I'm overdue for a switch to Bear Mountain, the third of three brands that I rotate in with tap water just in case they (*they!* It's always *they*) find out that one brand or another is filled with PCBs or radon or leeches plastic into the water or who-knows-what. You never know which source may be the killer. Gotta hedge! But it occurs to me as I stop pacing and rinse this cereal bowl in the sink, sometimes you can mix it up within one category all you want but it'll just be something else that'll get you. I've been using these bowls for years. They're Made in Mexico it says on the bottom. You just *know* they're still using lead-based glazes down there.

Anxiety is not the fuel that keeps the engine running but the engine itself. And yes, I've read the studies that anxiety causes cancer, heart disease and whatever else, the constant tension eventually wearing down the immune system. It's ironic though because I'm convinced my anxiety is what keeps me in shape. I'm slim and fit with a healthy heart, all because I burn so much energy worrying. As I put the bowl on the rack and sit down here on my couch, staring at the wall, I figure I'll worry up a good five mile run.

But I get up and re-continue pacing. I have nothing to do, nowhere to go yet today I'm too antsy to just sit here. (Post lesbian-conversion-coitus ambivalence will do that to you I guess). Of course, I have much to do, or could or should be doing but somehow despite all the urgency, I can't seem to do anything. My life has turned into one long exercise of procrastination, though I don't even know what I'm procrastinating until. There's just this vague feeling that somewhere, some point down the line, is where I should be and until I get to that righteous place I'm just going to waste time. (Of course, deep down, or rather, no, on the surface—actually, ok, I guess on every level—I know that the only way I can get to this vague, ill defined place where I'm supposed to be in my life is by actually *doing* stuff, playing music, looking for a new manager, recording new songs, something, anything).

I walk to the window and press my cheek against the glass with my head craned at a front row movie theater angle. Squinting, I look up beyond the sixth floors and rooftops of the two buildings that create the alleyway. A small, crystalline, light-blue square, infinite in depth is framed by the two soot-brown buildings—another miserable day of merciless sun and heat. I peel my cheek off the glass and turn back to the room, my rods (or is it cones?) working overdrive, my eyes trying to adjust back to the dim light of the apartment. Through a spotty haze, the Sony alarm clock's green digital numbers faintly surface. 11:27. I've just about successfully blown yet another morning. I think about making a sandwich but stick to the rule I've had to institute to keep me on some sort of schedule—using the term "schedule" loosely, of course—I can't eat lunch before noon. I plop back on the couch and wrestle with myself to not turn on the TV. But if I can't watch TV, how will I make it till noon? I wonder.

I decide the only way is to step outside and by a sort of homing pigeon gravitation find myself at St. Marks Bookshop a few blocks away. I go to my usual spot in the back and loiter near the magazines. I flip through the latest *Adbusters* and with resigned apprehension glance at the covers of the "alternative" music magazines. Irritated, I pull *CMJ* off the shelf. Look at those fays on the cover . . . with your artificial snarl and your derivative sound . . . I've heard your record—it sucks! . . . will the stylist at Atlantic let you keep your outfits after you get dropped? You better check, young-men-in-skinny-suits, 'cause this may be a short ride . . . *I* should be touring the nation; recording for half a year at Bearsville, indulging in five-day tone experiments on six guitars and four amps for one song; waxing philosophical in three-thousand word interviews poured over by swooning girls who think everything I say is obnoxious, funny, true, and . . . *I* should be wearing a stupid outfit on the cover of *CMJ*.

I shove the magazine on the shelf backwards and wander outside then make my way to The Strand. I spend forty minutes there browsing their alleged eighteen miles of books without reading more than a paragraph in any of them. Since I already was at The Strand yesterday I've broken my rule of alternating days between the bookstores I frequent; I'm embarrassed that the clerks will recognize me if I'm there too often. I decide to make it a trifecta and double back and hit East Village Books. It's my favorite of the bunch and I tend to dawdle endlessly in its cramped environs. I exchange nods with the bearded anarchists as I walk in then head down the aisles. Some dirtbags, a dude in dark jeans (a sartorial choice I never understood for August afternoons), and a butch lesbian all squeeze by me, the dyke's dangling wallet chain grazing me as I crouch between the bookshelves and thumb through the same copy of *Céline: The Crippled Giant* I do every time I'm here.

When I stand up there's a splotchy line across my shirt from the sweat puddle I accumulated while hunched. Whether it's the heat or low blood sugar, I'm feeling woozy. I head down the street and pick up a falafel. The joint doesn't have AC so I take it to go and try to eat and walk, spilling onion bits and unknown particles from the pita onto the pavement. Lifting for another bite I feel a stream of tahini sauce running down the side of my hand onto my forearm. As I lick the side of my hand

"Dan?"

"Mimi. Hi," I say as I swing my hand away from my face.

"What's going on?" she says cheerfully.

"Oh, not much. You know . . ." Mimi, whose name I always feel silly saying, is an actress friend of a girl I dated two years ago for about one second. I got sucked into going to a play she was in at one of those shoebox theaters with metal folding chairs. My ass fell asleep after ten minutes and I spent the rest of the play, which was some Harold Pinter-esq punishment, shifting in my seat trying to revive it. I couldn't understand why the acting sounded so fake until Sari, the ex, scolded me, "shh, stop fidgeting, it's supposed to sound this way." I never found out if she said that just to shut me up or if that's true. "What are you up to? In any plays right now?"

"Just got back from a summer stock in the Berkshires."

When you ask an actor what they are doing now and they tell you what they just did, the answer is: nothing. "Oh, that's great." I wasn't going to press.

"So, I guess we were due for our annual meeting," she says.

"True." Living in New York, there seems to be a small cadre of people you reliably bump into once a year. I was glad to see her. I felt these meetings confirmed a sort of cosmic order within the randomness of the city.

"Are you going to the Thataways show at Irving Plaza tomorrow?" Sari's now seeing their drummer.

It wasn't a Thataways show, they were *opening* for a big national band but I knew I'd sound like a dick making that distinction. Sometimes I have restraint.

"Yeah, maybe," I lie. I'm not paying twenty bucks to see a band perform that I'd played on the same bill with umpteen times.

"What about you? Any shows coming up?" she says.

"Not sure. I might be going to Europe, I'm talking with a promoter," I say trying to sound convincing.

"Cool. Well, see you tomorrow."

"Yeah, see you there," I say lifting the falafel as a cheers. But I think it just comes across as some weird gesture judging by the crooked smile I receive. As we part ways and I head down the street, my normal field of vision is suddenly replaced by a third-person view of myself walking, holding a falafel. And in this view I see a distress, an anxiety, some sort of unease on my face, even though I'm pretty sure in reality my face is straight. I'm watching a sort of Dorian Gray video of myself revealing what's hidden behind the façade. I shake my head and the image dissolves.

I come home and settle in to the couch. And I know the rest of this day will be like so many other days. The city, out there—the occasional honking cab, screeching tire, diesel-engined eighteen-wheeler ripping up First Ave., garbage truck sighing every ten feet, voices laughing, shouting, the atmospheric whir of an infinite army of air conditioners destroying the ozone layer, the sirens (that used to be just another voice—albeit a glorious, quintessential one—in the urban chorus, now, even though much time has passed since that day, stand out like an off-pitch solo soprano, each whirl flooding my stomach with a Pavlovian rush of acid so dreadful sometimes I'm rendered immobile for a half-hour as I wait, standing in the middle of the room, my head like a dog's, cocked just slightly to the side waiting to hear if there are more to follow, and if so, counting the different ones—*I think that's the third fire-truck. No, it's an ambulance; I can tell*—then ignoring the sirens and just hoping I don't hear a helicopter, because following sirens, if the police are using a helicopter then that means, at least potentially, something *really* bad is happening, again), cooing pigeons, skyscrapers growing, manholes ka-thunking under speeding tires, pavement crumbling under enraged jackhammers, buses' brakes' wailing, bike messengers' whistles' warning—all receding to a din, aural wallpaper, as the reels of my life spin forward like time-lapse photography in one of those nature documentaries on Africa, the panoramic shot of boundless plains and sky, hours worth of storm clouds gathering and dissipating in seconds with mesmerizing choreography, the sun seamlessly zipping across the sky, except in my film, in my life, the minutes on my Sony digital alarm clock furiously flicker by, hours going in finger snaps, while the rest of the frame is motionless except for when my body is seen darting supernaturally to the kitchen or the bathroom in that goofy old-timey-British-comedy way that sporadic movement looks in time-lapse, from its primary position on the couch, where excluding those comic bursts is as static and unremitting as the mustard glow from the fifteen-dollar Kmart halogen lamp in the corner.

And while I'm in this apartment, on this couch, I'm ashamed to say, I've been spending an inordinate amount of time watching TV. Every day I tell myself that today will be different, today I will not watch too much television, that I will not watch *any* television, that I will go outside, that I will converse with someone, that I will pick up my guitar, that I will write a song, that I will do something, anything, but somehow I am inevitably sucked in, like I am right now, as I'm ashamed to tell you, I've just flipped on the TV.

. . .

It was a couple months ago when I first realized the craziness with the notes. It was sometime in June because I remember it was one of those initial days of summer, real New York summer, when the city air takes on an entirely different quality of stink and thickness than it has the rest of the year. It was the middle of yet another random day of doing basically nothing when Jay buzzed from downstairs. He lives just a few blocks over on Lafayette in a rent stabilized studio, just like me, that chances are he'll never leave. Between finally getting a girlfriend (which at 28 I think was his first actual relationship), working in three different bands, and doing spot gigs with at least two singer-songwriter types (good bass players are always in demand), he hadn't stopped by unannounced like that in many months.

"Yo," crackled through the intercom.

"Load?"

"No, it's one of your other friends." I buzzed him in. He's such a dick sometimes.

Jay being nearly half-a-foot taller than me, we gave our usual awkward embrace, my arm reaching up around his back, him hunching over for a half-hug-half-pat. He had just shaved a mohawk into his head a few days before which made his awkward visage even more extreme—six-foot-three gangly frame; a snaggle tooth—the one next to the left incisor, whatever that tooth is called—that revealed itself whenever he smiled; huge feet in clodhopper boots that he was wearing even in June, look-ing like giant ballasts on the ends of his stick legs. He's one of those guys with a big Adam's apple that you're always looking at. His gaunt face was dotted with sweat.

"I do have other friends besides you," I said.

"I thought we got rid of the nickname?" Oh, now I see. He was pissed. It was a tit-for-tat.

"Load is a good nickname for someone who's last name is Loader! What else are we supposed to call you?"

"There's no we, Dan. It's just you." The scent of his everyday odor ac-cented by sweat hit me. To my surprise though, I found it pleasant in its familiarity. "No one else calls me that."

"Fine, fine. Whatever."

"I was just joking about the 'other friends' thing." He felt bad now.

"No you weren't . . . I don't care . . . I don't like a lot of people."

"And a lot of people don't like you."

"And that's fine," I finished without missing a beat. We both laughed. I watched the bump in Jay's throat bob. We'd been having this I-have-no-friends exchange since shortly after we first met six years ago through a classified musician's wanted ad. It hurts me a little every time we do it but now it's one of those *things*, those go-to inside jokes, the auto-banter that friends have so it's too late for me to stop it, it's part of our shtick and now I'm stuck doing it, sort of like that person at work you don't know but once waved to or smiled at when you walked past his desk, and five months or a year later, you still have to wave or smile or give a head-nod every time even though you'd rather not go through the motion (and worse, you suspect he feels the same way) but you have to anyway because you've been doing it for so long.

"Whoa, what the fuck is that?" Jay said walking toward the wall.

"Oh . . . it's . . . I don't know. Just some notes."

"Dan, you have like fifty of them on the wall," he said, marveling. "Music stuff?"

"No, not really." Just as I was about to intercept him from reading any of them, he turned away and plopped on the couch.

"Man you really are in your own world in this place, aren't you?" he said, stretching out and crossing his legs, thumping his boots on the coffee table then reached down and picked up *The Onion* off the floor. What I generally find frustrating, that Jay thinks of me as some sort of character, a weird loner-guy with lots of quirks, once in a while works to my favor. I was relieved he'd lost interest already, the notes quickly shrugged off as yet some other eccentricity of mine.

Despite his passing amusement, Jay's discovery nonetheless tipped me off that my place was starting to look a bit bizarre. I glanced at the wall and for the first time saw—as in really *saw*—that it was nearly covered in little post-it notes. Somehow over the preceding months—had it been months?—when they had been slowly accumulating I never took notice. *How could I not have noticed all these notes until now?*

"Dude, so check it out—my connection came through at Sound Designs," Jay said, blithely dropping the topic, shifting to his news-de-jour.

"The music house you were talking about?"

"Yeah. I already did my first rip. That's what they call the demo you make for a commercial."

"And you get paid for that? Just the demo?"

"Yeah. I get a few hundred bucks or more for the rips. Which is totally cool considering I have my home studio and it doesn't cost me anything to make them."

"Other than time."

"I've got time."

"Listen—"

"Aww, don't give me this shit."

"I don't want to say something as lame as 'you're selling out' but . . ."

"But . . ." he said, tilting his head back, flaunting his Adam's apple at me like he was giving me the finger.

"Fine, I guess that's what I'm saying."

"Oh, I'm sorry, didn't you sell out to a big label? It's the same thing. They're all corporations, it doesn't matter after a certain point."

"Jay, there is a difference between using my music in some ad to sell a bunch of useless shit versus being signed to a major label. I understand the label is part of some monolithic multinational entity but the difference is, the music stands alone. The only thing I'd be selling is the music itself. It's not being used as a tool to sell something else."

"No, the music's not the tool. *You're* being used as a tool to sell plastic discs for them. Which is worse? What if you make a video. That's basically a commercial."

"But it's a commercial *for* the music."

"Will you listen to yourself? I'd appreciate you not launching into a rant . . . You know—" he dropped his feet to floor and leaned forward, "fine, in a perfect world I wouldn't be making music to sell toilet paper or whatever but I need to pay my rent, to eat. I love music as much as you do but it doesn't always have to be some intense statement. Sometimes it can just be fun, it can just be whatever. I love that you take it seriously and that that's how you see it for your own stuff but you need to respect that not everyone sees it your way and that doesn't make them wrong."

He had a point and my silence let him know it; it was the best I could do.

"Besides, what do I care? The rips aren't even used in the commercials. I get paid even if they don't use it."

"*And* imagine if you actually land a spot," I said, feeling guilty and trying to be supportive, joining his side, "that's where the real money comes in. We're talking five figures. You know, with those residuals. Wait, do you get residuals for that?"

"I don't know. Whatever. Either way. I'm happy just doing the rips. A few hundred here, a thousand there. I don't ever need to land a spot."

"You'll be like those screenwriters who make half-a-mil a year selling screenplays that never get made." This prompted a snort from Jay. "I bet subconsciously you'll keep making the music just good enough to keep getting hired for the demos but just bad enough so it'll lose out to another demo so you won't completely be a whore having your music played in a toilet paper spot or some banking ad."

"Fuck you, I'm not a whore—"

"I was just kidding," I half-lied.

"—and second of all, if that's what my subconscious mind is going to make me do, I want a lobotomy. If I land one spot, I could live off that shit for a year." Yeah, it'll probably be more than I got for my stinkin record deal.

"You could totally land your music in an ad. Make some ambient, synth cheese for one of those phony-disease drug ads." I started singing an ethereal Gregorian chant-like "Ahhhhh." I slowly waved my arms around, then in a soothing pitchman voice, "'Do you ever get nervous? Are you sometimes sad?' Ahhhhhh."

"Very good Dan. Very good."

"Sorry." I can't believe it, Jay's going to get rich and I'm going to be stuck being me, a failure.

"I'm not trying to change the world. We've got to pick our battles. We can't all be pure like you living off our record advances . . . Anyway, what the hell are you doing in here all day?" Jay eyed the guitar in the corner. "Dude, when are you going to start playing again?"

"I don't know."

"Why don't you start gigging with some other bands or something?"

"I'm not a musician in that way. You know that. I'm not good like you or Alex."

"What are you talking about! Don't fish for complements. You know you're a kick-ass guitar play *and* singer."

"Thanks, man." I was surprised how good it felt to hear that. "I didn't mean it in that way . . . I mean I'm not a technician like you guys. Well, not you guys but those session guys . . . Some of them, it's like they might as well be mechanics or computer repair guys. They're just brought in . . . I mean . . . shit—" I got up off the couch and started pacing, "I don't mean that in a dick sense . . . I mean I'm a songwriter, a producer, more than I am a player. That's where my heart lies."

"So what? I like composing too but you can still play for other people, lay down some guitar tracks for someone, do some gigs, something. It doesn't all have to be *your* stuff." That's the difference between us. I would never say I "like" composing. Composing is the essence, the engine, the reason behind everything else, my life-blood. But I didn't want to get into it with him.

"I know. Maybe I should start doing other stuff. I do love the magic of just playing, that side of it, not just the creating side. I do. I just . . . I don't get the same joy, I mean, deep deep, like, God-level joy out of it as I do with my own stuff."

"Ok, fine, but can't you do other people's stuff in the meantime even if it's not your 'deep God-level' stuff? And why can't you do your own stuff anymore?" He sounded annoyed. "I don't understand."

"Neither do I."

Jay. Whenever I got too intense with him, if I even mentioned the *word* "deep" he often just shut off. It's not that he wasn't capable of getting into things, we had talks, he wasn't overly shallow but he had a sort of threshold for introspection, navel gazing, feelings. One time when I thought we were just having a good conversation he exploded, "Enough!

I was in such a good mood today. Can we just keep it light for once?" Like accidentally overhearing a conversation about you, it was one of those moments when you realize something startling: the way other people perceive you and reality may be quite different than how you perceive yourself and reality. "You wear people down, Dan. You can't just have a normal conversation," he said. He went on that I always led things into some sort of deep, and inevitably depressing, talk. That that was why Alex had been blowing me off ever since I got back from Chicago.

The musicians I've been around, like most artsy people, tend toward more existentialist talk than non-artsy people but even they have their limits. And apparently I didn't, I never got tired of this stuff. But I don't think it was just existentialist talk that I did that tired people of me. Though I viewed myself as a crusading realist, my tendency to harp on the futility of our dreams—surprise—alienated me from half the bands I knew in the city.

"People trying to make it" I said *make it* with air quotes, "aren't dealing in reality. I'm not saying that it can't happen. I'm saying in order for us to continue we have to ignore the reality of the situation."

"If we work hard enough and are good enough it'll happen," Steve Noblinsky, the guitar player for Thataways said as he lit up a hand-rolled Drum cigarette. We were in the dirty basement that was the "backstage" at Brownies, both our bands were playing later that night.

"Steve, that's not the way it works." I was looking down at the electronic tuner I had plugged into my guitar, plucking each string and twisting the tuning pegs getting the lights to align in the middle. "You know how many great bands there are that never make it. Either they never even get signed, or they get signed then dropped, or the record tanks, or they try to make it by grinding it out on their own but you know how that goes. Come on, man."

"Green, would you mind giving it a rest?" My low E finally in tune, I looked up at him. "You're a fucking downer, man," he said, slowly exhaling smoke toward the ceiling, his veneer of practiced nonchalance about to crack from my agitation. I took a strange pleasure in this, blasting people with harsh truisms as casually as they talk about a party they may or may not go to later that night. I was so desperate and afraid, how dare he not feel that way too?

"I don't get you, Steve. I know you guys have been at this for years . . . and didn't you go to like, Oberlin?"

"Wesleyan."

"Right. I knew it was one of those places—so it's not like you don't have the tools to get a quote, real job. To give up any sort of security, you've got to really want this yet you sit here smoking your hand-rolled cigarettes like all is cool with the world."

"Dude, I'm just relaxing before a show." I suddenly felt awful, an aftershock I could count on following a dark pleasure. A large part of me never wanted to make anyone feel bad, as bad as I did, and I hated myself for being a buzz-kill, the role I often found myself in. I believed what I was saying but I knew no one wanted to hear it. Shit, I don't even want to hear it, but for some reason—I do. I'm drawn to it.

"I know, I know . . . I just mean . . . I'm just wondering, are you really not worried about what's going to happen? Or are you as anxious as me and this whole chilled-out thing you've got going on is a façade?" It's as if I had no control. I'm like one step away from Tourette's syndrome.

"Green," he said and exhaled a long cloud. He paused for a moment then just laughed.

Looking at him I had a strange revelation: Noblinsky rolls Drums rather than just whipping out a Marlboro because he acts as if he has time. And people who have time aren't anxious. But I guess the question is: are the Drums a prop to prove his chillitude or are they a natural extension of someone who already is chill? I felt I was always wondering this basic truth about people. Were everyone's mannerisms and preferences and props genuine products of who they are or was it all simply who they wanted us to think they were? Or who they themselves wanted to think they were?

On some level I told myself that Steve and his ilk's prevailing ethos—favoring optimism to realism, insouciance to exactitude, laidbackedness to intensity—was in fact just a front. That deep down they were like me. Perhaps I needed to believe this for my own sanity. But what became apparent once I was spending large amounts of time in the recording studio was that this wasn't a mere persona for some of them, that actually, how they acted was a matter of philosophy; our differences went to the core.

. . .

I knew there'd be friction between Alex and me from the first day in Chicago when he snickered at seeing all the recording notes and charts I had spread out and was studying on the dining table after dinner. He and Jay were heading out for a beer and had come from downstairs to retrieve me, thinking I was upstairs putting on my coat and instead found me at the table, clearly not going anywhere.

"It's our first night. You don't want to go out for a while?" Alex was incredulous, almost hurt.

"Come on Dan," Jay prodded. In the corner of my eye I saw Tim, the producer, in the control room with headphones on, eyes shut.

I mustered a "sorry guys," half-looked up, then went back to my spread of papers.

I like seeing things in front of me, laid out, patterned. Unlike most of the musicians I know, I regularly have most everything figured out in my head, if not on paper, in some sort of chart or notation before bringing it to a band for rehearsal or recording. I've always been drawn to schematics, graphs, diagrams, and anything mathematical. Math is made for people who aren't laid back, people who take solace in definitiveness, structure.*

Alex was thin but cut, had a tattoo of eagle's wings on one shoulder and something resembling the Robert Plant symbol on the other, the leaf extending to the middle of his bicep, the design accenting the ridge between the two muscles. The toughness of the ink and his physique was offset by a boyishly handsome face. He had the requisite permanently tousled hair but on him it was a genuine result of laziness. In other words, he looked the way I always wished I could but never would—a little dirty, a little tough, yet still handsome, a zen balance of traits that makes certain girls swoon. But it was beyond simple lady's man appeal. It was more that he was one of those guys that had *it*, the looks and the relaxed, almost aloof air that only comes from confidence, that men and women alike are drawn to.

But as the days went by in the studio our vibes became more and more at odds with each other and my enchantment with him withered. Over so many years of songwriting, when I had been making detailed notes on how I wanted things to sound in the production of different songs, and even more so, in the immediate weeks before we arrived at The Watershed when I culled together much of the years' previous notes into thirty pages of color-coded charts for all the music, it never occurred to me that what I was doing was strange. When I was translating what I heard in my head to paper, scribing it out in my private argot of coded recording and performance notations, I was in an all-enveloping world of my mind's ear. I had no awareness outside of my creative process. But the world of my mind's ear, however fantastical, did not compare with the experience in the studio of finally hearing the sound from my head come *alive*. The sound waves in the air were of a hyper-reality so sublime

---

* I know, not all math is definitive and structured but I'm talking about basic math here not the high-end theoretical shit.

that the tools of our language are insufficient for describing what I can only approximate by saying I experienced them through a sixth sense of an alternative tangibility; the sound was not just audible, or even an illusion of being tactile, but experienced as some other heretofore unknown force. Unsurprisingly, after my first taste of this transcendence I was myopic and relentless in my pursuit of trying to experience it again, which meant often insisting on a militant adherence to much of my notes, to the frequent dismay and frustration of Alex.

I know Alex and Jay had talks about me. I overheard Alex complain, "Dude, he's not letting me decide anything," once during a break while laying tracks when I was in the control room and they were in the live room and didn't know the mics were on. Or, maybe they did. I know I drove them nuts.

I pressed the talk-back button down. "I *do* let you decide some things but I'm sorry, I want that tom roll in this spot."

There was a pause. Then, "You're like a dictator . . . Most of your ideas are cool, Dan. I really dig what's going on and I know you have this grand vision but sometimes you gotta bend," Alex's voice came in loudly through the monitors; he now must have been talking directly into one of the drum mics.

"I know, I'm sorry, I thought I have been." I really did.

I have only a rudimentary knowledge of standard sheet music and rather than learning it I developed my own complex system that not only transcribed actual notes but tones, instruments, effects, and other more nebulous sonic ideas. The song and production notes were a dizzying combination of different colors and symbols representing different mixing and tracking ideas. E.g. red letters <u>R</u>RG = heavy rock guitar panned hard right, brown <u>L</u>G = acoustic guitar panned hard left; different tones, e.g. lowercase "r" = classic rock guitar tone, capital "R" = heavy modern-rock guitar tone; all green pen was for effects, e.g. green PH for phaser, F for flanger, V for reverb, etc. Different sections of music like certain patterns or riffs to be layered or repeated within different sections of songs and throughout the album all had their own symbols whether acronyms or shorthand phrases or hieroglyphs. The elaborate ciphered details went on and on. One night, after an exhaustive couple hours of work, looking down at red and blue pen ink on my fingers, I remember thinking, I just don't want to die before the album is finished because no one knows what the hell all these symbols and codes mean except me. No one will be able to finish the album the way I want it to sound without me.

"Then let's try the other beat here instead of this thing you want on the toms," came back through the monitors.

I feverishly thumbed through a stack of papers, scanning through charts, momentarily lost in a language for one, as if seeing my idea on paper would legitimize my obstinance.

"We already did try it. I'm sorry but we have to stay on schedule. If we were here for six months then we could try everything but we're not." I was getting tired of pressing and releasing the talk-back button.

"Dan, it's a cool idea that Alex has, I don't know if we should just drop it," Jay offered, always the diplomat. His voice came in weak, being picked up by the mics at a distance. I wanted to scream at him and say that sometimes you have to take sides, (and of course, I needed him on mine).

"Look guys," I paused with my finger on the button and let out a sigh. I hated arguing with them. I just wanted everything to gel. "We don't have a lot of time. We have to finish tracking the bass and drums for this song *today*." I let go of the button and was met with a pregnant silence which meant I won.

They had more experience than me and I could tell they all, even Tim sometimes, were resentful of me being in charge. But fuck that, this was *my* project, my baby. Why are musicians criticized for being self-indulgent or control freaks for trying to mold things to stay true to their vision when it's not expected for painters to collaborate or novelists to sit around with five other writers coming up with a plot? Whether people loved it or hated it, even if the album bombed and was despised, or worse, met with indifference, I wanted it to be my sound. I had to get across what was in my head. There was something I desperately was trying to say and this was the only way I knew how to say it. I slumped in the high-backed captain's chair in front of the mixing board. I was glad Tim was out running an errand, he and I had our own battles and I didn't need him here for this one in case he weighed in on the other side.

I wanted to go down to the live-room to jam with the guys, patch things up while we were waiting for Tim to get back but I sat by myself in the control-room instead, afraid that going near Alex at that moment might have made things worse. I simmered in silence picking at the seam on the underside of the chair staring at the rows of lights and knobs on the board. After what felt like a long while of silence a four-count on the sticks cracked through the monitors then the bass and drums came in unison. My tom part thundered through the speakers.

. . .

There was a rivulet of sweat down the naked and nicked skin on the side of Jay's head. It was only June and my apartment already was sweltering. It portended a miserable summer. He was looking past me at the wall, staring at all the notes. "Dude, this might sound like it's from left field but, I think you're depressed. Maybe you should, like, see someone, you know, like a therapist or something."

"I've thought about it," I said, half-turning toward the wall for a moment, partly to show Jay my agitation and uneasiness with him staring at the wall and partly because I had to look again, reminding myself of the actuality of all those notes hanging there. I didn't want to get into this with Jay. "I don't know . . . I've seen so many shrinks over the years.

Ever since my parents broke up I've been seeing therapists. I think it's all bullshit. Ok, I mean, I'm sure it helps a lot of people . . . some people. It just doesn't work for me. I think I just need to figure stuff out on my own."

"Fair enough. You know, I just worry about you . . . Hey, you're lucky you don't have to work. Just remember that. You're living the life, man. You should be psyched." I knew he was trying to cheer me up, but hearing about how lucky I was and that I *should* be feeling good made me feel even worse, that I didn't even have an excuse.

"The advance is pretty much used up by now."

"How'd you blow all that money!"

"It wasn't that much," I said, pissed at his ignorance and feeling judged. "I don't think you understand—after the lawyers, and managers, and Tim and his studio—"

"I thought one of the reasons we went there was because The Watershed *wasn't* as expensive as the other places."

"It's not but it still ate most of the cash. Look at it as if I bought a Lexus instead of a Rolls. Cheaper but not cheap."

"I just thought Tim's place—"

I jumped on him, "I don't think you understand the amount of organizational and political bullshit I had to deal with between the label and studios and budgets to get the costs down to even where they were."

"That's what Sam was for. Maybe you should have relinquished some more control to him."

"Sam is a fucking opportunist! I never should have used him as a manager." I wanted to slap the bald sides of his head with a glove like men did when challenging someone to a duel. "More control? I should have done everything by myself! He was too high up, too much of a big shot. He didn't give a shit about me. I would have been better off with someone low on the totem pole but who cared about me or at least needed me to be successful. That's why the second shit started going south with the label Sam was nowhere to be found. I wasn't worth the bad blood for him, risking offending his contacts, whatever . . ."

"But it was still a lot of money?" Was he trying to piss me off? I had already spewed variations of this diatribe in the immediate weeks after we were dropped. I didn't understand why none of this was sinking in.

I was pacing now. "The point is with everyone else taking their cut— and don't forget I've been living off this egg, for what?, well over a year now—there's very little left." The truth is, and for some reason, I guess I was too embarrassed to tell him, "very little left" was actually "none left" by that time. Now, to my shame and much nervousness, I'm still not working and I've started taking cash advances on my credit cards to pay the rent and to live. Something in me refuses let go of what I wish I had, so I desperately and stubbornly live a lie, insanely not acknowledging that the money—and with it the dream—is gone.

"At least we're both rent stabilized."

"Got that right." I sat back down. "We don't even belong here in Manhattan anymore. Have you seen your street at night? The limos, the tools waiting on line at that club, whatever-the-hell it's called. It's just a fluke that people like us are even still here."


That night, in a wave of new-found self-consciousness thanks to Jay, I decided I had to protect myself and the apartment should anyone besides Jay—which considering my dearth of friends most likely only meant a random new girl I met somewhere—come over my place. The next day I went to the Kmart near Astor Place, bought some cheap bed sheets and nailed one up on the wall over the notes. During the day, even with my apartment's meager light the notes were still somewhat visible underneath the thin white sheet but at night they were fully obscured.

For weeks after that night every time I had a new note I would take the sheet off, stick the note up then re-hang the sheet. After a while this methodical activity became a chore but often during the ritual of it I began to wonder what these notes might all mean and perhaps, if anything at all, what they could or would be used for. Were they for an album? Were they for a book? A play? Some sort of avant-garde theater project? I didn't know. I just knew that these ideas, these notions, these scenes, sayings, aphorisms, platitudes, rants, characters, observations, charts, graphs, outlines, single words, punctuation and grammar-devoid hyperbolic scrawls, poems, lyrics, responses to questions that I only asked myself, rebuttals to arguments that didn't happen, letters to people I no longer talk to, grandiose plans, bullet lists, agendas, theories, suppositions, philosophies universal and personal, conversations I overheard, fading memories I wanted to catch before they slipped away, plots, treatments, schemes, song titles, book titles, cool names I wish were mine, pretty names and sexy names for girls I wish I knew, jumbles of words splattered in nonsensical pomo pretension, kept arriving in my head and I had to write them down. Not write them down because I knew or expected they would turn into anything necessarily, that there was some end result, some goal or project to lead toward but only, simply because I felt I owed it them (the ideas). It also wasn't out of narcissism that I was recording all these (perhaps disparate) thoughts; it's not that I thought everything I thought was worthy of permanence. It was that when the words flashed in my head I was commanded; the act of writing somehow had become not even just an impulse but an obligation. It wasn't clear to me whether in essence it was all more of a diary or more a collection of ideas, plans (for what I do not know)—both or neither. It was what it was: an unexplained compulsion.

Eventually I grew tired of what often was a several-times-a-day sheet ritual. These days, most of the time, I just leave the sheet in the closet except when I think there's an off-chance I may have a coed visitor, like when I'm heading out to a party like Andrea's. Every time I put the sheet up I worry it will be a Murphy's Law-invoking procedure, ruining my chances of having a nubile guest over later that night. Then I chide myself that there is no such thing as jinxing and continue hooking the sheet on the nails, obscuring my wall-o'-notes. I know having a sheet nailed on your wall is still disconcertingly strange for someone to see but I reason strange is better than creepy. A girl coming over for the first time to a guy's apartment she met at a bar at 2:00 a.m., perhaps a little nervous, with her guard up, would likely have her freak-detector set off if she saw all those notes. I figure: Sheet on wall = *kinda* weird, (and not that noticeable at night anyway with dim lights and through the haze of alcohol, lust, low self-esteem). Wall covered in scores of post-it notes = *scary* weird, as in "get-me-the-fuck-out-of-here-this-guy's-going-to-chop-me-into-pieces-and-put-me-in-his-freezer" weird.

. . .

We're having one of our staredowns again. Recently, they've been more intense and more frequent. I don't know how long it's been since I've been having them; there wasn't a declaration, or some definitive breaking point when I stopped playing. Like a lot of situations in life, I hadn't realized what the hell was happening until now, when I'm already deep in it.

The big explosions, the flare-ups, those are easy. It's the quiet, needling things, the details that slip by, the patterns that go unnoticed, time stretched like a strip of taffy; then you wake up one day and realize: I've been in a dysfunctional marriage for the past three years or Holy shit, I'm fat or I've been unhappy for so long I don't remember when I didn't feel this way.

Being in the middle of something in your life and not remembering or knowing how you got there, it's like when you've been swimming really hard with your head down and even when you take breaths your eyes are closed and then finally, you're really tired and you stop and you're doggy paddling and some snot is running out your nose and you look up and realize, shit, I'm in the middle of the lake.

I do remember a lot of specific days, specific times when I should have played but didn't. There were the days when I felt like I should, sensing it would be constructive or cathartic but guiltily I didn't because I just wasn't in the mood—I was too tired, too bored, too sad, too angry, too whatever (even though those were all the moods that used to be the impetus to play. [A long time ago every mood, every occasion was an impetus to play]). And worse, there were days when I *was* in the mood, when I desperately wanted to pick up that guitar, when the call was magnetic, intrinsic, near sexual in its pull but something, some vague sort of psychic energy, some distant queasiness I couldn't place was holding me back. — But along the way, strangely, all those days that I didn't play never added together for me. I had seen them as individual events and each slipped into the nebula of my memory not to grasped or connected to the present again.

Until tonight—as I sit on the couch, tahini-stained hand resting under my boxer's waistband, my back slumped against a scoliosis-inducing dead cushion, in the midst of yet another staredown. And for no other reason than I suppose it simply is time, those disparate days, the starry specs of disconnected memories are finally coalescing and now surging to the front of my brain, and I realize I haven't picked up my guitar, I haven't played or sung or written any music in a long, long time. Maybe since Chicago. And now all I do is stare. And I'm in the middle of the lake and I'm so tired from treading water but that's all I seem able to do.

It's a 1970 Gibson Hummingbird if you're wondering. It was the first thing I bought with my advance money. The day after I cashed the check I ventured out to Staten Island to the acoustic guitar mecca Mandolin Brothers. I walked in and announced to the salesguy, "I just signed a record deal. I have two thousand dollars cash in my pocket and I plan on walking out of here with the best guitar in the store." I knew it was a dumb statement, there's no such thing as a "best guitar" but I was delirious with promise and making a brash pronouncement felt deliciously right. I stayed there for five hours. I must have tried over fifty guitars—old Martins, new Taylors, dreadnoughts, jumbos, eight-thou-sand-dollar collectibles, four-hundred-dollar Korean-made mediocrities. The Hummingbird was far from being the most expensive, part of the finish was crackled, the stain was worn off on a spot on the back of the neck from use, and the chrome was tarnished—all "flaws" that in the fe-tishistic world of vintage guitars are seen as charming character builders, marks of authenticity—but most important, simply, and complexly, it felt better and sounded better than any other guitar in the place—to me.

On my way back home, on every leg of the nearly two-hour MTA extravaganza of a trip, riding the bus in Staten Island, the ferry back to the city, the #4 to the Brooklyn Bridge stop, then transferring to the #6 to Bleecker, I held the guitar in its sturdy hardshell case upright in be-tween my legs, my arms protectively, lovingly around the neck, with—if such is discernable—a look of terrified satisfaction on my face.

Looking back on that trip home from Mandolin Brothers it was one of the only times that all that money was for something purely good. I'd always been grateful for it but ultimately, and it took me a long while to realize it, the money was more curse than blessing.


The problems started when we got back from our stint in the studio. The finished album was being held in limbo (and eventually shelved) by the label and they wouldn't give us any more tour support. So aside from occasional gigs in the city, we were frozen. Touring wasn't possible because the label cut off the stipends to Jay and Alex, who then started playing with other bands again and working day-jobs as needed. I, on the other hand, had enough money left over from the advance that I didn't have to work.*

---

* Like a lot of solo artists started doing in the 90s, my band, Bryter Layter, was essentially just a vehicle for me as the frontman and sole songwriter. And as is not uncommon when a band clearly has a linchpin, the label only signed me; Jay and Alex were designated as employees. At the time, like so many New York musicians do, Jay and Alex were hedged, playing in multiple bands. So, when I got signed there weren't any hard feelings; in fact, as working musicians grinding it out in three, four, or five bands at any one time, they were just glad to be along for the ride in any capacity.

With the album finished and the label screwing me (by not putting it out and not releasing it to me), creatively and emotionally I was spent. My baby was being held in purgatory. Exhausted and demoralized, I found myself unable to do anything, and with a decent—(though having received the advance check over six months before, by that time already heavily dwindled)—cushion still left in the bank, for the first time in my life, I didn't have to.

Though trust funders and trophy wives may thrive, for me, not having to work became an existential disaster. Maslow's hierarchy. All my lower needs of shelter and safety were satisfied so I spent my days ruminating on my self-actualization which for me though, led closer to misery rather than transcendence. Perhaps more simply, the problem was Newtonian; I was an object no longer in motion and the more time I spent not doing anything and just thinking about things, the more paralyzed I became. I would have been better off being forced to work at least a few hours a week. Or, no: not Maslow or Newton. Kierkegaard! The anxiety of freedom. I had too much time on my hands, too many options. Having the "luxury" of time to think about things to the n'th degree was an imprisonment by the futility of circular thinking which led me to become more screwed up than when I had (the benefit of) the diversion of meaningless work. (Really, it's self-evident. Only someone with too much time and too many base needs already met could be this insular to self-educate on Kierkegaard et al. to explain why he was feeling the way he did).

THOUGH, perhaps I should acknowledge and mention that I innately have a tendency toward melancholy, brooding, and over-anxious thinking, and, oh, yes, there was the little matter that I had just been *dropped from my record label, annihilating my life's dream*, so I don't want to blame my poor mental state solely on bank cushion-induced idleness explained away by psych theory, laws of physics, or nineteenth century Danish philosophy. It's fair to say, I had what they call in medical euphemisms "contributing factors," a "predisposition," an "underlying condition" that just needed that little push. Like a suicidal teen handed a Cat Power disc or a copy of *The Bell Jar*, the tendency was there, it just needed the opportunity, the right circumstance to bloom, or rather, fester.

So here we are. Staredown time. I'm in the elevator-dimensioned claustrophobic's bad trip that is my studio apartment. The ceiling light is harshly reflecting in a spot off the tobacco-sunburst spruce top, phosphor bronze 12-gauge strings taut and silent. I can hear it; I can feel the mahogany back vibrating against my stomach; I see myself strumming a first-position G, every string in perfect tune ringing true, their harmonized waves dancing off the inside walls then exultantly radiating from the soundhole in a chorus brilliant and warm. I don't know why I can't get up and hold that guitar. I want to play, desperately so. But I will not. Instead I will stare and the Hummingbird will stare back and the Hummingbird always wins. And so tonight, I lose again. I finally blink, my eyes more bored than burning, and then look away.

People, I'm feeling queasy. I'm tired of sitting on my couch. I'm tired of Hummingbird staredowns. Why do I keep finding myself somewhere yet not able to know how I got there? Look at this wall, ridiculously covered, little flaps of paper like peeling shingles. My apartment has four walls and now one of them is fully coated in yellow post-it notes. (3M, oh how you've affected my life!)

I like writing on these small pieces of paper. Knowing there is finite space, the borders force me to be succinct, each square its own little world. I don't remember the first one but I know from the beginning I put them on the wall rather than in a drawer or a folder. It's like seeing my mind laid out into little pieces, all the notes on the wall. It's as if the foggier my brain gets the more I need to see it to keep track of things before they get lost. Or no, maybe it's not foggy at all. I'm on a tear, getting sharper by the day, reaching something, heading somewhere and

I'm just a poor man's stenographer stuck with these little pieces of paper instead of that nice long scroll they gave us in steno school, frantically trying to keep up and record it all. I'm a passerby taking snapshots of a crime?, a fire?, a stampede? roaring behind my eyes trying to capture, document whatever I can. It all happens so fast sometimes . . . I don't know why I keep doing this. Maybe just like with my music where I charted everything out, in essence, this—(my life?)—is the same; I need to see things in order for them to make sense.

I do have a general idea that this all—the notes and the guitar stare-downs—started around the same time which also was right around when I was dropped and my record was stolen. Look, I know it's not a coincidence. I know there's some sort of connection between all that. But what or exactly how, I don't know.

So looking back, the timing and the connections are obvious but so what? That doesn't mean I'm not still living this way anyway. Doesn't mean I know how to change things. Doesn't change the fact that I'm in the middle of the lake. Therapy's declarative precept that identification and analysis lead to solution is a dirty myth. Analysis just leads to more analysis. I know what has happened; I see where I am now; I've thought about it all a lot; and I am still unable to change. So, I ask you: what is the point of awareness without action?

So now here I am, humbled by the Hummingbird, cradled by yellow squares, growing a debt, alone on my couch.

II

It's early evening, the late summer dusk is overtaking the sky, and my stomach is burning again. I'm walking toward the Duane Reade on Broadway to pick up an old prescription for some fancy purple pills for my stomach and for added firepower, or rather *cooling*power, a bottle of Pepcid Complete, a pretty kickass OTC antacid I've gotten into recently. The eighteen months I squeezed out of my cobra health insurance after I left Antonelli's—the East Side Italian place, part of the Grubman Restaurant Group, (five places in New York, one in L.A. and one opening in Vegas)—finally kicked a few weeks ago. I'd been putting this off as long as I could, avoiding the outlandish price for prescription meds but the burn came back even in just these few weeks without the purple pill.

For the past week or so I've been drinking a cocktail of fresh ground ginger stirred into a Dixie cup of Pepto as a demented home-remedy for my acid reflux. Someone told me that ginger helps sooth the stomach but I think it just has made me numb, which was good as far as relieving the burn but worried me because I feared it was dangerously treating the symptom not the disease. The numbness was so prevailing that I assumed damage was still being done to my stomach only I couldn't feel it.

I'm walking to this store on Broadway instead of a drugstore closer to home because supposedly, walking helps with acid reflux, at least that's what I read in some article in the *Times* last week. Something having to do with peristalsis and gravity, they said. Really, if you don't have a bad stomach you don't know the different lengths (no pun intended) that you'd travel to get some relief.

(To make matters worse, and I won't get into detail, my ass has been bothering me too. So, as long as I'm there I might as well pick something up to help that situation as well).

I find myself squinting when I enter the store as I walk toward the medicines in the back. Even though I've come in from the over-lit city streets, the light in here is obnoxious and jarring, intense enough to meet safety standards for an O.R. "Whose idea was this?" A question I thought was secured in my head surprisingly mutters from lips. Some executive committee, after reviewing the data from a market research consulting firm they paid two million dollars, decided that indeed, blinding fluorescent light bewilders the consumer to a point that he inadvertently buys more deodorant or power bars or cheap hair-brushes.

Some easy listening song is raining from the shitty, no-bottom-end ceiling speakers like a vinegar mist. As the song plods forward, recycling into the chorus yet again, bursts of static and crackle begin to weave in and out of the music. (Can they possibly have the PA tuned to a radio station? How does a chain with this much money not have cable or satellite radio, or at least some consultant-created mix CDs? Maybe it's bad wiring). The static and the music together is a mix so caustic it prickles through the air and soars into my ear straight to my brain, so penetrating it's as if the standard filters and impediments of the outer ear and the canal aren't even here, as if this noise was purposeful in its intent, reaching its endpoint with precision like an Olympic bobsled staying centered on the track, nimbly avoiding the sides. Like a million needle-tipped sperm heading to my brain, their egg, they are attacking, infecting with their diseased DNA. It doesn't matter what song it is. It's always the same song. All the *You Light Up My Lifes* and *Dancing on the Ceilings*, the muzaked *Penny Lanes*—the sinister calculation of blandness, of inoffensiveness to the silent shopping majority—it's all one song.

There are four people loitering by the pharmacist's window in the back waiting for their drugs. I put in my order and the receptionist tells me it'll be ten to fifteen minutes before mine is ready. I want to plead that "he doesn't even have to *do* anything, my pills are already made, all he has to do is grab the bottle" but instead I muster a "thanks" and wander off to the aisles to look for the Pepcid. I pass the time by reading and comparing the ingredients of the generic brand products and the name-brand ones. Fleet Enema, Afrin Nose Spray, Tylenol, Advil, Advil Cold and Sinus, Advil Cold Sinus Allergy, Fibercon, Sudafed are all identical with their Duane Reade counterparts. I wonder how many sick people have touched all the packages I keep picking up and I absent-mindedly rub my hand against my jeans, not knowing if it's a symbolic gesture to appease my psyche or if it actually does something to sanitize my hand.

And it doesn't matter what store it is exactly. You've been here before, a thousand times. The Duane Reade-Kmart-Walgreens-Rite Aid-genera chain drug store. The mild though still requisite self-consciousness when you're picking up some personal hygiene product; the queasy pleasure of the blissfully artificial air-conditioning on a sweltering day; the trance-inducing fluorescent light beating down on and reflecting off the inter-changeable, over-marketed, plastic and cardboard contained products, the mottled white linoleum floor, and you. You grab your ass cream or zit medicine or fancy dental floss, the synthetic miracle they call "dental tape," no doubt the end-product of an R & D campaign with a budget rivaling a small African nation's GDP, and head to the front of the store. It's a long line filled with nobodies like you as the overweight, acne-faced failure behind the register methodically, dilatorily scans each item of the guy at the counter, six people ahead of you on line, bitterly strug-gling to even the score of her foundered life on the patrons in her store. She glances up at the silent, shrugging line with a sulky indifference while s-l-o-w-l-y scanning the next item. Her lot in life is not what she bargained for and we are being made to pay dearly for her frustration, her deprivation of her due. The same petty revenge of service workers everywhere, the bouncer not letting you in the club, the maitre d' con-descending to you at the trendy restaurant, the auto-mechanic charging for whatever repairs he wants because he knows you have no idea what happens in the mechanical bowls of your car.

I close my eyes and quietly exhale. I am walking in the hallway of my building, carrying my meds in the plastic bag, twirling it in a Ferris wheel watching the centrifugal laws of physics keep the contents snug in the bottom of the bag. I'll jiggle the key in the lock until it catches, then turn it and feel the deadbolt shift, and I am home. The apartment is dark and silent. I'll feel relief as I am finally back home, alone. And I will feel queer and unsettled because I will be home, alone.

As I step up to the register a Mariah Carey song comes down from the ceiling engulfing the store in a putrid, aural miasma. The production, the lyrics, her voice, stream down on me from these tinny in-ceiling speakers like acid rain. The chorus, some asinine platitude resembling "you are the hero/the hero is within" swells while overtop she vomits histrionic shrieks and abuses melisma as if it were the only means of expressing emotion, a soulless entertainer's shorthand for exclaiming *Passion* (and it is dutifully interpreted as such by her grotesque, disturbingly vast legion of fans). I'm picturing her hand quivering its way down with an ersatz religious fervor as she wrings the guts out of a defenseless note. Why must these stores do this to me? The tyranny of the lowest common denominator—the forced music in the modern chain store. Billboards you can try to avert your eyes, magazine ads you can avoid by not reading magazines, TV ads you can change the channel or just leave the room. But there's no escape from this.

I push the door on the right to exit and there's a person trying to enter on *my* side, the *exit* side. Is she that lazy that she can't open her door on the "enter" side? We bump, literally, into each other as I assume she'd let me out first and she assumed (rudely) I'd let her in first. The person leaving the store has the right of way, it's like the subway, you always let people *out* first. Irritated then startled from the bump I look at her, our faces inches away from each other. It takes just a moment to process. It's the girl from the stairwell in my building on the night of Andrea's party. *The* girl. Wrong side? Who said anything about a wrong side? As we pass, she seems to stall, if ever so slightly. Does she recognize me too?!

"Hi! You were at Andrea Leibman's party, right?" I exclaim, instantly regretting being so enthusiastic.

"Yeah," she says slowly. Her faces twists a little and her brow furrows as she looks at me. "Were you—"

"I saw you on the stairs," I interrupt. "I was coming down, you were going up."

"Right!" *She recognizes me! She's excited! There's a chance! I have a chance!* I'm staring at her. My face showing the sweet mania of a down syndrome smile. The harsh fluorescent light of Duane Reade is now somehow bathing her in a warm angelic glow. The bleeps of the cash registers are birds singing. Mariah Carey raining (and reigning) from the ceiling, now a glorious hallelujah chorus. "I guess we're always coming and going."

Three teenagers approach the door from outside behind her. They're in ubiquitous hip-hop attire, super-long shirts and jeans hanging below their waists, and despite the mild weather the middle one has on an XL "varsity" style jacket with leather sleeves. The one in front has on a pristine White Sox hat turned askew, its charcoal brim flat and stiff like a slate tile. He gives me a hard stare. *You win, you're tougher than I am.* I backpedal into the store and she follows forward allowing my new pals to enter then wander past us. I wonder if the Preparation H package (I told you I wouldn't go into detail) is visible through my bag. I clutch it nervously then hold it off to the side somewhat out of view. Just how opaque is this white plastic? That damn bold yellow and black packaging; everyone knows their logo. A black slip should be provided to cover any medicines having to do with your ass or other nether-regions like the black-out plastic cover on porno mags that are sent in the mail.

"So, shopping for some—" I turn around and see a rack of Halloween candy, "Halloween candy?" I pick up a bag of candy corns and dangle them. "It's only, what? Six, seven weeks from now."

"I'm buying some toothpaste if you must know," she says through a cute laugh and broad smile that swells her cheek bones and makes her eyes squint just a bit.

"To protect your teeth from all the candy you're buying?" I do a game show model hand-caress across the display.

"I'm not buying Halloween candy!" She's laughing, still! "It's the middle of September." Did I brush my teeth today? Shit. I can't remember. Her laugh dies down and there's a panicked silence.

"So, do you live in the neighborhood?"

"I'm on Astor Place," she says, motioning with a nod of her head in the general direction. "Where are you?"

"I'm on—I'm in Andrea's building. Remember?"

"Right! I'm such an idiot. Where is that? East Third?"

"East Fourth."

"Right," she says again and shakes her head. "I've only been there, like, twice or something."

"I'm between First and Second. Right next to Jeollado."

"What's Jeollado?"

"That sushi place."

"Oh," she says. She looks embarrassed and apologetic like a student admitting to a teacher she didn't do her homework, "I don't eat sushi."

"You don't? Either do I!" Calm down.

"You mean to tell me I've found the only other person in New York who doesn't eat sushi!" She says, her face aglow.

"Ahh. It's destiny then that we meet again."

"You mean again after this?"

"No, I meant 'again' as in right now."

"So, not again after right now?"

"No, well, that too . . . If you want."

"I do. Sure. Let's meet again."

"Wait. But does that mean we have to wait for destiny, again?"

"Hmm. Good point."

"We don't want to tempt fate twice do we?"

"Sometimes we need to take destiny into our own hands."

"I agree!" I'm smiling too much. Why can't I be cool?

"All right, Mr. I-don't-eat-sushi. What do you say we meet in front of Jeollado and then go out for Italian. We'll show them."

"Ok, you're on. I'm Dan by the way. Daniel Green."

"Lisa Arroyo." She fumbles around in her bag then hands me a business card. I glance at it then stick it in my pocket.

"You're a lawyer?"

"I hope so. I paid NYU enough money." She brushes her hair, which is parted in the middle and hangs down straight and perfect to her shoulders, with both hands off her face. For the first time I'm actually seeing *her*. It's like up to this point, when I had seen her on the stairwell, and even in this whole conversation until this moment, I hadn't really been seeing her. It's hard to explain. Does someone ever all of a sudden just look different to you? More nuanced, more real? ". . . Actually, I'm still paying."

I smile and laugh then say, "So, I'll call you?"

"I hope so," she says and gives my arm a light squeeze then walks past me and the candy racks then turns down an aisle and disappears into the store.


Too amped up to go home I swing by Jay's which is basically on the way anyway.

"Hello?" crackles through the intercom.

"Yo."

"Green?"

"Yeah."

"What's up?"

"I just met a girl. So hot. Can I come up?"

"Yeah, yeah," he says and buzzes me in.

When I get to his door it's cracked open, the deadbolt down preventing it from closing. I push my way in. Jay's on the far side of the room behind his decks.

"Yo."

"Yo."

"So, what's the story with this chick?" he calls to me from behind the table as I walk toward him. I give him the back-story—that I was at Andrea's, (I don't even bother getting into Amy's-friend-savior-girl), that I saw her on the stairs, I give a condensed explanation of the frozen moment phenomenon, then I give the capper—that I just *bumped* into her at Duane Reade.

"I don't know. It's weird though," I say. "She's the first Street Wife I'm ever going to actually go out on a date with."

"Cosmic."

"Hmm."

"What?" He says annoyed.

"What?"

"Your voice."

"What?" I say annoyed.

"*Hmm*," he imitates me and rolls his eyes. "Just go out with her. I know your whole life theory on Street Wives. You think I don't listen to you? I remember more of your shit than you do."

"That's probably true," I say through a chuckle. "I'm sorry, I can't get beyond it. Street Wife theory lives on. She's a corporate lawyer, man."

"Oh, really?"

"Yeah."

"So what."

"So, things are never going to work with me and some corporate lawyer. Not that I'm looking for . . . I'm just saying."

"Whatever Dan."

"I'm just saying. When we were on the stairs. It was perfect."

"Do you want real life or do you want perfection?"

"Can't I have both?"

"No."

"What about music?"

"What about it?"

"That's both. I want it to feel like it does when we're playing music. I want it to feel like that."

"That's not how it works."

"I think it does . . . or it *can* at least."

"It doesn't. I'm *in* a relationship. I can tell you, it doesn't work like that. That doesn't mean it's not great. It's just different."

"I don't know . . ."

"Just go out with her and see what happens."

"I don't know . . ."

"She's not even a Street Wife anyway. She's a Stairwell Wife."

"True." We bump fists and laugh.

"Hey check this out." He holds one earphone to his ear, cues one of the records then cricks his neck and cradles the earphone and spins both turntables. A female a cappella singer comes on chanting what sounds like Celtic rhymes. He swells the volume on the other deck playing a thunderous basic kick—snare—high-hat beat. He shouts over the music, "I FOUND THIS CRAZY IRISH FOLK SINGER. THEN I SLAP THIS 4/4 BEAT UNDERNEATH. IT TOTALLY WORKS!" He's rocking back and forward with the beat with his head still cricked to the side holding the earphone. He looks autistic.

"YEAH. VERY COOL." The floor is rumbling with each thump of the kick drum. His head is uniform peach-fuzz. He must have shaved off that ridiculous mohawk in the past week. I'm energized seeing him in his element, creating, happy. His joy radiates in near-tangible waves. The ever-present burn that I've been feeling because I don't seem able to create or play anymore that's been coursing through me like an un-remitting current buzzing through a glowing filament, suddenly, if only ephemerally, doesn't feel quite as bad. The sting is not diminished nor is it numbed, the filament still burns as bright as ever, but there is some-thing in some other part of me now that's offsetting its incandescence. Like a car's headlights on during the day, they're just as bright as they are at night, but surrounded by the light of day they don't seem so.

On the way home from Jay's as I walk the streets the rush of data begins. Words, ideas, computations flood my head. By this time I've taken to bringing a post-it pad with me whenever I leave the house in preparation for the floods but I've forgotten it today. I find an old MTA machine receipt in my pocket and grab the pen from my jacket. (I've been wearing a jacket a little sooner than the weather has necessitated just so I have a place to hold a pen; my pant's pocket, I quickly found was a bad idea). I stop on 4th between Bowery and Second and leaning on my thigh, I scribble away in microscopic font until the receipt is covered. I pull out Lisa's card, glance at her name then flip it over and continue to write until it too is full. I go to the deli on the northwest corner of 4th and Second. They know me because I'm in there all the time buying their discounted Ben & Jerry's pints, (which sadly are now 3 for 10, not the glorious old days of 2 for 5), so I don't feel bad giving a quick nod to the register guy as I swipe a napkin off the counter and run out. (Not that the napkins cost them much but it still would have been rude to just take one and walk out). Again I lean on my thigh and this time there's more space to write but I have to use larger print because of the porous material and I struggle to fit everything on there and to keep it legible. A girl walks by me and I'm aware that I probably look weird standing in the middle of the sidewalk writing on this napkin I'm holding on my leg but I don't re-ally care. I don't bother to look up, I just notice her pass in my peripheral vision as I keep writing. When I get home I toss the receipt, the business card, and the napkin on the table. I lay back on my couch and gaze at the wall. Later tonight I will transfer the text to post-its and stick them on the wall amongst the others.

． ． ．

I called her. Despite her Street Wife status, or maybe because of it. Forget about all my reservations and theories, don't listen to that shit. How could I not call her?

It's ten after five on the Sunday following the Tuesday that we bumped into each other at Duane Reade. I'm standing in front of Jeollado waiting for her. When I called her to set up the date, as an alternative to our pro-posed Italian dinner, I suggested a late-afternoon walk and she agreed. No doubt a girl like Lisa has been taken to fine restaurants, bought thirteen dollar martinis and picked up in cabs. Often. I can't afford any of that so why bother trying to compete. And who knows, a walking date might be something new for her.

For the past ten minutes I've been doing my best standing here trying to look occupied. These are the times when I wished I smoked. Around my late teens smokers stopped looking cool to me but they do still have one thing going for them: they look occupied. Somehow it seems not acceptable to be out in society doing nothing, just staring into space. Only old people are given a free pass to sit on benches and zone-out into the middle distance. I wonder if that's simply because they're old and they've earned it or if because when they were young it was okay to not be busy, so their behavior has been grandfathered in, as it were. What happened to good old-fashioned loitering? Leaning against a building with your hands in your pockets?

I'm standing here, hands in pockets, a living anachronism, feeling more and more awkward as it seems every person walking by me is on the phone. The cigarette of the 00s is the cell phone. The new prop. A cell phone on a Manhattan street is like the security blanket of holding a beer bottle at a party. But the cell one-ups the cigarette and the beer bottle, not only does it make you look occupied, it also shows how important you are. Someone wants to talk to *me*! I'm alone but I am not really alone. Look at all these people. It's as if no one can bear to be by themselves. Mustn't. Have. Any. Time. To. Myself. Must not, be, *here*, now. How can you let your mind drift, how can you truly absorb the streets if you're always talking to someone somewhere else? And so standing here, doing nothing but watching people stroll by, I'm the odd man out, the Luddite loser. All the grace in loneliness and being alone has been stripped from us.

Anyway, so here I am in my fidgety nervousness waiting for Lisa. Discomfited by the sidewalk scene, I turn to the window of Jeollado while keeping an eye on the street. It's surprisingly crowded for so early. East Village trendoids stuffing their faces with raw fish rushed to New York on a pollution-spewing plane from some distant, depleting sea. I turn back to the street.

Today, for the first time this year, autumn is palpable; the sun is still strong but there's just a hint of chill. And it very well may just be in my head but I think I can smell the season on the way. Things just seem different in the air.

I'm wearing my everyday jeans, Rod Laver sneakers and a three-quarter length softball-style t-shirt with dark-blue sleeves and a white torso with a crumbling silkscreen of a logo for a band I no longer listen to. My left hand is in my pocket and I've got my blue hoody zippered sweatshirt wrapped around my left arm.

I spot Lisa heading down the sidewalk toward me. She has a blank, if not, determined look on her face which only slightly breaks when she notices me. She too has on blue-jeans and she's wearing sandals that I've always dug, the ones with the wood soles and the one leather strap with the buckle across the top. She has on a burgundy long sleeve shirt with girlie trim around the plunging neckline and an unbuttoned cardigan of matching color on over top. Brown hair of flaxen quality and such shine rarely seen outside a shampoo commercial is casually parted in the middle and just kisses the tops of her shoulders. Alex Chilton is crooning the opening lines of Kangaroo in my head. She's not frail and is at least 5'4", probably 5'5", but she gives off the impression that she is more compact, somehow smaller than she is, as if cuteness were more aura than physicality. We hug hello. She has a curvy frame and feeling her chest press into me and the swoop of her lower back dipping out to her hips in my arm, as if it is an ergonomic groove specifically for me, is intoxicating. With one good squeeze, disciplined, I quickly let go, not wanting to skeeve her out with a lingering embrace.

"This is so sweet and charming, going for walk" she says.

"Well I wanted to do something different." And cheap. "I mean, how many times have you been out for drinks or to dinner for a date in this city. I thought this would be fun; a good way to chat a little and get to know each other."

"And without all the fear of 'is there spinach stuck between my teeth?'"

"Exactly." It's difficult even looking at her, she's so adorable. And funny! Now she's funny. Great—I don't have a chance. "And if things go horribly wrong, you can just run away. Being on the street has its advantages."

"I don't know, these things are tough to run in." She looks toward her feet and shakes her right foot around. "Maybe I'll just clunk you on the head if I have to."

"Kind of like a fight or flight thing. Head-clunk or run, whatever you need to do for your survival." This is too easy. It should not be this easy.

We head west on Fourth Street and pass Plate Techtonic.

"Oh, is this that trendy bar?" Lisa asks motioning to the brushed steel door.

"Yeah. Velvet ropes, the whole deal."

She makes a "hmph" sound but it's not clear to me whether it's a disgust hmph or a hmm type of hmph, in that she might want to go there.

"Man, I remember when it used to be this great dive bar right when I first moved here. Flannigan's or Finnegan's . . . something Irish like that."

"Oh, you're such a New York veteran. *I remember when* this *used to be* this," she says laughing.

"Yes, I'm an official New Yorker now. I have a wistful lament for the *old* place," I say giving air quotes to "old".

We turn south down Bowery. It's been a long time since I've walked down the street with my very own girl and it feels good. I ask her how she knows Andrea, wondering how this corporate lawyer runs in the same circle as super-coolster Andrea.

"She used to temp at my firm."

Aha! "Used to? She doesn't any more?"

"No, that was years ago."

"Oh," I say trying to hide my disappointment. I'm surprised how much of a letdown this is. God, I'm so fucking petty. "But you guys stayed friends, huh?"

"It's funny, she was there right when I first started. I hadn't gotten my sea-legs yet, so to speak, didn't really know any of the partners or associates well, and that place can be a real boys club, so we sort of bonded on that together."

"I can imagine," I say, not sure exactly what I was referring to. I just wanted to say something to let her know I was listening.

"We're not really close or anything, we sort of have different lives, and I'm so busy anyway . . . but you know, we talk once in a while. I was surprised when she invited me to her party that night."

"Glad she did." Ugh!—so earnest! I wish I had said something funny or witty but I couldn't think of anything fast enough. She smiles at me. I can't tell if it's a true smile or one of those obligatory flight attendant smiles. After a few tortured moments I let it go; otherwise I'll drive myself crazy wondering.

We chat about the change in the neighborhood, how Bowery used to be scary and now is pedestrian. "No pun intended!" I say as I take a few dramatic steps, (and she laughs!). We pass Spring Street where the meat market bar *Sweet and Vicious* is just off the corner and we both bemoan its lameness.

"Maybe if I was twenty-two *and* desperate *and* a total cheeseball I'd go there ... *maybe*," she says and makes this face where she rolls her eyes and the right side of her upper lip curls up. It's the type of quirk that would at best come across benignly, or more likely off-putting if exhibited by anyone else. But on her it's endearing. I feel charmed just for noticing it and to my inner embarrassment I instantly find myself eager for the next time she makes this face, as if it were a private treat just for me. People have no idea of all the little things they do, things they may not even notice themselves, that in their peculiarity, or even especially in their banality, utterly enchant someone else. I fight the urge to hold her hand.

As we walk I'm continually sensing the new air, this autumnal teaser. But my awareness of the weather is not a sign of distraction from Lisa rather it is an enhancement of her. All those things along our periphery that normally are a distraction (or our awareness of them simply a sign that we want to be distracted), every once in a while become a necessary part of our main focus, as if every single seemingly unrelated detail is essential, like a master artist's brush portraying every last nuance of a scene, and if any little thing were missing the painting just wouldn't be the same. I am able to notice everything around me—the weather, the sounds, the smells—yet I am still totally focused on Lisa. This is going to sound very corny but here it goes: it feels like the world right now is a symphony and she is the lead soprano, the city streets, the air, the cars, and the people we pass along the way are the orchestra, strings fluttering, light woodwinds sustaining a top note, somber brass in an adagio swell, all there to support the main theme, the prevailing melody, Lisa.

Or maybe, if I allow myself this thought, Lisa and me.

You know that condition SAD? Seasonal Affective Disorder. It's when people in places like Sweden or Seattle want to kill themselves because it's too dark and gray all winter. Its effect is so debilitating that Scandinavian governments subsidize trips to the Mediterranean in the cold months to avoid a population drop-off. We need light. We need sun. I know this.

Yet I know that I am not built for summer. It's self-diagnosed but I am fairly certain that I have Reverse-SAD. Summer is too bright, too excitable. There's too much pressure to be happy, peppy. You're guilty if you're not always *doing* something. If you sit inside all day you're a jerk. For me, too much sun kills contemplation and breeds misery. In summer the life balance between thought and action is fearfully tilted too far on the side with which I am not fully comfortable. I'm no ghost-skinned shut-in, I revel in my charge of vitamin D, but like a hyper-active child cranky and exhausted after a long rambunctious day, by the end of summer that light-generated pep has worn me down and I am eager for the relief of fall. Staying indoors is no longer a crime and even being outside, in cooler climes under blissful gray skies, there is no obligation to run, to lust, to *go*. Just stroll and *be*. (And by the way, autumnal reprieve doesn't count in LA or Florida. There need to be *leaves*, the kind that *change* and *fall* and there needs to be the musty odor of decay in the air. Nothing brings about contemplation like death).

And autumn is the only break in the year from a relentless onslaught of forced positivity. The Christmas cheer, the New Year's resolutions that never resolve, and worst of all, like a histamine-laden gust of pollen blown in my face, the grating irritant in the spring air of all the false promises people make, everyone pretending to everyone else (and to themselves) that they are going to have some sort of renewal.

There are no expectations in Autumn. My temperature has lowered, heart slowed, and the trees start to turn and get ready for their long repose. Autumn is like a whole season of that sweet time just before you go to sleep. Just as dusk is the most beautiful and thought provoking part of the day, autumn is the dusk of the year. With every breath, with every step, I can feel the acid in my stomach disappearing like Alka-Seltzer disintegrating in a glass of water.

Things are moving along so effortlessly that we've walked for a half hour without even feeling it. I ask Lisa if she has ever walked the Brooklyn Bridge and she says no. The onramp is just a block or two away.

"Once we start there's no turning around though," I warn her.

"Why can't we turn around on the bridge?"

"I don't know. It's just one of those things . . . if you start it it's almost blasphemous not to finish."

As we make our way from the ramp onto the bridge, she takes her shoes off and walks barefoot on the wooden planks of the walkway, her sandals dangling from her left hand. She lets out a small, self-conscious giggle. "I feel a little silly doing this," she says watching her feet, "but . . . I don't know," she says and shrugs happily. Our shadows stretch long on the path in front of us. I turn around and walk backwards for a few steps; the setting sun is peaking between the remaining towers, of which there are many, of lower Manhattan and in an instant is obscured by them then swallowed up by New Jersey and the Hudson. A thick breeze gusts off the East River but it is mild and I barely feel it through my sweatshirt. I wonder if Lisa might be cold though, as girls tend to get cold faster than guys do, and I offer her my jacket, with the disclaimer that I know that is one of the cheesiest moves of all time. Laughing, she accepts as I drape it over her shoulders.

"If only this were a varsity football jacket," she sighs, pulling it around her, "then I could complete my fantasy." I adjust the coat a little bit longer than I need to, reveling in our first real touch, (the hello hug doesn't count).

"Sorry, my only connection with the football team was being beat up by the quarterback in seventh grade. But I've got a whole arsenal of moves! Maybe we can go to a movie and I'll yawn and nonchalantly put my arm around you."

"Ooh, that's a good one. You know all the classics."

We make it to the other side of the bridge and stop at the flight of stairs near the end of the walking path. Lisa drops her sandals on the ground and leans on my shoulder as she wriggles each of her feet in. We descend the stairs and walk down the street past the Manhattan Bridge, turn onto Jay Street and head toward the water. The smell of lacquer fills the air as we pass an open garage door to a furniture finishing shop where two guys are hand-sanding a baroque looking chair. A few twenty-some-things with messenger bags dutifully slung over right shoulders are chatting away walking into Superfine, one of the new restaurants in the area, with the same air of belonging as suited men strolling into Le Cirque. A black BMW driven by a white guy with long sideburns talking into a dangling cell phone earpiece speeds by, the sounds of East Coast hip-hop drifting out his sunroof mixing with the trailing exhaust. We make a left onto Water Street and stop in the factory shop of Jacques Torres, the famed chocolatier. We share a cup of hot chocolate the richness of molten lava. For certain, they must simply melt a few of their regally epicurean bars in a kettle then pour the potion into a cup. No water, no milk. The flavor is so intense it makes a Hershey bar seem like sugared dirt.

And here I am, in the glorious autumn twilight of Brooklyn, New York. Lisa, my Frozen Moment girl, her nose hidden inside the cup we are sharing of the greatest hot chocolate in the world as she takes a sip is wearing my old navy-blue sweatshirt. Without thinking I put my arm around her and I am frightened and excited yet coolly at ease with what my instincts just made me do. For so long: I have felt the crushing disappointment of middling days; I've drifted away as if the only way to bear it was to watch my life from afar, frustrated and powerless, relegated to the role of mere observer of an insipid play. For the first time in months or maybe even years, I am present. I am here.

# OCTOBER

It had been a great day for a walk. In the past week the atmosphere had finally changed, the last remnants of filthy, dragged-out summer air were extinguished, sent south, or along the jet stream somewhere above the Atlantic, or wherever that air goes until the first gross day in June. There would be no more errant short-sleeve days. This was it, we were now officially on our way into a new year. Yes, a new year. Even six years out, after twenty-odd years of school beginning every fall, changing leaves don't feel like decay but the start of something new. I was leaving the G.I. doc's on Amsterdam in the West 60s. Even though when I saw him in late August he knew my insurance was to have run out by this appointment, Dr. Geller, the mensch that he is, told me to come in anyway.

"Daniel, I worry about you."

"I thought you said my stomach was going to be ok?" I said panicked.

"Your stomach is going to be fine. I'm worried about *you*," he said. "Come in for one last follow-up, no charge."

After Geller's once-over ended with a paternal hand on my shoulder send-off, I was on the street, with what I knew would be my final goodie-bag of purple pill samples in tote, (I had already almost gone through the bottle I bought last month). I was headed to the Columbus Circle subway station for the B train back home when a gust of poignant, Autumn air met me. I combed my fingers through my hair as the wind swept it back and I wore a broad grin not sure whether it was out of squinting necessity or out of a rare swell of quiet joy. As I made my way east I passed a frumpy but still dignified-looking woman. Her brown hair was frizzy and short with streaks of gray and she was sporting black slacks and a tweed Annie Hall blazer. I wondered what she was doing out in the middle of the day. Was she a professor, a housewife, divorced wife with a good settlement? When I'm out on a workday, I'm often guessing what people are doing, where they're going. I knew why I was out at four o'clock, but I had a safe assumption that stretching the last dollars of a record deal advance wasn't her story too.

As I continued east on 62nd I was still feeling a bit of a high from Geller's generosity and the clean bill of health he gave my stomach. The air felt good and I was dressed just right for the weather—jeans, a thin, waffle long-sleeve and an unbuttoned fleece-lined corduroy jacket. I wanted to stay outside in this air forever. When I got to Central Park West, instead of turning down toward Columbus Circle, I headed north a few blocks then turned into the park. Just ahead on my path, a smattering of early fallen leaves swirled off the pavement then funneled gently back down like a lazy tornado. Emboldened by my mood, I bought a hot pretzel, which as any New Yorker knows is a hit-or-miss proposition. The outside crust was warm but the inside was cold and the whole thing was stale. I took another bite then threw it in the garbage but I didn't mind. I felt empowered just for taking the gamble. On Fifth Avenue, a sophisticated mom in knee-high leather boots and a gray wool skirt emerged from a building pushing a stroller with an air of smug security that comes from being a mom who lives on Fifth Avenue and takes her kid for afternoon strolls. As I got into the 50s an M5 bus slowed ahead of me and for a moment I was going to try to catch it but I decided to walk the rest of the way home instead.

New York women hit their sartorial stride in October. The air is finally cool enough for them to put some clothes on. By this time of year, I've long since bored of summer skin and I'm pining for cosmopolitan coziness. It's not about SEX the way summer is; I can finally appreciate style; faces and hair take on a renewed prominence; I can imagine conversations and candle-lit dinners and going to the movies, anything really, the whole world has opened up again. Relief! Quiet rejoice as I slip into a rich world of fantasy as I walk the streets, no longer compelled, imprisoned purely by primal urges. The jackets, jeans, sweaters, skirts, shoes, boots in all their different styles and sensibilities, I don't care who they are, the midtown corpobots, the Marni Hill princesses, the society wives, the laidback Brooklynites, all are good for a gander. And of course my girls downtown, like the one ahead of me on the bench in Madison Square Park in her tight jeans and a jacket with those adorable furry donut cuffs and collar reading, is that?—yes,—Rilke —I love them all.

As I head down the Bowery I approach a new building going up, a grid of I-beams reaching toward the sky. Union guys have erected a giant inflatable rat on the sidewalk out-front and are blowing whistles and chanting. A delivery truck passing them honks manically like a Morse code tapper on speed. The men's voices on the street swell in response. I feel a surge fire through me and a lump in my throat. I have no idea the politics of the situation but I'm overwhelmed by the solidarity and community between all these men. I have a moment of delirium— euphoric and on the verge of tears. The sense that I don't have anything approaching a community or a team rushes me like someone swung open a door to a sauna in front of me. I think about me, Jay and Alex facing each other in a circle, my arm, near-dead chugging away on a chord, Jay is at the top of the neck on his bass, his fingers a blur, his eyes wide, his back arched, Alex is wincing, looking like he's on the verge of collapse, his arms flailing but tight and in control, at once chaotic and robotic, holding us all together.

When I got home my legs ached a bit from the long walk and I settled into the couch. I watched TV, stared at my guitar, and dozed-off killing time before Lisa, who is on her way upstairs now, was to arrive. She usually doesn't get out of work until eight or nine and even then, she often shows up later than whatever time she said she'd meet me. Earlier today, before I left for Geller's, I was excited when she called to tell me she would be able to leave early and be at my place by around seven.

"We could have dinner together," she added before blurting, "oh shit. I have to jump into a meeting. Seeyalater," and hung up. It's now 8:23. She hadn't called to say she'd be late and up until the buzzer thirty seconds ago, I'd been pacing the apartment starving and agitated, more pissed-off than worried that I hadn't heard from her. Yet when I open the door the acrid-churn in my gut is swiftly mollified. Her dark hair and warm eyes, even her clothes, her maple-brown corduroy jacket project a synesthetic gustatory presence of warm caramel coating my stomach. All is forgiven. And I hate myself for letting her do this to me. But I cannot fight it. Lisa, with flushed cheeks and silky brown parted on the side, not the middle part that it usually seems to fall into, is standing in the threshold with me inches away holding the door. It is one of those enchanted moments when you're near a girl who has just come in from the brisk outdoors—something tangible happens to the energy in the air. I can feel the cleanliness of cold emanate off her and collide with the warmth of the room.

Lisa has the large, deep brown eyes of a Disneyfied ruminant. She's not the kind of attractive where you hear the Hallelujah chorus when you see her—the beer commercial blond floating in the sky with her hair flowing back, the sultry underwear model commanding you. Those women are scary-pretty, cold-pretty. *Too* pretty. Their intense beauty or sexuality initially titillates, even shocks, yet ultimately wears you down with its severity. With an allure perpetual and overpowering, one can never truly relax around them. Lisa is safety-of-the-womb-pretty. Her beauty is compelling yet her features are just soft enough, just one shade humble enough to temper the intensity of her attractiveness, providing an almost impossibly perfect mix of arousal and calm. "She's a *perfect nine*," I told Jay after our first date.

"One day you'll get the perfect ten, Dan," he said sarcastically, "then you can retire. Then you get the gold watch."

"You don't understand. I'm not complaining. I was thinking about it—perfect nine is as high as it gets, there is no perfect ten."

"There're tens out there."

"That's not what I'm saying. What I mean is no one can act normal around a Ten. The hottest girl you ever want is a Nine. She's so attractive that you're consumed with desire yet not so much that you can't see her flaws. She's at the utmost limit of what is approachable, anything less and you will always want more, anything more and you will never feel comfortable, never be able to relax. It's a perfection paradox. Perfection makes people uneasy, so the perfect girl to be around can't be perfect, she has to be *just* below perfect."

"But the Ten still is perfect," Jay said obtusely.

"Yeah, but it's a theoretical perfect. An actual perfect can only be a nine."

I stare at my perfect nine for a prolonged second in the doorway and with agonizing awkwardness, I at once crave to hug her and am afraid to touch her. But because I must, I lean in for a squeeze. Her hair is shiny and filled with cold the way the ocean stays chilled through the beginning of summer. As I bury my face in it for a moment I am filled with the same joy as finding a new cool spot on a pillow.

She comes in and sits down on the couch. I take her coat, put in on a hanger and wedge it into my one closet. I never used to hang anyone's coats, I just chucked them on a chair but I feel nervous around her, like I have to act a little more mature than I really am. She is three years older than I am and works at a real job. So, I find myself doing things like hanging coats in a closet pretending that I live like a normal adult. She's wearing an off-white, soft and fuzzy sweater with a draping, luscious cowl neck. I don't need sex with her. I don't even desire talk. I could just leave her on the side of my couch like a giant stuffed animal. A big cuddly Koala bear.

"I'm exhausted," she says sunken on the couch.

"I thought you were coming home at seven?" I'm resisting the urge to caress her sweater gently with the back of my hand the way old people do when admiring fabric. I'm sure it's cashmere.

"I'm sorry, I had to work late," she says annoyed. "You know I have my review coming up and if I want to make partner I need to put in the face-time . . . Then I ran home first and changed."

"It just would have been nice if you called." Am I dating someone who uses the term "face-time" unironically?

"I couldn't, I was busy. I was helping out Jeff with a project."

"What about your life? Doesn't that have more weight than Jeff?" I want to nuzzle my head in her chest.

"Dan."

"What?"

"He's a partner at my firm. And with my review coming up . . . Besides, I respect him and if he asks for my help . . . Can we move on please?" How many goats were harmed in making that damn sweater of yours? You don't even care do you?

"Yeah, sure."

"So, where do you want to go to dinner tonight?" The Koala Bear asks.

"I don't know . . . You know I can't really swing anything above like ten bucks."

She lets out an exasperated sigh. "I know sweet thing. I'll pay for you."

You're probably thinking I've landed myself a bankroll. But I didn't. Except for one time when she said she wanted to because I had paid for our first couple meals together, she never pays for me, we always go Dutch.

"You don't have to," I say half-meaning it. "We just need to go somewhere cheap."

She let's out an irritated shriek. "Dan, I have a law degree. I work sixty hours a week. I earn a hundred and forty-five thousand dollars a year, and that's as an associate which I won't be by next Fall. I'm not eating at Burittoville."

I'm sorry to do this to you. But if you're disappointed in the "real" Lisa think how I feel. We started out having so much fun despite being so different—she's a corporate lawyer with a myopic determination to succeed; her world is structured; and I get the feeling she has a definitive life-plan; Christ, she was probably a grade-grubber in high school. I'm a twenty-seven-year-old neurotic, failing musician and broke. I'm quietly afraid I might be losing my mind and the only plan I have is to make sure I pay my rent each month. Chalk it up to a lingering sense of romance at the end of the summer, mutual loneliness or maybe just boredom but in the beginning at least, we did make each other feel good. And on top of that, we looked good together—our dark hair and eyes, our olive complexions (mine Jewish*, hers Spanish), we could have passed for brother and sister. That came out wrong, but you know what I mean: you've seen those couples—the scrawny, nebbishy guy with the statuesque trophy on his arm; the short chick with the six-foot-two guy, etc. They just look wrong together. We weren't that. We had a physical symmetry. But needless to say that's hardly enough.

"Okay senorita," I say raising my eyebrows. "Yeesh, with your Spanish descent and all I would have thought you'd be a little more amenable to the humble burrito."

"Burritos are Mexican!"

"I know, but you're all *Hi*spanic. Doesn't that count for something?"

She shakes her head and makes a disgusted grunt but I'm pretty sure she was disguising a chuckle. "Let's just order in some Thai and be done with it. My treat." She smiles warmly and grabs my hand, reeling me in for a hug. After a few mutual back rubbing moments we pull back and sit smiling at each other. Koala. I look at her and I am helpless.

"I'm getting a drink. Do you want some water?" She asks as she stands up somewhat abruptly, breaking the spell.

---

* I only consider myself Jewish in the Semitic racial sense, not a religious one. (Sometimes I call myself a Jew in the cultural sense, but that's more about how I assume others perceive me, rather than how I view myself. E.g. Why am I supposed to feel a connection to some Wall Street guy I have nothing in common with other than ancestry? Because we both eat bagels and went to summer camp? Whatever.)

"Yes please."

On her way to the fridge she stops and turns toward the wall.

"You have to explain to me what the deal is with these sheets again. I know you said you have these notes behind them and . . . I'm sorry but . . ."

"I told you, I'm working on something. It's just a project, lot's of papers and stuff, notes for things." She starts toward the wall. "Hey!" I say a little louder than I intended. "Please don't look behind the sheet."

"You know when you tell someone not—"

"I know," I cut her off, "it just makes them want to do it even more." We laugh and she wanders back from the wall and toward the fridge.

"I am curious though. What is this project? Why do you have to put stuff on your wall?"

"Imagine they're files but instead of in a drawer they're on a wall. It helps me to see things. The sheets just sort of keep things tidy."

"Yeah, this place is real tidy," she says kicking a lint ball while opening the fridge. "But I still don't understand, you didn't answer—what is the project?"

"It's. Well. To be honest, I'm not sure."

"Are you working on another album? Not like I'd know since you never play guitar for me."

"I told you I'm taking a break for a while. And I have tendonitis," I say flexing my hand and wincing as if that verified it.

"Well then is it song lyrics or something?"

"No . . . I mean, I don't think so. It's, it's . . . I'm not sure. I just know I'm working on something." I then add unconvincingly, "I think." I feel anxious at her questioning. Anxious because I don't want to have to explain any of this to her. Anxious because her questions are the same ones I've been asking myself and haven't been able to answer. But mainly, anxious because whatever it is behind that sheet is mine and mine alone. I don't want to share it with her.

· · ·

"Don't you want to pet Belle? She loves it when you scratch behind her ears." Koala picks up the calico one of her two cats and cradles her like a baby and starts scratching her underside. "And when you scratch her right here." She's speaking in that imbecilic voice people use when talking to pets and babies. "Oh my God, she's purring already," she stage whispers to me. She's hugging her now and rocking her arms side to side. She reverts back to the other voice, "but now Sebastian is all alone." My chest tightens. Sebastian, the black half of the duo is sitting by the door showing no interest in any of us.

"I don't think he wants to be picked up."

"I know you've said otherwise but you don't like cats do you?"

"No, I do, I do," I lie. "I'm just good at reading their signs. I think he wants to be left alone." Not only do I dislike cats, I'm allergic to them which for some reason I haven't told Koala. Despite the gleaming, white-tiled bathroom, the kitchen with its well-stocked refrigerator and sleek granite countertop, and that mornings in her bed unveil themselves with sunlight streaming through her twelfth-floor windows, I'm unable to be comfortable here. Yeah, yeah, not being comfortable in her apartment is probably just a sign of my unease with her. Or perhaps it's that being here forces me to blatantly confront the disparity between our incomes. But mainly I think it's the damn cats. Within an hour of being here my sinuses take this feline-polluted air as a call to arms. I imagine a microscopic bugle deep inside my nose sounding off the rallying *d-d-d-da-da-daaaa*[*] "charge!" as the cilia and capillaries and all else mucosal launch into their defensive stance of inflammation. I stopped taking anti-histamines a couple years ago because they never seem to work on me and they all— even the ones that aren't supposed to—make me spacey and zonked out (which I know for some people is a bonus but that's not my thing). Every

---

[*] for those so inclined:

night that I sleep here I am jolted awake by 2 or 3 a.m., gasping for air. I'm not one of those people whose body reverts to mouth breathing when his nose is stuffed. Instead I just lie here, asleep, on the verge of asphyxiation until my brain sends the shock-wave for me to wake up and breathe. I then sit up, still half-asleep, startled and confused taking replenishing wide-mouthed inhalations until I eventually come to. Then I pop another pseudofed and pace for a half-hour waiting for the airways in my nose to open to the width of those tiny, red, coffee mixing straws, enabling me to miserably, just barely, fall back asleep.

Koala had a power over me that seemed to override all my other senses and instincts. Over a month of being together and there wasn't all that much about her that I liked. It was pretty clear, at least on paper, that we had no business being with each other. And I'm not using "on paper" figuratively. Here's what I mean:

Starting with a brief fling with Debbie Witchowski in ninth grade (which lasted three weeks, ending with a denied attempt at third base after which I promptly decided she wasn't worth the trouble), I've always determined the potential of my relationships with two major categories: The Checklist and The Vibe.

The Checklist is an actual list of all the concrete traits I'm looking for in a woman. (I think the list is fairly universal. Our differences aren't so much in the items themselves but in our interpretations of those items. In other words, I think to a large degree we're all looking for the same things, it's just that we define those same things so differently). Here's my list for Koala; you'll notice that she has only three items checked:

| | | |
|---|---|---|
| Attractive | ☒ | **SECOND TIER ITEMS** |
| Smart | ☒ | Cool friends ☐ |
| Good sense of humor | ☒ | Similar (or respect for her) taste in: |
| Affectionate | ☐ | Music ☐ |
| Connection to and/or respect her work | ☐ | Politics ☐ |
| | | Artsy stuff ☐ |
| Connection to and/or respect her general world view | ☐ | |

Each item can also be broken down into sub checklists. For example, *Attractive* can be broken down into an anatomical sub list: Face, Legs, Breasts, Hair, Overall body; or a more categorical sub list: Sexy, Pretty, Adorable. Or *Smart* can be broken down to: Wit, "Deep" Thinking, Numbers/Finance, Street Smarts, Erudition/Book Smarts. And then there are sub sub lists. The level of minutia I break things down to is generally ruled only by how bored or how nuts I am at any given time.

So why would I stay with someone if she's only hitting three things on my checklist? This brings us to the second of the two major categories: Vibe. The Vibe is the more nebulous and enigmatic of the two categories. Vibe is that non-specific connection we feel with others. Maybe it has to do with pheromones or maybe something more new-agey like "energy" or "chakras" or whatever. I don't know. It's just that *feeling* we have with certain people. Some people, for no apparent reason, we just like being around. And they us, as The Vibe is generally two-way. (And when it's not, it's no doubt painful for the unreciprocated Vibe feeler).

So, what I do is create a graph of Checklist and Vibe. I take the two categories and put them on X and Y axes and mark the spot where they meet. This is often done in my head but—and yes, I'm a dork—not infrequently, actually written down. (I have a box filled with old girlfriend charts, including the very first one which was conceived and completed in a ninth-grade geometry class while pondering my failed fingering attempt on one cute but prude Debbie Witchowski).

To get the Checklist plot point I tally all the checked items on the list, then based on how many items are checked I know how high or low to mark the spot (e.g. if only one item is checked then the point would be only one notch up from the bottom). However, each item is weighed differently, often according to whim, so the whole thing's pretty inexact. But still, it gives a good general idea. The plot point on the Vibe axis is even less scientific; it's essentially just based on how I feel. (Nothing wrong with that!).

The far upper right hand corner, where both axes are at maximum is the best possible connection (marry at once); bottom left hand corner is no compatibility (this had better just be a one night stand). I draw a diagonal line, the *Compatibility Threshold Line*, from the top left corner to the bottom right corner and as long as the mark is above that line—though it's no guarantee—the relationship's got potential. If it's below the diagonal line, any attempts to make the relationship work are basically futile; I should give up and stop torturing myself. Here are Koala's indexes:

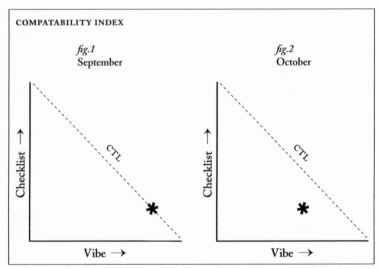

As you can see, in the beginning, (see Fig. 1), Koala and I had a very high Vibe rating which compensated for her lack of hitting very much on my Checklist (other than being attractive and smart, which while both are weighted heavily, are not enough on their own to carry the whole axis) and kept us just above—ok, teetering on—the Compatibility Threshold Line. As time has worn on though, (see Fig. 2), our Vibe, while still strong, is slipping, (perhaps the initial rush of meeting someone new has been wearing off), and with such a low Checklist score, we have now fallen below the C.T.L.

While for the most part the two axes operate independent from each other, occasionally there is a bleed from one side to the other. Even though we can have a great Vibe with people who we don't find attractive, (like sometimes I feel a great Vibe with other guys even though I'm not gay), every once in a while extreme *Attractiveness*, which is a Checklist criteria, can affect Vibe. Extremely attractive women can sometimes mesmerize me into thinking I have more of a vibe with them than I really do. Physical attraction can pull on enough unconscious, intrinsic Darwinian triggers that it sometimes can confuse one into thinking there is more Vibe than there actually is.

The whole thing can become a little confusing after a while but I'm telling you, if you're uncertain what to do in a relationship, the graph kills making a lame plus-minus list.


Sometime in the past year, right when I started getting deeper into this self-educating quest looking to Kierkegaard and the gang trying to come up with some answers for this state I've found myself in, I went on a Holocaust book binge. I read quite a bit by Elie Wiesel, and long after I moved on to other sunny topics one of the things he said continued to resonate with me: the opposite of love is not hate, but indifference. Now I don't mean to bastardize the intended meaning behind his quote, (the full text of which is pretty stirring by the way), but it got me to thinking in a larger sense than his specific point and I realized that most things in life can be explained this way. I had always thought of opposites as being on opposing ends of a line or the proverbial pendulum's arc. But that's not so. Opposites, in their most fundamental way, are one and the same, on top of each other. So forget the line or the arc and think of a *circle*. Starting on one spot on the circumference, as they travel and increase in intensity, the two furthest points eventually meet. The circle is not just for matters of the heart and morality as Wiesel was referring, but everywhere. Like in the fight or flight max tension/total-slackness-shitting-yourself I talked about before. Or when you touch scorching hot water, for a second it feels ice cold; and liquid nitrogen, which is *very* cold, will *burn* your skin. The most basic statements or questions are really the most complex and profound. When you get so deep into fields of thought like physics or astronomy or math they all start talking the same language. Somehow, seemingly opposing thoughts, fields, entities at their extremes always seem to converge.

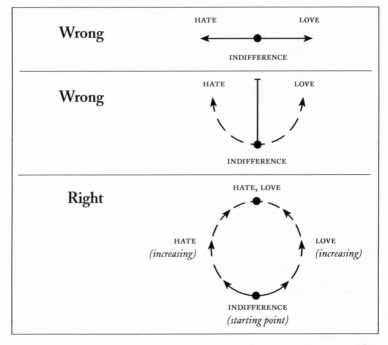

The reason I brought up the whole Circle Theory right now (besides the fact that I was already in geek chart mode) is that one of the few areas in life it doesn't seem to work with is the Compatibility Index. It's like the way general relativity explains the world but isn't compatible with quantum mechanics. (Ok fine, a bit of a grandiose analogy but still). When at their peak, the XY criteria may influence the opposing side (like the *extreme attractiveness* example mentioned earlier) but they don't *converge*. You could meet someone who has everything on your checklist but there may never be a vibe, and vice versa. The fact that compatibility doesn't fit into Circle Theory shows how incomprehensible, how *un*like the way most of the world works, compatibility is.

So here Koala and I are. As you saw in Fig. 2, we've now fallen below the critical C.T.L. and feeling this happen, (and *seeing* it happen on the chart) I am uneasy with us still being together. (I'd imagine she's uneasy too but we haven't talked about it so I can't say for sure what's going on in her head). I guess when you have a genuine Vibe with someone, which is so hard to find, even when it starts to disappear, it's hard to let go of that feeling you once had. Consciously or not, I've found myself clinging to that feeling I had that night near the Brooklyn Bridge even though I haven't felt the same since. I was hoping that no matter how much things were slipping, if maybe I stayed with Koala long enough I could get that feeling again. We can live our whole lives in service to those rare moments, the sublime, sometimes taking ourselves down lurid and mis-guided trails for years or even forever, trying to capture it again.

"Gosh, I know a lot of people don't like cats but I just love these guys," she says giving Belle an extra squeeze. Something about seeing Koala with her head down, shaking her dangling hair as she coos to this pet, and hearing her use a charmingly old-fashioned word like "gosh" *does* make me sort of like Belle. Just a little bit. But I'm not fooled, I know my temporary endearment toward this cat is for the same reason models are in ads—a little beauty always rubs off on whatever is around it.

I walk over to Sebastian and as I lean down to pick him up he nonchalantly walks away. I feel myself smiling. It's just as well; he knows my interest was a sham. Koala is laughing at my rebuff and I feel myself laughing too. I'm not faking the laughter but it still somehow feels fake, like I'm in a performance. In fact, this whole scene feels false. And distant. And in every second that is passing right now, as I stand here laughing, I'm becoming more and more aware that the past ten minutes in her apartment were nothing, not real, a show. And this is getting scarier and eerier. Because not only am I watching myself right now but I'm realizing how fooled I've been for the past ten minutes, that at least *now* I *know* my place, I can see this for what it is, that I'm watching this play unfold before me, I'm aware of my role. But earlier I *thought* I was in the real deal, the Now, (actually, I wasn't thinking about it at all, I simply was in it, which I suppose is the whole point), but I realize now, in fact I wasn't at all, that too was just a show, and it's freaking the shit out of me that for a few minutes I was an actor and I didn't even know it.


The next morning I wake up to her hunched over thumbing away on her Blackberry.

"What's the deal with that? You're not even out of bed yet."

"I know, I just . . ." she says annoyed without looking up.

"You'll be in at work in a half hour." She keeps typing away. "You treat that like a diabetic's insulin pump . . . the kind that's attached to their hip."

"Mm hmm," she murmurs, still looking down. Her thumbs are moving with the virtuosity of a twelve-year-old video-game addict. The flurry continues for a few more moments then she pauses, lets out a chuckle, and sends the email on its way, hitting the final button with a dramatic flourish, whipping her wrist after pressing it, then tosses the device into her purse on the floor.

Walking home from her apartment I get more and more irritated picturing her letting out that chuckle. What kind of fucking work email is she laughing about?

When I get back to my place the first thing I do inside, before I sit down, before I get a drink, before I touch anything is strip and throw my clothes into the laundry basket, a makeshift quarantine for all my cat exposed/infected clothes. I sit naked on the couch eating a bowl of cereal wondering if something is wrong with the rice milk because just for a second it tasted a little strange. And so:

- I have to throw this out, something could be wrong with it.
- Just keep eating it, it's fine. Don't be so neurotic.
- But I might get sick; it's not worth it.
- You know how much money you spend on this ass-blaster cereal and organic rice milk. You can't afford to just throw food out every time you go mental.
- I'm sorry, don't be mad, but . . . I think I'm nauseous. For real.
- That's only because you're psyching yourself out! Calm the fuck down and eat your cereal, freak.

And so yet another day wears on. Not much happens; all the usual boring shit. I watch TV. I look through my bills that are going unpaid. And I wait anxiously for my stomach to reject the tainted rice milk, bracing myself for an impending gastrointestinal situation—mild heartburn if I'm lucky, writhing pain, maybe death if things go the other way. The usual. At some point, while dawdling around, I spot a cluster of colored, folded-up pieces of paper on the floor. They're notes that must have fallen out of my pocket when I took my dander-defiled pants off. (I've taken to carrying a batch of blank notes in my pocket these days just so I'm covered when I'm out).

A few days ago, my post-it note supply in need of replenishment, I headed to The National Wholesale Liquidator, a local discount chain that's filled with gray market goodies. I've always felt good in the Liquidator—the cardboard boxes lining the shelves, thirteen-dollar Quasar toaster-ovens, the utter lack of any helpful signage—there's something refreshing about its bleak un-Americaness, its contrast to its sterilized and cheery mega-chain counterparts. As I meandered trying to find the post-its, I ambled down the aisles, past the canned fruit with Spanish labels, the surplus Quebecois cereal boxes (you can never have too much le fibre), and made my way past the cheap socks and underwear in weird styles that looked not like they were outdated but out-*placed* from a different land, like a former Soviet republic. When I finally found the office supplies section I came across the colored post-its, which stood out amid the standard yellow packs like a high-end item.

Now, instead of yellow, depending on my mood, I can choose between blue, light brown, orange, or purple for my notes. I thought about having each color signify a different category of note, creating a sort of system out of it all but it never came to fruition. The notes couldn't be distilled down to four categories. Sometimes I mix things up by using red or blue ink instead of my standard black pens but again, there doesn't seem to be anything systematic about it. The color is just for variety. And I must say, the wall is starting to look quite good now with its tri-colored ink and multi-hued squares mixed in with the dominant black-ink-on-yellow-square motif that started it all.

I pick the notes up off the floor and slowly read through them then walk toward the wall. As I am just about to stick the first note from this new batch in my hand on the wall, I feel a strange sort of calm come over me. The calm itself isn't strange as if it's some kind of profound zen. It's . . . I'm not sure . . . but I think . . . Yes—it's simply that I feel level. A state of normalcy for most but for me is strange and new. And as I stand here clutching these little papers in my hand, staring at the wall, scanning over all these past notes I have written—and I know them so well that

I know the full contents of each note just by just eyeing a random word or phrase on any single one of them—I find myself thinking of Koala. And I realize how far away she feels from me. And shit, it's not Koala but everyone, *everything*, which feels so far away. And I don't know why this is and oddly, in a vague sort of way it actually feels ok. The notes in my hand drop to the floor and I quickly sit down at my coffee table and feverishly begin writing on yet another little yellow square, (b/c despite having colored ones, yellow is still my go-to square), and as I write, the font gets smaller and smaller because I know there's so much I want to say and by a de-facto rule that I follow, except for extreme circumstances, it all must fit on one square. And as I continue to write, with every new letter formed, every next line down, I'm at once both overwhelmed with a sense of solace just by this simple act, yet inflamed with shame for feeling such deep solace from this action that I fear can only be evidence of some kind of deranged—or worse, embarrassingly immature—solipsism. And I'm mad at myself for not even allowing myself this peace, that no one is here, no one knows; it's ok if I'm a solipsist or a narcissist or whatever it is I am; that well, yes, I understand it's probably *not ok* in a larger sense, but SHIT, *right now it should be ok*, because this is all I have right now to get through whatever it is I'm going through and I need to just give myself this one thing yet I'm so fucking self-conscious that even when I'm alone I can hear the critics; I can hear everyone in my head pointing at me and saying "get a grip," "grow up" or some shit like that or they just groan out of irritation from witnessing such self-involvedness. I *know* what's going on, I *know* how all this introspection and then the need to record all the introspection must look but . . .

Come on man, you're by yourself, just let it go.

## SOMETIME (IT COULD HAVE BEEN ANY TIME, REALLY) BEFORE ALL OF THIS

. . . and I can feel the wood vibrating against my chest. My right pointer finger is bleeding, the cuticle shredded from too many wild down strokes. My left forearm is aching from being torqued in this position curling my hand around the neck for so long. It's chilly in my apartment but I realize I'm sweating now as I pause to rest and start dripping off my face onto the strings and the pick-guard. I watch a droplet crawl down the pick-guard onto the wood then well up on the white edge before it gains enough weight to drop off. I stare at the spot on the wood floor and feel my heart beating, it's just starting to slow down now. I become aware of voices talking next door and a TV blaring downstairs. But the noises are distant, foggy. The phone is unplugged, the shade is down and the room is lit a dark yellow from the halogen lamp in the corner. I am in a cocoon in my head and it's warm and bright. I am glowing gold. I realize at this moment, hunched over my guitar, alone, quiet, as I have at so many other moments just like this one, that this is the best I have ever felt and ever can feel. I am in a place of purity, clarity, blankness, oneness (name your spiritual euphemism) that cannot be reached any other way. This is not a frozen moment, time still is rolling, it's that the pain of time is somewhere beyond the glow.

Sometimes I can almost feel the moment while I'm playing, somehow latching on to it in a secondary part of my mind, but even that faint recognition in the outskirts of perception is still a corruption. Because the nature of the true moment is unawareness, only focused sense, feeling. So in essence, like now, as I lean over my guitar and watch sweat droplets collect on the floor, I can only be aware of the moment after it has passed. But even this after-the-moment moment has its majesty, like awaking from a dream, like post-coital glow, like the lip-smack *ahh* after you down the glass of water. And in a certain way, it's the post-moment

moment that is superior because it is the only one where you have the awareness to be appreciative. And I am grateful for being here, in this (post moment) moment that is now starting to pass and fade. The voices are getting louder, clearer. Steadily, the cocoon is dissolving like layers of a mummy's wrap unfurling. I don't want it to end but I am not sad that it is ending. I walk over to the stand against the far wall and gently place the guitar down.

O'Reilly's Bar, East 32nd and Third Avenue. Within the heart of the neighborhood Murray Hill. It's a popular after-work joint for midtown drones. I've been here once before when Koala asked me to meet her out with her work friends. It's Friday night and time for all the Erics and Steves and Brians to meet up with their buddies and toss back a few brews and the Staceys and Jennifers to get shitfaced on cosmos unwinding from another week of midtown toil. Next to me a Stacey is talking to an Eric about her job as a junior account executive at J. Walter Thompson; he nods pretending to listen while trying to decide how drunk she is and if he'll be able to get laid tonight. Stacey subconsciously runs her hand through her hair that she spends an hour every morning blowing-out to rid it of its natural frizz and curl. She tries to smile a lot and because the bar is so loud is glad that she has an excuse to now lean next to his ear to talk. Fakely unaware of her chin on his shoulder as she chats in his ear, she worries whether she should have only done one refresher spritz of perfume rather than three just an hour ago in the bathroom as she was leaving work. (She only needed one—the cloud of her *Obsession* or *Eternity* or perhaps more appropriate, *Desperation* [if only!] is surrounding her in a three-foot radius like the scraggly lines of perma-dust forever enshrouding Pigpen). Peppered not only in Stacey and Eric's conversation but flitting in gentle arcs like falling Nerf darts from countless mouths throughout the bar is the name Marni. When he worked briefly at a bar in the area, Jay used to joke that the neighborhood should be called Marni Hill because seemingly every other girl, as if they had come out of a press, had the same hair, clothes, shoes, and the name Marni. But I doubt he meant it this literally. I have a private chuckle on his behalf.

There are seven TVs all within earshot showing sports. Overtop the TV cacophony, they're blasting that Chumbawumba song which people are enjoying without irony. Spinning before this gem were the unfortunately-now-canonical 80s pop songs (does anyone really need to hear "Come on Eileen" ever again?) intermixed with moldy Madonna singles, and the errant Dave Matthews and top-40 hip hop track. There is no doubt in my mind, at some point within the next hour Steve Miller will unfortunately be flying like an eagle out of this PA system. This is the music of an empire in decline. This is the music of insanity.

"Like a Prayer" comes on, girls are singing along and clapping distinctly off the beat. A few guys in khakis with shirts tucked in are attempting to dance, though in a drunken, half-mocking fashion. Girls with shiny dark hair and faces like they're sucking lemons, wearing black tops, expensive jeans and pointy shoes bump into me as they make their way to the bar or head for the door packing their Marlboro Lights into their palms. Jeter just hit a home run. Guys clink beers. "Like a prayer, I'll take you there. Just like a dream to me . . ." Some fat bastard standing at a cocktail table is eating nachos, a glop of cheese and chili drops on his shoe.

"Hey baby. Do you want to go?" Koala sidles up next to me.

"Yeah."

"You look miserable standing here by yourself. I don't understand why you didn't come over and stand with me and my friends."

"I just wanted to let you do your thing."

"Well, it's a little embarrassing, you standing by yourself."

"I'm sorry. I think I'm just really tired. Are you ready to go?"

"Sure."

Out of nowhere, some choad in khakis with a goatee that makes his mouth look like a sideways vagina materializes next to Koala and puts his arm around her.

"Hey Lisa," Vagina Mouth says.

"Jeff!" she says, her face lighting up. They kiss *on the lips*(!). Ok—his lips may have touched *the corner of her mouth*. On purpose?! Accident?!

"This is Dan," she turns toward me.

He takes his arm off her and shakes my hand, "Hey, buddy."

I muster a head-tilt and a fake smile.

"Dan, this is Jeff. I think I've mentioned him before, he's a partner at my firm."

Look how happy she looks, all smiles. So, this is my competition? *This fuckin guy?* She probably wishes she was going out with this tool. What is she doing? He's wearing khaki pants and a blue oxford tucked in. *The uniform*, for God's sake! And he has a fucking goatee! I can't lose to a guy with facial hair that screams My Mouth Is A Sideways Vagina. I don't know what he does at that firm but he's definitely not a litigator, no jury would take that face seriously. But I'm sure *he* doesn't eat at Burritoville.

"Can I get you guys a drink?" Vagina Mouth asks. Oh, here it is; the big spender. Please say no Koala.

"That's so nice. A vodka tonic would be great." I thought we were leaving! Betrayal! "What are you drinking Dan? Do you want a beer?" She asks, barely turning from V.M.

Why are we together?

"Yeah, a beer. Thanks." Maybe she doesn't really like him, maybe she just wants to kiss his ass because he's a partner and her review is coming up, despite the fact that she has admitted to me that she doesn't even like her job. I'm not sure which case is worse.

"What kind, my man?" V.M. asks.

"Surprise me," I say in my best attempt at a *back off my girlfriend* tone.

"Ugghh," I grumble as he walks away.

"What? He's a good guy," K says.

The *Good Guy*. The Good Guy is the enemy. The Good Guy is everything that is and has been wrong. The Good Guy has been against me since I was born. The Good Guy smiles easily and emptily. He loves his girlfriend or wife but thinks nothing of the lap dances he gets on his big trip to Vegas. And she, his girlfriend, wife, swoons over him but she doesn't really know what it is to swoon. He's stoic, and late at night in bed, too often laconic which now that he's older he grudgingly admits, and this lame, belated morsel of self-awareness, the admission itself, not an attempt at correction, is enough for her. After all, recently he got choked-up watching a mainstream romantic comedy, though with an embarrassment that she found to be *so cute*. He's really opening up. But generally he just wants to watch *the game* with his buddies, maybe hit a few rounds of golf on the weekend. In the summer he tucks his Polo shirt into his shorts. He dutifully parts his hair on the side and it's always short enough to show the tops of his ears, it always has been, never occurred for him to wear it otherwise. And this is all fine with *her*. Because she loves the Good Guy because *that's how guys are, right?* And he duly bought her her diamond ring, even though he gave the obligatory groan about it to his friends, *But hey, what are ya gonna do, right?* That's the way it goes and the way it goes, he goes. And she has her ring and largely, that's enough. And when she chats with her friends or maybe her mom they laugh-off the foibles of Jonathan or Steven or Brian or Chris because, hey, *that's how men are!* And after all, he is a *good guy*. And once in a while she cries over him but *that is life and after all, he is a good guy*. Maybe Vagina Mouth does all these things, maybe not. The details don't fucking matter. I can feel it from him. I can smell it. These men are pervasive yet distinct, like bottled blonds with brown eyebrows. His blind devotion to normalcy piques in me a caustic resentment on par with that of a wrongly accused man before a kangaroo court.

I tell Koala that I'm overheating and that I'm going to step outside for a minute to get some air. I must be radiating misery; she doesn't protest. I make a stop in the bathroom first then head toward the door. I walk beside the long dark-wood bar where at the far end near the exit, Jeff is waiting among the throng to order our drinks. There's a burst from the crowd, something has happened with the game. The opening violin riffs of *Ants Marching* erupt from a speaker near my head.

"ALCS baby! It's happening, man!" Jeff says to me, seeing me on my way out.

"What is that?" I shout over the crowd and the music.

"What's what?"

"ALCS? You mean like, Lou Gehrig's disease?"

"Dude, *championship series*. Yankees all the way man."

"Oh," I say with an eye to the door, tantalizingly just a few feet away.

"Not a fan, huh?"

Oh, what the hell. I can't resist. "I think baseball sucks in general but the *Yankees* . . . I always figured saying you like the Yankees is the same thing as saying you like Golden Retrievers or something."

"What the fuck are you talking about?"

"It's too easy. What's the point? Everyone gets all worked up over it when they know that they're just creating this false drama in their heads. You all know that chances are they're going to win."

"No, no you don't know how hard it is. It's close every time."

"Not only do you people go for the sure thing, which is bad enough, you go for the sure thing while pretending, even to the point of believing it yourself, that it's not. The game is rigged, the cards are marked." Fucking corporate lawyer Machiavellian ass. "You probably were one of those middle school kids rooting for the bully to beat up the nerd. The American way."

"If I didn't work with Lisa. . ."

"The Yankees . . . it's like rooting for Merrill Lynch, or Exxon, or, or the mountain instead of the Engine That Could—the monolith!" Jeff turns from me back to the bar. I call to his back as I walk out, "there's no pathos" but I'm sure my voice disappears into the clamor.

I wander down the block to 2nd Avenue and loiter on the corner leaning against the wall of a white-brick apartment tower, my hands in the pockets of my corduroy jacket. After a few bored minutes, I go to the payphone I'd been eyeing in front of me and call my dad. I haven't spoken with him in over two months.

A little voice on the other end of the receiver calls out to the room, "Someone on the phone called Final Green is calling collect!"

"Accept. Accept it," I hear my dad's voice in the background.

"Ok, thanks Chloe, I got it. You can hang up now," my dad says into the receiver. His voice full of a sweetness and care that I don't remember him possessing when he was with family number 1. "Daniel" he whispers angrily, "you can't do that to her. She's only seven."

Final Green is an inside joke I've had with my parents since the divorce. My mom feigns some enjoyment in hearing it but neither of them thinks it's particularly funny, even though Jay and I do. I *am* the Final Green. When my parents married, my mom had been insisting on keeping her last name and only agreed to take my dad's last name if he shortened it from Greenstein. It was the early sixties and my mother, ever on the vanguard, and fresh to the emerging ethos, guised her demand as a women's lib endeavor but it really just sounded vaguely anti-Semitic and ignobly assimilated for my dad.

As pieced together from hearing the story repeated over the years:

"Lydia, there's no good reason to change it. My father will have a conniption."

"Harold, Jews' last names are a farce and you know it." She was always showing off her grad degree and how erudite she was compared to his more blue-collar roots. "The Germans imposed names on the Jews and when they got off the boat here, names were imposed yet again. You think the overworked undereducated immigration officer at Ellis Island doing their papers knew German or cared?"

My mom, a Gould, with comic absurdity felt her surname was more regal (and neutral, though she'd never admit to that) than dad's and resented that she'd be losing it. My dad changed the name, convincing himself it was a good start for them, a unifying gesture but he never forgave himself for doing it and her for putting him up to it. When they got divorced my mom went back to being a Gould and my dad switched back to being a Greenstein. He even threw a little party after he did it, the framed court documents hanging on his living room wall for the guests to see.

"Dan, it's easy! We can get the papers for you too in a jiff!" At the time, it was the happiest I had seen him, I think ever. Walking around his new apartment that evening, kibitzing (as he'd say) with his brother Steven and strange men I didn't know, and glad-handing like a politician the couples that were friends with both him and mom, he glowed.

"I'm not changing it," I said and got a rush expecting my response would thwart his mood but other than a momentary look of hurt on his face, he shrugged me off and went back to the other guests. He pressed me every so often for a few years on changing it, "but deep down you are really are a Greenstein, I made a mistake," but lost interest in the cause once he became involved with Sheila, and further when I became a disappointment to him.

"Do *what* to her Dad? What do you think's going to happen to her? It's just a joke. She knows you were a Green once doesn't she?"

"No, as a matter of fact, she doesn't," he says resuming his normal voice. "You're something else," he laughs. "So, what do I owe the honor of hearing from you?"

"I don't know. Just wanted to call and say hi. I'm allowed to do that, right?"

"Of course." I try my best to discern if he means this or not but standing here, squinting into the middle distance of Second Ave., I can't tell one way or the other. "So," he says breaking the silence, "what's going on with the band? Have you been able to move forward with lining up another record deal?"

"Everything's moving along . . . It's ok." He knows I'm lying. I contemplate asking him for money but suppress the urge. Things have been strained between my dad and me for years, basically forever. But since college, we really avoided each other, only meeting up a couple times a year, even though he was right in Jersey. My look, my demeanor, my life, in his mind don't fair well as an example for his new kids compared with my married-off and "successful" sisters, especially Jen bringing him grandchildren. I'm pretty sure they stop by his house often, as in, they are at the level where it's fine to show up unannounced. I, on the other hand, haven't really been integrated with his new family. Chloe, that gorgeous little kid, I'm certain would barely recognize me, and Lily, forget about her, she's way too young. To be fair, I think my dad and I both just feed off each other's bad vibes. He never approved of me not getting a quote-unquote real job, he almost seemed to take it as an affront. In moments when he makes the effort, he understands and I think respects what I am—(or is it "was" at this point?)—doing but those times are rare. He came from humble beginnings, worked his way up to owning three small, quasi-gray-market, wholesale electronics stores tucked away in nondescript strip malls, two of which are on the foul commercial highway Route 22 that my mom always groaned about driving on, frequented by dorky, electronics-savvy men, the kind who wore Hush Puppies before they became ironically hip. How could I, his only son, be so cavalier when he was so risk-averse? He *knew* what it took to survive in the world and I wasn't heeding his advice.

"Jenny and Laura—," he catches himself.

We both know they aren't a good topic between us. I laugh. "You're off the hook, dad. This is my own doing," I say. It's a bit of a non sequitur but he knows I'm responding to what's thought but unsaid. "I, me, who I am has nothing to do with you." Once more, a silence comes over the phone. I laugh again. "Nature versus nurture, you know, whatever. It's amazing I'm from the same family as my sisters. As I'm sure you're aware, just look at you and uncle Steve, more often than not, siblings are worlds apart. It's proof—I'm not saying a hundred percent, but for the most part—people just are who they are." A girl with shoe-polish black hair and blue eyes walks to the corner in front of me and waits for the light to change.

"Dan—"

"Dad, I gotta go. It was good talking with you. You know, uh, thanks for taking my call."

"Of course," there it is again.

"Ok, bye."

The girl is on her way crossing the street. Did she give me a look when she was waiting on the corner? Or was she just looking? I freeze for a moment, unsure if I should follow her, run up to her, ask her her name, ask her something, tell her something. I think of Koala and feel guilty, then angry. I walk back to O'Reilly's. Outside a Jennifer is on the sidewalk crying, talking to another Jennifer about something having to do with boys. Standing off to the side, courteously giving the sniveler space, I peer through the window. Whiff's of *Tainted Love* leak through the glass, swelling in bursts whenever the front door opens. A few girls are ineptly dancing in the back. They look ugly, unselfconscious, and they look happy. I catch myself sneering at them while my stomach churns with the rot of condescension and the sting of envy. I spot Koala off to the side with her gaggle. Through the glass she looks delectable and unobtainable. I don't know how I got someone so attractive. I imagine with distaste the conversation she's having, the certain inanity. Oh, the maddening ambivalence! A duplicitous surge rages through me, the warm wave of lust, delight, and gratitude for knowing she is mine that I felt just a moment ago now seems dishonest or dirty or wrong. Staring at Koala and her crew, I realize V.M. is not with them. I take in a sharp breath of November air and head inside the bar.

As the cab pulled in front of her building and the driver hit the button finishing the fare, Koala hesitated before pulling out her wallet. We'd gone over this ten times before—I don't take cabs, I can't afford them. If she wanted a cab, she'd have to pay. Yet she did that little hesitation with her getting her wallet. Was it on purpose? It had to have been. We entered through the revolving door and I gave a quick "hey" to Andre the doorman, a genial guy not too much older than me. He smiled back and as usual I wondered whether it was genuine or simply obligatory, disappearing instantly behind my back. I immensely disliked seeing the doormen in Koala's building. I was invariably left with the same feeling I have when a waiter at a fine restaurant is crumbing the table in front of me or how I imagine I'd feel if I were rich and had to converse with a maid. I've always had a certain awkwardness around service people. I want to say, "Don't worry, I'm one of you. I'm not really on the other side." I don't think it's money guilt so much as an awkwardness over being pampered, or the appearance of *enjoying* being pampered. I hated waiting tables and I would carry the divide I felt between myself and the patrons outside the restaurant. That demarcation has never quite been erased, it's just that I feel permanently on the other side. Nothing wrong with having waiters and doormen I suppose, it's just a hang-up of mine. As we strode through the lobby, under the chandelier Koala grabbed my hand and held it the rest of the way to the elevator and even inside the elevator as we rode up to her floor. Maybe she didn't hesitate in the cab; it was in my mind.

Later, lying in bed, her hands were all over me. A miserable night for me yet for her, all went well, she was completely oblivious. Or maybe she was aware of my misery, maybe even she was miserable too but didn't care or did care but was pretending not to care.

"My, you're so handsome," she said as she rubbed my chest. She used old fifties expressions like starting a statement with "My" sometimes, which I used to find endearing and we would get into a little in-joke fifties banter thing but now I just find it annoying. And it occurs to me that Koala is a bit of a hork (hot dork). "I'm so lucky to be with you," she coos.

There was a candle glowing on her nightstand. She shifted her body and in the dim light her face alternated from my undeniable Koala to a ghoulish doppelganger, strange shadows marking her bottom-lit face.

"I'll let you touch me even though you never pinned me, so we're not officially going steady."

"Gee whiz," I try to play along.

Eventually Koala cuts the fifties routine while we keep groping for the next few minutes. I open her nightstand and reach for a condom. "Dan, I haven't told you about this before," she says, "because I guess I wasn't sure what was happening with us but we've been together a while now, so, I want to tell you that I'm on the pill." She's fidgeting, moving in and out of the light again: Koala; evil twin; Koala; evil twin. "It's just, I didn't want to have sex without a condom until we were together for a couple months. I guess it's just one of those things, it's sort of another layer of protection," she laughs, "I mean mental, emotional protection. Besides, I know you're safe cause we talked about it." Maybe a month ago, while the two of us watched TV one night, some AIDS PSA aired and I mentioned off-handedly that I knew I didn't have any STDs because I had the doctor do a blood test on me during my physical that I had had in the summer. (Not knowing when I would get to a doctor again unless it was for an emergency, I had scheduled it just before my cobra was to run out. In fact, in the final three months that I had health insurance I lined up doctors to look into every ailment I had; four specialists in all, with the gastroenterologist, good ol' Dr. Geller, handling the bulk of my problems).

"I think this is a big next step for us," she says which hits me with perhaps the gravity and poignancy she intended.

I find myself almost accidentally, or incidentally, feeling closer to Koala than ever before and I'm disappointed in myself for feeling this way, for succumbing to the moment. *Come on Dan, don't be fooled by this. She's not a Koala, she's a wolf, a lawyer, a Jennifer; one of* them. *This, right now, is not what it seems. I mean* it is *what it seems in that this is real right now but right now is not real. You understand what I'm saying; don't ignore me.* Her head dips back again away from the light, her face safely out of the ghoulish shadows and now secure in Koala mode. I run my hand along her collar bone then down her shoulder, soft and curved like the head of newborn baby. I am powerless. *Maybe we do have something?—Energy, vibe, whatever.*

"I understand," I say. And I do understand. "I'm glad you feel close enough to me for us to do this." Fuck. *For God's sake, what about the bar tonight? You don't like this person! Remember?*

Koala leans up and kisses me and I slide in. Slick, warm, cozy. It's a sweet inebriation. Opium honey.

It's been years since I've been inside a girl without the dulling of protection and I'm overcome by how much better this is than I remember. Tactile liberation. I don't want to do anything for a moment; I just want to stay, still, in here. Then slowly, without conscious intention, we start to move . . .

*The pill? That's only like ninety-nine percent effective! And what if she has AIDS? I bet she has AIDS! She hates me, she's trying to kill me.* That's right Dan, let our old friend anxiety back in, he'll knock some sense into us. He never lets us down. Don't let her take you away. Don't drift from the engine, the engine is you. Any calm you feel right now is a lie.

But . . . *Opium Honey.*

Doesn't she see that we have nothing in common, that things aren't progressing, that in fact, they're regressing, that I'm slipping away from her?! *She knows.* She knows I'm slipping but she won't or can't accept it. I won't flatter myself that it's me she wants; she just wants *someone*. And I'm here.

The thing is though, she isn't really falling for me, she's falling for the first-date-me (and for a while I too fell for the first-date-her). No one is really themselves on a first date, usually even the first bunch of dates. Even if it's not a conscious act, we're the more charming, agreeable, and fun version of ourselves, suppressing all those other less desirable traits that don't reveal themselves until later. I can only conclude that while it became clear to me that our vibe was disappearing once I got to know the "real" Koala from the First-Date-Koala [see the trusty XY chart for further blunt clarification!], she has continued to lie to herself that I am still the First-Date-Dan, blocking out our differences and my failings because this delusion has enabled her to continue on her destined path. And I suspect this has taken quite a bit of effort, because although she's had moments of tenderness and affection toward me, they've felt forced because too often they followed hours or days of apparent irritation and frustration with me.

I remember a conversation we had one night. The same talk you always seem to fall into sometime early in a relationship where kids, a 'suburbia versus the City' debate, and money, and family and all those seemingly distant adult things are covered, and you're both talking about it coolly in the abstract but you both know that it's a thinly veiled abstract, that you're really talking about both of you, feeling things out, testing the is-this-one-a-keeper? water, even though you know it's way too early in the relationship to talk about any of this but you can't help it, you can't stop yourself from imagining the future with this person no matter how embarrassingly premature it is, that this is the twenty-something's version of the sixth-grade girl secretly writing her first name attached to her crush's last name in the back of her notebook. But as the talk went on, the requisite, collective cool-remove melted, so to speak, as the topics meandered from houses with lawns, to kids' names, to specifically, kids, because then pregnancy came up and she said something to the effect of, "at my age I would have the child if I got pregnant by accident, whether I was in love with or together with the guy anymore or not." And she continued in a snide, matter-of-fact tone that by the time a woman is thirty, each year after that her eggs are "steadily, if not, precipitously running out, never to return" and that *at her age*, seemingly regardless of the scenario or consequences she'd "very seriously consider, no, I'm pretty sure I'd just do it"—keep the child. Finally, I said, "So, you just want a sperm bank?" knowing that that wasn't exactly what she was saying but I still thought it kind of was. And, but just when things were getting a little weird and uncomfortable she diffused the conversation by touching my arm with her little bear paw and saying that we didn't have anything to worry about because that's not going to happen and this was just a hypothetical conversation and who the hell really knows what anyone is going to do in any given situation anyway.

But despite her conciliation at the end, that she was so emphatic, determinist with her life has stuck with me. Looking back to that conversation and now her affection for me here, tonight, in bed, and my certainty of her self-delusion that she really likes me, I suspect Koala would convince herself she liked a boyfriend almost regardless of who the guy was because shit, as she sees it, she is running out of time and things had better well go according to plan because this is what she wants, and she has always gone after and gotten what she wants. She took herself from a humbling adolescence in a shitty second-floor apartment in Stamford, CT, to a scholarship at Dartmouth, to NYU Law, to a white shoe firm in Manhattan, and the next item on her list was to just find someone (i.e. husband or even boyfriend) so she could have a kid and have him or her live the type of life she was deprived of growing up. BUT, if worse came to worst and she even had to skip the husband step, she would still not be denied this last part of her plan, and this all sort of seemed to explain her conviction to keep a baby if she got pregnant regardless of the circumstances. Sooo, and here we are having sex

*And FUCK, the pill is only 99% effective and for all I know she isn't even on the pill.* And I'm Grind. Ing. Away. And. It. Feels. Great. But. *Oh. God. This. Is. A. Big. Mis. Take.* But on the other hand: I worry about excessive intake of soy and I worry about radon in my water and I worry about how I'm going to pay my bills and about why I'm becoming more and more fixated on scribbling notes and sticking them on my wall and why I can't fall in love and I worry about why it is that I worry so much, that you know what, maybe Lisa's not so bad and she's just trying her best, like everyone else, to be happy and maybe she sees the good in me and can look beyond all the bad stuff and this is a genuine moment between us that I'm completely ruining by having this fucking dialogue running in my head.

Koala is deep asleep, her head peaking from the cocoon of the comforter with the intense, intrinsic adorability of an infant marsupial's head surfacing from the pouch. There's a widely held theory in science called Neoteny. It states that infants share similar physical traits—namely large eyes, small nose, soft features. And when we see these features we're hard-wired for them to trigger a paternal care-giving instinct. The trigger is there for our species' survival; our infants are helpless without us. The instinct is so strong it even stretches between species. There's a story of a child who fell into the gorilla cage at the zoo. The mom gorilla took the human baby in her arms and cared for him, protecting him from the other gorillas as if he was one of her own until the zoo-keepers got him out. She couldn't deny her flashing *neoteny!* alarm. It's why we love puppies and deer yet are repulsed by insects and rodents. There's no reason why we should find a deer more appealing than a possum, after all, deer are basically rats with hooves, they're giant rodents. But we can't deny that physical morphology—the large eyes, the small nose, perhaps even the dainty legs. It's all about looking new and soft and helpless. It's the *"awww"* factor.

So if we can go cross-species, it makes sense that the trigger extends to how we react to our own adults too, specifically women. Attractive women often have large eyes and some semblance other neotenous features—all key indicators of youth, and a component of fertility of course is youth. Naturally, there are many other traits and factors that make a woman attractive—the obvious va va voom stuff like child-bearing hips and an ample bosom, not to mention all the cultural i.e. learned traits, physical and otherwise—but it cannot be denied that apparently, a key characteristic in them we're subconsciously drawn to is a vague sense of helplessness. And for the ones like Koala whose features are heavily weighted with neoteny, it's beyond wanting to have sex with them; we want to take care of them (although, I'd hazard to say, except for biologists and freaks like me who think about this stuff all the time, this desire for care-giving/attraction to helplessness is not in the male's conscious mind when he finds a woman appealing). (And as an aside, this makes me wonder about how much of this innate tendency is culturally reinforced and amplified from the time of early childhood, in tales in which the evil person is always ugly, the wicked witch with the long nose and long chin and warts, versus the always comely, doe-eyed, high-cheekboned sweet princess. I.e. ugly = bad. Beauty = good).

BUT, *anyway*, the cruel and debilitating irony of all this is of course that physically, Koala, she of über-neoteny, of the large, wide-set brown eyes, soft nose, and prominent cheekbones that were it not for her cheeks with their hint of cherubic pudge to offset them would make her just a shade too pretty, severe, who elicits the *awww* factor of a Chocolate Lab puppy times 1000 is adorable almost to the point of pain, while *personality-wise* she's somewhere between the benign neutrality of a goldfish and the repellence of a, well, you get the idea. Her physical pull is always balanced against the push of who she is. We had a great vibe in the beginning, maybe because we both weren't quite ourselves, but it steadily eroded away. Now being with her has become a constant battle of my animal/instinct brain versus my advanced/thoughtful brain leaving me in a perpetual state of ambivalence and unease (psychologically and gastrointestinally). Internal chemical reactions are at war with each other, opposing neurotransmitters are sparking against each other like dueling fireworks shows from rival towns.

And lately I'm finding myself feeling guilty for letting this whole thing ride on the animal side. (And besides the animal brain thing, perhaps I've just been lonely and I like/need the attention from her and perhaps it's any one or combination of the whole host of other unhealthy reasons people stay with each other e.g. boredom, fear, masochism, sadism, Freudian impulse [getting back at your parents; trying to please your parents, etc.] etc. [And shit, who's to say what is "unhealthy" anyway? and now that I think about it, maybe these reasons that I assume are unhealthy are actually totally legitimate, healthy reasons for staying with someone. They make sense. We all have different motivations and needs. Who's to say? {But if I feel this conflicted, this uneasy, then isn't that a sign that this isn't right? <But, perhaps those uneasy feelings are just a defense mechanism against the fear of being hurt by letting myself get close to someone. Maybe my dislike of her is really just a construction. ⟨But, if something doesn't feel right I can't assume it's is an elaborate defense my psyche has created, I have to trust my instincts and go with my gut because in the end what else do I really have? ⟨But on the other hand, maybe I need to think this through because things rarely, especially things in our head, are what they seem yet . . . aaaggh! Stop!⟩⟩>}]). And so I have two hunches, one somewhat identifiable telling me to leave and the other a bit more vague telling me to stay and the whole thing is just pretty exhausting. Perhaps I'm overintellectualizing the whole thing, maybe all it really is, in the colloquial and crude parlance, a battle between my two heads.

3:05 a.m. I lay staring at the ceiling. There's a slight ringing in my ears from that shit music being played too loud at the bar. My nose is welded shut as if it's filled with cement, my sinuses in histamine-overload distress. Sebastian, sleeping on the end of the bed just woke up. He starts readjusting himself, his claws pricking my feet through the comforter. Reactively I jerk my feet in and lay there taking stilted breaths through my mouth. Then, after a moment I straighten my legs with a swift kick and feel the dark satisfaction of contact as he is plunged off the bed, landing with a thud on the hardwood floor.

. . .

Koala is in the bathroom doing her nightly routine of washing her face, taking out her contacts and brushing her teeth and whatever other maintenance and primping it is that girls do every night. I'm already lying in bed (I floss, brush and that's it). She's mostly out of view but every few moments she moves an inch or two to her left bringing her left side into view in the doorway. She's in panties and a little white top that doesn't quite reach their low-cut waistband exposing a thin line of skin between them. I remember on our second or third date she was over my place. We were still getting the basic facts, the general story down on each other and the conversation came to filling each other in on our families. She told me cryptically that her dad had "disappeared long ago" and she was raised by her mother, who now, for even more cryptic and apparently complicated reasons she doesn't speak to anymore. The only family she's in regular contact with is an aunt in Madrid. She was in dark jeans and I think the same white top she has on now. I was madly attracted to her and we hadn't yet had sex. My lust was at a boil.

"My mother has some addiction issues," she said plainly but with just a hint of haste, as if she was eager to get off the topic but didn't want to reveal that.

"Oh . . . hmmm," I responded, unsure what to say. I was trying to be sensitive to the fact that even tiptoeing the around the subject seemed to be uncomfortable for her. She was too blasé in tone and too short on facts; clearly she hadn't resolved all this stuff. She was sitting next to me on the couch and I had my eyes cast down acting like I was deep in thought, internalizing her words. Even though I knew her nonchalance was just a cover up, I played off it and allowed myself rather than making an overt show of sympathy (that she would have just dismissed) to fix-ate on the space between the top of her dark jeans that fit tight around her hips and the bottom of her little shirt that wasn't covering her fully; (it had crept up earlier when she reached for a glass out of the cabinet and she hadn't yet realized it). Did she know I was staring at her waist and she didn't care because she was glad I was distracted, or was she too stressed over the conversation topic to be aware of what I was doing? I wasn't obvious about it though. I looked back up to her face after just a few seconds, but in those few seconds I was lost in eternity absorbing the view. I was transfixed staring at this exposed section of her waistline, the little bit of olive-skinned pudge that swelled over each hip of her tight, dark jeans. Make no mistake, Koala is fit, this wasn't a jelly donut roll of fat, it was a perfect mocha bonbon on each side. Health, fertility, vitality!—it called to me.

And nearly in that same spellbound moment, just a flash of a second later, I thought about Amy's friend and how through a dog's eyes or if an alien came down to earth and looked at the two of them, he wouldn't be able to tell the difference between the pudge on one and the pudge on the other, that in fact it's quite subtle but to the male of the species, (or at least this male of the species), still definitive. Sometimes it's the subtleties that make all the difference, like every so often when you see a picture of a movie star's sibling, and you can tell instantly that they're related, they look strikingly similar actually, but the sibling is never quite as attractive for some indefinable reason. If you had to describe them ver-bally you'd use all the same adjectives but one millimeter of cheekbone, one summer of sun damage, one slight asymmetricality and there's the line between fame and obscurity.

And now as I look at Koala's left hip, it is mocha bonbon no more. It's not off-putting like Amy's friend, but in the same way that the difference between the two girls was subtle yet definitive, so is the difference between the same wedge of skin on Koala those months ago and what I see right now. And not only do I not feel lust but I'm unable to concentrate

118

on it; moreover I'm feeling unable to focus on anything.

In my periphery I see on her night-table the red message indicator on her Blackberry blinking. The bathroom light from the three naked vanity bulbs lining the top of the medicine cabinet mirror is beaming me in the face but I don't feel like telling her to close the door. Strangely, having to speak feels like too much effort. The light shifts from being an annoyance to actually feeling painful, like I've developed some sort of extreme photosensitivity. And off to the side, the tiny Blackberry light now has the force of an airplane beacon on its wing, a strobe set on slow, each flash hitting me not as light but as a pulse, a wave. I close my eyes. It doesn't matter. The light penetrates through my lids. I squeeze them shut, my face scrunched like a crumpled paper bag. My head is starting to spin. I can't breath properly. What's happening to me? Oh, wait . . . this might just be a sinus thing. Yes, it's a sinus headache. Belle and Sebastian are to blame. Those fucking cats! I'm going to be ok. It's nothing . . . But I still feel weird. Something feels off. I'm getting worse. It's not just sinuses. Something feels *very* wrong. I'm terrified now. I open my eyes and see the glimpse of Koala still standing there at the sink. I can't hear if the water is on or not. Am I deaf? Holy shit, I think I'm deaf now! I think I might throw up. I might be having a heart attack. Is there pain in my arm? Yes. I think I feel a sharp pain in my right arm. Heart attack, that's it. But why do I feel nauseous too? That's not part of a heart attack is it? Oh, I'm so scared. Will I ever be happy? My fingers are starting to tingle. It feels weird for me to say this out loud (on the page to you) but I'm very lonely. I'm very scared and I don't know what is going to happen to me with my life. I'm so tired. I'm so scared and I don't even know what exactly of.

"Lisa," I call out meekly to her from the bed. "I think I'm having a breakdown."

"Can you wait until I take my contacts out?" drifts from the bathroom after a long pause.

The tips of my fingers are numb.

## DECEMBER – ONE YEAR BEFORE

A bright gray Chicago sky is backlit by the early afternoon sun. Diffuse, milky light radiates through the windows sheathing the control room in diluted white. Tim is twiddling some knobs on the board, while Bones, his sheep dog, is curled up next to me on the couch behind him. Jason and Alex have left the studio for the remaining two weeks of the session while Tim and I track the final vocals and make adjustments to the rough mixes. Just a week before, the full band, string and horn sections, and Marty, the assistant engineer were all here. Now with just the two of us, a relaxed yet focused intensity has taken over the studio.

Ash, my A&R rep from the label has been calling two, three and four times a day pestering us with ignorant questions about the mixes. He had played some preliminary tracks we sent him for Aaron Stern, the new president of the label, and Stern apparently walked out of the room in the middle of one of the songs and told him to start looking for another band to sign. So, now Ash is living up to the old cliché of the label guy asking for the mixes to be more "radio"—which essentially means: raise the vocals, run them through the pitch corrector, and clean everything up in Pro Tools so there isn't one snare hit off the beat, one audible breath before a line, one guitar track that doesn't enter right *right* on the downbeat—sterilized for the masses.

When I got signed, the label had a different president who was close with Ash and shared his philosophy on signing (at least a few) unconventional bands that they would cultivate over the course of several albums and not worry about radio hits. Stern was hired as a slice and dicer, trimming the staff and the roster of bands, with a myopic focus on disposable hits to try to generate the quarterly profits the brass demanded. He isn't going to push the album (or any albums) unless he hears a hit. Ash is actually a cool guy but he wants to save his job and says if I want a chance I "need to come up with at least one radio friendly track."

The phone rings. Tim and I groan and look at each other.

"Green, it's Ash." Tim passes the phone to me.

"Hey Ash," I say, my voice sinking. "What's up?"

"Oh the usual. Just wanted to check in on you, see how the mixes are coming. I was listening to *If When* and I was thinking . . ." he sounds tentative.

"Don't start a fight Ash."

"I'm not but I've been thinking about it a lot—after that bridge section with the strings, you could bring everything home with the chorus, *that's* the heart of the song," he pleaded, "rather than that outro."

"Yeah, uhh . . ."

"I *love* the outro," he bursts, "you know, and, we could have that version of the song as a b-side or a web-only type of thing. But I think you need to end strong and the chor—"

"Ash we've gone over this before, man," I cut him off. "I'm not altering the structure of that song. And besides, we're not working on that track right now, were mixing *Infinity Pool* so my head's in a totally different place." Ash has been relentless ever since Stern did the whole walk-out on him.

He knows very well that my music is all about grandiose epics and exploring strange new sounds—hardly the ingredients for a pop single. Nevertheless, there is little attempt at disguising his mission. Call number one of each day, the butter-up call, usually entails him going on about the "vibe" of the record or some other nebulous concept that he uses as a shorthand for *I'm a music guy; I'm on your side.* Then the truth comes out. Calls two through four always contain the words "hook" or "chorus" and the phrases "can you make it any shorter?" and "why don't you try doubling the vocals in the *chorus*?". The whole scenario of the new president and my A&R guy harassing me is so cliché Major Label Rock that it feels more a right of passage than a twist of fate.

"I think you should try it. Tell Tim I want him to try it—" I hate that he's trying to pit Tim against me.

"Listen Ash, I gotta go. We're in the middle of mixing," I say, then hang up.

I suggest to Tim that we unplug the phone and don't check our email for the next week which he graciously and eagerly accepts. I don't begrudge Ash or even Stern, they just want to ensure a return on their investment. I just happen to disagree with their premise that you need a hit single to sell records; I think there are enough people out there looking for something different, they just need to be exposed to it. Just put me on the road, get me some press, whatever, that's their job to market the album— and the records will sell; they should be more creative than just worrying about radio. And success aside, I've been writing music, dreaming this album up in my head for so many years, I'm not blowing my one chance to make it real, to record it and bring it to life, by changing it for some businessman. Because chances are the album won't sell, ninety percent of the albums released don't sell, so I might as well fail (financially) on my terms than shame myself with some lame radio-friendly track and still have the album tank anyway. They're just trying to do their jobs but I'm just trying to do mine. So, in short: they need to leave me the fuck alone.

"How about raising the rock guitars another two db?" I say to the back of Tim's head. "And on second thought, let's leave the kick where it is. I think that room mic we juiced up is giving it an extra push." Tim moves a couple faders on the board and types some notes in the computer.

"Ok, you ready for the rock?" Tim asks.

"Bring it." I love that he always adds "the" (with no irony) before "rock," as if *rock* required the extra respect of a preposition, as if each time we heard music through the studio monitors it wasn't just *music* but Music with a capital M, a grand event, a force.

Tim hits a button and the two-inch tape fast-rewinds, slows down to a crawl, then re-engages the magnet and starts spinning forward. The SMPT time-code on the tape locks in with the digital tracks in the computer and we watch the digital tracks scroll on the screen as the physical tape rolls, one giant, unified system of analogue and digital tied together through a Medusa's hair of wires and cables. A wall of sound hits us with visceral force through the floor-to-ceiling monitors. Thick power chords from guitars layered five deep pound in unison with the bass and drums with military precision. The effect is as if this sound were all one instrument, or rather, one entity, one statement.

I sit frozen and feel a hint of a smile inadvertently push the corners of my mouth as the sound surges from the pulsing speakers. Every day we work the music is becoming tighter, more alive, closer to the sound I've heard in my head for so long. I don't miss Jay and Alex at all. I've always been more of a one-on-one type of person and now I'm relishing being here alone with Tim. But the first few nights at the studio Tim and I, both intensely passionate and controlling, clashed and I worried whether I would make it the full six weeks, especially knowing that Jay and Alex wouldn't be here at the end. I remember thinking, I'm stuck in this studio with this guy and I'm supposed to be recording an album, tapping into every emotional and creative resource within myself and I don't know how that's going to happen if I'm expending all this energy fighting and being frustrated. Tim and I argued basically from the very beginning. On the first day of tracking we spent half the day debating what snare drum to use and the second half of the day arguing over the tempo of the track, ninety bpm or ninety-six bpm. Alex and Jay chimed-in at the start but after a while dropped out and left Tim and I to slug it out. Now though, after all these weeks, Tim and I have reached a sort of cruise control set at a hundred miles per hour. We still argue at least once every day but we both know the arguments are based in love for the project and that ultimately, debating things is bringing out the best in the music.

The song shifts into the breakdown section, the volume drops and the different instruments split apart from each other surprising the listener with relief from the onslaught of the unified playing up to that point.

"You hear that?" Tim shouts over the music, "I spread the toms out a bit more and I put an ambient panning thing on your guitar."

"Oh yeah, everything's really opened up now. Fantastic." It sounds like there are a half-dozen Native American drummers encircling the room pounding away. The guitar is dancing around the drums, like a strolling minstrel slaloming the drumming tribesmen.

"Get ready, here it comes, we're going back to the head," Tim says excitedly and almost with a hint of fear. I remember my dad sounding the same way preparing me for when a wave was about to hit when I was around ten and we were down the shore. He would take me many yards out in the ocean, the lone kid with the adults and teenagers to body surf. Hovering near me as I was treading water, my legs too short to reach the bottom, wide eyed he'd shout, "Get ready Dan!" Then he'd command "over" or "under" before the wave would crash. Tim peers out the door toward Dalia, his "on-again-off-again, it's complicated"-girlfriend who's on the couch in the living room. She's been around the studio a lot recently taking care of their other business, selling an obscure natural hallucinogen called Salvia Divinorum on the internet. She is so unassuming though, that in essence it still feels as if it's just Tim and me in the studio for this final stretch, even though I walk past her in the living room ten times a day. Except for an occasional kiss, communication, interaction is sort of superfluous for them I've gathered, as if simply being near each other is enough. He jumps up and closes the door to the control room just as the song shifts back to the head and the wall of sound hits with even more volume and impact than in the intro, all the instruments and sounds coalescing into one force again. I'm sure he was closing it out of courtesy for Dalia but it feels now, with the door shut, that it was more for us, so we could be alone with our creation.

Unlike the sterile catacombs that most recording studios are with their hermetically sealed air-lock doors, immaculate blond hardwood floors, and dark gray soundproofed walls, where you come in, do your work and then go back home or to your hotel, Tim's studio, which he has dubbed The Watershed, is also a home and decidedly not of the corporate antiseptic milieu. It's a live-in studio, meaning that musicians actually live there while recording. Tim has an apartment somewhere else in the city, (I think), but he's never there. He's slept on the couch in the control room every night since I've been here. Downstairs, where the brick on the walls in the front room is crumbling in spots and the whole place frankly would benefit from a day-long vigorous cleaning by a professional crew of five, there is a bedroom and several sleep lofts, and the three live-rooms where all the performing takes place. The large front room has angled, ten-foot ceilings with movable sound baffles suspended from them, a checkered tile floor with Mexican rugs, and two special, triple-pane glass windows looking out onto the mostly desolate street. The "live" acoustics in that room are magic for creating giant drum sounds. The two back rooms, carpeted and with brightly painted sound-proofing foam on the walls have no windows, echo, or any contact with the outside world, offering not only mental isolation, but the opportunity for anything put to tape to be isolated, pure—no room-sound, or sound of anything at all other than the instrument making it onto the track. When you're in there you could be in Chicago, Prague or the proverbial Timbuktu—that's the point. The only awareness you may have, with the kitsch psychedelic lights, the eccentric painting scheme, and a vast store of musical instruments and equipment scattered around is that you are in The Watershed; nothing else matters. Upstairs is the control room, living room and kitchen. It's the only studio I know of where the control room doesn't look out onto the tracking (i.e. performance) rooms. A foot-wide, insulated pipe carries a bundled sheaf of wires connecting the all mics and other equipment from the basement up to the control room on the second floor. When you're downstairs, with visual contact eliminated, communication with Tim is through your headphones and mics only. Not seeing the control room or the engineer behind the board is the final element in creating the focusing isolation that the back tracking rooms provide. Tens of thousands of dollars worth of amps, mics, instruments, and other equipment in winsome juxtaposition with the low-tech decor rest on the funky checkered tiles and shag carpeted floors of the three tracking rooms. Most of the building, up- and downstairs is dominated by a groovy lighting aesthetic—chains of Christmas lights drooping from the tops of the walls, psychedelic lamps in corners, a black light that I always leave off because I find its glow sickening after five minutes, goofy illuminated toys resting on top of amps and the piano, and an errant, naked blue or red bulb in the ceiling or sconce socket.

When I first arrived at The Watershed, I'm ashamed now to say, I was initially disappointed at the looks of the place. I had always imagined myself in one of those gleaming corporate facilities, that's what I associated with really "making it," and after all, I did have a deal with Warner Brothers Records. I felt jipped. I had often heard or read about musicians complaining that they need the right *vibe*—the most important word in the musicians' argot—to feel relaxed and to be creative but I always figured those complaints were hollow, akin to some rock star whining about the rigors of the road while he was screwing models and staying in five-star hotels. Tim had pitched his place as being the antidote to the lack-of-vibe endemic in corporate studios, saying the high-end studios are too cold and inhuman for most musicians to get into their vibe. I agreed in theory. Still, I couldn't shake the vision I had of what I needed, what I deserved, for my major label recording session. But once there, I quickly learned that Tim was right, that what makes The Watershed work is that its dreamy and almost whimsical atmosphere lulls you in; you can't help but feel relaxed and creative in this place. Despite its low-tech, low-gloss aura, The Watershed is ultra-high-tech where it counts. It has all the modern equipment (not to mention Tim's expertise behind the board) to pristinely capture the magic on tape. It's the perfect combination of warm and cold, old and new, comfy yet professional.

Now, here alone with Tim after weeks of twelve and fourteen-hour days, of thinking about nothing, *nothing*, but music, of scarcely seeing the sun, I don't want to leave. I can't believe my foolishness in ever feeling different. I still dream of touring, and adulation, and success but that dream is vague, distant, it does not captivate me. In here, a rare focus, or not simply focus, but sphere in which to view the world, to live my life has taken over, the future is of little if any interest or attention, my full world is this, here, right now, the sublime totality of immersion in creating. There's a part of me that senses, that not touring nor money nor any of the other stuff but that *this*, being sequestered with a few musicians, an engineer, and a Brinks truck worth of audio equipment is the real dream and I am living it. All the sounds that have been swimming around my head can finally be brought to life. Tim and I are like explorers of outerspace or the deep sea, for the sounds in our heads and the possibilities of all this equipment are infinite. I love everything about this place and I'm reminded constantly, with every new playback in the control room, with every new pass I make on a vocal track, with every new tweak that is done to a mix, that this is my home, nowhere have I ever so deeply, so rightly belonged.

The beginning of this realization came over me on the third or fourth night. It was the first of countless times when Tim indulged and cultivated my tendency to dork-out on esoteric audio-science stuff and more importantly, it was also the first time that we both saw in each other what we saw in ourselves, (or maybe more accurately, I saw in him a version of myself I aspired to be) and nothing has been the same since:

We'd been recording virtually non-stop since ten-thirty that morning until around eleven at night when, exhausted, we all decided it was enough for the day. By twelve, Jay, Alex and I were downstairs in the sleeping lofts. Yet, on verge of drifting off, a new guitar part filled my head. I climbed down from the loft and picked up the ES 135 that was leaning against the wall. On tip-toes I darted to the front room to not wake up Jay and Alex, sat down on the drummer's stool, and started plucking out the notes that arrived in my mind's ear moments before. Now it's 2 a.m. For the past two hours I've been up going over the part, perfecting it for tracking tomorrow, near euphoric that I've figured out a third guitar track. I can hear it in my head, sprinkling arpeggios panned hard-left entering during the bridge of *Zoetrope*, the seven-minute epic the band's in the middle of tracking over the next couple of days. I'm nearly overcome with sleep yet simultaneously feel exceptionally focused as I'm hunched over, picking the unplugged electric guitar, its unamplified strings twanging weakly like an emasculated Dobro. It's a bizarre state, being sharply awake yet on the verge of passing out, my body's chemicals and signals clashing, diverging, it is not a balance between the two states, there is no yellow light; green and red are both commanding me. My mind and body is confused, my blood made of a billion magnetic particles all repelling each other as they course through me. I wander upstairs to make some tea in the hope of tipping the chemical balance to the awake side. I just need another half-hour and I'll have the part nailed down. Walking back from the kitchen toward the stairs I notice Tim in the control room through the window on the door. He has headphones on and is staring straight ahead, his hands on the faders. I enter and he turns to me, not startled or surprised that I'm here, as if it's normal that we're both awake at this time after having worked for over twelve hours straight today. He pulls off the headphones and a hiss like the "snow" sound from a no-signal TV is audible from them laying on the deck.

"You hear that?" Tim says.

"White noise?" I ask confused. I walk over and put the headphones to my ears for just a second and am blasted with ***shhhssshhhss***, like having a firehose roar in my ear (minus the water of course). "Jesus," I reflexively toss the headphones back on the console, "were you just listening to that?"

"Hah!" he says as if he caught me like I moved my feet even though

Simon didn't say to, "it's not *really* white noise." He looks like a hipster version of a mad scientist. He has on black horn-rimmed glasses and is wearing his hair, which normally hangs down straight, shoulder-length like Bono's circa *The Joshua Tree*, (only his isn't as shiny and straight and feminine looking), with just the top pulled back into a ponytail with the back and sides hanging down like you see on those European soccer players. He's sporting a Hawaiian shirt unbuttoned half-way down his bare chest, paisley pajama bottoms, and is barefoot. This is not a look that someone cultivated trying to be cool, this is a look that developed over ten years without leaving the confines of a recording studio. "What everyone calls white noise is really just snow, static, it most likely isn't covering the full spectrum. *True* white noise is a sound that contains every frequency in equal amounts within the range of human hearing. This is close," he aims his thumb to the headphones, "but it's not it. Plus, I purposely pulled out a few frequencies. Can you guess which ones?"

"You're not serious?"

"It's something I mess around with. After I mastered perfect pitch this seemed like the next thing."

"Jesus, Tim."

"You've got good ears Dan. You could do it too, it would just take some practice."

"Really?" I humor him.

"Oh definitely." His faith in me is flattering and unnerving. "Anyway, actually I'm not just messing around. Recently I've been thinking about getting into mastering, not as a serious thing but just for fun, on the side. I think playing with the white noise stuff will prove really good for that, fine-tuning my ear to subtle frequency changes."

"But wait, can we go back a second?—I'm confused. How can you ever hear true white noise because every set of speakers or headphones produces a different character of sound? Doesn't that mean then that they all produce different frequencies? Or is it the same frequencies just in different timbres? Like white noise out of a little TV speaker is different than white noise out of towering five-way studio monitors with sub woofers and those are different than in-ear headphones and the way they produce bass response in your ear canal, and so on. They all not only give different frequency ranges but the character, the timbre of the sound is vastly different. So, in a way, I guess I'm saying that no one can really hear *true* white noise, because true white noise, if I'm allowed to sort of extend the definition, I would think not only covers every frequency but also every timbre. It can only be theoretical."

"Yes yes yes! I see! You have a point!" Tim's knee is bouncing. "I should have known, you with all those crazy charts. You get it, you've got the bug, like me."

"The bug?"

"Yeah, the bug. You get it."

"Actually, I don't really understand any of this."

"You do . . . You're missing the point anyway. It's that we're talking about it."

I feel like a fraud that Tim thinks my mind works on his level—and I desperately wish it were true—but I don't want to dissuade him from thinking that and I don't want to lose this connection with him even if it's an illusion, so I let it go.

"Word," I finally say. I hate that expression. Unless you're from the ghetto it's always seemed fake to me but for some reason it slipped out and it sounded right. "So you're moving the faders, testing yourself? Practicing?"

"No no no, I'm not really practicing. Like I said, the mastering stuff is just for fun. I'm really working on something else. Something big," he says and stops his knee, refocused. "Ok, so: white noise is sound occurring in every frequency. *But* what people perceive, what they actually *hear* is more high frequency content than low. We hear it this way because each successive octave has twice as many frequencies as the one preceding it."

"Ok, I'm with you. There's an exponential advantage to the higher end frequencies."

"Right! That is until it goes beyond our range of hearing. So, but the thing I'm curious about is what would *true* white noise sound like. And by true I don't mean the technical definition but I mean what would it sound like if we *could* hear the lower frequencies at the same perceived loudness as the higher ones. Sort of like a white noise structured to compensate for human hearing. I'm doing some experiments trying to pull down the upper frequencies and push up the lower frequencies to get a true, well, *perceived* true white noise. So I guess it's not white noise then. I should call it a True Noise or something like that . . . I haven't really thought it through. I'm just playing around."

"Oh."

"Our world, man. We're hearing one thing but the reality is, something else is actually there, in the air. All those lower waves, they're being drowned out. Just one more example of how reality and how we perceive it are two different things."

"Sure. But isn't reality whatever we perceive it to be? There is no reality, blah blah blah."

"Don't get into that shit with me!" he barks through a smile. "That's not important. Don't you want to know the True Noise! Sometimes we have to compensate for our own humanity."

"Hmm."

"You really should try the salvia." I notice the little, glass pipe on the console. "It just totally opens up what you're able to perceive. It gives you an extra sense."

"Maybe it just makes you *think* you have an extra sense perceiving more."

"Ahh, you bastard!" He says shaking his head. "Who cares? What's the difference?"

"Are you high right now?" Is it *high* or is it *tripping*?

"No, no. I wouldn't be talking with you. It's way too powerful for that. I just think you should try it. I'll be your sitter."

"Ok, maybe," I lie. "But, uh, I'm not ready for that now." I remember how I had palpitations after I took two hits off a joint in ninth grade. I haven't done anything more adventurous than drinking since.

Tim slides the main fader down silencing the *sshhhhsss* leaking from the headphones; I'd forgotten it was still on in the background until this moment. "Hey I'm sorry we haven't been getting along," he says. "I think we both just care a lot about the music."

"I'm sorry too. I get kind of insane when it comes to this stuff."

"It's all right. I don't expect either of us to relent in our upcoming battles . . . hopefully there won't be too many though," he says and smiles.

"Both of us are coming from a good place."

"We're going to be all right. We're going to make some magic."

"I just. . ." Out of nowhere a lump swells in my throat and I find myself fighting back misty eyes. "I want this so badly. This is my dream here. You know how the business is, this may be my only chance to really make things happen." I take a deep breath in and on the long exhale there's a hint of LLQ (Lower Lip Quiver). All of a sudden I'm overcome with fatigue. It somehow was pushed aside once I got talking with Tim but sleep chemicals rose up, they would not be ignored any longer. I fight against the wave, my conscious mind battling my body's instincts and finish what I was saying. "It's been pretty scary for me these first few days. Just with the gravity of being here and then on top of that you and I arguing from day one."

"I know," he says reassuringly while giving a warm and knowing nod, "I can see how intense you take it all . . . Don't worry about the arguing, it's nothing . . . we're just working toward something. I know we talked a lot about it on the phone before you came out here, let's just focus together on getting that magic sound."

The first time I called Tim, as an informal interview of sorts deciding whether I was going to go out to Chicago and record with him, we ended up talking for four hours. It had been taking months for me to find a producer and studio to record the album. I had an unusually small deal for a major, which until I got hooked up with Tim, left me in a catch-22 because the only producers and studios I could afford with my advance, the label considered not up to their standards and wouldn't authorize using them, yet my advance didn't give me enough of a budget to afford a recording studio and producer they would accept. I first argued with the label for weeks because I wanted to produce the record myself, only relenting if I could get a producer from a ridiculously pretentious short-list of name-brand guys who were way out of the budget. I eventually agreed to co-produce if it was with someone I trusted and respected. Once we got the producer issue somewhat settled—not *who* but at least that there would be another one at all—the next problem was finding him and a studio that would somehow make it under budget.

"Sam, it's like this deal was designed to make me fail!" I had complained to my manager. "You told Ash I'll go to a cheaper studio, that I want to produce it myself, which is *free* by the way, that I'm willing to go *under* budget—right? I just want to get in the studio and start recording already."

"There's little I can do. That's the deal Gar got you." Garland Stable was my lawyer, who like Sam, also stopped returning my calls after I got dropped. Though with Gar I was always routed to one of the associates who, even with their disingenuous encouragement for me to "hang in there" because "Gar's very busy but you *are* important to him so just try him again in a few days," were still better than being thwarted by that bleached-blond L.A. imbecile Jill at the reception desk in Sam's office. "The contract is what it is," Sam finished. To Gar's credit, after I got dropped at least he made an effort shopping my deal around to other labels to buy it out but I was a long-shot at Warners to begin with and the deal was structured so lopsidedly against me that no other big labels would want—and no small labels could—buy it out anyway. Whereas with Sam, not only did he drop off at the end, I knew there was trouble with him right after I signed with him, when within two weeks after he got his advance (off of my advance) "he's in a meeting" quickly became Jill's mantra to me.

Among musicians, Tim has always been known as an indie rock producer, someone who has a great talent for making interesting and sophisticated left-of-center music. In the past couple years he's produced a string of independent records but on the phone we mostly talked about his work with Suede Potato, a quirky four-piece from the Florida panhandle, whose songs while on the surface were whimsical and often comical, were in actuality complex affairs filled with all sorts of time shifts, sophisticated arrangements, and wildly innovative production. Tim and The Potato, as he referred to them, lucked into a fluke novelty-song hit-single and with it he and they scored a platinum record about six years ago. Ash had told me that, "within the industry he's been riding the coattails of that album ever since, with his agent still pitching him as a hit-maker. You and I both know he's more of an inventive producer rather than a straight-up pop/radio guy but Suede Potato, man, multi-platinum. I think Stern may go for it." Ash knew that Tim hadn't produced a hit album since then and in the past couple years the major label projects had started to dry up. Tim had the industry cred but we would be able negotiate a good deal within the budget.

At one point during the call, after talking endlessly about the finer details of the recording process and with delicious minutia about the sound I was looking for, Tim just bluntly said as if it were a confession, "I really want you to come out here Dan. I think we can make something great together. I want to bring your vision to life." Some of the other producers I was put in contact with, even one guy on my dream list, made overtures to me but they all felt vaguely insincere, like their motive to work with me may not have been completely self-serving but it was pretty damn close. Maybe it was because besides the huge upfront fees they required, they all demanded what I felt was an offensive amount of (royalty) points on a record *I* spent the past years slaving to bring to fruition, playing an endless number of shows to empty clubs, writing parts, hundreds of them, for every instrument, crafting detailed production ideas for in my head. None of them seemed to make a real effort to want to understand and pursue the sound I was looking for, rather they all had ideas on how to craft my music into their own visions. Maybe Tim too had his own agenda—he was getting a decent flow of work from the indie community but according to Ash their budgets were barely covering his expenses, he needed the money and/or he wanted the cred of landing another major label project—but he was the only one who I sensed meant it, from a musical perspective, when he said he wanted to work with me and that he cared about creating the sound I had in my head. Yes, we would collaborate but only for the purpose of him helping me achieve what I wanted. (At The Watershed our clashes were mainly about how to get that sound, what I wanted, and on Tim's insistence periodically—and rightly so—that I "just try" his way because "there may be a sound in your head that you may not even know is in your head until you hear it." It was a shrewd way of getting me to listen to his ideas and implement some of them without feeling I was compromising my own vision. In other words, even if an idea was his, if I listened to it and liked it, it de facto became my idea, not in the sense of origination or ownership but that if an idea of his was ultimately what I wanted, then by default how could that then not be my vision as well).

"Think about your main vision," he continues, trying to calm me down (no guy likes to see another adult guy with LLQ). "What are you trying to do?"

"I don't know . . ." I say, searching for some sort of encapsulating answer. I am so tired it feels like darkness or blankness is overtaking me as if I am in a dimly lit room after having been outside in the snow and my eyes can't adjust. But it's not that I can't see, it's that the blackness has overtaken my mind and my body. I zone-out for a moment, not thinking of anything. "I just want it to be *total fucking power*. You know what I mean?" I add sheepishly.

Silence.

"I just want to destroy people the way I've been destroyed by my heroes. You know? I want some fifteen-year-old kid's head to explode when he hears this record. If that's not my goal, it's like, why even bother. You know what I mean?"

"I do," Tim says, then laughs. "Total fucking power."

"It feels good to say, doesn't it?"

"It does. Instead of Elvis's TCB we should get TFP tattooed on our arms."

"It's a motto."

"A way of life."

"I would do it, don't tempt me. I've always wanted a tattoo but nothing, no symbol or picture or words have ever meant enough to me to do it. But TFP," I picture it on my arm with the Elvis lightning bolt underneath it, "I think this could be it." I'm seriously contemplating this.

"What are you doing up anyway? I thought I was the only one who stays awake this late."

"Just working on a guitar part that popped in my head before I fell asleep. Are you always up this time of night? You seem wide awake and like you weren't surprised at all when you saw me."

"I'm up most nights."

"How can you work *all day* and then keep working through the night?"

"This isn't working," he says almost apologetically, and like a nervous guy on an interview fidgeting with his hands, nudges the headphones on the console.

"Isn't your mind tired? Do you ever kick back and watch TV or something?"

"TV? I don't watch TV, it makes me bored," he says with regained confidence.

"Yeah, me too but I watch it anyway for some reason . . . holy shit, I'm exhausted." I'm suddenly hit again with the feeling that I could pass out, as in, about to fall down right here. "I'm heading downstairs," I say. On the way out, one the verge of being overcome I turn back to Tim while leaning in the doorframe, "How late are you staying up?" I ask incredulously. "Aren't you tired?"

"I don't know . . . just feels natural. I only need four or five hours of sleep."

• • •

"So," Tim says after the final seconds of *Infinity Pool* fade out, "what do you think?"

"It's great, man. It's great," I say still coming down from the rush of the music, my body faintly tingling. "What do you think about that guitar in the second chorus?"

"I was thinking the same thing. Bring it up a db?"

"Totally."

"There may be one or two other little changes I want to make."

"All right, just don't do anything major!" I say finally emerging from the afterglow of the song, the tingling having subsided. "You know how nervous I get futzing with anything once we get it to a certain level."

"Oh don't I know it," he says and let's out a small chuckle. "Just trust me."

I step from the control room out into the living room. Tim gets up and re-closes the door so the dust from the mountain of dried salvia leaves that Dalia is de-seeding and crunching into powder—which has made the living room nearly opaque—doesn't circulate into the control room and damage the half-million dollar's worth of equipment. (I wonder for a moment if that's why he jumped up and closed the door while we were in the middle of listening to the song; perhaps it wasn't as a courtesy to Dalia nor to help us bond, but just to protect the equipment). There are a half-dozen four-foot tall burlap sacks lining the walls, all filled with leaves sent from Mexico. I think about the people who grow and tend to this plant and how far away they are from this frigid West side of Chicago. If the dust can damage the equipment I don't see how it's not damaging my lungs. I hold my breath as I walk by Dalia through the living room to the kitchen. But the air inside the kitchen is nearly as cloudy so I give up reluctantly and breathe.

Tim wanders in a few minutes later as I'm staring at my veggie burger slowly rotating in the microwave. He checks on the solution in one of the many beakers that line the kitchen counter, part of a frighteningly and comically elaborate chemistry set-up he has created complete with test-tubes, centrifuges and spiraling, glass pipes dripping deep purple liquid into said beakers. Tim does not have a college degree and taught himself how to create and operate this set-up through reading some advanced chemistry text books he picked up at a used book store over on Milwaukee Ave. According to him, he has developed a technique on how to refine Salvia leaves into a concentrate that can be smoked in tiny doses producing a short yet incredibly intense "trip" unlike the traditional method employed by native users of the plant where a massive amount of leaves must be chewed for the high. Apparently, the refining technique Tim developed is quite revolutionary because he is now, with the help of Dalia, selling hundreds of packages of their extract each month off his website to people around the world who are in-the-know about this sort of thing.

"You must be pulling in serious money with all this," I said during my second week at the studio when I had my first experience seeing a shipment arrive. The chemistry set-up was impressive but it wasn't until the living room was taken over by giant sacks of fragrant leaves that I absorbed the full grandeur of the endeavor.

"We're doing pretty well," he said. "Sales are really up from last year. The community's really starting to spread." Not satisfied with the quality of processed product he was receiving from other middlemen, Tim started the distillation experiments to improve the potency for his own enjoyment. Through a lot of digging and detective work he was able to obtain a shipment of raw leaves from their native region in Mexico to experiment with. But when he experienced firsthand the results of how good he was at processing the leaves he knew others would want his product too. I made the mistake of asking what the trip was like. Tim was happy to talk about the drug but let me know his aversion to using the word "trip" to describe the "natural" experience you have on the drug. "Unfortunately, *trip* has all sorts of negative and artificial connotations" he said, associated with acid and other "destructive" drugs. "Salvia is not about recreation, it's about something much deeper." He said when you smoke salvia—(I wouldn't know, I refuse to try the stuff)—"you are able to see the world from a different angle and you are actually able to see yourself as if you are floating outside your body." He went on to say that the floating though, was not only in a literal, physical sense but also many times or at the same time in a non-physical, more of an emotional or spiritual sense. (The effects are near impossible to put into words; which essentially is the point of taking the drug).

At some point later in the month, when it was just Tim and me in the studio, he confided to me that besides a genuine belief in the wonders of salvia and that he wanted to be a part of "enriching people's spirituality," the reason he got into selling salvia was to supplement his income (from recording) which had dropped off in the past couple of years. "The way the industry is going, I may end up doing this full time and just recording bands for fun once in a while," he said.

But the money truly does seem, if not secondary to, than certainly not more important than the personal satisfaction Tim gets from being a part of the saliva community. "The Mazatec shamans are genuine healers. These are a noble people. The problem is as salvia gets more popular I fear eventually the American government is going to schedule the plant. There's all sorts of talk about it on the web, the DEA knows about it. You know, and if the U.S. government schedules the plant that would of course prompt the Mexican government to probably do so too and go after the Mazatec and destroy a way of life . . . this is an integral and beautiful part of their culture . . . this is their spirituality. Centuries! These people have been using this plant for centuries," he trailed off and shook his head.

Tim's description of the salvia "trip" got me thinking about my own out-of-body experiences I'd increasingly been having. The sensation had been freaking me out enough as it was; it didn't help matters that the one person I could relate to about it experienced it as a result of a drug, whereas I had no control, my mind was going to strange places on its own, against my will.


"Dan, I think the track is ready if you want to go in and check it out," Tim says as he lightly swirls the beaker, squinting at the liquid as it sloshes around. "I edged up that guitar just a db, you might not even notice but I think it makes a difference."

"Great," I say. The microwave beeps and I grab the patty, burning my fingers as I toss it onto the roll on my plate. "I'm just gonna take a bite or two of this thing before I head in. I'm dizzy with hunger." *Or is it dizzy from the dust? Oh god, I don't want to get high on this crazy shit.* I've already asked Tim at least three times if there's any chance of getting high from being around all the leaves and dust and he has reassured me that that is an impossibility, like someone getting drunk just by smelling the hops in a brewery. I'm tempted to ask him again but suppress the urge. In its natural state my head is scary enough for me to deal with, and at times seemingly out of my control, so I've always had an aversion to mind-altering drugs; I don't need them. Jason used to tell me I talked with the depth and strangeness of people on heavy psycho-pharmaceuticals, (I'm pretty sure he meant this as a compliment), and that if I ever took acid I would either go insane never to return or I might figure out the meaning of life. One or the other. My constitution wasn't designed for an explor-atory drug trip. I'm quite afraid of losing my sanity, and while having any sort of figuring-out-the-meaning-of-life epiphany is ostensibly appeal-ing, I think I'm equally afraid of that too, if for no other reason than the latter may very well be indistinguishable from the former.

I take a few bites of the veggie burger that I've smothered in ketchup and mustard and drop it on the plate and head back into the control room. (This was years after my meat fears and morality issues started, yet before my soy fears began so tofu "not-dogs" and soy-veggie burgers were a pretty standard part of my diet then.) I listen to the track a few times through and take some notes for little adjustments here and there that I want Tim to make. I've learned a lot about how all the equipment works just by standing over Tim's shoulder but I would never think of attempting to make the changes on my own. Confronted with this much technology, I am afraid to touch anything without him in the room for fear one wrong button-press could be catastrophic, wiping out an entire track or sending a computer or piece of gear into the sort of hackneyed comic-overload with smoke coming out of it that you see in TV shows or movies. I call out to Tim to come back in when he's ready but he says he's fried right with this song for the day and wants to take a couple hours off before getting back to work on a different track.

I step out of the control room to find Tim sitting Indian style on the floor two feet from the TV screen playing Sega. Tim has mastered all thirteen Sega games he owns. He buys a game, learns it, and gets to the top level usually within one day. This is Tim's idea of relaxing.

"Do you want to play?"

"Nah, I don't know how to play any of this stuff. I won't be much of a match for you."

"Yeah, I guess you're right" he shrugs. He's not being rude, he just spends his whole life in this studio and doesn't have the social acumen to bother to soften the honesty of his statements. "Do you want to play some chess?"

"Sure, but again, not gonna be a real challenge for you."

"I'll give you ten minutes on the clock and give myself five." This is the handicap arrangement we've seemed to have established for our chess matches. He still wins every time. Tim springs off the floor from his lotus position and bounds over to the kitchen table where the chess board resides. He sets the clock as we both sit down and after a minute of staring at the board, I make the first move, hit the clock and we start playing. His arm darts so quickly when he moves each piece on his turns that I get flustered not knowing what piece he moved where. After a few minutes of playing he turns his head away whenever it's my turn, staring into space or at Dalia, as if having to study the board anymore is an embarrassment. Unconsciously, his fingers twitch while he's looking off to the side, barely able to contain himself until it's his turn again.

His whole demeanor in the game is making me nervous as hell yet strangely in a way that doesn't feel unsettling. Tim has been my confidante and supporter ever since that first conversation on the phone. The whole time at the studio and especially now with just the two of us here, (excluding invisible Dalia), I feel like I'm able to tap into whatever it is he has; that through equanimity and creative respect, he knowingly or not has somehow opened up his energy to me and is letting me harness part of it, enabling me to capture some element of him and take it on myself. I've been a sort of supernatural voyeur, absorbing through osmosis a touch of whatever it is I'm seeing and feeling being close to him. He is at once frantically busy yet utterly relaxed. Instead of the person who is hyped-up, bouncing around, anxious with the pressure to do everything, he is coolly manic, a fine machine steadily running at a comfortable hum, knowing that he *is* doing everything. Perhaps it's his being occupied that provides his peace; that when you're always busy there's no time to brood or ponder or worry or most importantly, feel guilt over not doing enough, over wasting time.

He check-mates me and offers me another game but I say, "I think I need a break from your break" and head downstairs to the tracking rooms to play some guitar. In the back room I pick up his Martin D-45. I sit down, close my eyes and start strumming. The guitar is pressed tight against my stomach, the top edge nestled into my solar plexus. The sound is warm and large and the vibrations of the wood resonate through me. I keep playing the same first-position G-chord over and over, and slowly become entranced, at once surrounded by and within the sound. This is my favorite chord. It uses the whole guitar, except for the A-string which I mute. Some people play their G-chords with a finger on the second fret of the A-string (adding a low B into the chord); I never do; it adds too much color. What makes this chord perfect is its simplicity to the ear, its three octave Gs and just two harmony notes, the third and fifth. In some ways, the more there is going on in sound, the faster we tire of hearing it; ear fatigue. It's only something so simple and pure as a drone, the intrinsic lure of a single thread for one to hold on to that can bring you to the point where in a way you are not actively listening yet the music is still moving you forward. If you look at a blank canvas you can see what it is your inner mind wants you to see; if you keep listening to a drone, you will hear what it is you want to hear. Strumming, strumming. I keep playing the chord, keep playing the chord. Lulling myself into abstraction. Sound. If only I could be inside. If only I were small enough to crawl inside this beautiful guitar. Keep strumming, keep strumming. Sound. It swirls around me, the vibrations from the wood penetrate through me. Harmonic waves, I can taste them, burnt sugar into my brain. I am sound.

Eventually I stop and open my eyes, and see the red digital numbers of the clock in the corner reading 4:55. There are no windows in this room but I can feel the newly settled darkness outside. Something about this disquiets me and I feel a little sad or is it lonely? or is it nervous? I don't know. Something just feels off. Maybe it's knowing that another day has gone by and I can never have it back; it's our hardwired signal that time is implacable; the daily nudge that the march is on and you have no recourse. Maybe I'm just afraid of the dark.

I look at the TV set in the corner that's been sitting dormant since I got to the studio over a month ago. Except for some walks to the supermarket and one mandatory day-off two weeks back when I wandered around the neighborhood, I haven't left the studio since my arrival. I was perfectly content—(and I mean that in the literal sense; my contentedness was *perfect*, complete, total)—in my cocoon. It was understood on an unconscious level that TV would have distanced me from the zone I was in inside my cocoon as much as walking outside; it never even occurred to me to turn it on. I saw it and knew it was there but I never noticed it, the way the A-crowd kid doesn't know the name of the dorky girl he's been sitting in front of in homeroom for the past three years. All I've wanted while I've been here was to stay, locked in the zone, and think and feel nothing but the music. I stare at the TV in silence and realize that my left hand is still holding the G-chord position on the guitar even though I stopped playing minutes ago, just before I opened my eyes. This is the longest I've gone without watching TV in as long as I can remember. And since Tim never watches, only using the one upstairs occasionally for Sega, I haven't even seen one on inadvertently. Yet, I can't seem to pull myself away. It's as if I've used up all my power from being in the zone, power that made me impervious to the set, as if it weren't even here. But now suddenly, for an unknown reason, my defenses are down, my power reserves low, it has appeared. I get up and turn it on.

The TV is set to some upper-level cable channel showing a rerun of a contrived family drama that ran in the 90s. The lead teen couple, who are clean and intensely but generically attractive in the way that teens are on TV are in a *serious* conversation. Both of them are doing lots of brow furrowing. I had forgotten about this actress, that elfin face, the long, sheeny dark hair, the exaggerated chest perched on the svelte frame. "But I don't *want* to leave!" she whines. My head aches and I feel myself squinting for some reason, as if maybe the TV's too bright or too color-saturated or maybe too loud. *Who are these people? What do you want from me?* Sitting here watching, it's like I have detoxed from a drug then relapsed but I'm not prepared for its potency, the first hit is too hard. *Your emoting is an insult. Yet soured with guilty prurience I continue to watch you.* I'm ashamed and depressed that I'm leering at this person, who at least as this character on the screen, is so abhorrent. Like experiencing the bursting flavor of a twinkie after having spent a month on a vegan organic diet, the intense artificiality of not only the show but the TV, the medium itself, is jarring.

I lean forward and turn it off. The silence in the room is pointed, stark. I've committed a sacrilege bringing this disease into the room, into the studio. The cocoon has been breached. I stand up still holding the guitar in my left hand and walk behind the set and yank the plug out from the socket. I gently lean the Martin against the wall, turn around and walk across the room. I turn on the Marshall half-stack connected to a black '72 Gibson Les Paul. I swing the guitar over my shoulder, its solid block of wood dead-weight, the strap heavy on my neck. The amp warms up, the vacuum tubes are buzzing. I pluck a muted string, a sort of tapping-my-hand-on-the-iron I often do to test sonically where things are at before I start to play, and it's deep and louder than I expected. Judging by the volume on my muted pluck, the singed palm as it were, I should turn the amp down but I don't. I stand my ground five feet in front of it. My right hand is on the strings muting them. If I take it off for one second the amp will wail in feedback; it's turned up so loud the pick-ups have gone microphonic; I can almost hear my breath through them. I stomp on the distortion pedal at my feet and the buzz from the amp now is even louder. It's just waiting, waiting for me to slip and take my right hand off from muting the strings. *Just one second* it says, *give me one second with your hand off those strings and I'll tear right through you.*

It's all potential, all this buzzing, potential energy waiting for the opportunity to do what it's supposed to do, to be what it's supposed to be. I lift my hand off the strings and just before the feedback squall assails the room, I don't so much strum as slash the pick across the strings hitting the same G-chord I had been playing on the Martin acoustic. I hadn't thought about doing any of this; sometimes we're just on a track and that's the way things go. On some subconscious level I had to keep going; I had to keep playing. If only I could keep playing the same thing, my same G, it'll all be connected from before. And maybe if it's loud enough I can wash it all away: The noise. The breach. The weakness I had. I have.

Glorious sound fills the room, four twelve-inch speakers rumbling, my ears crackling, the sound surging like a shock-wave. Inside the amp, vacuum tubes glow unyieldingly, so hot to the touch they'll steal your fingerprint. More. **I WANT MORE SOUND YOU FUCKING BASTARDS.** I frantically yet methodically start pounding out the chord, my arm churning, my face tense, resolute. *If I can just keep doing this, if I can just keep doing this . . .*

Sometime later that night Tim called down to me by way of flickering the lights. In The Watershed where everyone was in their own worlds with headphones on or in soundproofed isolation booths this was the only logical way to get the musicians' attention downstairs. Relieved and spent by the G-chord catharsis, I had put the guitar down several hours before, and I was now fine-tuning some lyrics for vocal tracking the next day.

I bounded up the stairs two at a time as I always seemed to do at The Watershed. Mr. Bones was at the top of the steps to greet me up on his hind legs, front paws heavy on my chest. I grabbed hold of his delicious shaggy hair in both hands and gave him a joyous shake.

"Hey Mr. Bones! Hey Mr. Bones!"

I've never been much of a pet person but the appeal of Mr. Bones is undeniable. Rarely rambunctious and never mean, he's a blob of shag resolutely content simply loafing around The Watershed. The type of dog that elicits lots of "*good dog, good dog*"s from everyone around him. Mr. Bones followed me into the control room where Tim was on his back underneath the patch-bay singing "Mr. Boneman" to the tune of Ozzy's *Mr. Crowley*. Mr. Bones jumped off me and scampered over to Tim. "Dan, I'll be out in a second, I'm just fixing a few things with the wiring. Everything's all set with the mix. I've been working on it for hours." It was so humbling to be around someone who not only knew how to operate all this equipment but also how to fix it. Over the course of the six weeks in the studio no less than five times was Tim on his back behind the patch-bay or hunched down behind the wall of rack-mount gear or sitting in front of his computer holding the motherboard green cards of hardware in his hand, screwing and unscrewing, twisting wires, soldering, and running diagnostics with metal probes attached to different metered gauges.

"Goddamn, you're like the race car driver and the mechanic all in one," I said to his feet. "I don't understand how you know how to do all this."

"You just learn as you go I guess," he said then slid himself forward from underneath and behind the rack and stood up.

"You're so . . . I don't know what word to use . . . empowered."

"There's this theory that we all have underlying stress because we don't know how anything in the world around us works. From a toaster to a computer to a toilet—we are surrounded by machines functioning in ways we don't understand. You know, it's like why religion came about—to explain the natural world to people who had no idea why it was raining one day and sunny the next. But there's no story to explain the machines so you just have to do the work to figure it out."

He took a breath, looked me in the eye and said with solemnity, "*Coming Down* is ready for your ears." Then, with his eyes closed, in a hushed, almost reverent voice, he whispered, "Total. Fucking. Power." Then walked out.

*Coming Down* was one of my favorite and most personal tracks on the record. There's an adage that songwriters' songs are their children, so of course you love them all but inevitably, some you just feel closer to than others. Every song I write I try to tap into something powerful and something true. For whatever reason though, some songs are just able to convey those feelings, that *truth*, better than others. I've seen plenty of out-of-tune singers at open-mics and young bands at small clubs who you can tell really *mean* it as they're belting it out up there on stage, but the ingredients, whether it's talent or luck or something else aren't there, and that *truth* just doesn't come across. I know that being honest is not enough. It's a rare gift when the same emotion and energy that went into the creation of a song purely transfers to the listener on the other side. I didn't know how it was going to hit anyone else but to me at least, *Coming Down* seemed to communicate the feeling and energy I embodied when I wrote the song in as pure a channel as anything I'd ever done.

I stood in the center of the control room, somehow both calm and vibrating with anticipation. Mr. Bones was a shaggy blob on the floor next to the couch. I gently nudged him toward the door with my foot. He got the hint and dejectedly trotted out and I closed the door behind him. *Sorry buddy,* I wanted to say to him, *I need to be alone for this.* Through the door I heard a slight whimper then a moment later a flurry of tapping nails on the hardwood as he happily scampered away. The rebuff was forgotten almost instantaneously. There must be Prozac in his Alpo.

The overhead lights were dim but I decided to turn them off completely. I shut the computer screen off too leaving the room lit only by the airplane cockpit lights of all the rack-mount gear—scores of tiny red, blue, green and yellow lights, some blinking, some constant, others swept side to side, as if they were communicating with each other, and with me, saying, We're on, we're alive and we're ready when you are Dan, just hit play. I felt as though I was in the future. Not a scary and cold Kubrickian future but a warm one where we figured out how to harness technology in service to our souls. All these blinking lights, all this equipment, all this electricity running through the room, all the zeros and ones flowing from one piece of silicon to the next, it was all there for me. Not just to be used by me but as if it existed just for me. This strange world in this room was *my* world. I thought, When I press *play* this room will become me. I was surrounded by an extension of myself. The speakers, the tape, the amplifiers, the latest Macintosh whirring away, processing data at rates inconceivable to the human mind would speak for me, speak with a voice that I am unable to have on my own. This room of the future, of utter artificiality gave me a feeling of more connectedness, or perhaps more precisely, more *power* than I had ever felt by way of shared humanity through interaction, for it let me extend my own humanity, to be more than myself.

I decided to stand in the center of the room rather than sit in the captain's chair where Tim always sat as he mixed at the board. I wanted as much of myself open to the air as possible, as if I anticipated being able not to just hear, but to absorb the sound through my body and having my back and legs covered by the chair would be like wearing earplugs. I took a step forward and hit play on the deck then pulled my foot back and stood at attention, legs at shoulder width as I waited for the pre-roll to rundown. Distant guitars so heavily drenched in reverb and other effects that they were nearly unrecognizable as guitars slowly escaped from the speakers. Complex triplets of notes fluttered from one speaker to the other, the patterns repeating and collapsing in on themselves. Flanging strings, eerie, distant and distorted chimes, and other manipulated sounds started appearing, some mirroring the guitar patterns, others laying down the root as a pedal drone, a soft and constant bed underneath all the dancing notes from the guitars.

The music began to coalesce. The guitars, diaphanous, like vapor-trail ghosts, whisking around the room seemed to solidify and become emboldened, wrapping around the drums that were starting to build. The pedal bass drone swelled, getting both louder and larger. The ambient strings and other unidentifiable tones from the ether swelled too, their numbers multiplying like water fast coming to a boil. My instinct to stand was prescient, as the music now took on form beyond just being in the air. It was as if the concept or the physics of sound gained another property, exceeding being something we simply can hear or bass frequencies moving air we can physically feel. Because now the music not just filled, but embodied the room, enveloping all the space where air used to be and the music was one force, an organism alive from another dimension but now part of our own world. And within that one force I could feel and hear every disparate sound within the music shining separately but still feel and hear them all together as one.

As the music played everything looked a thousand shades of blue. I was underwater. Yet not in the traditional sense of "being underwater" because nothing was muffled. I'd say I was floating, weightless in ethereal air, or drifting, suspended in dreamy, amniotic, slow motion. But neither of those are accurate. It was more that things like floating and weight and gravity were irrelevant. I was in outer space or rather *another* space where everything is smooth and black and pure and right. Yet of course I knew I was right here on earth and I knew that the earth and this world and my life were from another world or in some way connected to another world where everything is bathed in blue. From radiant cerulean skies to the darkest black-blue of the deep part of the sea, life was a spectrum of blue.

Cool, dark, mysterious, bright—blue. And during that time I understood that magic was possible, that it was real.

Through the wires and into the air, the music, the room itself was me reincarnate. I somehow had become alive in this other dimension. Finally, I was free from myself. What man has always dreamed of. I was free to fly, to float, to be. To be something other, something more than myself.

I was so small; and the world was so large; and quietly, I wanted to explode and be everywhere.

## DECEMBER

"Finally," Koala says as the waitress puts our plates down after we had been waiting an eternity. Old Devil Moon is half full sometime after eight on a Thursday night. It's one of her favorite restaurants and she insists on coming here at least every week or two. I hate it here. I can't eat Cajun food because of my stomach but she doesn't seem to care. "Just order a burger" she always says. I don't even like burgers which she keeps forgetting (or knows but doesn't care). And besides, ordering a lame burger at a Cajun place feels stupid, like ordering a salad at McDonalds.

"Well, at least it's good," Koala says as she chews a bite of her blackened catfish. She doesn't completely close her mouth while she chews, a nasty quirk of hers she lets out too often, and I can hear the bovine *myuck myuck* mastication of the food being tossed from side to side by her tongue, ground by her molars, mixed with her saliva. Once again though, I'm amazed that something I would find disgusting coming from most anyone, is at worst, neutral coming from her. Attractive women, they can get away with anything. I'm annoyed that she gets to coast through life like this. I'm annoyed with myself for not being disgusted, for giving her the free pass. I'm annoyed with myself for being annoyed.

"How's the chicken?" she asks.

"It's really good, actually." I generally avoid eating meat but tofu isn't exactly a southern specialty so before we left I had downed a cocktail of Maalox and Pepto, brought some Pepcid Complete pills in my pocket for after the meal, and ordered the Cajun chicken breast po-boy. "You know I love Cajun. I mean it tastes great, I'm just gonna be paying for it later."

"But you took all that antacid stuff. Won't that help?" There's a drip of sauce on her lip. If she spit her food on the table I'd eat it.

"I don't know. It's hit or miss with my stomach these days." I feel the springs in the shitty old booth bench I'm sitting on poking into my butt.

I slide over a little but then sink into a hole where all the padding underneath the red vinyl covering is gone. I'm a few inches lower now, feeling like a little kid at the table. I'm too lazy to move and Lisa is too interested in her meal to notice. I look around the place at all the random crap—a saw, a deer head, old postcards on the walls; the decrepit booths; and the uninterested staff—our waitress in a Winger concert shirt and the other waitress in '80s leg warmers and Capezios chatting with each other near the kitchen while the guy at the table next to us has been trying to signal his server for the past five minutes. What's the deal with this place? Is the décor kitsch? A purposely shabby chic thing? Is the around-the-world beer collection on the back wall some sort of campy nod to those meat-market, frat guy pubs in the West Village? Or is this simply what it is; take it at face value? Who the hell knows anymore.

The guy next to me gives up signaling them and puts a hand to his head before turning back to his friend across the table. I try to catch his eye to give him a fraternal smirk and head-shake of disgust but he doesn't notice me. I look back at the waitresses and squint trying to read the concert dates on the back of mine's shirt. It was a big tour, there're about fifty cities written in what must be 8-point font. I wonder how much she paid for that shirt. I'm thinking forty dollars off of ebay, more if she got it at some boutique in the city. Like, *I get it*, it's cool because Winger are not cool. Pretty subversive stuff—really stickin it to those earnest hair metal fans!

Koala and I eat in silence (aside from the chewing) until our waitress eventually comes by and saves us. "Do you want some more water?"

"Lemme ask you something," I say. "Do you *like* Winger?"

"Dan, don't start in on this," Lisa says exasperated. The waitress discharges a nervous little laugh. She looks confused and stands there for a moment, the perspiring metal pitcher dripping onto the table. She leans in and pours our glasses with a constipated grimace on her face. Lisa is staring at me, I'm staring at the waitress, the waitress is staring at the glasses and then turns her head without looking at us and walks away.

"What?"

"Just leave the girl alone." Lisa is cutting the fish with the side of her fork, pressing unnecessarily hard, her face tense with effort.

"Why? Why should I leave her alone? I want some interaction. I want to know—does she genuinely like hair metal bands from the late '80s."

"Maybe she does. Maybe she has all their albums at home."

"If she does they're just another prop in her whole shtick. It's beyond clothes, she wants people to see all the CDs in her collection. She probably even listens to the Winger disc alone, ecstatic in her own private ironic bliss. It's not even about showing other people; they do it for themselves. That's how deep they take it. This whole irony, kitsch, camp, whatever-the-fuck it's called—it's a way of life for some of them. She's thought this through. Kids today, they're very thorough." Once I hit twenty-five, twenty-six, the people in Williamsburg and the East Village started looking very young. Since then, with little awareness or condescension I've been referring to them as "kids." Now, at twenty-seven, I feel like an old man around here. It's just a few years difference, I know, but I think there was some sort of generational tipping point between us. I'm on the tail end of one, they're at the head of the next. Or this all may just be in my head.

"You're exhausting. There's nothing new with what you're saying. I know, I get it," she says tiredly, "irony is crushing us, distancing us from ourselves. It's easy and cheap to knock something down with distanced derision but it takes courage to support something you believe in and to show that support earnestly. Shall I continue? . . . I get it. I just want to eat dinner." *Must. Fight. The Neoteny.* Don't look at the Koala. You can't fight with her and look at her at the same time.

"I'm just saying . . ." I trail off and put my sandwich down.

"Hey sweetie, I don't want to fight."

"Then why are you giving me a hard time?"

"Why are you giving the waitress a hard time? You're always giving everyone a hard time."

"I don't give you a hard time."

"You do too!"

"Then why are you with me?"

"Because . . ." *Because you're thirty-one years old and like most unmarried women your age, you're lonely and afraid.* "Because I think you're smart and funny and handsome." Oh? "But you're always tearing everything down."

"No," I jab, "that girl, she's tearing everything down. I mean, society isn't coming to an end because she's wearing that stupid shirt but *come on!* I'm just fucking exhausted by everyone. I'm not trying to be a pain in the ass, honest. I genuinely feel like I don't understand what's going on anymore."

"Maybe that's because you spend all your time thinking and writing those notes instead of working like everyone else."

"Oh, so the key to understanding is to not think."

"Dan, what are you doing?" She puts her fork down. "What are you doing with your life? What are those notes?"

"I told you, they're just notes I write about things."

"Yeah, that's called a journal."

"It's not a journal. They're ideas or just . . . ideas about things. I don't know, maybe some of it is a journal but that's not what it is. I don't know, I can't" or is it don't want to? "describe it." My right eye suddenly is burning. *Did I just rub my eye with this fucking Cajun spice on my finger?*

"And I still don't understand why they're on the wall. It looks creepy, it's weird. But I've never complained."

"*Oh,* so—"

"At least have them lead to something—a book, a play. *Something.* An album. Can they connect to another album?" She pauses. It wasn't rhetorical. "Oh forget that! *You've never even played guitar for me.* Not once!"

This is about you isn't it? You're thirty-one years old and you can't date a guy who doesn't have some semblance of a career path. I was interesting and fun for a while but let's get serious here, I'm not going anywhere and that fact doesn't fit into your plan.

"What does that have to do with this! . . . The notes aren't about that . . . Why does everything have to lead to something? Why is life about the result instead of the process?"

"Oh, spare me the aphorisms."

My eye is blinking furiously. Does she even notice this? I pour water in my hand and lean over and cup it in my eye. This relationship was one date that wrongly got stretched into three months. A perfect first date, we should have left it at that. We should have stopped after the Brooklyn Bridge . . . No—the frozen moment. I should never have seen her again after that moment on the stairs. *How does she not see what's going on with my eye?!*

I get up from my seat which requires more effort than I anticipated due to my being so low to the ground from the pad-deficient bench and wander slightly disoriented to the bathroom. I have to see what's going on with my eye. I close the door and look at myself in the mirror. My right eye is completely red. *How could she not notice this?! Or notice it and not say anything?!* I should have asked her for her contact lens solution, that would have helped. Besides my eye burning, I realize now that my stomach is ablaze. I take a Pepcid out of my pocket and chew it, the chalky remnants like spackle, left in all the grooves of my teeth. I turn on the tap and cup water into my mouth and swish it around. Then I cup water into my eye, blink awkwardly for a few seconds, then pass both hands under the tap and run them through my hair. I can taste bile in the back of my throat. I exhale slowly and take a step back. My back is flush against the wall and I stare at myself in the mirror. I have a bloodshot eye, water looking like sweat after an August run is dripping down my face, and my lips have white powder on them from the Pepcid pills. Blank. I want my mind to be blank.

*I walk back out to the table and Lisa is gone. There's a twenty on the table and a note written on the back of the check:*

Dan,
This isn't working out.
Lisa

*Despite everything swirling around my mind, I'm glad she left twenty bucks toward the bill.*

I open my eyes, my right one still burning and stare uninterested at myself in the mirror. I walk back out to the table. The back of Lisa's head, straight, shiny dark hair, just slightly curling under is visible above the back of the booth seat. Her head is a giant, chocolate-brown croquet ball. I imagine taking a mallet and smacking it off the top of the bench, watching it fly across the restaurant landing in someone's bowl of gumbo.

"What's going on?" K says making her signature face, rolling her eyes and curling the right side of her lip ever so slightly. I remember the first time I noticed this quirk. We were walking down East 4th on our first date. I thought it was so endearing then. I couldn't wait to be closer to her. How I craved the delight, the privilege(!) of knowing all her eccentric charms the way you only can of someone you've been with a long time. I wanted time sped up, fast-forwarded to the good part where we already knew each other, where we could sense each others' thoughts, where we already had formed a bond through so much shared experience, where we had created something between us that was larger than ourselves. Now I'm there and all I can think is I want to take that key lime pie on the dessert stand across the way and slam her face in it, a heavy glaze of custard and cream obscuring every feature, every muscle twitch.

"What do you mean 'what's going on?' Do you see my eye? It's totally fucking red."

"You didn't have to just get up from the table."

"Yes. I did." Neoteny, losing, power! "Listen, I don't know if I'm ever going to have a real job. I don't know what's going on with me. I don't think you want that."

"You have so much potential to do something, to have a good source of income. You're a smart guy, you just have to channel it to the right place."

"I am channeling it in the right place, I'm just not making money from it."

"I know you want to do your music thing," *music thing?* "or your notes or whatever but you can't live off that."

"I don't think you know anything about me. I don't know what we've been doing for the past few months."

There are tears in her eyes. "Well, I guess 'wasting time' is the right response."

Must. Fight. Neoteny. "It's not . . . it wasn't a waste of time." This is not easy seeing Koala cry.

How can she really have these feelings for me? Why is she crying? Why is she this upset? We're nothing alike!

"You know what your problem is? You're a dreamer not a doer. You just walk around criticizing everyone, including yourself, including me—I know what you think of me, of what I do; I'm not an idiot . . . You're going to spend your life daydreaming. Those notes—that's just daydreaming. You're not *doing* anything."

And so that was it. The end is a little hazy to me now. I said something dramatic like, "One thing I *can* do is walk away from this table," and got up and walked out. Heading home down Avenue A, I missed her already.

# JANUARY

As I approach 9th Street I look up at One Fifth Avenue, the grand apartment building one block down on the southeast corner of 8th and Fifth. The top of the building is lit up by the late day sun, the limestone façade painfully reflective in blunt contrast to the sidewalk which is cast in shadow. Seeing the light on the top of the building, I instinctively cross over to the other side of the avenue seeking warmth where the sidewalk is caught in the full light of the bleak winter sun. Deep in our primal brain we are told that light equals heat but in an affront to my instinct, the light today is a mere illusion, a mindfuck. The January sun offers no warmth, only the false promise behind light. Now, walking on the west side of the avenue, instead of being merely cold, I am cold and squinting. In Alaska, cruelly, the coldest days are the ones that are clear, when the sun is streaming down lighting up the world; it's the cloud-cover they say that actually retains some of the heat on the ground by acting as a ceiling of insulation.

I feel a little depressed having been duped by the winter-sun trickery. I remember walking down this street just a couple months ago crossing to the sunnier west side and getting the wonderful treat of a five-degree bump. I let go of my collar which I had been holding up to keep my neck warm, and put my hand to my forehead to shield my eyes. I look like a soldier giving an impromptu salute to the statue of ol' G.W. I'm fast approaching as I cross Washington Square North and head past the Arch into the park. The naked trees in the park, frail like old women, look cold, their bare limbs trapped in a Parkinsons quiver in the persistent wind. I work my way along the asphalt paths walking diagonally to the southeast corner of the park. The frigid square is devoid of life. Even the scattered business-types heading to meetings or late to the office and the couple of NYU students I pass are moving briskly and stiffly with the pained, morose faces of people you'd see in film clips of life behind the iron curtain.

Only the homeless man pacing in front of a bench, shouting at no one, is animated. At the corner of the park I set out east on 4th Street holding my collar again. My hand is red and raw. Only an idiot doesn't think to put on gloves in January. I let go of the collar and decide to leave both hands in my pockets. It's become a game of three-card monte, shifting the pain from one spot to the next. With my neck unprotected, my head shrinks into my shoulders like a turtle. When I hit Lafayette, instead of continuing east toward my place, I turn left and head toward Jay's. I hadn't contemplated the change of direction, it just happened. And as I continue up the block I wonder if I've turned on Lafayette because I'm feeling lonely and want to see Jay or more obviously, I'm so damn cold that my body sent me on an involuntary path to the closest indoors relief. As a fierce gust whips down the street and I hear the flags in front of the Public Theatre in the distance rippling violently, I decide it's the latter; the thought of traveling the extra few blocks to my place seems as daunting as the Iditarod.

"Yo, it's Dan. Buzz me in," I say panicked and weak.

A surprised, "Hey" crackles out of the intercom. "I was heading out. I'll be right down." I wait a few moments but there's no buzz. Fuck! Why doesn't he just buzz me in?

After a minute I break. "Just buzz me into the hallway while I wait," I say exasperated, my finger trembling on the button. There's no response so he must be on his way down the stairs . . . he better be on his way down the stairs. I hit his buzzer in a manic childlike flourish anyway, like high-strung people do waiting for an elevator.

An eternity later Jay appears in the hallway. "Hey, what's up?" he says cheerily as he opens the door.

"Are you trying to kill me? Why didn't you buzz me in while I was waiting?"

"Oh, right. My bad."

"Yes. Bad."

"Sorry," he says without sufficient remorse, giving a minor shrug. "I'm going to Starbucks up on the corner. Wanna come?"

"Starbucks?" I say like I'm a Klan member in 1940 Alabama just asked if he wants to go to a colored restaurant.

"It's too cold to walk all the way to A."

"Good call. Even I have my limits supporting the little guy." Dutiful lefties that we are, we always go to Alt.coffee, a mom n' pop joint on Avenue A.

"Don't worry, I won't call the hipster police," Jay says and claps me on the back.

Starbucks is packed—students hunched over textbooks with highlighters in hand, guys in suits looking over papers talking on cellphones, the requisite strange middle-aged man with dirty, unkempt hair, frumpy slacks, and worn-out Rockports, and twenty-somethings like Jay and me in some variation of jeans, vintage sneakers, and nerd-cool glasses, who all for whatever reasons—freelancers? trust funders? unemployed dot-com-ers?—aren't at work mid afternoon. It's an agitating, and I reluctantly must admit, invigorating atmosphere of bustling activity and incongruent vibes. The homogeneity of our standard Alt.coffee crowd for a moment seems kind of lame. I don't share this sentiment with Jay.

After a frustrating wait on line getting bumped constantly and clucking my tongue and making lots of *tsss* and *pfft* type noises as each order ahead of us seems to involve a Byzantine procedure using multiple machines, button pressing, and lever pulling, I finally get my chamomile tea and he gets his venti organic free trade Mexican blend. We lumber through the crowd in our winter gear until we find a teensy table with four people crowded around it getting up. Jay, with his six-foot-two frame (bass players are always tall), who normally is pretty imposing, now is a monster in his giant down jacket. As we sit down he's reduced to comic folly as he struggles out of his zaftig coat, nearly rocking out of his chair in the process.

"Watch it, you're gonna knock over the table," I say, realizing though that

I'mmoreworriedabouthimknockingintothegirlwho'swalkingbycautiously holding her topped-off cup, envisioning a scalding grande latte dumped all over me. The place is so crowded you wouldn't know there were three other branches within a two-minute walk from here. He finally wrestles the coat off and drapes it on the back of his chair, half of it on the floor.

"Hey, I'm a big guy. What are ya gonna do?" He shrugs. "So . . . You and the Koala Bear, no more, huh?" I had told him about the nickname.

"Yeah," I say tiredly.

"So, how ya feeling?"

"I'm not sure. I can't tell if I'm depressed, lonely, or just bored."

"Hmm." He takes a sip of his coffee. "Are you looking for other girls?"

"Nah, not really."

"What have you been up to?"

"Not much. Just been wandering around a lot lately. But I think I've had enough of that now that it's so damn cold."

"Maybe you should start playing again."

"Yeah. Maybe."

"Seriously man. You gotta start playing again."

"Yeah," I say distracted. Sheryl Crow's *Soak Up the Sun* is beaming from the PA system. "But why? What's the point? This is the crap that people want to hear."

"We both know that's not why you make music."

"Well, I don't know what to do with myself, how I'm supposed to make a living. This is what the labels want," I say. Then holding my arms out, "This is what people want to hear." *Iiiiiii've got no one to blame. For every time I feel lame, I'm looking up.*

"This music makes people happy."

"Jay, it's the middle of the Goddamned winter and they're playing *Soak Up the Fucking Sun!*"

"Right, they're trying to pep everyone up on this cold day. What's wrong with that?"

"Everything is wrong with that!" The truth is I really like this song. I could never resist a great pop hook, no matter how insipid. In fact, sometimes the more insipid, the better. *Gonna tell every one- to- light- ten- up*—love that F# minor climbing to the A-flat minor and on up to the B major! But I can't stop myself, I'm on a roll. "Everything is wrong with this song."

The song goes to the outro where it's just Sheryl and an acoustic guitar. "See—they have this thing compressed like a brick."

"Don't get into your compression diatribe again," Jay moans.

"Can we sit down here?" Two girls, one homely, one half-decent, probably NYU students, are standing at our table.

I look up at them. "Girls, do you know anything about compression? Do you hear that?" They smile awkwardly and look at each other.

"Sit down, sit down," I command.

They hesitantly set their coffees on the table and settle in to the empty seats next to us.

"Do you hear that?" I say pointing a finger at the ceiling. "Her lone voice and acoustic guitar—it's the same volume as the peak of the song five seconds earlier when there was a full band with a drum kit and like five guitars and three thousand vocal tracks harmonizing the shit out of that chorus until syrup oozes out of the speakers."

"Dan—" He tries but knows there is no stopping me. At the same time, the homely one says, "What?" sporting the obnoxious, confused teenager *excuse me?* face.

"That's the problem with all the music today, girls. They compress everything! There're no dynamics. Everything is just *loud*, all the time. Even the soft parts are *loud*. Radio stations are afraid people will change the station if the music dips for a second, and stores, with their consultant-designed mix CDs or satellite or however-the-fuck they're piping the music in here, they're afraid that if the volume bumps up for one second people will freak out and run out of the store. They all demand flatness! Chop all the peaks, boost all the lows and level it off. We have to keep everything flat and *loud*, all the time. And the bands, hah! They compress everything on the disc too because that's the only way to get it really *loud*, so the music's ruined before it even reaches the radio. The poor songs are compressed over and over, every stage squishing them some more. Don't even get me started on your computer sound files! Do you understand what I'm saying? You understand, right? It's just like how they're leveling off the West Virginia mountains from all the coal mining—I know, it's not covered in the media but it's happening—except with this not only are the tops lopped off but the valleys are filled in too. Look at a sound file, that's what it is. Flatline. This is the soundtrack of our lives, everywhere we go, every fucking store, office, wherever, this brick of sound. I don't know if they've done studies or not but there is no way that this is good for you. The real world, the natural" using air-quotes on *natural*, "world is filled with dynamics. Only once in a while do our ears really get blasted like if there's a boom of thunder or if a huge dog is barking in your face, or something. But no, we walk around, we're in an office or a waiting room where some jerkoff has Light FM on the radio all day, or you're in your car—though at least in your car it's music you want to hear—it's all a brick, you're listening to a brick. Everywhere we go we've got a brick smacked on our ears. This can't be good for you."

At some point the girls had left the table. Jay is sitting there with a blank expression, not quite pissed, not quite amused. "Some people like it loud," he says, which I'm pretty sure he did just to rile me up again.

"No they don't," I continue unabated, eyeing the girls a few tables away. I call out to them, "they think they do but they don't." I turn back to Jay. "Put on a Black Sabbath album or *Nothing's Shocking*; that's some of the loudest shit there is but the CDs aren't loud. Why? Because the music has dynamics and it's the dynamics that make the loud parts even louder. When everything is all smushed together like they do now . . . in a way, if everything is loud, nothing is loud. It's just noise. It's just bullshit."

"Hey!" he says annoyed, finally having run out of patience and done being entertained. "I've heard this all before. Do you want me to get Ash on the phone for reinforcements? So you can argue with him about this again for three weeks?"

"Thanks man. Thanks Jay. I really needed to be reminded of that era of my life."

Sometimes I wonder if this ultimately was the reason I got dropped. I wouldn't relent on them compressing the dynamics, the life out of my album. After the recording was finished at Tim's I was sent to Silver Sound, one of the top mastering houses in the country. (Mastering is the final step of making a CD, after all the recording and mixing, sort of like putting varnish on a wood cabinet you just built). I had had a long conversation there with Craig Gerby who TOTALLY agreed with me on what was best for my record.

"The volume wars are killing music. It's really an epidemic," Craig said.

"Though it makes your job easier, right? You just slam everything. As long as it comes back hot on the CD—those idiots, that's all they want to hear."

"You've got a point," he said, stroking his white goatee. "But it's becoming too easy, this bullshit is eventually going to put mastering engineers out of business. People will just hook up a Finalizer and be done with it."

Man, Craig Gerby was such a cool guy. He even looked cool, in his jeans and t-shirts, short, brown hair on his head thinning like David Letterman's with the remaining tuft in the front, center, and his white facial hair[*]—it gave him an air of relaxed authority, the elder statesman. It felt good to have him as an ally. Then, a few days after our first meeting, I came back to check on the tracks and noticed that everything sounded different. Everything was flattened out and tight, there was no air left in

---

[*] Unlike Vagina Mouth Jeff, Gerby could pull off a goatee.

the track. It was so compressed, the digital displays on the monitors that show the waveforms of the song looked like solid rectangles, whereas if the track was left more natural the waveforms would look like something more akin to the zigzag line on a heart monitor. As the first song played, Gerby looked at me abashedly, smiling awkwardly and fiddling with his goatee as the music rolled by. I got up and turned it off.

"I'm sorry Dan. You knew the label wouldn't let this stand, you knew they weren't going to let us do it our way."

In my naiveté—at the time I really *didn't* know, actually—I thought I had some control, especially at that stage of the process. But no matter how savvy I thought I was, my excitement over recording the music my way, bringing the sound to life the way I wanted it, seemed to have over-ridden my common sense. "But you're the mastering guy! You're a fuck-ing legend for God's sake," I cried. "You don't take orders from them."

"They're paying the bills, Dan. They're the client."

"I thought I was the client."

Over the following weeks I argued with Gerby, Ash, and anyone else who would listen. I really pulled some shit with Ash. I'm talking, top-of-lung screaming, spit flying type of shit. I remember what I think was my last confrontation with Ash: I howled into the receiver, "Are you fucking kidding me! You're ruining my fucking album! You're ruining it, you're ruining it!"

"D—" he tried to cut in.

"You're fucking with my dream! This is not the way . . ." I felt myself on the verge of collapse and hung up the phone. It wasn't long after that that Warners shelved my record. The irony was, they fought me so hard every single step of the process, yet they never even released the damn record. If they weren't going to release it anyway, they could have just let me be and make the album the way I wanted.

"Would you lighten up?" Jay says after finishing off his coffee. "I'm your friend. I'm just messin' around. Trying to get you to take it easy."

Ok. He's right. He's right. I've got to take it easy, must relax . . . but *No.* I can't. I love Jay to death but sometimes I fear whatever he says is the exact wrong thing. His life is the exact wrong example . . . Or maybe his life is there to be a counter-weight to mine, to show me the other side, to balance me out, give me perspective . . . Oh, fuck it. I don't need that perspective. I don't want to take it easy. Taking it easy means I have failed.

"Ok. Ok." I feel myself coming down anyway.

"They *do* have good coffee here," Jay says trying to get me off the subject.

"The tea's not bad either. But, you know—it's *Starbucks.* I feel guilty if I enjoy it."

"I didn't want to come here either but it's too cold to walk anywhere else." A guy in slacks and an overcoat walks by us blathering into the dangling earpiece from his cellphone, his hands moving around as if he's giving a presentation.

"It's funny how people still move their hands when they're on the phone."

"Yeah, I guess it's one of those things," Jay says as he glances at the guy then turns his attention toward a table of two youngish looking girls.

"Hey, you have a girlfriend. Eyes off."

"I can look. I'm allowed to look." Both of the girls have notebooks open; probably NYU students. This area is crawling with them.

"How does someone study in a coffee shop?" Jay is entranced and not listening to me. "Too much noise, you know? I need total silence if I'm going to do anything." I think there's drool coming off his lip. "Jay! Are you listening to me?"

"Yeah, yeah, coffee shop," he turns back toward me. "Speaking of girls . . . I have a bomb to drop on you," he says, his voice solemn.

Holy shit. Jen is pregnant. Abortion, obviously. I hope. Jay, you can't be a dad right now.

"When my lease is up in the summer, I'm moving out to Willy B. to live with Jen."

"What!" This somehow feels worse and more shocking than if Jen was pregnant. "What about Cindy?"

"She's going to move out. And her room was made with one of those temporary walls so we'll knock it down and just have the one bedroom and a huge living room. I think she might be moving back to the west coast. Apparently she hates New York."

"Wait a minute. You're leaving your place?" I'm still trying to compute this. "But it's rent stabilized, you can't leave." He's making a terrible mistake. This is a terrible mistake.

"Yeah, yeah. But, at some point, life moves on, man. I've been dating Jen for over two years."

"So what? There's no time limit to things." He doesn't even love Jen. This is a disaster. I can't let him make a mistake like this. Jen is a total dud. A zero. She's bringing him down. She's refining his edges, wearing down the spunk, the funk, the life in him. But. He's an adult, this is who he is. If he likes her then that says something about him. I can't solely blame Jen even if I'd like to. He knows what he's doing. I'm not going to change his mind.

"*Two and a half years* it'll be come May. It's time."

"Ok, ok. Hey, if this is what you want to do then I'm behind you," I lie. "Can I just ask you something?" Don't say it. "Don't get mad, but, are you even *in love* with Jen?"

He makes a pfft sound and shakes his head in disgust but then surprisingly, actually gives me a response. "*Yes* . . . yeah . . . well, what is love anyway?"

"I mean, I know you love her but are you *in love* with her?"

"Dan, there is no difference."

"Yes, there is. That's the problem, you don't see that."

"No, that's the problem with you. You're never going to find someone because you are waiting for some magical feeling. I think you're confusing love with lust."

"No, Jay, I think you're saying that you fall in love with someone just because you've been with them for so long, *two and a half years*—" I imitate him. I'm such a jerk sometimes, "—because over all that time you grow attached, you need each other. So being in love just means being needy. You know, it's like you have all these shared experiences and over time it's like your lives are so intertwined, you have so many shared memories and there's all this familiarity of each other's quirks and whatever else. I know this shit man, I went through it with Lisa, and believe me, it was really hard when we broke up. I was surprised how much I missed her even though I couldn't stand her at the end of things. It's like even though I stopped liking her, she became this part of my life, this part of me."

"So what? So what if time and neediness and whatever it is you're saying is part of what love is? That doesn't make it any less real."

"I don't know . . . is being attached to someone, familiarity, the same thing as love? All I know is when I think of the way I felt when I was out at The Watershed working on the album, *that's* what I think love feels like, or should feel like."

"It doesn't. As you get older you just have to accept certain things. I'm not talking about settling, I'm talking about understanding the reality of life."

"Is that why you're doing the music for the commercials and not working on your own stuff anymore?"

"I'm still working on my stuff." No you're not! You haven't played me any of your own music in months! "But I need to make a living. I need to get practical. And I think you could use a good dose of practicality. Is that a word? Life isn't just about dreaming. I went through that phase. I did all the drugs, I did all the other crap."

"I don't know. I just don't view love that way."

"Then I don't think you're ever going to be in love."

*Don't say it, don't say it.* "I think you're making a mistake. I think this is a mistake." Fuck.

"Unlike you, I don't want to be alone forever." *That's not a reason to stay with Jen!* He doesn't realize that whenever he talks about her it's always about how great she is *to him*, not how great she is as a person on her own. And now this 'we've been together for two years' bullshit. "I think I make good decisions. I'm doing the best I can."

"What does that even *mean*? I never understand what 'doing the best I can' *means*. Everyone is always doing *the best they can*." Jay's looking pissed, he doesn't want to hear me anymore. But he has to; it's for his own good. Or it's for my good because I want this off my chest. Either way, there's no stopping me. "Whatever way you live your life, that's the best you can do. By default. Whatever someone is doing, that's their best. You know what I'm saying? It doesn't matter if they have potential for more. People are too easy on themselves. It's too easy to just say I'm doing the best I can and convince yourself, even on a subconscious level that that's the case. The *best*" in air-quotes, "is totally arbitrary. Unless you're talking about something you can measure objectively, like taking a test and how long you studied for it, or how many hours you spend lifting weights, or whatever, then it doesn't mean anything. Because for the rest of stuff in life there isn't a gauge, you can't measure effort on most things. I'm sorry, I just feel like that is the most BS expression."

"Whatever . . . What am I doing? I don't need to apologize to you."

"You're right, you're right." I give up. Why beat on my one friend? "I think I'm just bummed you're not gonna be living near me anymore. God, everyone lives in Brooklyn now."

"I know but that's where it's at. Manhattan's over. Too expensive. Look at the East Village. Look at these people," he says motioning with his head. "It's all bankers and rich NYU students now. Another few years and it'll be like the West Village."

"The nature of cities, I guess. Neighborhoods change . . . shit, we can probably just say all of Manhattan. It's weird, I'm always changing how I feel about it here, I can never decide. It depends on the day or even the hour . . . sometimes it still feels magical. But—and I hate to say this—I can't shake the feeling that its heyday has come and gone."

"You think?"

"It's still got *it*, that spark, that energy, don't get me wrong, but . . . I don't know. I feel like we've missed something . . . And Brooklyn, it might be cool now but it never has struck me as magical. There's a difference."

"There are other places besides Manhattan and Brooklyn."

"Nah. The whole world is going the same way. It has to do with capitalism, globalization, homogenization, you know. The whole deal."

"Oh God." He rolls his eyes.

"What?"

"Nothing."

"I mean, seriously, as New York goes, so goes America. The city, the empire, it's on the wane."

"Maybe you're right. Whatever Dan." He goes to take a sip of coffee then realizes it's empty. "I'm not worrying too much about all that . . . I hear you, man" he says quickly as if he's cutting me off, though I haven't said anything. "I hear you. Totally. I just, you know. Whatever."

"Yeah, fuck it. Here we are. So be it . . . So. Williamsburg—I think you're too old to move there. I think you need to be under twenty-six, *may*be twenty-seven to live there. We're over the hill my man."

"Always cheery," he says shaking his head. "What do you want me to do? Move to the suburbs? I'm not making a life statement. I'm just moving in with my girlfriend. Not everything has some giant meaning."

"Really? I wonder about that all the time."

"You're not joking. That's the scary part," he says snickering. "No one's watching me, no one's judging. No one cares. Everyone's too busy worrying about themselves to care about where so and so lives or what he's wearing or whatever."

"Don't tell me you're immune to worrying about how you appear."

"I'm not. I'm not saying that. It's just that I can only care so much about it."

"Ahh, oh well," I say, giving up. "I can just hop the L."

"If you didn't have *your* rent stabilized place you'd have moved out of the neighborhood a long time ago. Maybe you just should. Maybe it's time for a change."

"Let me tell you something, another month or two and I'm going to be kicked out anyway. I think I can eke out paying my rent for another month or so and that's it. I'm so broke and so in debt now."

"I'm sorry to break this to you but you've gotta get a fucking job man."

"I know. I know." I crumple my napkin with the teabag soaked through it and shove it in my cup. "Hey, you ready to get out of here?"

"Yeah."

It's 9:30 a.m. and I've just munched down my obligatory colon-cleaning bowl of bran. It was the first bowl I've ever had with almond milk. Fuck rice and soy! I need to diversify even more. I saw the almond milk at this new health-food market on University. It was mixed within a huge display of all the various boxes of "milk." Wheat milk, buckwheat milk, hazelnut milk, rice milk, soy milk, rice-soy combo milk, chocolate soy milk, vanilla, regular, enriched, low-fat, on and on. Why the hell do they call them all "milk?" Why try to be something you're not? Just call it "____ water" or "____ liquid." Maybe it *is* milk, you know, technically, etymologically, semantically speaking; depends how you stretch the definition. But I don't care, call in whichever linguistics scholar you want, I still think the whole milk tie-in is bullshit. No doubt, some marketing consultant asshole came up with calling all these liquids "____ milk." I can picture his PowerPoint presentation to the company, the different lines of white or yellow text zipping off the blue screen transitioning to each new slide:

---

**Naming Your Brand**

[Whoosh, off the screen]

---

**We need to ease the consumer into new product territory.**

Our data shows that consumers are more likely to embrace a new product when it bears some resemblance to an existing product.

[Whoosh]

Consumers desire old products
but with a new twist.

Never introduce a product that
is drastically, completely new.
The consumer fears this.

[Whoosh]

Often, a new product name will include
some textual element of its derivative
product category. In the Breakfast
Liquid Accompaniment category We
must use a familiar name as the suf-
fix so the consumer knows what to do
with the product. Consumers obviously
are reluctant to purchase a product of
which they don't know its purpose!

[Whoosh]

[Whoosh]

If we just call it rice water,
the consumer won't know
what to do with it.

[Whoosh]

It's just like the radio. The new hits always sound kind of like the old
hits they're replacing, usually with just a little twist of difference. New
but not *that* new. Unlimited choices of limited variety.

Anyway, the almond milk was good. It actually tasted like almonds!
But when I look on the ingredients *natural flavors* is listed. And you
know *natural flavors* is a total lie. It's just a euphemism for *chemicals* because even chemicals at some basic level are from nature and that's how
they *(they!)* can get away with calling anything they want *natural ingredients*. It's true, they do this. Oh, it's all such bullshit! They're just lying
to us all the time! Well, whatever. I give up. It did *taste* good. If it's going
to be fake it might as well taste real. *Right?* No. Wait. Anyway . . . Well,
it gave my body a much needed break from the rice and soy that most
likely were killing me.

**winter**

The almond and wheat and hazelnut "milks" all cost more than the cheapo brand of soy milk and at this time I'm well below being broke but fuck it. You reach a point when you are so broke it just doesn't even matter anymore. I don't know how I'm going to dig myself out of this. I'm taking cash advances on my Visa to pay my rent each month. I'm a disgrace. I know I need to work. *I know, I know.* I just can't. And I know what you're thinking. You're thinking I'm a total baby, a whiner, a complainer. *Get a fucking job you lazy, faux-artist slacker.* And it's not as if I'm enjoying myself. Jason, Lisa, all of you, you think I've got it easy, who am I to complain! But I can't enjoy this. I'm nervous. I'm sick. I'm diseased. (Or am I well and everyone else is sick?—Hah!). I know, I'm insufferable. This is going to come across as a cop-out response but the truth is if you haven't lived this type of life then you just won't understand. I don't want to be like you. I don't want to work for the next thirty years at some bullshit job. I'm trying to *do* something with myself here. (And no, I'm not sure what it is exactly, but that's besides the point!) I have other motivations beyond the pursuit of security. I know you think you do too but let's be honest, you're never going to do anything about those little urges you get once in a while to make those changes with your life. I can tell. You're going to stay married to that spouse you don't really like so much anymore, you're going to keep working at that job that is draining away the best years of your life, you're going to keep living in that same lame-ass place even though you've been telling yourself for years, (years!), that you're going to move . . . Ok, maybe not all of you, I know not all of you, but some of you, most of you. This is why I am lonely. This is why I am alienated from everyone.

It all relates to the lottery test. My mom's advice and world view haven't been the most constructive but this is one of the things she said that I still return to. It's nine years ago, mid summer, my mom has already moved out west, I'm alone in the house in Jersey for the final month before I leave for college. My whole senior year she had been taking trips out west—northern California, Seattle and Bellingham, Boulder—deciding where she was going to "start the next and perhaps final phase" of her life, as she put it. She hadn't met George yet but she sounded already settled and fully in her element on the phone from her condo near the CU campus.

My parents were never meant to be together. "We were a one-night-stand that lasted twenty-one years," she told me when I was twelve. (When I repeated this to my dad he said it had something to do with her being stuck in the "I'm Not OK, You're Not OK" stage, which of course was of great relevance to a sixth grader). She married Dad because he seemed like a dependable guy and probably showed some flare when they first met but all along it never felt quite right for her. She was more of a free spirit, reckless, loner type. But she went with Dad because that's what she thought she should do "it was 1963 and things were quite different then, and I wasn't brave." But she never forgave herself and she had a mean streak and she made Dad pay for her regrets and self-hatred, starting with the whole making-him-change-the-last-name power-grab bullshit.

So anyway, I have my mom on the phone. I've just broken up with Jillian Schlotzker, my girlfriend of the past three months because we're both going off to school and it seemed like the right thing to do. But I'm second guessing myself, having all sorts of crazy thoughts that graduating seniors with girl/boyfriends have, like that we could actually stay together and make things work, that we can "do our own thing" in college but ultimately we'll get back together after school's over and maybe get married, that I know this seems unlikely but maybe it's just turned out that I met my wife in high school, etc.

"How are things holding up back east sweetie?" She never called Jen or Laura sweetie. My mom wasn't particularly maternal but she had a soft spot for me because I was the child she saw some of herself in—the brooding, the anti-social tendencies, and the gravitas, if you will.

"Oh, doing ok mom. The house still feels weird with all these boxes around and all the missing furniture. I'll be glad to get out of here in a few weeks."

"It's such a bad house! I feel like a new person out here. You'll do so much better once you leave too."

"Hey mom—remember that girl Jillian? I think I told you about her."

"Yeah . . . yeah," I pictured her searching the ceiling trying to remember.

"She's the girl I've been dating," I said annoyed.

"I knew that."

"Mom."

"No, no I did. I remember her."

I sighed.

"We just sort of broke up but I'm thinking I may have made a mistake."

"Why?"

"It's kind of complicated . . ."

"Don't tell me why you think it's a mistake, tell me why you broke up." She had an almost pathological keenness to support anything that propelled my independence. Maybe subconsciously that's why I told her; I wanted my decision validated.

"Because we're both going off to college and—"

"That's a very sensible reason" she jumped in.

"It is, right?"

"Yes. And don't take this the wrong way but I think she was a bit of a lightweight for you. Very nice girl but I could just tell, not a serious candidate for you."

"Really?"

"Daniel I've learned a lot over the years. People like us, we're different. I don't want you to make the same mistake I made when I was young. You need to just go out there in the world and do your thing. You can't be tied down with one person. And beyond girls, just don't listen to anyone, listen to your muse." Mom forgot to mention that the world order was more complicated than just following your bliss. I wish I could go back to this conversation and ask her how following my muse was going to pay my rent. But, despite her callow advice I know she meant well. She was just overcompensating for her own failings.

"Have I ever told you about the lottery test?" She said.

"No, I don't think you have."

"You're not ready for it now, don't even bother using it with any girl you meet in the foreseeable future but when you're ready, when you're a little older, you're going to need this advice. And this seems like a good time to tell you, prepare you for down the road."

"Ok," I said tentatively and slightly weirded-out. This was shaping up to be the closest we ever came to an actual "life" talk. Perhaps it was because she felt freed by her move or perhaps she was feeling sentimental because of the milestone of me leaving for college. Maybe she hadn't yet acclimated to the altitude. I realize now, that until she moved, she had restricted a lot of herself during my junior high and high school years. Though periodically they bubbled to the surface, she kept her criticisms of dad to a minimum, and she kept most of her larger life views from me, or at least the more venomous core of them. And even with her affection for me, my mom has a more laconic nature than I do, so imparted wisdom over the years has been scarce. Though I speak a little more often with her than my dad these days, the conversations are generally brief. She supports whatever it is I'm doing and chooses not to hear any downside of my situation. I'm a musician in New York City who was signed to Warner Brothers Records and was flown to Chicago to record an album—that's all she needs (and wants) to know. In some vicarious way, this rosy soundbite version of me is a vague semblance of the life she was supposed to have lived. But hey, she does love me, and she does care, which is nice to know; it counts for something.

"When you're an adult—not now, because you're not an adult yet. I know they call you *young adults* but being in high school or college is not the same as when you're out of school, on your own . . . you're going to be dating a lot more women over the years. Just like this girl Jillian, you can't let yourself be caught with someone who ultimately is not the right person for you. Because I know what type of person you are. It doesn't mean Jillian's not a wonderful girl but when you're older, you're going to have to ask yourself when you're with a woman does she pass the lottery test. You've always followed where your heart took you, that's what I love about you . . . I love you because you're my son," she corrected, "but . . . you understand. The hours and hours and hours you'd be in the garage playing music, all your report cards and teachers saying that you seem distracted and that you have so much potential but you choose not to use it, except for Ms. Kellinger, she knew what talents you had, you loved that class. What I'm saying is, when you're older you're going to be one of those people whose work defines them. I know you will. Have you ever heard the expression, who you are is what you do?"

"No, I don't think so."

"Most people don't love music the way you do. Most people don't care and think about things the way you do. I know you already knew that but . . . What I'm getting at is, you will never be truly satisfied with a woman that doesn't also share that passion, or a passion in her life. You need to ask yourself, if this person won the lottery would she still be do-ing the same job she's doing. Because most people, and I'm not saying they're bad people, they're just not like us," we both know she's talking about dad, "they would quit their job in a heartbeat. But I know you, you could be given a million dollars, ten million dollars, it doesn't matter, you'd still be playing music, you'd still be wondering about things, always asking questions. Most people simply work to pay for themselves and their families. And again, there's nothing wrong with this. But it's just different from who you are, or who I think you are. Work, even if they like it, is ultimately just a means to an ends. If people were offered their paycheck every two weeks but they didn't have to work, very *very* few people would still work. But a small percentage of people would. There's a small amount of people in the world where work isn't just about the ends, I mean making money, it's about doing the work. People for whom what they do is an inseparable part of who they are, an essential component to them feeling they are living a full life. These are very different ways of living." Considering this advice was coming from a person who for the previous fifteen-plus years lived off sporadic uninspired teaching gigs at a local community college and mostly her husband's salary then his alimony, I assumed my mom was exempting herself from the "who you are is what you do" philosophy. So I can only suppose she meant it to be taken more in the theoretical realm. Or, is it possible that she did in fact mean this as actionable advice? And as a byproduct this was her way (consciously or not) of letting me know that she failed her own philosophy and I am expected to bring to fruition her unfulfilled dreams? Ah, how clichéd mom! But really, I don't know; my mom has always been and still remains a bit of a mystery to me.

"Oh," I said looking around the empty living room.

"You either pass the lottery test or you don't."


Goddamn, that almond milk really did taste almondy and I can't even enjoy it because I know the almond flavor is solely from the chemicals. It's people like that jerk Jeff, who get paid two hundred grand a year to defend these companies from anyone who questions the legality, the validity, of calling something natural ingredients.

I turn on the TV, something I swore to myself I'd never do during the day but do every day now anyway. I'm stealing cable I spliced in the hallway from outside Dayna's apartment next door. But for some reason it only goes up to 13, which is the for the best anyway. This way I actually settle on something which no matter how bad it is, somehow seems less destructive than scrolling through a hundred channels for hours on end. The TV's on 2 and I start flipping my way through the networks and curse all the talking heads, those insipid baby boomers pedaling the latest crap on the morning shows. That insidious Katie Couric. What's with adults who still use cutesy abbreviated endings to their names, the "ie"s, the "y"s, (the Janies and Billys and Joeys and Tammys)? Some producer twenty years ago probably decided that *Katherine* wasn't as personable for the audience. And that thespian Matt Lauer . . . I don't even have the energy. Ugh. The two of them just lying to us day after day. You're not my friends, so cut with the jokey chumminess as you stare into that teleprompter inside the camera fooling a million fools on that deep, inaccessible, un-turnoffable level of the id that thinks one is being looked in the eye. The profound dishonesty of it all. The only thing more sickening than this charade you perpetrate through your counterfeit smiles and deceitful good cheer when you're playing the role of the *Fun-Morning-Pal-to-Help-You-Start-Your-Day!* sampling some shrimp dish just grilled on camera by the latest celebrity chef de jour pimping his new book or that phony, solemn tone you take on when you're playing *Mr.*- or *Ms.-Grown-Up-Newscaster* reciting the latest hard news for a minute and a half so stay-at-home moms can pretend they're well informed are the rubes from flyover country standing outside the studio in the frigid weather with signs saying "Happy 40th Birthday Janet!" cheering on cue when the P.A. tells them to because the camera is on them now as the producer gets ready to cut to commercial and you are not an observer anymore, oh no siree! you are a part of the show now, you're behind the glass, you've come all this way to be on the other side and damn it, you're going to do your part to be part of the show and you are going to dutifully cheer on cue because somehow on some level you understand that you are not a fan anymore, you are now an actor playing a fan, that this is not reality, that nothing about this is real even though you all pretend it is.

I flip over to PBS, the only station tolerable, and the Teletubbies are on. I hit mute on the remote and pace around my apartment waiting until I feel the need to shit. I turn on my stereo and hit play on the CD player, not knowing what's in there. Electric guitars sounding like slithering cellos play mournful lines juxtaposed with jumpy syncopated beats from a drum *kit* morphed to sound like an ailing drum *machine* while the man sings of "the next world war, jackknife juggernaut" and being "born again." I sit back on the couch and sink into one of the long-since beat-up cushions and stare at the screen while music of postmodern alienation takes over the room. The minutes disappear, time somehow both stale and cruising right along as my fuzzy friends frolic on in their Martian land and the band plays on or rather the recording of the band playing plays on, on this winter day, like so many days before it, of no consequence. And in some parallel universe kind of way, this morose, brilliantly confused music feels surreally, sublimely perfect as the soundtrack to the nonsensical goings-on of these deliriously cheerful, furry, pastel creatures on the screen. For once I don't feel anxious or scared, something just feels terribly off. And I don't seem to care all that much.

*So, this is depression.*

The show ends and I manage to conjure the willpower to just-shut-the-damn-TV-off. I start pacing the apartment again, and feel nature's broom beginning to sweep through my system. I keep pacing, waiting. I look around the apartment. The notes are covering almost two full walls now. All my yellow squares, hanging there, reminders of me, hopes for who I want to be; dreams that are evidence of delusions and/or admirable bravado; revelations that are deep truths and/or mere platitudes. And I am embarrassed and emboldened, ashamed and proud; and I am plagued with self doubt, and I am a narcissist; I am glorious and I am afraid as I bask looking at all the yellow squares, hanging there, that however they are perceived or received, are most certainly me.

**winter**

## LATE LATE WINTER

Gotham was in full force as I walked up Irving Place at 1:30 a.m. on a Friday night. It was still winter-coat-and-hat cold but in the past week there had been a break in the frigid front of Canadian air that had taken over much of the Mid Atlantic states for what seemed like weeks on end. The weathermen warned that although temps were in the forties we may get one more spell of Arctic or Canadian or just plain *Cold* air in New York before a genuine spring thaw was irreversibly on its way. It takes extreme acts of weather to keep New York's streets barren and the recent insufferable cold was enough to do so but once the temperature swooped a full ten to fifteen degrees up, as it did a few days ago the city was back.

Smatterings of couples wander by me, many with the women's arms hooked though their man's arm with his hand in his coat pocket. A guy with a sweater and no jacket stands outside a bar smoking a cigarette trying his best to look comfortable as his hand shakes. Random individuals, mainly men who look like they are on their way home from bars, and less common though still prevalent, females, some of whom carry that perma-fear-induced attempt-at-looking-stoic middle-distance stare and others who actually make eye contact with passersby, are walking up and down Irving and crisscrossing the side streets.

The night sky is a light gray so cinematic in its glow that I find myself frustratingly, repeatedly detached by its majesty because the point of comparison my mind is referencing is some vague amalgam of the New York of comic book films with their futurist-retro cityscape like twenty-second century art deco, mixed with the classic 1940s New York of Alfred Steiglitz photographs or some Cary Grant film. Mists of roaming cloud-cover are back-lit by a strong moon like diffuse Kleig lights. A thousand shades of crystalline liquid gray illuminate the city, the eloquent light so commanding that I look down at my hands seeking the beige of my skin to confirm that the whole world hasn't turned black and white. Because New York City tonight is in black and white. As I look up and around, the buildings, the street lights, the cars, the people, including me, all feel almost like props doing our part to bring a clichéd, Old—not era-specific, just *Old*—New York photograph to life. And it feels not antiquated but simply timeless. Majestic. And endearingly ominous, the top of the Chrysler building, the emblem of this emerald city night, moving in and out of the fast moving low-level clouds. American flags hang at soft angles off Federalist townhouses that line Irving Place framing the view up to Grammercy Park. Pre-war residential towers with gargoyles and near-ostentatiously ornate carvings in stone facades surround the small park, ensconcing young wealth and blue-blooded denizens grandfathered in from the era before real estate hit hyperspace.

I am not tired nor am I manic, I am simply compelled to remain in this crisp dream. And so I turn around and start strolling south. I meander one block west and continue down Lafayette past Astor Place where punk kids are sitting under the Cube while skaters attempt and fail repeatedly at their ollies off the cement island in the crossroads; past the Public Theater, past the giant semi-circular Crunch sign and the neon Jivamukti Yoga studio sign just beyond it. I cross Houston, a mini-Times Square now, overwhelmed by oversized illuminated billboards, some on the sides of buildings, others standard issue highway-style billboards perched on massive steel columns erected on former gas station lots like the garish and monstrous Yahoo sign adorned with blinking red bulbs and a kitschy glowing globe. I cross Houston towered-over by the painted cityscape inside the letters DKNY ten-stories tall on a brick wall facing north. I continue south to Broome, make a right then make another right up Mercer, somewhat unconsciously, seemingly heading me back toward home, the call of fatigue ringing ever so slightly in the recesses of my body. The streets here are near empty as the hour in some sort of tipping point has grown much later. As I began up Mercer and crossed over

Spring walking on the west-side sidewalk, I saw a standard-sized street poster, the kind slapped-up in the middle of the night that advertises upcoming local concerts or album releases or the latest internet site or tech gadget glued on particle-board walls with **POST NO BILLS** stenciled on them in front of construction sites and derelict buildings in cities all over the world. The poster looked like this:

Who put this poster here? Why? Was this someone who tried for so long to "make it" and this was a project done in a darkest hour after years of heartache? I know from putting up my own lame posters for my band, which was tedious enough that a far superior poster like that, with all the fonts and a designer's eye to detail and the Marilyn picture, then to pay to print them in color on the quality, standard issue, professional poster paper, then to plaster them (assuming there are more elsewhere) up—this was not done on a whim. This involved serious time, effort, love/anger. Ahh, the refreshing bleak honesty! Every ad promises a better future; for once there's a message telling it like it is. And although the message is not cheery, I am gratified by it for its truth and its lack of commands. And though my aims weren't specifically to be famous or a big star, I am relieved and comforted by the commonality of failure I feel with whoever put this up here.

I stand here facing the poster, that strangely hangs all by itself. It's the only one plastered on the boards of a temporary walkway in front of a building under renovation. I keep thinking about who made this sign and put it up here. I think he or she would feel good knowing that I was standing here right now, alone. I walk up closer to the bill, searching the bottom, the perimeter, then all over for a logo, a web site, a signature, some sort of signal of ownership but there is nothing. Whoever did this is not promoting a product, not even themselves, just an idea. All the obvious, shock-seeking ads that hit you over the head and even the ads and posters that seem clandestine, if you take a second glance, you'll see the website, the logo, the product name, *something* for sale. The fact that there was nothing for sale, not even a signature from some artist seeking recognition for his or her work added a power and poignancy to the poster that I realize now would have been greatly diminished were it there. It felt pure. What true art, true communication is or can be— when all that really matters is your idea—not selling it, not knowing who's going to view, hear, or absorb it, and not even caring to take credit for it. There are little things like this poster all over the city—recurring painted figures on the sidewalks, small posters and stickers on walls and lampposts with nothing but a picture or oblique text—that after some time of living in the city are easy to spot yet just as easy to miss. It all depends if you are looking, even if you aren't *looking* but rather if you want to see them or not. If the desire's there, if it's in you, you'll see them, at once hidden yet everywhere to be seen. These are the last bastion of pure communication. A monologue (or dialogue) between anyone willing to take part; a community of anonymity. Quiet, almost secret reminders for us in the group that we are not alone. A faceless conversation with more depth and sincerity than a thousand exchanges I've had with acquaintances and fellow employees, party-goers, or barflies. Our shouts silent to all but those who choose to hear: I AM NOT ALONE. I AM PART OF SOMETHING. AND I HAVE SOMETHING TO SAY.

A sad yet valiant cab rumbles past me, its shocks furiously abused by the unforgiving cobblestone. Stones that no doubt were laid and re-laid scores of times over the past few hundred years. How many cabs have passed over these very stones over the years? How many feet have passed over these cobblestones? How many Reebok sneakers and aggressive stilettos and suburban-worn Rockports and artists' black leather boots and gentlemen's loafers . . . ?

I turn right and watch the cab head south, the dark driver's head turning side to side, like a modern-day hunter scanning the terrain, looking for a fare. In the distance and just partially obscured, the Woolworth Building stands proud, almost winking at me renouncing its ownership by Trump. The downtown sky misses the Twin Towers, Woolworth and a few nondescript other buildings forced to take up the slack, which they do so feebly. In a flash I see them on fire as I stood in Washington Square Park that morning. When the second plane hit and a ball of fire blew out of the north side of the tower my mind could only compute the event as a CGI created scene from some blockbuster. Hollywood special effects my only reference point. In the recess of my mind I figured people had just died but the surreality, the cinematicness of the event distanced me as I continued to watch the event unfold as an enthralled observer in awe of the spectacle with a vague yet unnerving guilt over my intuitive detachment. I turn left and sixty blocks to the north, its magnificent spire unobstructed like a beacon, the Chrysler Building again anchors the northern sky. Men's hands, strong hands that I know nothing of, built all these buildings and I love them for it.

The comparatively stout Cast Iron buildings all around me on Mercer and its adjoining Soho blocks, up close, nevertheless loom like giants, eight and ten proud stories tall. It's hard for me to understand when I hear some people talk about the size of the city, how the buildings overwhelm and frighten them and make them feel claustrophobic. These Soho buildings surrounding me here on this desolate, wee hour, Saturday morning block protect me. I imagine myself as a ten-year-old kid and they are my sixteen-year-old big brothers looking out for me. The whole city, every glorious building, every last one is here for me! And despite That Day they are still defiant, "Dan, we understand! We may block out the sun sometimes, and whip up fierce winds in our valleys on certain blocks but we're here for you and we are permanent in our limestone and granite, iron and steel. Don't ever believe anything different." Every façade carries with it a history and every room behind each window there is a different person with a different life, a different story to tell, and behind that window carries the ghosts of all the lives and stories of all the people before that person in there today.

People who live in the mountains must have a similar feeling of history, humbleness and protection being surrounded by structures so large and old. Yet mountain folk feel their connection with nature, (or more likely, with God, through his work), whereas the man of the city, of great structures, buildings and bridges and tunnels feels his connection with man. Both of us though, drawing our solace, our strength from knowing we are part of something more than ourselves.

Two model-tall women click-clock by me, their expensive heels providing little cushion, if not outright opposition underfoot. One is Asian with shoulder-length hair the slick, muted appearance of a wet paint-brush, pulled into a low pony-tail held together by a large silver barrette. Her companion, black, with glistening deep red lipstick, I decide may be a transvestite but it's too hard to tell. Maybe they were coming from Bar 89 or maybe a friend's loft around the corner, I wonder. As they disappear down the block, silence befalls the street again and I stare at Marilyn and look at the buildings some more. I've been here for almost seven years and it still all feels new, wondrous. Will I be here in thirty years and still feel like some guy from Jersey?

A man dressed in all black with smart, wire-framed glasses and close cropped gray hair walks uptown past me barking into a cellphone. *Is that Hebrew?* No. Maybe Aramaic—does anyone even speak that anymore? Something guttural, forceful anyway.

Almost a shadow, a black blob the size of a small football struts unhurriedly, defiantly on the sidewalk across the street before slipping comfortably into a hole under the steps of a building. Even him, the reviled rat seems a justified and proud New Yorker.

I look uptown again. Oh, those marvelous illuminated hubcap slats! The Chrysler spire, direction anchor in the sky for wandering urban dwellers. The irony that the Walking City's greatest building was paid for with car money and built to symbolize a car! When I think of the myth of Gotham, it is always shrouded in art deco. A design somehow at once nostalgic and of the future. Its rounded edges, its stately yet progressive fonts, deliberate and capitalist, lean yet privately ostentatious in its self-assuredness, of confidence in man, confidence in the future. *We've figured it all out and we're in charge! The engine of this experiment we call America will roar on!* New York in its grandest, most ambitious, most urbane, sophisticated will always be art deco in my mind.

The longer I'm out, the milder it feels. I take my hat off and dig my fingers through my matted-down hair and shake my head like a dog. My scalp tingles, virgin to the air. The City is ALIVE! Waves of energy are nearly visible, palpable, pulsing through this quiet and majestic night. I unbutton my coat knowing it's not warm enough for that but I want to feel cold. I want the clenched-fists bite, I want the bone chill misery, I want to brace myself in this last remnant of stark winter air! Because winter is waning and I am nostalgic already for the season almost gone. But I am not sentimental; there is nothing to reminisce. Rather, I am nostalgic for a time I wish I had, a life I wish I had lived. Nostalgic for Time I wish I could get back. Those peculiar days when you feel the weather change for the first time in a long time, the break, the jolt, even when it's just a teaser ahead of the season, it's the time-code on the bottom of the editor's screen, the almost audible click of the odometer, the flashing lights in the theatre before the show, the wakeup call: **life is passing you by Daniel Green.** You can't get it back, any of it. As sure as the earth's orbit will not be stopped. I hold my coat open with both hands, trying desperately to take in the last remains of cold. I hate this fucking winter and I don't want it to go. I'm begging! Bring me back, let me make it right. Because another month, another season, another year has gone by as we spin inexorably, elliptically around the sun, and I am not where I want to be. I am not who I want to be.

A young woman walks by me, hands in pockets, her face forward and resolute. We share that peripheral glance that New York girls know how to do so well. Was she afraid of the freak spinning around, holding his coat open to the world? If she only knew! *Don't be afraid!* I call out to her in my head as I watch her round the corner onto Prince. Yet again, (yet again, yet again) my heart sighs because I think that just may have been my wife. A subtle but determined carbonated fizz of despair begins to well in my solar plexus, burning, eroding me. Because the girls, they sparkle and shine, they sparkle and fade. Because I will forever be in anguish because I am a glutton because I am a man because I want them all. With each one comes a promise that they've never been able to keep. They make me feel down, always leaving me sad as they disappear down a street or deep inside a crowded bar or slip off across the way; yet the minute she is gone I am seeking another, to fall in love all over again, if just for a moment, because in that moment is everything. The glorious immobile moment. Where the world gleams with clenched, unforgiving beauty, where I am at once inside and released from dream, where everything and nothing is real. Only to be left alone again. Ah! But there will be another, there always is. And the promise will be upon me once again, to be broken once again. But maybe, *just maybe*, it won't.

I start up Mercer Street steering my way back home. Soho, the insufferable mall during the day is exquisite in quietude *very* late at night. The cast iron buildings, their rude merchandise safely hidden behind dropped gates and locked doors for the night; their artists mostly, long since gone to Chelsea, Williamsburg, wherever; their factories and warehouses relegated to Jersey, Brooklyn, Mexico, and who-knows-where are silent, in repose. These buildings know their role, which is never to move, never to crumble yet to roll with whatever new cultural wave comes their way. They envelope me in their brotherhood as I walk alone among them, beneath them. I look uptown, the glowing peaks of the Zechendorf in Union Square, the Con Ed clock, the towers of Midtown and beyond—We did all this! Man! Look what we have created!

And frankly, it's inevitable, unthinkable to be other than this: the buildings immersed in all the energy of the city are alive themselves, have an energy all their own. As do the streets, the pavement, the tunnels, the bridges, the cabs, the lights, the sewers, the manhole covers, the antiquated townhouses, the cookie cutter residential towers, the tenements, a proud Roebling exclamation, a brutally minimal Mies Van der Roh façade, the Robert Moses highway disasters, the structured, manicured plot of Olmstead—they're all alive. One living, breathing, pulsing organism. Energy emanating, bouncing, reverberating from the people to their creations and back again in a feedback loop forever or until a (or is it "the"?) great catastrophe makes it all go away. New York City protect me! New York sometimes I hate you, I fear you, in desperation I need to escape you but that's only because I love you. And you are my home.

. . .

There were times when you thought you were fighting for what you wanted, what you needed, only to look back a long while later and realize that there was no fight at all. You thought you were working toward something but they knew better; the outcome was already known. The whole scene was like a child toying with an insect, the creature scurrying frantically only to be flicked, plucked, prodded, or burned again, its meager instinct-based brain doing the best it could, thinking perhaps it had a chance, never aware of its impending conclusion on the sole of a sneaker.

Maybe I'm being unfair to them, maybe some of them did care, did actually contemplate giving me a chance. But I don't think so. I thought there was a possibility of making it happen, so did Tim. Even Ash was on my side (briefly). But I never had a chance. All along, or at least once Stern arrived, my record was merely an accounting stipulation, a net loss to be crunched and manipulated into a tax deduction by someone wearing khakis. And now they won't fucking give my album back to me.

"Come on Green, you know how this shit works," Ash said to me near the end when it was becoming clear that they weren't going to release the album. "Stern's an MBA, he's not a music guy. You guys, The Frames, Pete Salinger, you'll all just be write-offs for the next quarter."

"That's not really how this works," I said half knowing better but half not quite believing it either.

"Yeah, it is," he said bluntly but wearily. I knew he was sad over the whole thing but I wasn't sure how much of his sadness was for me or for his own career which clearly was in jeopardy. I didn't blame him. "Listen, Green, this is off the record but I'm talking with some people . . . I may be starting my own indie label, probably as an imprint connected with—" he cut himself off. "I can't discuss it yet."

"Saving your ass while you have the chance, huh? Sorry for trashing your career. Next time I'll make a hit single."

"I'll take you with me. I'm talking with my lawyer [yes, A&R guys all have their own lawyers] about whether you'll be able to exercise the key man clause in your contract."

"I thought if you leave, that's it, I automatically get released from Warner Brothers. We fought for that in the negotiations."

"I know but I have my own employment contract with the label that has its own sort of reverse key man clauses in it that I can't take any artists with me. It's fucked up but my lawyer is reviewing things."

"Great. So the clause in my contract is negated by your contract? Fucking lawyers."

After that conversation Ash never mentioned starting his own label again. I called him about it once a few weeks after I was officially dropped but he brushed me off. Last I heard he's still at Warners. The Rubies, his other signing around the same time as me, are still on the roster. The music supervisor for some piece of shit teen soap on FOX is friends with the guitarist in the band and had been playing tracks from their self-released CD and an advance version of a track on their forthcoming Warners album on practically every other episode for the whole season. I'm sure that was enough for Stern to green-light the record's release and for Ash to keep his job.

I know I seem pathetic now, wallowing in inaction, but when the shit went down I fought like crazy to survive, to get the record out there somehow. I didn't give a shit what label would do it or how it would happen. I tried every avenue I could think of but my support team, (the managers, lawyers, handlers), all with their own agendas and relationships with the power structure to worry about, collapsed around me toot sweet once they knew I was being dropped.

"Sorry Dan but things just didn't work out," was all I got out of Jill, Sam's dipshit assistant. For three weeks I had been trying to get him to return my calls. Apparently, Jill finally was authorized to bump up her stock response "he's in a meeting" to something more discouraging.

"Jill, this is complete bullshit. You tell Sam I don't care who else he represents, I'm not go—"

"Please stop calling here! He'll get back to you when he can," she said before disconnecting me. A week later I eventually got a call from him. He said he had been "working-it" for me, talking with people at Columbia and pursuing some other options but no one was biting. I was used goods and the main line was that I was "too out there," a non-commercial "integrity signing" (an act a label signs not with the goal of earning any real money off of but mainly for the purpose of appealing to other bands they want to sign or retain, as evidence of being committed to "serious" music). "Everyone is cutting back. It's just a bad time in the industry," he meekly offered. I didn't believe him that he even bothered to call anyone for me but I was so desperate for any acknowledgment at that point that him just going through the motions with me and feeding me some bs felt like a victory, albeit a petty one. He had his couple cash-cow acts, I wasn't worth the effort.

In a way, all this is my own fault though. Sure, the label and all these other guys fucked me but no one put a gun to my head to sign on the dotted line. I knew what I was getting into and I still went for it. To me, with my type of music and the way things had gone for so many years, it seemed I had no choice. Scratch that, in a way I did have a gun next to my head. It was either sign with these guys or wait tables the rest of my life, and never have my music see the light of day. By the time Ash first contacted me, we had spent years being ignored by every label big and small and our crowds for the most part weren't getting any larger. I was on the verge of quitting and Jay knew it. He used to say to me, "Things are changing, you don't even need big labels anymore." We'd get into a whole argument—that amazingly, after all we've been through, with being signed, recording an album, and then getting dropped—we still have nearly verbatim today.

As I sat on the couch this morning, staring at the TV, he called.

"You're breaking up with Jen and staying in the city?" I said by way of a greeting.

"You're such a dick."

"What? I thought maybe that's why you were calling."

"No," he said and sighed. "I'm calling to see how you're doing. I haven't heard from you in ages and I haven't seen you at any shows. What the hell have you been up to?"

"Nothing really. I'm sort of waiting the winter out."

"Waiting it out for what?"

"To do something."

"What are you planning on doing, planting a garden? You have to do something now, Green. You're going to die in that apartment."

"I've been going for walks now that it's getting a little warmer."

"Good," he said like he was talking to a retarded person. "But lonesome walks aren't enough. You need to *interact* with people. Stop feeling sorry for yourself. I don't care if your record got shelved and you got dropped."

"I didn't say anything about the—"

"It doesn't matter," he cut me off, "that's what you've been using as your excuse for half a year now. Let's get real here. Who cares about big label deals anyway? That's so *last century*," he said laughing, amused at his term. "You can record at home or somewhere else for cheap, the technology's changing everything, you just need to catch up. Hey, I know I just have Cubase but I've got an SM57, that's all we need to lay some tracks down. You were spoiled at The Watershed."

"I wasn't spoiled, that's what I need to get things to sound the way I want. Am I going to bring a string quartet into your apartment?"

"Yes. If you want to."

"Jay, we can't record a string quartet with one SM57."

"Fine. Whatever. That's not the point. The point is you need to start playing out or recording again. There's no excuse. You can play out solo-acoustic if Alex and I aren't free and you can't find anyone else. Why does every gig have to be a full production? Can't you just get out there and do it? Why does the recording have to be perfect? So it won't be as good as Tim's. Whatever."

"What do you mean, *whatever*? The whole joy for me is getting things to sound a certain way."

"Listen, you're using your misfortune as a crutch. Getting signed and then dropped is really just the beginning. It happens to bands all the time. You know how many bands are out there doing it on their own. You can put your shit on the web, that's what everyone's starting to do now. Your music was never meant for a big label anyway. Your not playing anymore has to do with *you*, not with a recording studio or not wanting to play solo or whatever else. If you really loved music you'd be playing; it's that simple. Everything else in life would fall into place."

"Thank you, I guess I can expect a bill in the mail. I didn't know you have an MSW. No seriously, thanks for explaining it all to me."

"Sorry to be tough on you," he softened his tone before things escalated any further, "but you need to hear this." Then he added as an afterthought, "I'm worried about you," with a sincerity that scared me.

"You know I could rebut every one of your arguments. I can't play solo because that's not my sound. I need a full band and I need at least a couple string players. I can't record at home or in your place for the same reason. I can't tour because I don't have the money. I have a big sound, I'm not some troubadour." I felt better breaking things down in a cold way. I knew I had been a hermit for most of the winter but there wasn't *really* something wrong with me. It all made sense why I wasn't playing anymore. Right?

"If you feel like you need all those people and a special recording environment and whatever else then that's all the more reason why you need to get out there in the scene and make friends with people who will hook you up. You should talk with Noblinsky and those guys. They have a phat studio in Greenpoint. It's beautiful there."

"Noblinsky hates me."

Jay growled. "God damn! Fine. That's not the point. Just get out there. Be social. Make it happen. You've got so much talent and it's all going to waste."

"Ok, ok. I'll see you out soon. Maybe at Arlene's this weekend," I said placating him.

"That's Jen clicking through on the other line. I gotta go. I better see you soon," he said and then hung up.

Jay was right of course. About all of it. But for some reason the pain I felt hearing that line about my talent going to waste, instead of spurring me into action just made me feel more paralyzed. I can't explain it.

I know I've been under an illusion for some time now. What I thought was embittered perseverance, is really just embitterment. Staying angry is not the same as doing something, it only feels that way because you use so much energy. But being anxious and depressed has been my M.O. since forever and I guess the turn of events made it all too easy to slip back into my hole. You'd be surprised how many people are just one bad year, one unfortunate event, one trying situation away from spiraling to disaster, a latent tendency waiting for the right, (or wrong, as it were), circumstance to be brought to life. Like the soldier who suddenly goes nuts during the war and slaughters an innocent family in some unknown village; or the insecure teenage girl who absorbs one cruel comment too many from the assholes in the hallway at school and falls into drugs or anorexia or promiscuity; or the lost and susceptible guy, who for whatever reason, after reading the pamphlet given to him by the cult freak on the corner, decides to attend the meeting promoted on the bottom of the last page and that's it, he's sold all his possessions, given the proceeds to "the leader" and moved into the compound in rural Michigan. If I could control it I would. I want to keep playing. Desperately. I want to forget it all and just move on but . . . I just don't seem to be able to. So much energy, so much love went into that album. So much potential, finally, was about to be realized. I wasn't dreaming of sold-out arena tours. My fantasy was to have a small loyal following, I'd go on modest but still successful club tours for six months every year, and maybe I'd be really popular in one country, like France or Japan, and in interviews in the states I'd talk about how fun and surreal it was to go there and play some fifteen-thousand seat venue after having been on the road in my own country playing to a few hundred or in one or two big cities a thousand people a night but that I love America and I'm so lucky to have the fans I do and as long as people still show up, I'll be out there on the road playing clubs for many years to come; I don't have an estate in Bel-Air but shit, I never wanted that anyway; I'm doing all right. And people will read it and think I'm totally cool and humble and just some talented guy making a respectable living. Maybe I'd even have a modest hit single off the second album that all the loyal fans would be ambivalent about, having heated discussions in chat rooms, one side feeling good for me that I'd make some money and get some mainstream recognition, the other side bemoaning all the guys in baseball hats who'd now be at the shows, how their exclusive thing would now be exposed. This seems like a reasonable thing to have hoped for, right? This wasn't some outlandish fantasy? Ok, eliminate the being big in France part. Playing clubs around the country to a few hundred people a night, that would have been enough. That's the dream.

Shit, even if the record tanked, even if the tour was a bust, if I failed totally, at least I would have *known* that the dream wasn't possible, that even in its humility it was never meant to be; I would have felt ok on some level because at least the answer was there. Even if it was an answer I didn't want, it still was an answer. It's the not knowing what could have happened that hurts so much. It's an absence so boundless that it cannot be reconciled. I just needed *the chance* to get it out there. And now all I see are music notes, thousands of them being sucked into a black hole, spinning, colliding, tumbling into a void that swallowed up what was supposed to be my life.

The TV has been on quite a bit these days. When I step out my door it's chaos, noise, frustrations, delights, and people people people, the sensory overload of the city. It's loud out there of course. But even when I'm home, like I am right now, ensconced in my thimble of an apartment, everything still *feels* loud. Regardless of the sense, everything seems to trigger a response on a direct path to the part of my brain that recognizes *noise*—the transient swatch of sun gracing the floor each morning; the radiator hiss; the vague citrusy and minty scents wafting from the Pepcid, Pepto, and Milk of Magnesia bottles that I dip into daily; footsteps and voices in the hall; and the walls with all these notes—the yellow paper, the tireless scrawl, the charts, pictures, and endless words, so many words—all form a unified assault—sight, sound, smells—it's all one kaleidoscope of noise that won't go away. In fact the only thing that is quiet is my guitar, coated in dust leaning against the wall in the corner. Its spare wooden frame somehow too heavy to lift, it just sits there. Stop staring at me, fucking Hummingbird. Look at you sitting there on the stand, like a museum piece. Look at me, playing a role, a laughable poseur like people who put books they haven't read on their shelves just so everyone can see them. It's clear—the guitar is just a prop now. My apartment is the set of some shitty off-Broadway play and I'm putting on a performance, and there isn't even an audience, that is, except me. I've been performing for me! How sad is that. This room, I am inside a diorama, a little action-figure with my turn-of-the-millennium accoutrements of the young urbanite, my not-quite-stable Ikea bookshelf, my 1-800-Mattress, my frost-encrusted freezer box in the top of the fridge. My guitar. I'm below the normal phonies whose concern is fooling others. I'm the lowest kind: the self-deceiving phony. This whole life—music, my apartment, this city—I don't belong here. I'm just pretending. I'm not a musician. I'm a pontificator, ruminator, a lounger, a TV watcher. That's what I do, this is who I am.

Yet there's so much I want to do! So much to say! I can't even enjoy my lethargy. I just sit here filled with guilt and anxiety. That sickening feeling you had in college when you kept procrastinating, hour after hour, before studying for that big Chemistry final, you *knew* you had to study, you *knew* you were wasting time and you felt sick over it but you still did it anyway—that's how I feel, all the time.

It's not just the guilt over not doing what I feel I should be doing right now but the ceaseless, consuming desire to do *more* at some indeterminate point, a fixation on the future, on potential, and a responsibility to live up to that potential that burns, that stings relentlessly like an electric needle threaded into my solar plexus emitting a brutal, unremitting current. Sure, I lost my record deal but that's no excuse. Even if I have to work a day-job again I can still record somewhere. Jay is right. I should just put the shit on the web. People will find it, somehow. And if they don't I'll work ten hours a day emailing every goddamn person I can find to tell them to check out the MP3s online. I can tour even if it's just me. Who cares, at least it's something. I can move to LA; no, Europe. Somewhere, anywhere but New York. Maybe I'm just in the wrong place. There's so much I can do, it's endless. I just need to start. Why can't I start?

In a way, anxiety is the opposite of depression. The depressed person feels he can't do anything, doesn't want to do anything, or would like to do something but feels he isn't good enough so doesn't bother. Anxiety is knowing you *can* do something, that you *should* be doing something but you haven't or you can't, something or someone (perhaps just you, though perhaps not) is holding you back from doing these things that you are supposed to be doing, these things that in the most solipsistic and egotistical of mindframes, when you are drunk with entitlement, feel like you not doing them is a profound injustice. Which leads the anxious person to wondering the reason *why* he hasn't fulfilled his potential. Is it out of sheer bad luck? Or even worse, is it simply because his expectations are unrealistic, unwarranted? (Which if that's the case makes him question how well he knows himself. How does one know how much to expect of oneself? when does one know when to say "when?")—and thinking about this of course causes even more anxiety. BUT, the irony is: the sheer burnout of this continual anxiety, this frustration of unfulfilled potential, eventually often leads to depression anyway.

> Anxiety is the opposite
> of Depression
>
> YET
>
> Anxiety leads
> to Depression

"You can't be ambitious without being anxious," I told Jay one day, tossing off the pronouncement as we were packing up our gear after a rehearsal. It was over a year ago. We were in the final weeks before heading to the studio to record the debut. Although I was ecstatic about having a record deal and the imminent recording, to my surprise, my anxieties only seemed to increase. My newly garnered ego and empowerment from the deal only led to feeling the burden of more responsibility. If I had the advantageous platform of a record deal, with all the money and resources that came with it that would enable me to work solely on my music, plus all the connections with other creative people that (I assumed) were bound to materialize, then I had no excuse to not then achieve even more: the record *would have* to sound a certain way, Anything Less Would Be A Failure; once the album was finished I would have to start work on that film idea that had been floating around my head for years, Anything Less Would Be A Failure; within a year or so I had to land a gig scoring a film, something I had always thought my orchestrating skills would be well suited for, ALWBAF; in a few years, surely I had to make a second album even grander and more experimental than my first, yet it would still be effortlessly listenable and would awe people with its ingenuity and passion, ALWBAF; and years later if my career had really taken an upward swing and I had serious money after a couple successful records and tours and whatnot, I'd have to use it wisely, I couldn't just buy some asshole mansion or hobnob with other jerks at some exclusive resort in the tropics, I'd have to funnel a zillion dollars to Greenpeace or Amnesty International or, no, I'd have to start my own charity or maybe just buy vast swaths of forestland to save them from timber companies or suburban sprawl, how could I not? ALWBAF; and finally, of course, it might take a few tries but ultimately there would be no excuse not to land the perfect girl, at that point I'd have come into contact with so many interesting, inspiring people, how could I not? ALWBAF. There were so many things I had been dreaming of doing and now that I had the record deal, the first step, there was no excuse for not achieving all of them. With my new position in life, to not pursue and accomplish all these things would be a shameful embarrassment, a disgrace, an affront to myself like a Harvard graduate not being able to land a job. The deal made me more anxious and miserable than I was before I got it. There were no excuses anymore. Everything I ever wanted to do, now had to be done.

"That's ridiculous," Jay said then zipped up his gig bag with a sharp swipe of his arm, the *zzzzzziip* serving as an exclamation point.

"No, it's true. Think about it: if you have ambition, that means you have desire, right?"

"Yeah . . ." he said tentatively.

"And if you desire something then that means you are not satisfied

**late late winter**

with where you are because you cannot at once be satisfied and have desire because the definition of desire means you want more, and the definition of satisfaction is fulfillment of desire, i.e. not wanting. You can't feel them both at the same time; they're mutually exclusive," I said without looking up. I was on my knees placing my different effects pedals in the black gym bag I used to ferry my cables, pedals and other performance necessities around to gigs and rehearsals.

"I'm pretty happy with where I am," he said, slinging the gig-bag over his shoulder. "But there are things I still want . . . I'm allowed to be happy." I had to love Jay. It was amazing how game he almost always was to dive into yet another one of these of conversations that centered on some new theory or axiom I read about or more likely, concocted (or at least thought I concocted) myself.

Ambition =
Desire =
Not being content =
Anxiety

Ambition = Anxiety

We left the room and crossed the linoleum-floored hallway to the elevator. We waited as it came up from the lobby where Alex had gotten out a few minutes before. The minute rehearsal was over he had bolted, off to meet some new girl he was seeing at The Mercury by 9:15. Drummers, they always have it easy for rehearsals, all they need to bring are their sticks.

"See, but you're not *really* happy or you don't *really* want more. If you're happy that means you're content and if you're content that means you don't want anything. I'm talking about these feelings in their essence, their core. There's a difference between wanting and *really* wanting, I mean like at such a deep, intrinsic level that well . . . I guess it's not wanting anymore but needing. If you're really passionate about something and so desperately want it to happen, which is what true desire is, then you can't be satisfied or happy with where you are. And if you really desire something deeply then you must feel anxious because anxiety is intrinsically linked to worrying about whether your desires will be met. It's all connected."

"I still disagree with you."

"How can you disagree with me? This is airtight, man," I said as we got in the elevator.

"I don't know how to argue it with you but I just disagree. That's all."

"You *cannot* have ambition without anxiety. Dude, this is basic philosophy or psychology or . . ." I paused, unable to find whatever word I was looking for, "*something*. It's airtight. It's law-of-nature stuff. The definitions collide. You can't be full and hungry at the same time."

"You totally can!" The door opened and we headed through the vestibule onto a quiet West 37th Street. "You've never eaten a huge meal and you're stuffed but you still want one more bite because it's so good?"

"No, you're missing it." Jay was such a fool sometimes. "You might want to eat more but you're not hungry. You just like the way it tastes."

"Exactly. I'm full but I still desire more."

"But the wanting more isn't about hunger. It's about the taste buds! You just want to taste more. I didn't say you can't desire food and be full at the same time. I said you can't be *hungry* and full at the same. There's a difference between desiring food and being hungry. Sorry. Bzzzz! You can't argue this with me."

"You win. I won't argue with you."

"But I want you to actually believe me, agree with me, not just give in."

"Give it a rest. It's not about winning. Why does it always have to be about pulling someone to your side?" We turned down Broadway and headed south to the 34th Street N/R.

"I don't need anyone on my side, I don't care if people agree with me, I just need them to understand what I'm saying, get where I'm coming from. It just so happens that in this case understanding what I'm saying means that you also have to agree with me. Once you understand it you have to accept it."

"That's convenient."

We passed one of the countless off-market perfume stores that line the streets in the area. Its gate was down but in the middle there were spaces between the metal rungs and you could see the front window. How do all these places stay in business? I wondered. Is there really that big of a market for bootlegged Calvin Klein Eternity made in some guy's bathtub? No, no all this shit is made in China, giant factories. "I just can't see it or live it any other way. Ambition—anxiety. I can never relax, it's never ok. I'm in pain. It's like some kind of paradox or cycle or . . . what's the term for this? It just feeds on itself, keeps building, it never ends."

"So just learn how to embrace the pain," he said and punched my arm.

"Ow! Dick!"

"This is who you are, Dan," he said. "Why haven't you figured that out yet? You'll never not be like this. Can't you just learn to accept it? If it's possible, try to enjoy it, otherwise . . . I worry about you. You're gonna have a fucking a heart attack. Just chillax. You're twenty-six, there's plenty of time to do everything you want to do."

A flash of acid scorched through my stomach. There wasn't time.

I stretched-out my strides, trying to keep in synch with Jay's long-legged gait but I couldn't do it. I felt like a kid with his older brother. I thought of that Simon and Garfunkel album cover where Paul barely comes up to Art's shoulders. I felt a little better. We crossed 35th and Jay asked if I wanted to rent a movie.

. . .

I've never been one for drugs. Even liquor doesn't suit me; the way rubbing alcohol feels on an open wound is the way drinking alcohol feels in my stomach; and anything hallucinogenic, narcotic, or illicit, I simply (as if you couldn't tell) don't have the disposition for. I'll say it—I'm afraid. Who knows what could go wrong. And, so, like I am doing right now, I watch TV all the time. It's the non-pharmaceutical way for me to clear-out or at least drown-out or maybe just tire-out this sonic fuzz infecting my head until the noise fades down to its essence, a near subsonic, a-harmonic hum: my anxiety engine. Vroom Vroom! Here we go. I'm on fire baby and I've got everywhere to go! I have so much to say! So much to do! But you wouldn't know it by watching me. I'm still here, sitting in my apartment watching TV. I'm just a sloth curled in the corner of a couch. But let me tell you, inside that sloth is a dynamo. It's like the dream where you're screaming but no sound is coming out. That's my life. Inside this immobile figure you see before you, his eyes vacant, staring, his feet in three-year-old slippers with the fur lining all matted down, in his boxers and t-shirt, with the light of the set flickering on him as if *he's* a screen in some abstract art exhibit, is a person running around the world. Please imagine the damage being done to this body. There is a person inside running, laughing, arms flailing like Keith Moon doing a solo—all this is happening inside this immobile body.

Potential.

I'm a Ferrari with the rpms red-lined but the gear is stuck in neutral. Pop the clutch! Please, I need to pop the fucking clutch already. I want to peel out and scream down the blacktop. I want to floor this fucker and blow everything down in my wake. But I am still right here. I keep pressing harder and harder on the damn pedal and it's down as far as it can go and the tach needle is pinned to the right but I'm stuck in neutral. And I'm getting scared now because

**late late winter**

smoke is starting to come out from under the hood. And I could almost take it, being stuck, if only I weren't burning all this fuel. And what happens if I run out of fuel before I can get into gear? So I've got to just ease up on this pedal until I figure out what the hell is going wrong here but I can't, I keep flooring it. And so the engine is roaring and I am going nowhere. I am stuck right fucking here.

I'd say I was the horse at the starting gate, getting ready to explode when the bell rings and it flies open but that's not quite right because I'm not waiting to explode, I *am* exploding; I'm just not going anywhere because the Goddamn gate is stuck. So really, I'm the horse galloping in place—[Yes, yes, follow me with this analogy!]—head down, ramming against the metal gate, pushing, braying, a patch of blood is visible where I keep making contact, giant horse nostrils flaring in desperation as the trainer looks on in horror. OPEN THE MOTHER FUCKING GATE. I am wasted potential. I am the sperm in the bottom of the condom. I am the spoiled food never to be served, the honors student hit by a drunk driver, the husband and father lost at sea.


I can't have sound on the TV anymore, it's just too much; I keep it on Mute all the time now. But I'm sitting here, staring at the silent screen and all the action, all the flashing, the powder-faced talking heads, the closing credits, the insipid, irritating, endless visual cacophony of commercials, the car chase explosions, the talk-show inanity, the show for the young and "prized" demographic always discernible by its jump-cut assault, the histrionic courtroom/emergency room/living room drama— it's all streaming in front of me and it all *feels* so loud. *Why can't I turn it off?* I know the sound isn't on but I can still hear it. Every flash, every cut, every scene, every light is a new sound. Synesthesia, baby! I'm losin' it. I reflexively mash the *mute* button on the remote seeking relief and am jarred like a salted snail when blaring sound comes on. *Jesus, I'm trying to mute a TV that's already muted.* I laugh to myself, or rather, I laugh out-loud and I am by myself. Something tells me it might be a wise move to shut-the-damn-TV-off now but instead, I meekly hit the *mute* button again. I'm so lonely, that this flickering box, even in all its repugnance, somehow is a consolation. I'm tired of thinking about time; I'm afraid of all the time I've wasted, that I *am* wasting, and cruelly the one way I seem to deal with this is to waste more time with the TV.

But what exactly have I been wasting time until? I always felt like I've been burning time until some specific point—a sort of optimism in the midst of a depression. One day in the future the music might come back to me. It'll be like the old days, when glorious sounds filled my head as I walked the streets, or was at crowded bars, or when I sat alone staring at the wall. And then finally I brought those sounds to life at The Watershed. Where is the music now? It must be out there somewhere, I just need to find it because it no longer is finding me. Maybe all these notes will amount to something. *What the hell are all these notes?* I don't even know what I'm writing. I don't even seem to know *when* I'm writing anymore. They're just appearing, more and more, growing like a paper fungus on the walls. Keep wasting time until . . . It may be misguided but I keep thinking in a vague, borderline-subconscious sense that "it," that *something* is going to be better at some point in the future. This profound nagging sense that I'm not myself but soon, if I just hold on, sooner or later, I can finally be me. Instead I am this hideous imposter, a third-rate understudy not playing the role the way it's supposed to be played at all. Where is my life? Who stole my life?! This has all been a vicious joke and if I can just stall my way through this, just zone-out a little longer, if I can just take a nap and wake up as the real me, the me I am supposed to be, my divine right, when the planets are aligned the way they're meant to be not this interstellar chaos that we must be in now—it will all be ok.

My reviled box, its sordid light despicably pulling me in, calling to me with a false promise of solace we both know it can't keep; but it does keep me company and even though I know it's a lie, I'm game to be deceived.

**late late winter**

I'll keep watching because it's the only thing that lets me burn time, if only just a little longer until I'm there, until I'm me.

I'm a little embarrassed to tell you that as I waste away staring at this flickering light, thoughts of Lisa surface like hazy memories of a dream. Because thinking of her—a Vibe chart failure, after all—seems like a weakness. But I realize it's not Lisa that I miss. It's the feeling I had when we first met, when we strolled the Brooklyn Bridge, and everything was still unknown. Or maybe it's not even then that I miss, but the first time I saw her on the stairs. It's *that* moment, the frozen moment, that I miss so terribly. The connection, no matter how illusory in the end, was real in that moment.

---

FM* experience is not innate? →
Language of film/TV is so powerful that it alters perception of special moments in real life. →
Having ingrained 20+ years of slow-mo scenes in movies, (which generally signify *this is an important moment*), has my mind simply been trained to experience/see important moments this way?

---

Film literacy not merely alters but <u>limits</u> our scope of perceptions?
→ Are there other more nuanced and multi-sensory reactions we could be having but they've been squelched and replaced by the filmic slow-mo experience? NB— still photos in essence *are* FMs. (Photos have even more influence on perception than film?)

---

Too complicated! Need to study relativity and break down string theory to try to understand the FM? (Infinity, or the Gray Goo scenario related to FM? No—they're just more concepts I don't understand that flood my head when I try to figure out the FM.)

---

Maybe there is some sort of special energy in the air.
Or maybe I really am transported to an extra dimension (string theory!) that exists simultaneously with ours.
Time is as amorphous as Dali's melting clocks.

---

\* Frozen Moment

. . .

You. **YOU.** You fucking bastards. You demand action. You protest: *When are things going to happen?* Where's the thrust, the suspense, the plotline smoothly unfurling like a red carpet unrolling for the Queen? No more thoughts! No more authorial asides, expository bursts, extended internal dialogues!

You all demand Goddamn ACTION so I've got to keep things moving.

Yet to tell the story streamlined, the way stories are told, the way they must be told, feels like a lie. Giving only the highlights—and that is what a story is—feels like a betrayal. For me, maintaining the streamline, omitting down-time and eliminating detours from the action seems to be as much of a lie as any fabrication. (And btw, believe it or not, I *haven't* included all the detours I wanted to; you think this has been meandering and tangential? Hah! It's endless where we could have gone, every page could have been its own book's worth of transgressions. I've left out so much!). I want desperately to go beyond the highlights but I'm aware you're here and I'm aware of your need for things to keep moving, for things to keep happening, for things you can see. So I'll take you to the action soon, I know it's been a while, but there is something I need to tell you first.

I am so tired of being lied to by all this fiction around me. TV shows, movies, books; and all the ads everywhere—in magazines, on TV, billboards, clothes, even in the urinals—we're surrounded, it's all fiction, and it's all a lie. Not because of what they show us (though plenty of it is blatantly fake) but because of all that *isn't* shown. It's the Fiction/Action-Falseness Dilemma. The nature of fiction—things must be condensed. We know this. We know when we are told a story—whether it's a novel, a movie, a friend telling you about her day at the beach, even a one-page ad in a magazine (that too is a story)—that we are getting just the main facts, the action. (Though at least when we are talking with someone we have some say in what the essentials are—we can ask whether the beach was crowded, if there was a lot of traffic getting down there, etc., if we're interested. But everywhere else—TV, books, movies, billboards, magazines[*]—we don't decide, we have no say. We're stuck taking in their stories, forced to absorb them in whatever highlighted version they want to tell).

So. Fiction is all around us. And we know on an intuitive, obvious level that all the fiction we are absorbing is really highlights, by its nature it can never be as lengthy as real life. By our powers of cognition we know that when the screen slowly dissolves from one scene to the next that time too has been dissolved. A few moments into the new scene we realize that now the story is picking up a week later or the next night or the next year; whenever it is, we know that *stuff happened* in that unshown time of the dissolve. We know this. But my concern is the difference between processing the unshown time, filling in that blank, and being shown the actual time. What if: when a novel has *Three Days Later* written at the top of the page, you actually read about those three days; when there's an ad in a magazine showing a young couple relaxing on a beach on vacation, it's preceded by a three-page photo montage of the drive to the airport, the four-hour flight to the Caribbean, the waiting on line at the hotel check in; when the ER TV drama instead of showing non-stop mania shows the doctors sleeping or sitting around bored for at least half of the show, reflecting the reality of time in an ER?

We've been telling stories to each other for thousands of years, whether listening to tales around the fire, attending plays, or reading the next weekly installment of Dickens' latest novel. During those thousands of

---

[*] Even the news, reality shows, investigative journalism. It doesn't matter that what we're shown is "true." It's what we're not shown that I'm talking about. All information received through a filter, rather than you living it yourself, is fiction. Not fiction in that it is necessarily made up, but that all retelling of events (made up or real) is the result of editing, of putting certain info in and leaving certain info out.

years a relatively small amount of time was spent taking in these stories. Most of the time people were in reality—working, eating, conversing, resting, fighting. Now however, our waking lives are engulfed in fiction—the hours and hours of daily TV viewing, the movies, every ad we flip by in a magazine, every billboard we pass. Its shadow is omnipresent. And I'd hazard a guess that there are days, many days, when I spend more time being exposed to fiction than I spend living in pure reality.[*] And this does something to me. And I'm not even talking about the content of all this fiction (that's a whole separate well-trodden territory), what I'm trying to talk to you about here is all the content that is left out. The *Three Days Later* and my cognitive ability to process it in relation to my own life.

On a certain level, when I'm presented with *Three Days Later* and young couples on beaches in ads and a thousand filmic dissolves nearly every single day, for many hours every day, actually *living* the three days, *living* the week that was "dissolved," and sitting on the four-hour flight to the Caribbean has all started to feel awkwardly boring, and time-wastingly dull and guiltily uneventful. Look, I understand that in fiction things are left out by necessity, and I understand that in my life nothing can be left out, there are no dissolves, I actually must live those three days that the screenwriter or director or novelist deemed not eventful enough to warrant being shown. For thousands of years we mainly just compared ourselves to each other and only occasionally to fiction but that ratio has flipped, and it makes sense that if nowadays we're constantly comparing ourselves to fiction—and this certainly must be the case because we spend so much of our lives immersed in it—that our basic cognitive ability to process the *three days later* narrative shortcut versus going through the

---

[*] And of course there is no such thing as pure reality because even when we're interacting with other people (and not watching a movie or reading a book or eyeing a billboard) we're still to some degree in fiction b/c we and everyone around us have been so overexposed to fiction that the way we all act and think is a direct reflection of that fiction, so even just plain conversation or work is really an indirect fiction anyway at this point. It's too late.

**late late winter**

real three days in our own lives will be worn down, distorted, off kilter. (And to make the dilemma worse, generally by default, while you're taking in all this fiction you can't be making your own real story. You can't have sex, run down the street, enjoy a conversation or play guitar if you're sitting on the couch reading or in a theater watching a movie. So it's not just mental, it's a physical time thing—you generally can't be making your own action if you're watching someone else's). I guess what I'm getting at is, there's a sort of inherent self-loathing I've developed in having to live those three days when I've spent so much of my life immersed in fiction that never shows them.

To help combat the Fiction/Action-Falseness Dilemma there should be a law that forces all the TV stations to have a mandatory minimum number of hours each day or minutes within each program where we see the characters just watching TV. There has to be some sort of proportional representation of reality. If it's a half-hour sitcom and the episode's story takes place over a week, then a solid five minutes of the twenty-two minutes of the show must show the characters just sitting there watching TV. I know, it's going to hurt to have to watch this, but it's the only way to keep it fair, to—(sorry for using this expression but I have to)—keep it real.

And this my friends, takes us to a point where I have something uncomfortable that I need to share with you. I've been keeping something from you from the very beginning, and in connection with all I've just been talking about, I simply must tell you. And what I need to tell you is this: my life is not exactly as I've been describing it. I've left out one giant, GIANT element to all this: I've spent the better part of this year that I'm telling you about watching television. A lot of television. Perhaps not more than the average American but that's still a lot of television. We're talking maybe thirty or more hours a week. And I know I've given you a couple scenes of television watching but it's not the same, it's not enough because to give you the story without giving you all the time I sat there alone in my apartment watching TV just doesn't seem right. Because all that time watching TV has had as much if not more of an effect on me than all this stuff that actually happened. Watching TV was to a large degree, my life.

If it was up to me you'd be reading the word "TV" for a hundred pages. It'd be the only way not to lie. And it *is* up to me. But I won't do that to you. You'll just have to take my word for it: for the most part, nothing really happened; all I did was watch TV. I can dump buckets of purple prose on you talking about wasted time and time spent doing nothing but it's still not the same as actually taking the space in actual pages to show it because proportional representation matters. Nothing connotes time like time. Descriptions are inadequate. Some things we simply have to slog through in order to even come close to truly feeling them. Descriptions of time are cheap and dangerous because we fool ourselves into thinking we *got* it, but we don't. You must slog. The only way to do it right would be to give you page after page of TV viewing but I won't do that because who wants to slog? Who wants to read that? I just don't feel comfortable making one of those books where the joke is on you, where it sucks to read it but the difficulty and boredom you'll encounter with the text and the content is *wink wink* the point.

But since I'm not doing that I ask a favor of you: when time elapses, when it's to be understood that weeks or days or even hours have gone by, put the book down for a moment, and with a concerted effort imagine me sitting in my apartment watching TV, doing nothing. Since I won't make you slog, all I ask is that you make this extra effort. Because in a little way that will help make all the omissions of that time a little less of a lie.

Ok. I take it back. I need more than just that favor. Because missing the proportional representation is so huge that I need you to do more than just making that extra effort to imagine the omitted time. You may understand but you won't really *know* that omitted time; our brains can only do so much. And you know what? The point of all this is for you to *know*, for me to at least *try* to get you to know what it is I'm talking about, trying to say here, in this whole story of my recent life. Because I have something I'm trying to say but I don't know how to say it. So, I will make a deal with you. You just need to give me a small concession. And it is this:

**late late winter**

TV

# III

## EARLY MAY

Kelly Christie. I met her in Washington Square Park early one bright afternoon. She was sitting on the steps that ring the fountain reading *A Farewell to Arms*. When the weather started getting warmer I had taken to going to the park during most days for at least a few hours. Even with my TV addiction, without having cable, the daytime options were so limited, the programming so poor, that for at least part of the day my disgust overrode my depression/anomie/laziness—whatever and I was compelled to get off the couch and go outside. I was depressed and anxious that I didn't have any money and was ashamed and guilty that I wasn't doing anything about it which in turn made me more depressed and anxious which in turn made me more . . .

What can I say? I was in a rut. People get in these sorts of ruts, you know. Jay would tease me and say that I had it made, how could I complain? I didn't do anything but lounge around. "Yeah, yeah, I know you're depressed" he would say, (and he did mean it with sincerity), "but you gotta get your ass in gear. Stop going to the park every fucking day, stop watching TV or whatever else it is you do in that pit apartment of yours." Anyway, like I said, *(and as you very well know),* I was in a rut and sometimes people just don't know how to get out. So anyway, Kelly. Yes, Kelly Christie. I sat down a few feet from her on the steps that ring the fountain, not really noticing her at first. Or maybe I was trying to not notice her; I didn't want to be *that* guy ogling some college girl in the park. But as time wore on as I sat there, I couldn't help but turn my head, ever so slightly and glance down at her legs. Taut, long and smooth, so sexually and also simply, aesthetically alluring that to describe them any further would reduce me to hyperbolic food adjectives (e.g. delectable, delicious, etc.); they were *just barely* pressed together, perhaps even a millimeter of space between them, as if they were conscientiously closed tighter when she first sat down, as women do when wearing a skirt, but eased open just the slightest bit as she became engrossed in, or at least distracted by, her book. She was wearing a white tank top and the straps of her white bra, laying just to the outside of the tank-top straps, were exposed on her shoulders. She could have gotten away without wearing a bra, her breasts no more than perky B cups (educated guess) but seeing the straps was far sexier than not so I was glad for it. Her skirt, which came a few inches above her steeply bent knees, pink, snug, and silk-like with lace trim on the bottom, like a slip, worried me that it was being pilled or snagged by her sitting on the concrete steps. I don't know why I think of these things.

*What can I say to her? Anything I say will be construed as a line, a cheesy pickup attempt. But I must talk to this girl. Blonds normally aren't my type but a pretty, youthful thing as her . . . some looks override anyone's general taste. I must talk to this girl.*

"So, what do you think of the book?" I blurted out, trying to hide the quiver in my voice. This is good. It wasn't about her looks. I read; I'm smart; I'm safe.

"Oh, it's ok." She looked up at me, surprisingly relaxed, not startled. "I don't think I'm that into Hemingway but I have to read it for this American Lit class."

"Yeah, he's a bit manly for my taste. Although, there are some nice scenes in that book. When he's in the boat with the girl; what's-her-name?"

"Hey, don't ruin it for me! I'm not there yet."

"Right. Sorry." Ummm. "So . . . do you go to NYU?"

"Actually, I go to U.N.—Nebraska—but I'm doing a summer class at NYU."

"Summer? Did the spring semester end already?"

She laughed. "Yeah, it just ended but I got here early anyway, before my classes start. Figured I'd get a jump on the reading."

Her blond hair, of the geographically appropriate corn-silk variety, was pulled into a ponytail held with a cute, metallic, pink barrette. A tress of hair from the front of her head that couldn't reach the barrette was hanging down the side, slightly curling under her chin delicately framing her face. She tucked the stray hair behind her ear. I've watched her tuck those errant strands three times already. Once just now, and twice when I was, what I think was discreetly, eyeing her before we started talking. Periodically, as she was reading or when she would take a break and look up from her book for a moment, it would work itself loose and reappear dangling, and when she noticed it or got annoyed by it, she again would tuck it behind her ear. Women! How can you not love when they do little things like tucking stray hair behind an ear! The ponytail often brings to mind a kind of priggishness, the hair, (sometimes appearing painfully so), tautly pulled back into a band, repressed, bound, held in place. But(!) that ponytail association is completely changed, or more specifically, balanced, when there are those itinerant wisps dangling free in that stray bundle in the front. There must be the strays(!), for then all the roles of freedom and submission are apparent: the prude with a hint of desire for abandon; youth and developed wisdom; pulled-together and falling-apart; the proverbial naughty librarian; etc. It's such an encompassing representation of all the paradoxical (and one could argue, unfair, limiting and demeaning—but nevertheless, very real) expectations of femininity in the Western world that I believe it should be our culture's universal symbol for *Woman*. Instead of the stick figure with the skirt, on the Women's Room door there should be an outline silhouette of a head in profile with a ponytail coming out the back and a thick black line coming down off the forehead slimming to a thin point at the bottom where it's slightly curling under the chin.

Proposed International Symbol for Woman*

"That's smart. So, Nebraska, huh?"

"Yup. Born and raised. But I love New York. I came here on a business trip with my dad when I was little and ever since then I've wanted to come back. When I graduate I'm moving here or Paris. I've already decided."

"So you're not much for the football team and all the wholesome Midwestern stuff?"

"Nah, it's fun an' all but I think I'm a New Yorker. I've always liked the more artsy stuff and that doesn't float too well in my town. Not that we're hicks or anything like that! You know, it's just different though." *Those teeth. Look at those cute, perfectly straight teeth. I wonder if she had braces? Nah, probably just good Nordic genes.* "So, what do you do? Are you from here originally?"

"Uh . . . to be honest I don't really know what I do right now. I'm a musician. Or I used to be a musician. Songwriter. Whatever." The smile fades from her face and she looks at me blankly (or is it intently?) for a moment.

"Oh my God. Wait. This is going to sound really dumb but are you in that band *Bryter Layter*?"

---

* I know, there are women with afros or shaved heads etc. but I stand by this symbol. (After all, not all women wear skirts and that pictograph is basically universal).

**early may**

"Yes. I am," I answer almost suspiciously. This is unprecedented. I can't believe she recognizes me. I've never once been recognized by a "fan." "How do you know my band? We never even played outside the East Coast." I think I may be more weirded-out than flattered.

"This girl, Julie Kemp, who transferred to my high school senior year from New York, Westchester I think—is that what it's called?—She saw you guys play in the city a bunch of times. Julie, my friend Tamara and me were the only ones in my school who were into, you know, like, underground rock and stuff like that."

"Wow. That's, that's . . ."

"Yeah. We used to listen to your EP all the time. That's how I recognize you. From the picture on the back." She's beaming. "Actually, probably not from the CD but from your website. But that's been down for like a year now. But hey, wait! Didn't you guys get signed to like, Atlantic Records or something?"

"Yeah. I mean no, uh, Warner Brothers," I stutter. "Sort of. But that didn't really work out."

"So, you're not playing anymore? I don't understand. Did you guys break up?" *Wait; I actually might have sex with this girl.*

"Well, it's kind of complicated. The label basically stole my album."

"Wow! That's so terrible. But you guys still play out and stuff, right? When can I see you play?"

"Well, I guess we sort of broke up. You know, the band wasn't really a band, it was really my thing." I don't know why I feel the need to tell her this. "I wrote all of the music; the label just signed me." I pause for a moment. "It's a whole complicated thing. I'm just taking a break now I guess."

"Oh, sure. I understand," she says more subdued now in an attempt at a knowing tone.

A crowd had been forming beyond the other side of the fountain. Two black street performers are riling them up, doing syncopated dance moves to an old Michael Jackson track. "Have you seen these guys before?" I say nodding my head in their direction.

"No."

"They're great. Tic and Tac."

"You know their names?"

Oops. I probably shouldn't tell her not only do I know their names but I know every line and stunt in their whole routine because like them, I've been in the park nearly every day since the middle of March. "I've seen them a couple times."

There's an awkward pause. The crowd erupts, thankfully filling the silence between us. Peering over the heads of the crowd I see Tic (or is it Tac?) stretched horizontally laying on his partner's head being spun around. "I think they call that The Helicopter."

"No hands! That's incredible. How does he balance on that guy's head?"

"The magic of Tic and Tac."

A hot red flash rises through me from my feet to my head like blood being pulled into a syringe. I instantly start sweating as if I can feel the directive sent from my brain down my spine then in a lightning-bolt lattice out to every pore. "So . . . would you like to go out sometime?"

"I'd love to," she says and flashes a huge smile. She goes to tuck her hair again behind her ear but it's already there so she ends up doing a kind of reinforcement tuck, running her fingers along the top of her ear.

I try to play it cool; I fear I might be smiling as wide as she is. "How about tonight?"

"That sounds great."

• • •

I offered to pick her up outside her dorm on 10th and University at nine. Rounding the corner on 10th and Broadway heading down the final block on the walk over, I'm hit with a minor wave of pity and self-consciousness. I remember when I was a senior in college feeling like a loser hitting on freshmen girls. This situation doesn't bode well in comparison but to my relief, as I approach the dorm, it looks like any other apartment building, no prominent NYU signage and my nerves over her being too young (or me being too old) suddenly feel unnecessarily masochistic and silly. The negative nerves swiftly reverse direction like a full sail violently and completely shifting sides as the boom sweeps across the boat converting themselves into a surge of antsy anticipation of seeing Kelly. I'm excited in a way I haven't felt since eleventh grade when Sabrina Tartino, (one of those under-the-radar pretty girls who somehow avoided being in the A-crowd, whom I'd had a major crush on since tenth-grade English when I used to stare dreamily at the back of her head), after having revealed that both her parents worked during the day then asked if I wanted to come over after school. It's an excitement of not only foretold requited lust but of a clean hope, a promise of being alive . . . Ok, maybe it's just lust. But still—under the initial spell of girls like this the whole world does seem better, brighter, like when the *Wizard of Oz* shifts from black and white to color.

As I near, I see that she's outside waiting for me. She has on a thin, long flowing white cotton skirt with flip-flop clad feet peeking from the bottom, and a light-tan tank-top with little pink flowers embroidered on the upper left side. I wave to her as I cross the street. And. As I walk up to her, every step is dreadfully further confirming something until it is irrefutable as I am now next to her: She is a good two inches taller than I am. Shit. I didn't realize this when we were in the park. After I took her number I left her sitting there on the steps, she never got up. I should have known—*those legs*. I decide that she's wearing the flip-flops almost apologetically, knowing that she'd be taller than I am. Neither of us acknowledge the height situation and I lean in (or is it up?) and give her a kiss on the cheek. Why are *they* so tall? And why are my people so short?

I curse my gene-pool, offer a, "You ready?" while holding out my arm pointing west, then lead us down 10th Street.

Ever since Koala, I'd decided all first dates should be walking dates. This could become my forte, I think as we stroll west toward the West Village. I can't believe I'm walking down the street holding the hand of a 5'11" blond. It's not something I'd been striving toward, I never wanted to be the Billy Joel or Rod Stewart, (and certainly not the generic schlubby banker with the trophy wife on his arm), the lack of symmetry always struck me as looking silly. Not to mention the way those couples look to everyone else, their cold motives—beauty seeking money, money seeking beauty—as if they are somehow more shallow than the rest of us. But walking down the street with her, to my surprise, I like it. I'm *that guy*.

Impressionable Midwestern coed, Kelly is the perfect foil for me to play tour-guide, Mr. New York. I steer us down Tenth Street, then weave us through all the choice blocks west of Seventh Avenue, nonchalantly pointing out an Eighteenth Century townhouse here, an ornate iron gate there. The sounds of the city all but have disappeared as we wander down Barrow and Commerce, antiquated little blocks so charming nothing short of one of us getting hit by a car would dissolve the sweet haze cast over us on our little walk. I take her inside The Grange Hall, a restaurant and bar way out of my price range but tonight I don't care. It's a perfect spot for the charm tour, adult and refined yet not stuffy with its cheery art deco decor. It's just another forty-dollar dinner for the middle-aged ad executives or the magazine editors at the tables but it's an anomalous treat for the Nebraskan college girl and the broke, failed musician. We sit on stools at the handsome dark wood bar, resting our feet on the shiny brass pipe running along the bottom. It occurs to me that she's not even twenty-one. I ask her what she wants and order both of our drinks so she doesn't have to talk to the bartender. He makes two vodka martinis and as he places them down in front of us, it may just be in my head but I think he gives me a knowing glance, a *nice-move-landing-this-one* guy-to-guy-camaraderie kind of a look. Yeah, she's probably not twenty-one but I gotcha brother, here're your drinks. Cool satisfaction is on me like a Xanax halo; I know my stomach will be fine. The vodka slides down with benevolence, pooling in my gut with the neutrality of ice-water.

"So, I don't understand the whole thing with your record label. What does that mean, they *stole your album*?" Kelly asks as we're half-way done with our drinks.

"Eh, it's all this legal shit. I stupidly signed my life away with them," I say and take another sip of the martini that despite not (yet at least) killing my stomach still tastes like rocket fuel. "I was so fucking excited when they wanted to sign the band that I was willing to make all sorts of concessions. It's not even like I didn't know what was going on but I just . . . I almost had no other choice. I'd been playing in near-empty clubs for years, then the band started doing ok, we actually had some people showing up but it never grew beyond that . . . I mean, I was thinking of quitting basically, it wasn't happening, we weren't going anywhere. Then this guy, Ash, who works at Warner Brothers got a hold of one of our demos and was interested and it was like, after all these years of every label ignoring us—and I don't just mean big labels, I mean every indie label too, no one gave a shit—when it seemed like nothing would ever happen, this guy wanted to sign the band. I had to do it, it didn't matter what the contract said."

"But I still don't understand about the album."

"They own the rights to the masters. That means they own the album. And I know this sounds crazy but even though they won't put the album out, they won't let me have it either because they basically paid for it. Most people don't hear about this stuff but it happens all the time."

Kelly's eyes are focused on me, as they have been since we arrived. Her drink is near empty but only because she'll turn to it take a gulp then immediately turn back to me, as if continually taking little sips would be too much of a distraction. Her gaze is near unending. As I talk, to maintain concentration I waver between making eye contact and having to stare into my drink or at the icy-blue bottle of Bombay Sapphire straight ahead of me on the wall behind the bar. It's still hard for me to believe that I'm sitting here with her. I catch my reflection on the mildly distorted, antique mirrored wall amidst the bottles and for a moment, in what feels somewhat pathetic, I am depressed. Because as I talk away and soak in her attention I realize that this is just the most teensy weensy taste of what it must be like to actually be successful, to have people know your music, not to mention specifically having her, the type of girl who was too cool and too attractive to ever be interested in me in high school and college, swooning over me. It's like a little window on what my life could have been. But my self-pity dissolves as quickly as it appeared, as I turn back to her and look at her face, so fresh, excited, so *pretty*. Normally a face like this I can only look at in a passing moment on a street, in a bar, in a store, and then I must quickly turn away before I cross that line from subtlety into something wholly inappropriate, but what a luxury, what a gift!, that I can gaze for as long as I want, that I can study every freckle, look into each eye trying to distinguish in this indoor light if they are very light brown or is that a hint of green or maybe some other color too mixed in, (and yes, I believe there is), and focus on the roots of her hairline, discerning each strand as it leaves her scalp, following it as long as I can before it disappears among the rest.

"God, I can't believe that," she says. "You guys are so good! I don't get why they wouldn't *want* to release your record?"

"And you wouldn't believe what's on the album—it's totally different than the live band. And you know that little bit of strings on the EP?— the album has that times a thousand. I mean not that they're strings all over the place but that it's just . . . it's just really lush, there's a lot on there."

"So what are you going to do? I mean you're not going to just stop making music."

"I don't know. The world is filled with idiots. People don't want anything different. They want to hear the same thing. These big companies, it's the tyranny of mediocrity. I understand where they're coming from. They can only put out something that's going to appeal to millions of people, otherwise its not worth their time and effort and money."

"I guess you're right. But you can't stop making music. You can sell it on the web, you can tour." I know she means well but I hate when people tell me to just "put it on the web" as if you just make a website and poof, thousands of people start buying your music. "There's this great band, *The Reigns*—ok, they're not great but they're really good—who are from Lincoln and they have a recording studio and I think they put their records out themselves; no, I think they're on Saddle Creek, you know that label?"

Did I just say "tyranny of mediocrity" and she's still looking intently at me? And not only that, she put her hand on my knee when she said, "you can't stop making music."

We continue on talking through a second slow round, only pausing from the conversation now and again for an extended silent gaze or smile. The longer I am with her, the more confident I feel just being myself. I don't want to come off as some pretentious tool but every time I delve into my life philosophies she genuinely seems interested. I'm running with it.

When both our second glasses have been empty for quite some time I ask Kelly if she's ready to go and she says sure. Feeling like a big shot, as we get up to leave, I slide two twenties to the bartender and say, "Don't worry about it," and give him a subtle wave of my hand over the bills like you do above your cards when you "stick" at a blackjack table. Then I regret it because the drinks were eight dollars each. For months I'd been ordering plain instead of veggie slices to save the extra dollar, getting taco-locos instead of the "premium" guaco-locos at San Loco, and basically penny pinching any way I could—it felt like I just left him a C-note.

We step outside into the now late night. I could steer us toward my place but that doesn't feel right. I want to be out on the town with this girl. I'm twenty-seven years old, I live in the greatest city in the world (as far as I know), and I'm on a date with a pretty girl who, to my sickening delight, has been listening intently to me as I prattle on about compression and Sheryl Crow; the oppression of irony; the privatization of public space; simulacra and the illusion of choice; television; advertising; and yes, the tyranny of mediocrity. I know it's not new stuff here, folks, very little is after all but sometimes, when you find the right person, when you speak with conviction, with impassioned articulation, when that person is able to really *feel* what it is you're getting at, that you mean it, that you *really fucking mean it*, that you have no agenda other than the truth, that you're not just regurgitating something you read somewhere, that you're not just reciting what you think some phantom cool crowd somewhere approves of—then it sticks. Then it is real. Then, no matter whether they've heard it all before or they have been in the dark just staring at those Platonic shadows waiting to be shown the proverbial light—it means something. Because to care means something and people—especially irony-infected people of my generation (*I know,* whateverthefuck "my generation" is/means)—deep down of course want to be around people who are willing to take a chance to show they actually care about trying to do, be, or seek something genuine, something deeper, something larger . . . than this. We're dying for it. The jaded ones and the simpletons. We're all dying for it. Because anything less is to not truly be alive.

"So, where to, tour guide?" Kelly asks as she squeezes my arm as we stroll down Greenwich Street.

"I don't know. I say we just keep walking and see where we end up. Whadaya say?"

"I think that sounds great," she says and gives my arm another squeeze before letting go and grabbing my hand. Her hair is down tonight. It's shorter than I thought it would be from when I first saw it pulled back. But it's still long enough to not be considered short. I can see the layers in the front, the ones that didn't reach the ponytail and I wonder if she was/is trying to grow out bangs. For a moment I picture her with bangs and am repulsed by how young that would make her look. I realize that without her height, between her face and her demeanor I would feel much more awkward about her age. But somehow her being an inch (or so) taller than me is enough to allow myself to feel tricked into being comfortable with the whole thing.

We continue down Greenwich for a long while until we reach the old World Trade Center site. There are some suburban looking teens in front of the blockades near the pit. A boy from the group wearing a basketball jersey is standing with his back toward the pit while a girl, maybe his girlfriend, is holding a camera getting ready to take his picture. "Make sure that you can make out my numbers in the picture. Ok?" The boy says. "Don't worry Jordon it'll come out good. Ok. Ready? One, two," the boy flashes a big smile, "three."

The surreality of this kid's comments and that he smiled for the camera is more than I care to address and I just give a sort of tug on Kelly's hand for us to move on. As we wander away from them Kelly asks the inevitable. "Were you here when it happened?"

"Yeah. It was a bad scene," is all I seem able to muster. Not that it's too painful to talk about but that it's too large to talk about. I don't want to change the mood of our date. Kelly doesn't pry and just says, "I can imagine," and leaves it at that. I sense that she isn't saying anything about it because she thinks it's too upsetting for me to talk about, that that'd be rude. I feel a little guilty for not clarifying that that's not the case but I play along. And interestingly, this little moment doesn't bring the mood down but acts as a strengthener on whatever it is we are establishing between us. The sweet haze continues.

We meander along the perimeter of the site and keep walking south until we hit Bowling Green.

"Well, this is it. The tip of Manhattan. The only left to do is to dive in," I say as we lean against the railing and peer out into the black Hudson and beyond to the lights of Jersey and Staten Island.

She laughs. I feel a tinge of regret that I don't have the guts *to* just jump in, partly because there is something in me that wants to—I've always wished I was more free, more open to doing something foolish, something extreme, even if just once—but perhaps more so because I want to be someone I think she wants me to be. If she's been impressed up to now, I could become a legend in her eyes if I do something spontaneous, something crazy. On the other hand though, I reason, something too crazy could also turn her off, frighten her. I quickly feel better about not being filled with more reckless bravado than whatever little bit it is I have. I wonder if I occupy that perfect spot for her, just right on the edge of excitement—a musician, a New Yorker, an older guy, yet not someone she should be afraid of, not taking her to some party where people are doing lines off a kitchen counter, no overly aggressive moves on her, no jumping in the Hudson. She said when she called her best friend from UN to tell her about meeting me, her friend was very apprehensive about her meeting up with me on a date. I could be a psycho her friend said. "But I decided to go for it anyway," Kelly had said and elbowed me in the side.

"Wow, we've been walking a long time," she says looking at the water.

"Are you tired?"

"No," she says defensively, worriedly that she'd given the wrong impression. "I could keep going all night!"

"I know just the thing for us. It's one of the last great free things you can do in this city." And with that I take her hand and walk us toward the Staten Island Ferry.

I'm surprised at first that the terminal is crowded at 1:15 a.m. but then it seems perfectly normal, to make sense. This is New York. We ride the ferry standing outside on the deck in front, the spray from the river misting us every so often. When we reach Staten Island we get off and run from the exit area thru the terminal back to the loading area and hop on the boat as it gets ready to depart back for Manhattan. With the strong breeze off the water and the spray, it's much colder on the boat, especially this trip back, than it had been walking.

Even though I'm cold I don't want to go in. I don't want to be anywhere but right here, outside in the night air on the water. But as we stand hunched, our elbows on the railing, Kelly's huddled against me and I wonder how she's doing.

"I'm kind of cold. Are you?"

"Yeah."

"Do you want to go in?"

She pauses a moment, then still looking forward finally says in a voice neither forceful nor coy, just softly and matter-of-fact, "No."

"Me neither," I say without turning toward her.

The lights of the city glitter, the multitudinous yellows and whites, the errant red, green, or orange, some flitter, some are a steady glow, yet all taken together they seem to vibrate in a unified hum. It's a marvelous sight. I wonder what someone from the middle ages would think if he saw this; he'd think the sky had fallen to the ground. I stare at the space in the skyline where the twin towers should be. For some reason I'm certain she's thinking about the towers too, their absence simply looms too large to ignore, but neither of us say anything.

"When it gets really hot in the middle of the summer I used to come down here a lot to the ferry and ride it for hours back and forth. Sometimes when I couldn't sleep because my apartment was sweltering without air conditioning I would ride the ferry all night and doze off leaning on the railing on the deck." This is not true. I've ridden the ferry only once before but I'd like for this to be true and so would Kelly so I find myself lying about it. It's strange but it's as if the more enamored with me she is, the more I want to impress her.

"It's like free air conditioning," she says.

Everything up to this point has been the truth and she has fallen for me on the merits of who I am: my charisma—and for her being from Nebraska, what's probably exotic—my anxious and garrulous personality. She's been hanging on my every word. Yet something here on the ferry has made me want to be more. In a way, I don't want to impress her as much as I want to impress myself. I can see how excited she is and I want to feel the way about myself that she does.

We take a cab back up to the East Village. I didn't ask her if she wanted to go home. I just called out "East Fourth and Second" to the cabbie as if there were no other option than for us to go back to my place. But when we got out of the cab I still wasn't ready to go home. Perhaps because I hadn't gone out at night for so many months, perhaps because I hadn't been with a girl since Koala, I didn't want the night to end even if the ending meant being in bed with Kelly; I wanted to be out there, in the city.

Standing in front of my building I turn to her and ask if she wants to hit another bar.

"Yeah, that sounds great," she says, unsurprisingly.

"There's a decent place a block over. It's sort of a couches-and-candles type of place. Is that ok?"

"Sure. Anywhere."

We wander to the Opium Den on East Third.

The place was filled with Eurotrash in leather pants trying to impress each other with their smugness, a DJ spinning obscure drum & bass trying to impress them with his hipster musical acumen, and bankers running tabs on their Amex cards trying to impress overly made-up women who were trying to impress them with their looks. I am only slightly less out of place in my jeans, Rod Lavers, and three-ringer t-shirt than Kelly is in her J-Crewesque Cape Cod ensemble. But no one seems to notice or care. Knowing that taking a cab and hitting these expensive bars has essentially been financial false advertising, I bring a couple beers back from the bar and let Kelly know the truth which is that my wallet now has two dollars left. She of course doesn't mind and happily offers to pay for the next round.

Because I rarely drink due to my stomach, I'm a complete lightweight and so I am already buzzed after the first beer. The couple martinis earlier in the night, despite or maybe because of the miles of walking and the late hour feel as though they never fully left my head. As I get drunker I launch into another impassioned societal rant, drifting into that gray area between veering too far from quietly romantic talk and making sure that I am *nothing* like any guy she has gone out with before. I've found someone who's interested in and excited by my world theories; I'm gonna run with it.

"I was hoping this place wouldn't be too crowded but I guess it's still popular," I say sitting back down on our Victorian red velvet couch after having to wait for three people ahead of me at the bathroom.

"It's amazing, everywhere is just so filled with people. I guess if a bar doesn't close, people don't leave."

"The world is too fucking crowded. I love the city but sometimes I think it would be nice to get a break from being around so many people all the time."

"I know what you mean. But I do love the energy."

"I know . . . me too. That's why I'm here. That's why we're all here I suppose."

Kelly nods in approval. She looks dark and sensual in the dim candle-light of the bar. I scoot a foot away from her and draw a long swooping "J" in the velvet with my finger.

"Have you heard of the J Curve theory?"

"No, what's that?"

"It's this theory, Malthusian theory it's called, that says the world eventually is going to run out of resources for all the people. You see, the population is growing at an exponential rate but our resources only grow at an arithmetic rate. Exponential means things double, like 1, 2, 4, 8, 16 and so on," I point at the vertical part of the J, "see, this represents the doubling. But arithmetic means 1, 2, 3, 4, 5, 6 and so on," I draw a long diagonal line, "so obviously, look, it can't keep up." What the fuck am I doing? Why am I getting into this right now? I look up at her. My rods* working overtime in the weak, flickering light, I try to make out the expression on her face. She's staring intently at me. How is this possible! I'm pushing the envelope with this, baby. I'm fearless delving into this crap on a date!

"And the J curve can be applied to technology and tons of other stuff too. It's like here's the wheel, then here's the stone age," I'm pointing at successive points along the long gradually sloping bottom line, "bronze age, whatever the next major thing is after that, this stuff is over hundreds or thousands of years. But then you see, once you reach the corner," I say as I trace my finger on the curve, "as we've done first with the industrial revolution then with computers, the growth rate is virtually vertical. I mean these major things like the phone, TV, microchips, they've all been happening in the metaphorical blink of an eye." How am I getting away with this? And during all this professorial lecturing I am holding her hand. I've somehow been able to be cerebral and romantic at once. "Who knows what's going to happen next? In ten, fifteen years biotechnology, nanotechnology—they're going to make today with our Microsoft Windows and whatnot seem like the dark ages."

"Nah, we'll still probably be using windows," she says.

"Touché!" I wipe my hand across the seat. "Don't listen to me!"

Eventually we close out the Opium Den at 4am and wander out onto the street. Like college kids on a binge, (ok; for her it's not "like" a college

---

* I looked it up—rods are for low light and cones are for colors. Always learning!

kid), we grab two Bud tallboys from the corner deli and pop them open on the street, toasting through brown paper bags. It's still completely dark but you can feel dawn approaching, the sun somewhere over the Atlantic gliding closer to the east coast of the United States. Determined to see this date to its rightful conclusion, which is not sex but the far more meaningful, sunrise, I take us up the stairs of my building, continue past my floor and push the fire-door open stepping out onto the roof. And there we lay, our backs slightly propped against the two-foot ascending lip on the edge of the roof. I've finally shut up and we lay there in silence save the occasional gulp of the tallboy. As we stare at the censored sky of New York where only the strongest stars shine through the halo of a million manmade lights our bodies are side by side, the only contact two pinkies locked together.

To our right, at first, ever so slowly, below the roof lines of the East Village, black portrays just a hint of a turquoise glow. Then in J Curvian exponentiality, time quietly roars forward, night ceding to day as the turquoise sky begins to dissolve into a pale yellow. And at the first spec of bright orange light peaking above a nondescript building somewhere in Alphabet City, my head foggy with exhaustion and alcohol I stand then pull Kelly up with me.

We give bleary-eyed grins to each other then cross the roof toward the metal door. As I open it, it gives off a creak that in the early morning silence surprises me because it's *not* jarring but strangely invigorating bringing some life and levity to the stillness of the hour like an urban rooster. As the hinges whine, I turn around and our faces meet sharing the same smile and wee chuckle, like the laugh version of a mumble. We walk down the cement and iron stairwell to the second floor. I unlock the door and we enter my studio apartment. Perhaps I'm too tired to go through any coy motions or more likely, I act on what feels like the only sensible thing to do; I turn toward Kelly and without saying a word lift her shirt over her head then untie her skirt and slide it off her waist and let it fall silently to the floor. I'm shocked and nervous for some reason, her body exposed in just a white bra and underwear. Her body is starkly beautiful with its balletic figure, its fawnlike grace. Its defiant contrast to voluptuousness, while not sexually alluring in an obvious way is aesthetically transfixing, (and does carry a dignified undercurrent of sexuality all its own). Before me are limbs so impossibly long as if she's from a different species than me. She is not frail or sickly like a runway model, she has a healthy, strong fragility, like a fine couture garment or a British sports car. Though she does not possess the tight yet curvaceous build and the warmth of dark hair that has always excited me, these traits aren't missed with her. Her appeal is so consuming that whatever she *isn't*, doesn't matter. That's the magic of women: when one truly captivates you, whatever her look—a coffee-skinned pixie with cascading curls or a blue-eyed, Dutch giant with hair like dry wheat—it becomes for that moment on the street, or in a party across a room, or standing in front of you, naked, in a dim apartment, everything. All else you thought that mattered is forgotten. Nothing is lacking. It is not a willed delusion of satisfaction, it is a rejoice in the universal perfection of the individual, nothing is relative because there is nothing else but this.

She pulls my shirt over my head and there's a new seriousness on her youthful face, the features right now a combination of solemnity and lack of guile that is devastating. I watch her, her long outstretched arms bent ninety degrees at the elbows form a diamond between us as she works the buttons on my jeans. She shimmies them down leaving me in my boxers with my penis at full staff pushing against the fabric. She reaches her hand through the left leg and massages my balls. She then takes both hands and hooks them under the waist-band and pulls it out from me, stretching it as far as it will go, clears my staff and slowly pulls my boxers down. She drops to her knees and takes me in her mouth. Her left hand is back on my balls and her right is on the shaft. Between her mouth and her fingers, slender and so long gripping me, I am encompassed in way that renders every other blowjob heretofore a clownish warm-up for this main event. I softly grab her hair and drift into bliss. After a few moments, or maybe more than a few, it's so hard to tell in this woozy up-all-night state, I gently pull back and lead her head to stand up. I unhook her bra and gently slide her panties down, my fingers trembling on her goose-bump skin as I tread oh-so-lightly guiding them all the way down her very long and thin legs. As I rise back up from crouching at her feet, my right knee softly cracks. Just when I fully stand, she turns from me and curiously, almost pruriently, without looking back, walks away from me. She then climbs straight onto the bed waiting on her hands and knees, her long thighs extending her ass high in the air. I am shaking now. Is it the alcohol? Am I over-tired? What is happening to me? I stand for a pregnant moment then scurry toward this figure of pure carnality and grab a condom from the drawer next to my bed and put it on.

I climb onto the bed behind her. The room is beginning to swirl, my left hand is resting on the small of her back, my right hand is unsteady as I attempt to hold my penis getting ready to guide myself in. At once now, things are happening in slow motion and in a vertigo, sort of sped-up time. This is it. I am about to fuck Kelly Christie, this willowy beauty, the prettiest girl I have ever been with. From behind! That's all folks, nevermore. I can retire after this! God, Jesus, Buddha, Allah—whoever is in charge up there—you have shone down on thee and I thank you for this gift! A hundred thousand years of genes and evolution all converging, culminating in this moment. The supreme fundamental urge of all living creatures—This is why we are here, this is why anything is here—to make more of ourselves. I am following the plan, bringing its course to fruition, the ultimate satisfaction of achieving our only true mission, *the* only mission coursing through me . . .

And then I miss.

Her legs, miles longer than mine . . . unable to steady myself, unable to reach, I had plunged forward yet "landed" in midair between her legs, precious inches below her. Then I promptly came. In midair. The expectation of bliss was so great, I came on assumption. Then—perhaps it was from the alcohol and exhaustion or maybe it was through a sort of unconscious will generated by ferocious embarrassment—the world spun upside-down, I fell backwards on the bed and everything went black.

**early may**

"So, what does she think of those crazy notes?" Jay asks as he thumbs his unplugged electric bass while sitting on the couch.

"She loves them. She thinks I'm brilliant."

"Oh God." Jay rolls his eyes. "Didn't she freak out when she saw your apartment? You're like a psycho killer or something." He starts singing the chorus of the *Talking Heads* tune, playing his bass along with it.

A part of me sees myself the way I think Jay does at times—an eccentric guy who's always spouting a bunch of bs about the world. But maybe I am on to something. I mean, shit, why else would a girl like Kelly be so smitten with me? Even if a part of me knows or fears I am saying nothing new, that I *am* nothing new, I still believe in it anyway. And maybe that's all that really matters in the end—not being original, but simply, truly trying your best to keep learning. I can keep worrying that my life is a cliché, that my thoughts have all been thought, that my words have all been said but worrying about this doesn't bring me any further from unoriginality. So I have to just let it go. And what's so bad about not being original anyway? How about being connected to those things that are universal and trying to tap into them, isn't that more rewarding?

"No. That first night, when I passed out—*and I don't want to hear anymore shit about missing the target! I was very drunk and she's very tall*—she must have wandered around the apartment. I had the sheets up on the walls but she peeked. She read everything. And I don't know . . . Later the next day I woke up at around eleven and she was lying next to me and she just had this glow, this sort of besotted gaze on me. And she told me how she was sorry for peeking behind these sheets because clearly if I had these sheets up then what was behind them was meant to be concealed but obviously she didn't realize that it would be all my notes, she figured it was like, who knows what she thought it was, and then once she saw all these crazy post-its and stuff she had to, you know, just had to read it. It's fine though. It was about time someone saw my work."

Jay shakes his head then stifles a chortle. "Dan—I mean this as your friend, not trying to be a dick or anything, but is that really *work*? Writing random things and sticking them on your wall is not work. I mean I know it's *work* but not work as in," he lifts his hands from the bass and makes air-quotes, "work."

"I don't know . . . Whatever," I say sulking. "So it's not work."

Jay takes a deep breath and goes back to picking at the bass.

"I know, I know," I continue, "thoughts are not work . . . No, that's not true" I correct myself, "they are." Jay's head is down and he's plucking the theme to *Night Court*, which is to bassists what the riff from *Wish You Were Here* is to guitar players—something you learn when you're fourteen and you'll be playing it absently the rest of your life. I keep going anyway, "I make no claims for greatness, for universality. Maybe all those notes are just for me. It's that—I am trying to say something. Desperately. And I don't even know what it is I'm trying to say. I just know I have to keep trying to figure out what it is and how to say it. Do you get what I'm saying?" I call to the top of his head. "And even if ultimately it is only to myself, I don't care; I just need to figure out what it is and how to say it." Just to hammer it home, I call out again to the top of his head, "I have something I'm trying to say, I just don't know how to say it."

"Hey, I hear ya, man . . . I'm not trying to give you a hard time," he looks up. "I just don't want you to get a big head or anything with this chick falling all over you. She just wants to smoke the pole of a rocker."

"That's not true. You don't under—"

"Yes, I do," he cuts me off. "I'm just fucking with you. Would you relax? Look, you know I think you're smart. I just—" He trails off and goes back to picking away at the bass, which is starting to annoy me.

"Anyway," I say undeterred, "—and I know you're going to kill me for saying this but—despite, well, I guess maybe it's because of the whole way she is about me, I just don't know how connected . . . how much of

Kelly I can take." Ok, here it comes. Brace yourself Dan.

"AH!" He stops playing and grabs the neck of the bass. "That's it! Either it's like Lisa who was a corporate bitch just because she didn't go for all your dreamy loner world-theory stuff or Kelly who's not connected to you enough because she likes you too much, even in all your weirdness! You are just looking for excuses not to be with someone."

"That's not it. I just don't want a protégé for a girlfriend. It's very flattering, it was, it *is*, but I need more. It's like if I wanted to go bungee jumping tomorrow or cliff diving, whatever, something stupid, she'd do it. You know what I mean? I don't want to be that in charge. I need something back from her, more than just yeses . . . It's just, I want someone to make me feel the way I feel when I'm making music."

"You don't even make music anymore."

"Yes I do. I'm just taking a break."

"A break is a week, maybe a month. You haven't touched your guitar in a year."

"It hasn't been *a year*," I whine. "And how do you know anyway?"

"Dan," he says getting up and walking toward the guitar, "this thing hasn't moved in fucking ages." He leans over and blows a puff of dust off the headstock. "Hey, can I borrow it? Seriously. It's not getting any use here."

He's right of course and I should let him use it but I give him a look like a man would give if someone asked to borrow his wife. Having that guitar near me seems to be the only thing tethering me to something real, some part of myself that I wish I was, I wish I could get back to. Jay runs a finger across the harshly out-of-tune strings, sending a shock of a discordant clash of tones in the air. I feel sick. "Suit yourself," he says finally. "My Yamaha will get the job done."

I'm about to say, Just take it, but instead I sit there and say nothing.

"Let me let you in on a little secret," Jay says standing, towering over me while I'm on the couch, "no one is ever going to make you feel the way music makes you feel. You need to understand that. That's not what love is. It's a different thing. It's about caring about someone, knowing them inside and out and they know you inside and out, and you know that that person will do anything for you and vice versa. Listen, I'm not going to talk to you like I'm some love expert. I can only tell you from my experience. People and relationships are complicated, it's not all excitement but over time it's really special." Am I this immature that I can't buy into what he's saying? Is there something really wrong with me?

"I always figured I'd know I was in love when it felt a certain way. I've been excited by girls before, I mean more than just excited, really connected. But it's never the same as . . . I don't know. Life just seems so crazy and fucked up so much of the time—and making music, when I'm in the zone, it's the only time, it's this feeling of total certainty that doesn't exist anywhere else in my life. It's like a drug or a high. But it's not even that, it's more than just feeling amped-up or mellowed-out, it's . . . it's the zone, man. You know what I'm talking about. I've always assumed when I was really in love with someone, *really* in love, that it would feel like that. But if love is what you're saying it is, that it'll never feel that way, then maybe I'm just not interested. Because nothing compares to that."

"You know you're really smart about some things but other things, it's like you're in dreamland like a child or something. That's your problem Dan. You live your life in your head. Nothing in the real world will ever be able to compete with whatever it is you have going on in that head of yours." He grabs his bass and sticks it in his gigbag. "Anyway man, I gotta go. I've got rehearsal down on Ludlow in ten minutes."

With Jay out the door I sink into the couch. But a moment later, in a fit, I pop up. I pull the case from under the bed, open it, and feeling faint and sweaty, walk to the front corner of the apartment. I grab the guitar and quickly but gently, as if it were a ticking bomb I needed to secure in a lead box, carry it back across the room and place it inside its velveteen lined case. I then clamp the case shut, locking-down each of the three latches, and shove it under the bed. Standing there, my heart punching through my chest, pulse throbbing in my ears, I give the case a quick nudge with my foot and it slides an inch further out of site.

The day after she had slept over the night of our first date, eyeing the guitar in the corner, Kelly had asked me to play for her. But I told her, somewhat convincingly I think, that I had tendonitis from playing too much and couldn't even think about picking up the guitar for a month. "Doctor's orders," I added for good measure.

That night, just a few hours after Jay left in his huff and I stowed the guitar out of sight, Kelly came over. Almost instantly after walking in, she noticed it was gone and asked where it was.

"It kills me but I had to sell it," I lied. "With the record deal over and . . ."

"That's terrible! *I'll* buy you a guitar." She looked stricken. I felt myself dissolve.

"No no no," I downplayed, nervously waving my hand, "There's still some money coming to me from Warner Brothers, my lawyer is just working some stuff out with them. Once I get that check I'm buying it back from the guy I sold it to. He knows it's just temporary. He's sort of just renting it." The levels of shame I felt—for lying to her, for not being who I think she wanted me to be, and most of all, for not being who I wished I was, a musician, because I wasn't a musician anymore—are so obvious it's not worth getting into.

• • •

It's a warm day. Kelly and I are strolling. I finally have one on my arm and all I want is every other girl I see. The girls—they're all out today in slinky summer-wear. Faces recede as if interest in them is some form of antiquated chivalry, all that matters are bodies—bare legs everywhere, breasts in camisoles suspended like cantilevered shelves, nipples trying to surface through tank tops, bra-less sets exposed just-so in flimsy halter-tops. Orbs. I am simple. I just want to squeeze all of them. I am not ashamed to admit it. I'd say it's a disease if it weren't ingrained in the male DNA. It's not my fault. This is all for procreation! Why should I apologize? I'm tired of feeling guilty. But—it feels like a disease, a crippling addiction, a craving that consumes and is never quenched. I'm nauseated, exhausted, disgusted with desire. It's a curse, carrying the xy. Women: everything you fear is true—we really are this maniacally myopic (at least on certain hot days). And it's torture. When does this end? I thought this would have ended by now. I am a disgrace. I'm not proud of this but I can't turn it off. Bring on the burkas, I need to be saved!*

It's a symptom of something else of course. All the women, filling some psychic hole. If I was happy or satisfied in life I wouldn't feel so miserably tempted by all of them. Maybe it's not that. Maybe I'm trying to distance myself from Kel, from all of them, too afraid to be close so I objectify them, take away their humanity. Ironically of course, I am so fucking lonely and viewing all the beautiful woman around me as objets d'art, and everyone else as extras, all of them characters in some play, calcifies my role as the observer, the less I engage, the more I observe. Hah! Is that it? Where are the shrinks! Gimme some psycho babble! Tell me what's wrong, I don't want to be this way anymore. But even if that is it or the shrinks do have some other answer, then what? Having the answer and being able to do something about it are two different things. I've had all the answers for a long time. I know exactly what's going on

---

* I'm aware this is a patently unfair clarion call, that if I have a problem with objectifying and being over-stimulated by women that *I* should be the one who has to sacrifice. I should be wearing a blindfold or forced to stay alone inside versus calling for *them* (women) to have to wear cloaks to accommodate me; so, yes, *of course* I am against the Islamic (and other religions') sartorial demands on women. But imagining them all in burkas, misogynistic a wish as it may be, is rooted in pedestal-placing adoration, because adoration and belittlement confusingly and complexly overlap at times (circle theory!), for it is natural to deride those who wield so much power over you. In other words, it really would be nice to be given a break from all the stimulation.

but so what. I'm tired of learning, of thinking, seeking answers. Answers Don't · Do · Anything. Just knowing the reason why something is happening doesn't mean you can stop it from happening. In fact, having the answers just makes everything worse because then I have to live with knowing what's "wrong" or why it's wrong while still doing it anyway. It's like when you're driving and you take the wrong exit off the highway and all of a sudden you're on some new highway and you know instantly that you fucked up, that you shouldn't have gotten off but it's not one of those exits where you can just loop around and hook back onto the highway, there's no where to turn around and now you're stuck, flying down this new highway going perpendicular, or diagonal or who-the-fuck-knows-where away from the road you should have stayed on and there are no exits in sight and there's nothing you can do. So what do you do, you keep going, only now, you're agitated, nervous, and you're really pressing the pedal, bumping it up to seventy, seventy-five, maybe eighty, and for a second you worry about getting a ticket but you can't stop, you're so far away from where you are supposed to be but the only way to get back there is to go even faster and farther until you find an exit, and this exit, my God!, better have a U-turn, it better not be another exit like the last one throwing you onto yet another new highway with no U-turn in sight, holy shit then I'm really fucked, Ok, I can't worry about that now, I can't even *think* about that being a possibility, I have to just keep going, faster, faster in the wrong direction.

I glance at Kelly's minis, hanging free behind an open-backed silky top cut deep in the front with thin straps tied around the back of her neck. Her breast plate is level and open with a dew of sweat running down the middle. Just suggestions of mounds lie out of sight, covered by her top, unrelated to the broad plane directly below her neck. Even here, an utterly modest endowment, what should be an escape from the disease, is still devastatingly, exhaustingly feminine. The id is in overdrive and does not discriminate—all is beautiful and I want it all.

As we're heading back on Fourth we pass what used to be Plate Techtonic. The windows are covered with newspaper.

"I can't believe this space is changing hands again. The bar that was here just opened within the past year."

"Hey, look the door is open," Kelly says.

There's a guy, younger than me, not more than twenty-three, twenty-four tops, wearing a sport jacket and a crisp, unbuttoned collared shirt, jeans, and black loafers milling around inside.

"Hey," I call out to him through the dusty dim and hanging funk of stale beer.

"Tsup," he offers, uninterested or just preoccupied, looking at the ceiling.

"Do you know what's going on here?"

"Yeah. I'm the owner. I'm turning it into a bar." He says proudly, sauntering toward Kelly and me.

"I thought it already was a bar."

"A better bar. A vodka bar."

"Oh."

"It's going to be a Soviet-themed place. *Hammer and Sickle*. All Russian vodka. Very high-end."

"Are there enough Russian vodkas to fill a whole bar?"

"Yeah, there're plenty," he says snottily, defensively. I didn't mean it as a challenge, I genuinely was trying to imagine a whole bar only serving Russian vodka. What do I know. Whatever; screw this guy.

"When I drop in for a Stoli martini I'll be sure to wear my CCCP jumpsuit," I say. Touché dickhead. Both Junior Trotsky and Kelly are silent. (Wait: are they too young to get the joke? *You* remember when people used to wear those shirts in the 80s, right?) I smirk to myself—sometimes I forget that irony didn't start in the 90s. With Kelly's silence I wonder if I've saved face by defending myself against this guy or if I just look like a jerk for getting into it with him. Being testy with people is rarely flattering. I try to tone things down, "No, that's cool," but it comes out more sarcastic than I intended. "It sounds cool, man," I try again but it still doesn't sound sincere. I really don't know how to talk with people.

I look around, scanning the place for a moment until my eyes meet Kelly. I reach for her hand and we walk out as she half-turns and flashes a weak smile at J.T. and gives him an unsure wave like a student nervously volunteering an answer.

"Great," I say to her as we continue back down the street. "The place went from being a cool local dive to an Upper East Sider-fest and now it's going to be i-bankers and bridge and tunnel." What is coming out of my mouth? Bemoaning trendy bars, complaining about neighborhoods not being edgey enough—how trite can I be? Sometimes I really hate myself. I let out a sigh. "It's the nature of cities, I guess. I just wish it weren't happening on my block."

"You're so right. Even in Lincoln that's what's happening. There was this bar, Crops, that was, like, totally gross, a total pit—everyone used to call it Craps—I know, it's stupid but people thought it was funny I guess . . . I never went there, I was too young. Now it's this fancy coffee place."

I know she's trying, and to be honest, she does obviously get what I'm saying but her response still feels unsatisfactory to me. And I feel like a pretentious jerk for thinking this but I can't help it because she's not offering me anything new, I don't just want confirmation, I want elevation, inspiration! Is that too much to ask?

"A coffee shop doesn't sound bad, as long as it's not a Starbucks."

"No, no, I mean, the coffee shop's cool . . . I just meant that the bar was—"

"No, I hear you," I say not wanting to give her a hard time, and also, reluctantly, (why is it reluctantly, what the hell is wrong with me?), I do see her point. "I feel like in a weird way, sometimes it's just hard seeing anything change."

Kelly is too tall for me. I'm over the novelty of having the stalky blond on my side. Now it just feels awkward. Plus, she looks so young. She *is* so young. I'm that creepy older guy. And she's too blond, too lanky; next to her I am dark and smarmy. I looked good with Koala. We looked good *together*. I had a couple inches on her. Her dark hair, her brown eyes, there was a synergy, or is it unity?, whatever—we had that *something* in our look together.

Is Kel's hand bigger than mine?

She's got to sense it too; she must feel strange with me . . . I'm her New York Jew novelty. It'll wear off soon enough. I feel like I'm in a latter-day *Manhattan*. For a moment this thought delights me and I decide that we'll rent it tonight, as I'm sure she hasn't seen it, and that can be one more chip for me. But then I reconsider, thinking we're both just watered-down versions of Tracy and Isaac anyway.

– *What are you talking about, watered-down?*
– I have all the bad parts of Isaac but none of his success.
– *You're better looking than Woody Allen.*
– Girls like Woody. Or they used to at least. Some of them . . . Plus, you know, Kelly is in college not in high school. It's not as extreme.
– *Umm, isn't that a good thing?*
– Yeah, in the older-man-as-creep sense . . . But still, less dramatic. It's never as dramatic as the fucking movies is it?
– *It was supposed to be sad and funny.*
– Was it?
– *[Sigh]. It's not something to emulate.*
– And, but . . . *Mariel Hemingway*, come on, man! Kelly may be as pretty as her but Mariel's in black and white.
– *Can't compete with that.*
– Right! See what I'm saying?
– *Will you listen to yourself? . . . Actually, don't listen to yourself.*

– Why am I relating to movie characters anyway? Isn't that unhealthy?

– *. . . [long exhale] I'm not getting into this with you now.*

– I should just be taking this as it is, living life, purely, cleanly. No reference points.

– *Ok—you know no one does that.*

– I just feel like a cliché. And it's only because of films and guys like Philip Roth.

– *Maybe the cliché is in so much Fiction because it's so present in real life.*

– Yes, maybe . . . but maybe it's in real life only because it was there first in Fiction.

– *We're not getting into this now.*

– I should just be in the moment with this girl.

– *So—be in the moment.*

– It's hard.

– . . .

As we stroll down East 4th holding hands I can feel the sweat on both our palms. The front of my white t-shirt is dotted with moisture. Kelly looks comfortable in her flimsy top, cut-off jean shorts and sandals. I wish I could be a girl, just for a day, maybe a week. I've thought it ever since I was in second grade and had a crush on Alison McGuiness. I spied her climbing on the jungle gym, her fine hair hanging limply to her waist. She was so pretty and fair, it seemed to me that she floated through life, as if she were lighter than the rest of us, or at least lighter than me, dark-haired, and a boy. She wasn't the most popular girl in class, that was Catherine *something*, can't remember, she moved away the next year, but little Alison had a magnetism, all the adults treated her well, I could tell.

I take my free hand and run it through my damp hair. It feels good sweeping it back, like I've just scratched an itch. I see myself doing this, as now I'm hovering above the two of us, off to the side. Why must this happen? Every second, every stride (which we take in unison, through some conscious effort on my part) is a slide preserved in my memory, though it's like I'm remembering this while it's happening.

*Oh God. What is that?*

"Something just dripped in my eye."

"Are you okay?"

"I think it's air-conditioner fluid," I say panicked. "It's hot out. Right, right. It's definitely from some guy's window unit, probably ten stories up." I let go of Kelly's hand and I'm covering my eye now, tilting my head back looking up at the buildings with my good eye. Window units are everywhere, hundreds of them! sticking out of the façades like cancerous warts. "Poison! **Poison** is in my eye!"

"Can you see? Are you okay?" Kelly asks.

*This is it. I'm going down.* I hate New York.

How is this legal? Why don't we hear more about people being blinded by dripping air conditioners? I'm sure it happens all the time. The silent epidemic. There should be something on the news about this. There was—I think I've seen a segment once!

"Yeah . . . Yeah, uhh, uhh, I don't know." I'm still walking but I've slowed down to baby steps now. "I think I'm okay," I say unconvincingly. *What are you doing Dan? Pull yourself together. Don't do this now. Not with her.* I can't help it! Freon is burning my retina, and now through my mucous membrane the chemical is entering my bloodstream! I'll have to wear a glass eye; no, a patch! Forever. And I'll get cancer!

"It's just water Dan." She's patting me on the back laughing.

"No, no. It might be Freon or worse, it's probably rusty water mixed with Freon. I . . . I think I'm seeing spots."

"Take your hand away from your eye," Kelly says laughing harder now while she pulls on my wrist trying to uncover my eye. "How do you know there're spots when you're covering your eye?"

"I can see them through my lid." She wrestles my hand away and I open my eye. "I have blurred vision now," I say in a panic. I stop walking and stand there blinking my eyes fitfully, my whole face spastically twitching. "I hate air conditioners! It gets one degree above seventy and everyone has their stupid air blasting, destroying the environment. Destroying my eye! I'd rather suffer in the heat. My air conditioner broke three years ago. And you know what—I never bothered to get a new one. It just feels so fake, so *artificial*. I'm better off! I'd rather suffer."

"Well, you're suffering, all right. Let me see," Kelly says as she brings her face in, our noses nearly touching, eyes with irises of gold, brown, and green bursting from a pinprick pupil like a nebula, looking into mine.

Freon. That shit is like liquid nitrogen, the stuff the dermatologist used to burn a wart off my foot when I was twelve. I knew an air-conditioner repair guy once and he told me that if just *one drop* of it hits your skin, it'll burn it. If just a *molecule* hits your eye, you're blind for life. How is this legal, these dripping air conditioners!? But . . . Kelly? Wait . . . her face. It's right here in front of me. It's clear. I can still see! If I can see then it wasn't Freon. It's not even blurry anymore.

"I think it was just dirty water! Condensation." I exclaim in Kelly's sweet face an inch from mine. "I think I can see. I'm ok."

"Poison!" Kelly shouts, imitating me, and laughing uncontrollably. And the thing is, I don't think she's laughing at me. She gives me a big hug. She thinks I'm funny! "I have never met anyone like you," she's says with a huge grin. Can it be that she finds my neurotic antics endearing, not annoying?!

"Do you think I'm crazy?" I may have ruined everything. I'm a freak, a wimp, a neurotic Jew, the stereotype dies hard.

"No," she grabs my arm. "Yeah, well, maybe a little," she says still grinning.

Coney Island. Kelly and I are on line to ride the Cyclone. Through some strange shameful twist I've never been to Coney Island before and am very excited to ride the famed old coaster. I'm not much for the big amusement parks with the steel-aluminum behemoths and their triple loop-de-loops; I don't need to pull three Gs to have a good time. Not to mention the soullessness of the naming tie-ins—The Batman Ride et al. The Cyclone's got the funk. It has history, it's made out of wood, it doesn't go upside down, and it's not named after a superhero. I take more pleasure in the fear associated with riding a rickety wooden coaster, wondering if I'll die because the thing is going to fall apart than I would in riding one of the gleaming tubular monsters with all the fluid in my body pushed into the top three inches of my head as I'm upside-down at the apex of its tenth loop. I'm not testing for NASA here, I just want some speed and a little rumble. The new coasters don't give any rumble, you need the rickety wood bracing for that.

Seeing one man operate the release of the coaster with a wooden lever sticking out of the floor is at once refreshingly quaint and terrifyingly archaic. *I like that this thing is old fashioned and all but—Shouldn't that be done electronically?* The operator, doing his part to further remind us we're in Brooklyn and not at Magic Mountain has on the decidedly uncorporate uniform of filthy jeans and a wife-beater that covers less than half his gut. His obesity is one step beyond grotesque, inducing morbid fascination, like rubbernecking a horrific accident on the highway or seeing a girl on the internet getting screwed by a dog—you look, cringe, look away, then quickly look back again. The delicious and confounding attraction-repulsion paradox.

The coaster pulls in and we climb into the third car. I had wanted the front car and was willing to wait longer for it but Kelly was looking fidgety so I silently gave in to the debate that never happened. "This is going to be great!" I blurted.

Kelly grinned and said, "you're so cute," a phrase that's always irked me but was charming coming from her Midwestern smile and it filled the air with wholesome mirth. Scrunched together in our seat, I pulled the bar down and we quickly kissed on the lips.

The fat man pulled the lever and the coaster slowly rolled away. I started stomping my feet really fast. "Whooh! This is great! This is great!" Kelly blushed at my outbursts and squeezed my hand under the bar. But it wasn't a "be quiet, you're embarrassing me" squeeze, it was a "I love that you are *alive* like a little kid, unashamed to be excited" squeeze. The coaster started its initial and paramount ascent, the classic clank-clank-clank-clank of the cars being pulled up by the linked chain resounding around us. My hands gripped the bar tight in anticipation. In the corner of my right eye I could see Kelly, her face in a taut smile of terror and excitement, her sun-kissed hair blowing gently forward covering part of her cheek. The heat had been intense that day and for the first time since we had been in the park I felt relief as the breeze grew stronger as we climbed higher. As we edged toward the top the clanking seemed to slow as if I was watching a film and the projector's motor died and the reels were decelerating. And then there was silence, so complete not even the wind was in my ears. And it felt like we had frozen at the peak, one of those magic dragged-out moments, the gravity of it so heavy, that not that time itself is slowed, rather, our mind's are put into a special sort of perception-mode where we are able to read time in a new way, where we are able to stretch it, where we are able to see what we used to not be able to see; the world is still the same world, we're just catching it from a new angle, a new lens, the seconds constipated, where we are at once able to be inside ourselves yet also flying above. In a surreal tranquility, our car in what seemed like a permanent stall on the peak, so so far from the ground below, I looked out to the edge of the city/world, beyond the boardwalk and the beach and all the people and saw the ocean waves breaking on the shore; I saw the infinite blue of sky and then . . . SOUND, SPEED, MOTION, a sensory explosion, the film is back at regular speed, the foley man has cranked the ambient noise, the uplifting soundtrack theme is about to kick-in at full volume. All the audience cues are here, the director is shouting at us through the screen, shaking us, his hands on our shoulders, drama, life, emotion, *Feel It Now, Damn It! Feel. Now.*—Gravity takes hold, the world, my life, time resumes, the coaster drops.

After a stroll on the boardwalk we wandered down to the beach. We navigated our way through the crowd passing overweight Hispanic moms in spandex shorts, bickering children with plastic shovels, teenagers drinking forties covered in brown paper bags, and a smattering of white hipsters, pale and skinny in too-small t-shirts promoting variously, Kentucky bourbon, bands, and *Seth Schullman's Bar-Mitzvah 1988*. We walked barefoot in the sand and I worried about whether there were shards of glass or needles or worse waiting to be stepped on. I kept thinking about the Cyclone, the rush of the centrifugal force pressing my body into the seat as the coaster roared upwards after a big dip, the violent shaking of the car as it rattled along well-worn tracks, the cacophonous roar of the wind and the wheels grinding the rails. I couldn't help but wonder if those antiquated sounds and inefficiencies were an inevitable function of a hundred-year old ride or if those elements could be fixed— the bracing tightened, the rails greased, the wheels aligned—but were purposely left that way, or worse, made to be that way for some sort of simulation of authenticity. People don't ride the Cyclone seeking a sleek, computer-designed, modern marvel, they want the charm of the antique; the owners must know this. I'm saddened that I'm even pondering something like this; that so much out there is fakely authentic that I am unable to experience anything remotely old or original without questioning whether it's a simulation or the real thing. (Arguments about what constitute "real" aside). I think about the surreality of the Frozen Moment before the drop, the out-of-bodiness of it; intense and *real* as it was, its very intensity forced me into a sort of unreality. Not meaning that the experience wasn't very "real" but that it was that different dimension, alterna-universe type of real which in a certain way is not viewed as "real" in the classic sense. And I realize the only thing that was definitively *real*, "real," REAL, Real—whatever—was the physicality of the ride, the adrenaline rush of the G-force and speed and the innate(?) pleasure of the wall-of-wind in my face, that my exhausting internal dialogue over everything has rendered me impotent to experience anything without a three-layer deep argument over it in my head, killing any sense—or is it lack-of-sense?—of being in the proverbial *now*, that the only thing left for connecting me to the *now* is the primal and the sensory.

"I want to be real, Kelly," I said as I dragged my heels toward me in the sand making two trenches. This is why I love being with her, because I can drop lines like this that would nauseate just about anyone else but she embraces their juvenile sincerity, their ambition. She seems to enthusiastically take in all my declarations, my expressions of modern anomie and observations and indictments of our world as excitingly fresh (in the same way some of you were once excited thinking about these sorts of things). But I fear what I'm saying is sophomoric and I wonder if the only reason she is interested in it and "gets" it, is because she is young and she will soon mature beyond it (either by outgrowing it intellectually and experientially [surpassing my own rube-like level of philosophical sophistication], or regressively by becoming one of "them" after having made it into the "adult" world, having lost all but the most passing interest in anything spiritual or existential in nature, like she'll ponder this stuff after she randomly comes across a philosophical article in the Sunday *Times* or watches some high-minded, sci-fi movie, but by an hour later she'll be right back to the business of being a consumer/mom/worker/etc. and whatever she was ruminating on will have been basically forgotten.) And thinking that Kel only is enamored with me because she's too young to know any better brings on a pitying sadness for myself. After all, Lisa thought my obsession with all things existential and societally critical was a bore, I'm just an irritatingly callow angry young man, and frankly, now that I think about, excluding Jay, pretty much everyone else seems to think that too. But(!) despite this self-pity I must admit, I retain, perhaps delusionally so, but nevertheless, a driving suspicion that I *am* on to something, and just about everyone else, as good ol' Jim Morrison would say, are just a bunch of slaves. *On the other hand*, though, I wonder whether this enthusiasm Kelly has is not just some temporary stage she's passing through but *is* her nature and will remain a part of who she is as she gets older, and thinking this, I shamefully find myself filled with condescension toward her, that when I finally have found someone who wants to hear what it is I have to say, is excited by who I am, who "gets" it on a real internal level, I assume she must then just be a rube, a well-intentioned simpleton, someone annoyingly earnest and unsophisticated, what I fear myself to be. Yet, almost conversely, at the same time, underneath this condescension burns a jealousy over her apparent ease and lack of self-consciousness through which she exhibits this enthusiasm. (Does she not know how other people view incessant talk about this stuff? Or does she know but doesn't care?) I *also* wonder if maybe her "getting" me is neither temporary nor permanent, that perhaps she only *appears* to be "getting" it/me, and that it's not being done to purposely deceive but her excited questions and responses and at times near-shaking-canine-like head-nods of approval are only evidence of her interest not her understanding, (which while appealing and comforting to some degree does not offer the same and desperately needed connection of someone actually knowing what you're talking about, being on the same level so to speak). *OR* maybe, and I'm just being a little crazy here, she has the capability to get it but not the interest, and her enthusiasm is a finely crafted ruse just to make me interested in her b/c she assumes that I would want to be with someone who fawns over me and what I have to say. But all this being a ruse seems pretty damn unlikely because why would she go through all this trouble pretending to care and be deeply exited about what I say/who I am just to make me like her, because if she doesn't really care about and isn't deeply excited about what I say/who I am then why would she want me to like her anyway? What exactly am I offering her besides my antics? Is it possible, in a gender role-reversal, that all my jabbering and pontificating and weirdness is basically stuff she puts up with and feigns interest in only because she thinks I'm hot, that I'm some older guy living in New York that she can use as a notch on her belt and this whole experience with me is just something to tell her friends about back home or for her to catalogue in her head as evidence of having really lived-out her New York experience? My imperfections don't matter because they'll all be edited out—and not necessarily even in a knowing, psychotic manner but in the more common, unconscious embellishing and sweetening of memories our minds often do; I'm just a launching point, an idea to be crafted to fit into an already-reserved sepia-toned memory slide titled *Summer NYC*. I know it seems farfetched, and I don't genuinely think she's capable of such behavior, but people do this shit, I'm telling you. *And so*, after running through all these aforementioned possibilities, I am further shamed and frustrated for even having this internal debate. Why must I run through all these possibilities in my head! The whole five layers deep thing is just embarrassing and exhausting. *When does it end? When can I stop?!* And besides all the layers of the internal/micro analyses and dialogues, recently, I'm just as exhausted with all my external/macro shit, i.e. my never-ending societal and existential observations and theorizing etc. (And something I've realized is: all my external/macro debates and theories *are directly tied to* my spiraling internal/micro debates and theories over Kelly's intellect, psyche, and motives, because my internal dialogue over her is basically all about her relation to—her "getting" or "not getting"—my external/macro shit; it's all intertwined). But the Kelly shit is just the latest offshoot; it's the macro that's doing me in. I've grown just enough to become embarrassed by the sheer sophomoric platitudenousness of my thoughts and pronouncements but not grown enough to have moved beyond needing to be in touch with their basic sentiments. It's a terribly uncomfortable spot I've lodged into and I don't know how to get out; I need to either give up caring about any of the things that I care about or I need to become smarter and figure out a more sophisticated view of things, neither of which feel very possible to me. I keep thinking if only I were smarter, if I could just figure out a little bit more, I think I'd be closer to something. I'd be happier or I'd live deeper, richer. It's dangling right there in front of me but I just don't seem to be smart enough to grasp it.

God. Look at those legs, tan and lean. I'm fairly convinced at this point that her physical attraction is not purely sexual, it's almost more of an aesthetic lure with a vague copulatory undertow. I simply want to look at her and that is enough.

"I want to make something so that there is something out there in the world beyond myself, my own body," I said as I dug along the already deep trench lines with my heels. Kelly stared at me through squinting hazel eyes in the June sun, sweat beaded on her lip and forehead. Was this a blank, empty stare or was there more behind it? Despite her clear enthusiasm over my general charismatic (i.e. passionate and humorously neurotic) demeanor, she often gave this sort of look when I got deeper into my sophomoric/profound pronouncements. The platitudes and my (at least what I hoped were) more original or complex ideas excited her which in turn excited me because it was flattering to have someone interested in me/what I had to say and because it temporarily would fool me into feeling less alone, into thinking that someone understood me, but often times whenever I got into the deep stuff—and by the way, I'm well aware, *painfully* so, that you may be reading this snickering (or worse) to yourself over me complaining about this girl not "getting" my, what

I consider[d] to be "Deep" thoughts, as in you ruminated on "I want to be real" type stuff when you were twenty years old after doing a bong hit or something*—she would just look at me, not even wearing a look of confusion (or even condescension if that's where her head was, although I don't believe it was) but a look of *nothingness*. I could never tell with her but ultimately this look again and again had to be taken not as a sign of contemplative wisdom (and, come-on, it certainly wasn't distanced, veiled derision) but as for what it is on its face—the expression of nothing, no thought. I hope I don't sound like a jerk saying all this, putting down Kel (I recognize that I might), but it's the truth and I'm trying to convey what was going on. I was seeking some sort of response from her: from wide-eyed sycophant fascination to interested engagement even to amused (or annoyed) condescension. Just give me *something* here, Kelly. "And you know what," I said, taking my heels out of the trenches then sweeping my feet sideways across the sand filling the ridges in, carefully patting the new sand down, "it doesn't even need to be tangible like a book or a CD, it just needs to be out there, floating, like an idea."

Whether it was because I was upset by her look-of-nothingness or maybe because on some subconscious level after having filled in the ditches I felt a sense of completion and I was ready to acknowledge bodily functions, (like when you're watching TV and the commercial break starts and you suddenly realize that you have to go to the bathroom), seemingly out of nowhere I realized that I had to pee. I informed Kel of the dire urinary situation and told her to, "wait right here for me on the beach, I'll be right back."

---

* of course, if you weren't snickering and you actually are/were engaged in a genuine sense with what I've been writing then I've somewhat ruined the purity of that connection (between us, i.e. me and you) by acknowledging that others may be snickering, (although, perhaps if it [the connection] is really genuine then nothing can ruin it, certainly not my self-conscious acknowledgment that others may find what you find to be deep, new, exciting, not deep, new or exciting at all). Ok, enough! Sorry . . .

"Hope it all comes out okay," she said and gave my ass a smack as I got up.

At the urinals behind the boardwalk I stood between a balding and hunched old man and a fauxhawked twenty-something kid bizarrely in near-identical outfits of beige Havana shirts and madras shorts. I considered making a joke but decided against it. And either it was from relieving myself, or my amusement at seeing proof of the fashion adage "style is cyclical," or maybe it was just that the few minutes wandering alone to and from the bathroom seemed to clear my head, but the distanced, anxious, lack-of-connection feeling from/with Kelly that I was experiencing now seemed to have dissipated quite a bit. All the players in the five-layer-deep argument in my head seemed to have tired each other out. They weren't gone but now they were just sort of looking at each other, grunting derisively but otherwise finished with the whole thing. I really was starting to feel ok again.

And as I was walking toward her she was looking in the middle-distance at the waves, and in the corner of her eye noticed it was me coming near her and: under the gleaming, afternoon sun bearing down on her (not just sexual, but youthful, so-full-of-life) delectable body and super-duper pretty, faint-freckles-across-the-bridge-of-her-neotenous-girl-nose face, on both of us, on everyone on the beach, on everyone on earth, she turned toward me—And despite all my disconnect I felt with her and the defeating exhaustion I felt from the internal dialogue over the whole thing, she did something that in some ways wiped all that clear, made it irrelevant and it made me wonder if ultimately, none of this shit really means that much (in regards to me being connected to or happy with her or maybe even in life or with anything) because:

then she smiled

and, **whoosh**, or is it **wham**, or . . . shit, I can't come up with the right word and these onomatopoeia words aren't really accurate because there isn't a sound but more of, well, I'll just use the film reference/analogy (although it's not really an analogy b/c it sort of actually *is* happening that way) again—the tape slows down, the sound drops out, and here we go again with the Frozen Moment and the world slowing down but not really slowing down but I was just able to perceive the world in this new way, from a new angle and all the magic particles and all that stuff . . . And I'm thinking "maybe this is enough. Maybe all I really need (or all I'm really able to get) from her or women in general is this FM sort of feeling. And in the end, that feeling—(bearing in mind the semantic shortcomings of the word "feeling")—is everything."

In those moments when we can escape ourselves (although perhaps we're not escaping ourselves at all we're just tapping into a different part of ourselves), when the whole world, when life itself is presented in a way that carries so much weight, is so indescribably enormous, ambrosial, sublime, awesome (and I don't mean awesome in the "dude, that's awesome" sense, I mean literally paralyzed with a *sense of awe*) that it actually *is* (or feels like it is, but is there really a difference?) freezing time—I mean something has to be seriously fucking heavy to stop the clock—how can I not, not only think about those moments and make some sort of attempt at figuring out what they're all about, but how can I not live my life in servitude to those moments, to the memories of ones passed but more so to ones that have not yet come, to live for and strive for in any way I can that magic again? My whole life is about chasing the FM. In a way it seems as though maybe what makes the FM so worthy of reverence is that when you're inside the FM it very much seems to embody, in an abstract incommunicable way, everything. As if in that one delicate moment I can behold life itself.

FM → just a primal, reproductive urge manifesting itself in a distorted fashion beyond its functional role?

I.e. Is the FM just some abstract, indirect sign of sexual desire? An unintended side-effect of lust?

The FM is NOT simply an offshoot of sexual desire! While the FM is mainly brought on by women there are other triggers:
– Music
– Sensory overload
– Wistful moments of rare and extreme profundity

After I break out of my FM and I'm back in regular old reality, I'm still feeling kind of tingly. We're both sitting there under that gleaming sun I was talking about before. And I say, "This might come across kind of weird but Kelly, I feel like we have some sort of force together," and I really do believe this, although I sort of don't believe it in a way too, "like there's a wall around us sometimes, a shield." I am certain I'm saying something very true yet for some reason I feel like I am lying. Ok, there *is* a Force, there is something there but maybe it's just the FM remnants still lingering. Shit, maybe it's just neoteny. Shit . . . No; this is real, it's not a lie.

"*I know, I know!*" she says. She seems almost relieved to hear me say this, as if she's known this all along and was just waiting for me to realize it or to come out and say it. "I've felt this way from the first time I met you. We have something really special." She says this with such solemn intensity that for some reason I feel bad. It's like her sincerity has repelled me or maybe just brought out the truth from me which is: I'm lying. This whole thing is a fucking lie. What the hell is wrong with me? Is it a lie? Can something be both at the same time?

"You know what it is, it's like a force field around us, protecting us, putting us in our own little world." I am a bad person.

"I know. I can feel it," she leans in and hugs me. "Dan, our Force Field."

· · ·

That night we came back to my place. I was withered by all my doubts and internal debates but the thought of not being with her, at least that night, made me sick. Good vibes, lust, loneliness—who knows? Whatever it was, I wasn't ready to let go. So we're in my apartment and we're in bed, and there's this warm glow in the room (though the "warm glow" was probably more in my head than reality because now that I think about it, the lights were off and a sickly whitish light from the fluorescent bulb in the alley that the super recently installed due to some fire-code regulation now cast a pallid light through my window, because even though I have blinds, I had the window open a good foot to let a breeze in, and the blind was only pulled down to the bottom of the open window itself not to the sill so the breeze wouldn't be blocked) but anyway, in my head there's this warm glow and our bodies are warm under the sheets but not too warm because despite the heat during the day things cooled down nicely that evening, it was June after all, we hadn't made it into the real misery of summer yet, and we're looking at each other lying on our sides, naked, our legs intertwined, and she gives a sort of half-smile the way someone does when they're feeling romantic and calm but still really happy, and I think I was giving the same romantic-calm-happy half-smile back, only behind my half-smile was all that anxiety and uncertainty that you already know about, and I hate lying on my side and I'm basically uncomfortable and just hoping my left arm won't fall asleep but I don't want to move because the creamy pleasure of having my legs mixed with hers—(after all, like the strange intrinsic joy of seeing fresh cement or the satisfaction of scooping out a spoonful of pudding, what's not to like? I know shaved legs are a cultural thing but it must be in our genes: smooth = good)—is outweighing my potential nerve damage, and my right hand is gently scratching her back, I'm making these squiggly motions starting from her neck working my way down imagining my fingers are the teeth on a rake and I'm making jagged lines on the just-groomed dirt of a baseball diamond, and we're both giving each other these seemingly identical smiles *and but the whole time this is happening* I'm not really there, I'm sitting in a theater alone watching all of this, and there's something almost repulsive about seeing myself up there so large on the screen canoodling with her, it's not appealing like seeing it in a normal movie, instead it feels awkwardly invasive like stumbling in on a college roommate with some girl, there's even something graphic about it even though there's nothing profane to see, the profanity is in witnessing the scene itself, its intimacy and privacy somehow violated by me watching myself with her.

## LATE JUNE?

Things at this point are getting foggy, tough to remember. I think it was late June but I can't say for sure. The psychic drain of ambivalence had worn me down. I cared deeply for Kelly but I feared it was only in so much that she fawned over me. I felt guilty just being with her, knowing that things weren't equal, that she had begun to depend on me. I realized that the responsibility for someone else's happiness is more than I can bear. Or at least if that someone is Kelly Christie. Or at least if that someone was Kelly Christie at that time in my life, in her life. Are things not working because it's you or her (*the people* involved), or maybe you're the right people but it's the wrong point in one or both of your lives, just bad timing? You never can quite tell, can you? You know when you feel that imbalance in a relationship, when you know one of the two of you is in charge? Some people want that, some relationships need that imbalance, but for me there's an inherent discomfort in playing either role. Things (d)evolved where she was at my apartment every night, hung on my every word, agreed with whatever I said. Discussions generally broke down into lectures. Or maybe things didn't change this way, maybe it was like that from the start but *I* changed, my perception or tolerance of the relationship changed. I don't know; there's no way you can know for certain these types of things.

My life seemed to be getting away from me at that point: I thought being out there in the world would change things, being in **action**, not slothing around my apartment, living in my head. But being *out there* (in the world, doing things) just felt fake. I couldn't bust out of my actor role, so it (being out there) just seemed pointless after a while. If I'm just playing a role, and while playing that role I'm stuck watching myself in that role, and watching Kelly (the actress) (not Kelly, the person) playing the female lead opposite the me-actor playing the male lead—(which was cool in a distant sense because I was proud to have a pretty girl playing

my love interest *but still*, it was just someone *playing* my love interest)—
and watching everyone in their roles, and everything, the world, my
whole world as it existed, as I was able to grasp it was the Shakespearean
"all the world's a stage" thing taken to its utmost, brutally literal dissociative conclusion, why bother going outside (my head/my apartment)?
I was stuck. No matter how hard I tried, I couldn't engage, I couldn't get
*inside* the Action. Whether I was floating above, seeing it happen on a
TV screen, or the most removed, sitting in that dreaded theater, I was
watching myself in "real time" doing all these things—talking, eating,
walking on the beach—and it seemed like fun for that guy Dan Green
but I wasn't Dan Green I was just watching Dan Green. And the longer
I ("I" as in the "real" Dan Green, the one watching, not the Dan Green
doing all this stuff) have been watching myself talking and eating and
walking down East 4th and sitting on the beach and so much else, the
less likely it seems I'll ever get out of whatever this place is that I'm in.

I didn't want to get into this with you too much before. I know I
clued you in a few times like the night after the Cyclone and at least
once when we were walking on the street but I wasn't going to stick
some clause like, "hello dear reader, just letting you know that I'm floating above right now" every single time it happened, but I'm letting you
know now that for much of the time I wasn't there. Things have gotten
so bad these days, (it's been happening within the first few moments
after I wake up for God's sake), that I had to take a step back now and
acknowledge it (to you). By the way, it's not that every moment of every
day I was separate; for example, as you should know, when I was on the
Cyclone roaring up the track (especially with the FM* at the peak) I was
*There*, oh man was I there(!), but those non-separation times are starting
to become anomalies.

---

* Btw, it should be clear but is worth mentioning: the FMs and this watching/separation
situation are two very different things. An extremely rough way of putting it is: the FM is
the most *in* one can ever be in ANR (Action/Now/Reality), while the watching one's self
as if you are an actor in a movie is the most *separated* from ANR one can be.

**late june?**

And just so you know, there are gradations to the separation. Yes, they've been that frequent and each time that prolonged that I have a nuanced perspective on it, it's not just on or off. I am a Goddamn expert on not being in the Now. If they're looking to do a case study on this shit, I suggest the PhDs call me. The way the Eskimos have forty words for snow, I need my own vocabulary for this because just as the Arctic environs were their world, the separation has become my world. But instead of forty words I can break it down into three main stages— (the floating, the TV screen, and the theater). The dreaded theater. The floating, at least I'm there, hovering right nearby the action; the second stage, watching it on the TV screen I'm usually nearby too, if the Action is indoors then it's an easy step for my separation doppelganger to hop on the couch and watch it all on the tube, (though sometimes while I'm outside I get transported to my couch watching it on the TV screen, which in those circumstances is basically just a junior version of being in the theater); which brings me to stage three—the theater. Being in the theater makes floating above seem like just a warm-up, like the difference between snorkeling and being eighty feet deep SCUBA diving. Like if someone thinks that floating above is bad, ha!, they don't know anything about being separate from the world because in the theater you're not even floating in the vicinity like some sad ghost, you're completely somewhere else, walled-off in a different room, like that night after the Cyclone. Let's revisit:

I'm in bed with Kelly but an element of myself—in the room there with her, in the Action/reality—is operating on auto-pilot. Sitting here in the theater it's all being manipulated from my seat, I have some sort of mind-control like I'm tugging invisible marionette strings connected to the Dan on the screen that rule not only my/his movement but what he says and feels. And I feel sick and angry, half because I'm looking at this guy Dan Green on the screen wondering what his problem is, why he can't just give a genuine smile and feel it a hundred percent rather than suffer the ambivalence I know is behind the grin. (Even though I'm looking at the same Dan Green that Kelly is seeing right in front of her, I'm somehow able to see what is behind the smile in a way that she can't, like when I went to a lecture at the MOMA last year, and even though we were studying the same painting, [I think it was a de Kooning], the art historian was able to see something in the figure's face that I wasn't able to see [unless she was full of shit, which is possible with those art people but I'm trying not to be cynical about it]). And the other half of me is sick and angry not because of what's going on in Dan's head and how he's acting on the screen but more broadly, simply because I'm in this damn theater at all, that I don't want this perspective anymore, not that I ever did, but now I really don't want it anymore, and I'm scared and uneasy, and I'm sort of trembling a little because just as I'm naked in bed on the screen, I'm naked in the theater but there is no blanket, I'm just sitting here with my bare ass on the seat, but mainly I'm trembling not from being cold but because I feel as though I'm about to cry because I'm so damn lonely sitting in the theater watching my life, watching life itself, and for too long I've basically just been living in the theater suffering through a feature film that never ends, day after day of this, my separation from the Now more and more solidified, and it feels I might as well be dead because if I am not really there, lying in bed with Kelly, and the possibility of getting back there is more and more remote, what is the point of anything. And now I'm out of my seat and I'm running down the aisle, my body awkward, exposed, genitals flopping, the way they do if you run naked, and I reach the front and I am pounding on the screen. LET ME IN! This guy on the screen, THAT'S ME!, he's stealing my life! Let me in! LET ME IN THE FUCKING SCREEN! But I can't get in.

And there's a whole other type of separation too. No theater or floating above, in fact there's no omniscient/third-person watching at all,

**late june?**

rather I've been separated from the Now so many times because I've gone "somewhere" in my head, *thinking*, getting lost in infinite layers of internal debates. And the more infinite the world in my head the more difficult it has been for me to engage, to get *into* Action/Reality, which has sent me further into my head which in turn made it even more difficult for me to engage, rendering me even more of an observer instead of a participant in Reality which in turn . . .

I was scribbling notes about every Goddamned thought that popped into my head. Kelly thought I was a genius but I knew she was wrong. I wasn't brilliant, I was just losing it. The noise of the world crackled around me like a thousand TV screens in a Circuit City showroom all playing snow. The simplest things were somehow being processed as profundities. The way a cab rolled past me down the street, the stitching on the hem of my jeans, the staggered pattern of bricks on the side of my building fascinated and even confused me. When people talked to me I had trouble taking anything they said at face value, at times it seemed everyone had some alternative agenda, the guy at my corner deli, some random dude I'd chat with in the back of the Mercury Lounge, in particularly bad moments even Jay and Kelly, no one was telling the truth, they all had on faces. A chance encounter with Andrea simply saying "hi" to me would send me into near paralysis as I ran through infinite possibilities of what she *really* meant. And conversely, the philosophical, theological quagmires for which there are no answers ridiculously somehow seemed almost in my grasp. I had started a long time ago but in recent months, and even more so in recent weeks, I had spent hours nearly every day, even while I was with Kelly, sometimes staying up till three or four in the morning reading every social, psychological, philosophical theory I could find, bouncing from one website to the next. I scoured East Village Books and the half-price street tables near the cube on Astor Place buying dog-eared and highlighted Nietzsche, Marx, Frankl, McLuhan, Postman, anyone that seemed to offer some new angle or overarching frame in which to view the world. I wasn't *quite there* but as my index finger frantically tapped the mouse as I scrolled through site after site and as I skimmed the hyperbolic blurb on the back of some media ecology book I was about to buy I couldn't deny the giddy, psychotic rush I felt as if I were about to crack the code of what life meant, as if there were some schematic for the world and each new piece of information I absorbed was like filling in another word on a crossword puzzle, at once deliciously tying in to what was already there and leading to what was to come. Everything was backwards. I was totally fucked.

---

THEORY

3rd person watching of my-self →

caused by overexposure to fiction

FICTION DEPERSONALIZATION SYNDROME

---

If so much of my life is spent watching fiction (TV, ads, movies, magazines, etc)—it seems inevitable that I'd start to view reality itself as fiction. I'd view others, and ultimately myself, in the 3rd person. The brain so used to this mode that that becomes all it can understand.

---

Maybe all the time spent watching (instead of living in the Now) can induce a chemical change in the brain. Or maybe a physical change—like if you wear the wrong prescription glasses for a long time, after you take them off your regular vision is all messed up.

---

"I have a present for you," Kelly chirped through the receiver.

"A present?"

"Well, um, it's not really a present, but it kind of is."

"Wow." Coils of anxiety constricted my stomach. "We don't see each other for two days and you're already getting me reunion gifts!" This is not good. Kelly, don't do this.

"You know this is the longest we'll have been away from each other since we first met in the park five weeks and four days ago. Not that I'm counting."

I had told Kelly that I was helping Jay record some new tracks at his place in Williamsburg and that I would be working from early-morning until late in the evening, so it would make sense for us to take a few days off. The truth is, though, I never left my apartment. I loved being with Kelly, not with her as her boyfriend but simply in her presence. I was attached to her aura/energy/whatever you want to call it that made me feel so warm, yet I had grown distant from her as a person. As if who she was as a person and her vibe were two different things. And each time I was with her the weight of my dilemma, this cruel dichotomy became harder and harder to bear.

"How's Jay doing? How's the recording going?"

I stared at myself in the bathroom mirror, nodding. "Oh, he's fine. He just uh, ran out for a sandwich so I figured I'd give you a call." I knew she didn't have caller-ID in the dorm room so I was free to call her from home. *I'm not doing this to hurt you, Kelly. I'm sorry for this. It's just that I need some time to myself. There's something wrong with my head.* "Listen, I gotta go. I'll see you tomorrow sweetie."


In light of my ambivalence over the relationship and my increasing inability to connect with the *now* in any sense—(i.e. my losing of Daniel Green to some actor playing Daniel Green), this basic looming insanity (defining "insanity" as not being able to be in the *now*/reality, which may or may not be included in the DSM definition) (although and btw I always thought that if you were going insane you're not supposed to be able to be aware of your insanity, that if you are aware of it then you can't be insane because if you have enough presence of mind to be aware of it then you are still [somewhat] connected to reality but I was learning woefully that was not the case) as I made my way through day after day of sinking deeper and deeper into my seat in the theater as a forced viewer of the actor playing me, which we all do from time to time, I think, (watching ourselves on the screen, *not* the terrified pounding part), but now things were reversed, the standard ratio had fully flipped for me in that I was spending almost all my time in the theater watching, clawing the red velvet seat cushion, my face portraying the duress of extreme constipation, and only from time to time was I breaking *out* of the theater and into the screen/reality—I was planning on ending things with Kelly. It was clearly for both our own goods.

The next day Kelly buzzes me from the vestibule downstairs. I'm getting ready to start in with an elaborate explanation that I've worked out in my head for the breakup. I'm going to talk about where I am in my life and that I love her and that it's not her but me but I just can't seem to focus on anything right now and I'm depressed and anxious and therefore, "I just can't continue with us anymore" which is all true, *but* I'll leave out the fact that part of the reason I'm breaking up with her is that ultimately we just aren't on the same wavelength. (And while yes, there probably are some people who can understand someone else's wavelength without being on it themselves, those elite people pack such intellectual, emotional, intuitive power to have the virtuosic sense of empathy necessary to truly "get" someone else's wavelength that was not their own, that they're operating on a different level than most of us—but let's get real here, Kelly did not pack that kind of power, I didn't know anyone who did). She did offer me a lot by way of her vibe and connected to that, she was a hell of a lot of fun at times but ultimately, really, I couldn't get beyond that what she mainly offered me was sycophantic, panting puppy-dog type adoration which while important for my ego ultimately was making me feel more lonely and screwed up; but telling her all that seems needlessly hurtful.

But while I don't want to be hurtful I can't escape the feeling that only mentioning my anxiety and depression (and excluding the wavelength/ adoration stuff) as the reason why I was breaking up with her felt less like an omission and more like a lie, albeit a well intended one, which was making me feel disingenuous and therefore, extremely uncomfortable. Further, maybe I'd be doing her a favor by just telling her the whole blatant truth, that while yes, I was A&D and having psychic "reality" issues totally separate from her that were so bad at this point that I could barely function around other people let alone a girlfriend, and that I needed some time alone to try to sort this all out, but also, "just being honest, part of the reason I'm breaking up with you is because I don't feel you're on my wavelength, you're more like a protégé." Maybe that would help her grow as a person because she'd learn something about herself (what exactly I'm not sure though) because we can always learn more about ourselves from the truth than from a lie and so maybe the whole truth for that reason is always the best policy. (Although, on the other hand, perhaps in many circumstances it says more about them [them = the people telling the ugly/hurtful truth], that they feel the need to flex their sense of superiority by telling others something "for their own good" than us [us = the people being told a hurtful truth about ourselves] and in fact hearing the whole truth in many circumstances is not helpful or illuminating at all, it's merely a guise for the teller to say something hurtful [even if it's not purposefully hurtful] to the tellee, and that it takes more energy and dignity to not tell someone something that while true is still hurtful and unless it's essential for their wellbeing they'd probably ultimately be better off not knowing it). So, yes, after weighing it all out, I decide that I should leave out all the protégé/not-on-my-wavelength stuff and just put all the blame on myself and just harp on my A&D and reality/separation issues.

AND but (get ready, here we go) I get so deep in the lie/omission I've concocted in my head, it's so convoluted so as not to hurt Kelly's feelings, putting all the "blame" (of the breakup) on myself and my "insanity" and none on her or rather, on us, for our lack of connection, that I start to get confused, mixing up how I really feel with this lie/omission I'm preparing, that I'm not sure what the truth is anymore, that in crafting it and repeatedly going over it in my head, trying to make it sound as believable and sincere as possible I have actually started to convince myself of the lie/omission and I have to sort of step back and keep reminding myself that, *no, this is not the case*, which is needless to say really scary. And so then this Breakup Lie turns into yet one more layer to slather on top of the already myriad layers of confusion and fear about my Reality situation. And my depression, anger, insecurity, anomie, ennui, weltschmerz, laziness, near-paralyzing-self-doubt-paradoxically-mixed-with-an-undercurrent-of-delusional-overconfidence; vague, ever-present, base-line anxiety; and—whatever, you-name-it—general all around mental fucked-upedness were, to put it succinctly, putting me on the fast track as a candidate for some very strong psychopharmaceuticals (which I just recently started considering as a "remedy" for my current condition but know I will never take because however afraid I am of my mind— what should be a healthy synthesis of neurological chemicals, like the successful results of a junior-high chem. experiment resting securely, triumphantly in a test tube, is instead something resembling a bubbling, smoking, fluorescent green and yellow toxic goo leaking out of an abandoned, rust-coated, deteriorating tin drum illegally dumped somewhere in a vacant lot covered with weeds in Seacaucus, New Jersey; that, let's face it, those synapses aren't quite firing the way they should—I am even more afraid of altering it with a pill [which I recognize isn't necessarily— {although I believe there may be some serious validity to it}—a wise position to take but that's a whole other schpiel I'm way too exhausted to get into right now]).

Whew. Umm. Ok. Breathe. Now,

So anyway, all this shit is swirling around my head and I'm trying

**late june?**

to wipe it clear from my mind as I hear her ascending the stairs toward my second floor apartment. I do a couple arm-dangle shakedowns and slow exhalations like a swimmer before he gets on the starting platform. *Ok, just relax.* I let out a lawwwwwwng exhale. I'm more nervous than I thought I'd be.

As she knocks I can see in my mind her smiling face behind the door. When I open the door she immediately embraces me, her lithe arms wrapped around me like cables.

"Ok, sit down Danny Boy. I have something to show you." Ugh, she's so effervescent, so alive, so happy. God, she looks good. *I'm not doing this.* If keeping this girl from being sad means living a lie then so be it. It's wrong. This girl should never ever be sad. I need to know that she exists this way; the world needs her to exist this way. This is the way things should be. I'll just stay with her forever . . . Or at least till the end of the summer.

"Wait. Before you do anything I need to talk to you." Ata boy, stay strong!

"No! You have to see this!" I wish you could see how animated she is; it's really heartbreaking.

She then turns around, takes off her shirt and across the small of her back is a tattoo in black ink in a gothic font that says

## 𝔉orce 𝔉ield 𝔉orever

I wish I could say that was one of those moments where time froze and all that stuff but instead it kept rolling, mercilessly. My stunned silence was enough to tell her what she didn't want to know. As we stood there, unsure what to do, I halfheartedly recited some Erich Fromm quote that I had memorized for the occasion, "If a person loves only one other person and is indifferent to the rest of his fellow men, his love is not love but a symbiotic attachment, or an enlarged egotism." I tried to conjure my (by then, standard) professorial, near patronizing tone but mainly the quote came out as an ashamed mumble for saying such a thing to her at that moment. I even sort of drifted-off at the end of it.

There were days of tears, (both of ours), and meek fists pounding into my chest, and her face behind a sobbing curtain of shame and disbelief, so beautiful it stung and . . . that's enough. *I don't want to talk about this. Ever again.*

. . .

I don't know about you but I need some levity right now. Or if not levity, at least something to distract me, something concrete, cold, math, science, stats, charts. Charts! Yes! Did I tell you that there are sub charts to the main Compatibility Chart? There is so much to analyze, to think about, every plateau is made up of an infinite number of steps, mini-plateaus that got us there. Every answer is built upon answers before it and those answers were built upon other answers before them. Of course the main chart is not the only one!

Branching underneath the main Compatibility Index (which is comprised of Checklist and Vibe) there are layer upon layer of sub indexes. As you may recall, sub indexes however are only made of checklist criteria; Vibe, due to its ill-defined nature cannot be sub-indexed. A sub index example would be: *Smart* on the X axis and *Heat* on the Y axis. (See diagram below). (*Heat* btw is basically the same thing as *Attractive* [and uses the same sub-checklist criteria] except of all its sub-criteria it weighs sexiness the most. [Because some people can be attractive without really projecting any sexuality]).

And of course there are sub sub indexes. (E.g. the *Pretty – Adorable* Index is one of the many indexes that comprise *Heat*). Even though sub indexes do not indicate overall compatibility, they do give me insight into the checklist itself. Does any of this make sense? Diagrams are below.

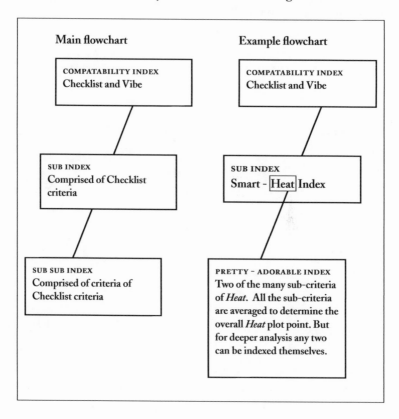

Now that Koala and Kelly are both behind me I'm consolidating them onto the same charts for easy comparison. Koala is represented by the paw and Kelly is represented by the ear of corn. I know, it's a little *too* cute, believe me, I'm sickened but in times like this I need to amuse myself no matter how juvenile the method:

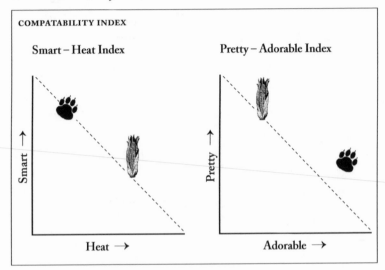

Aside: On the Main Compatibility Index one might think that Vibe should be weighed heavier than Checklist, that the balancing of the XY Axes is inappropriate; that to rely on Checklist equally as much as Vibe is to not go enough with your heart and too much with your head but the cold reality is that lack of a strong positive Checklist, while not essential initially, will affect and eventually erode Vibe. Because no matter how much Vibe someone has with you Vibe alone cannot sustain a relationship that doesn't have the more boring yet still essential nuts and bolts and common ground. I.e. you don't need to be doing everything together, wearing matching outfits when you're on vacation and eating the same entrees but over time it will be alienating and frustrating when

**late june?**

you're forced to listen to your partner's horrible CDs on a four hour car ride (and she doesn't want to listen to yours) or you have to get together *again* for the umpteenth time this year with her lame-ass friends Michael and Pam or she always seemed just slightly below where you needed her to be physical attraction-wise and you didn't really care in the beginning all that much because you didn't want to be shallow and she seemed really cool but man, that nagging feeling you have every time you pass a girl on the street who's just a little hotter just won't go away. And of course, if you have a great Vibe then none of these (negative) checklist things really matter singularly but if there's a whole bunch of them, it'll make your day-to-day life with this person, if not alienating, then at the least, a pain (because you won't be doing things together that you both enjoy) and if things start feeling like a pain too often then a lot of those good Vibe feelings will, if not erode, than at the least be squashed down below the surface as you deal in the day-to-day realities of spending time with someone.

Here's the main and final Compatibility Chart for both Koala and Kelly. The final plotting point for any relationship/girl is not the plotting point when the relationship ended but the average of all the points from throughout the relationship because ultimately it (generally) is not how things ended that one should focus on but the overall feelings from the duration of a relationship to get the fairest charting of compatibility.

(Note: there is a circumstance where the final plot point can be above the CTL but it still was the right move to end the relationship. This occurs when the aggregate of compatibility plot points over time is above the CTL but by reviewing the chronology of charts a clear downward trajectory of the plot points is visible. Meaning that things may still have been good at the end but you knew that the relationship was on an inexorable decent. These are the toughest relationships to end because you're relying solely on projections based on the downward pattern, [aka foresight], to kill something while it's still good. Ending a miserable relationship is easy, it's ending a relationship that's still good yet you know inevitably is doomed that's hard).

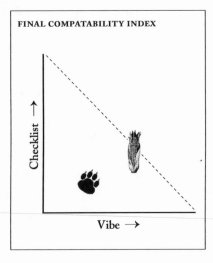

And you may be wondering: but what is the value of all this analysis?

Ok, I know this might be coming across as a bizarrely clinical objectification of women (and puerile and emotionally dysfunctional) but listen, I understand that life and people are never this simple, this categorical, but breaking things down really does help make sense of things sometimes. Besides, I can't stop it, this is what runs through my head, I can see these graphs and I think maybe it's my mind's innate tendency to try to quantify, rationalize, and yes, *objectify* something that is highly complex and esoteric because I am not a man of faith, I am not someone who can just accept the unknowns. I feel compelled to at least *try* to understand these things, the unquantifiables of life. Tim was right, there is a certain underlying stress in not understanding things, it's just that it's broader than not knowing how a transistor works or how a DVD actually plays a movie, (I mean I know digital is all zeros and ones but what exactly does *that* mean?), it's not knowing how emotions work or thoughts or feelings, all the seemingly non-rational (even though they probably all are rational at some level) strange things that people do. And no matter how futile (and perhaps destructive) the mission, I still can't stop myself from making an attempt to make sense of things. Everything. Sometimes I do it through charts like the XY Index for Compatibility but mainly, lately, for everything from why are some people such assholes to why are we physically attracted to certain people to why the hell do I act, think, and feel the way I do, it's been through reading, thinking, ruminating, re-thinking, re-ruminating, re-reading . . . and then obsessively recording the results of the whole process on little notes. (And yes, I recognize all this is a problem in the sense that I can never seem to *stop* analyzing and *stop* thinking and that perhaps all this analyzing and thinking causes even more stress than the not-understanding-things-stress that I'm trying to alleviate, the whole "the cure is worse than the disease" thing. People, it's not easy).

I wanted to do a series of charts where there would be a flip-book animation of a bear walking backwards on the Vibe axis of the Compatibility Chart—mapping the descent of my Koala Vibe (and hence relationship). There would be a different cell on each page with the bear incrementally "walking" backward in each cell. You'd flip through the thick bunch of pages, (say, maybe sixteen or so), with your thumb on the edge and view the animation. But upon further reflection, I've realized that devoting that many pages in the book to the animation would have added too much weight (figurative and literal/physical) to it, assigning an inappropriate amount of importance at this stage of the book to the Koala relationship and its demise. (This is, in a sort of abstract sense, not dissimilar from the Time representation dilemma I talked about earlier with the "TV"-on-the-page thing, in that inherent in the number of pages in a book devoted to anything there are all sorts of issues regarding representation and perceived duration of time and issues regarding the perceived importance of events, scenes or anything else written about in correlation to the amount of pages used for and actual duration of time spent

**late june?**

reading about a certain span of time, or event, scene or anything else written about due to our, i.e. the reader's [conscious and perhaps more so, subconscious] perception of time and importance of anything written about.) BUT, despite these issues I still think the animation is important (for reasons detailed two paragraphs down), so, as a compromise, instead of sixteen pages of the book devoted to the animation, the animation is still included but only as twelve cells on two pages.

Directions: cut each frame out, then arrange them with the upper-left-hand frame on top followed by the next one to the right, working your way across each row going down, ending with the bottom-right-hand corner as the last frame in the stack. Put two staples on the left edge of the stack. Then put your thumb on top of the right edge and flip the stack like a deck of cards and watch that bear walk backwards! (Of course I recognize that the time and energy expended on doing this project exceeds the time it would have taken to have just flipped through sixteen pages already in the book but still, due to the reasons detailed above, I cannot justify using that many pages in the book for this stupid animation. Devoting sixteen pages to it would have lent the animation too much importance relative to the rest of the "regular" content in the book, not to mention taken away the novelty, too much power and impact from the "TV"-on-the-page device [using the word "device" not in the derogatory sense here] which is of far more emotional-thematic-spiritual importance to the book than this animation. Somehow, *you* devoting [relatively] a lot of time to making the animation seems less misleading and less guilt-inducing for me than *me* devoting all those pages to it, even though that would have been a lot faster for you.)

So, it is imperative that you deliberately and consciously think of all this ("this" meaning the time and energy spent on the cutting and stapling and flipping) as more of a pacing and emotional break, an arts & crafts digression, rather than attribute (consciously or subconsciously) a corresponding amount of importance to it via your actual "real" time

**late june?**

spent on it relative to the time you have spent and will spend on the rest of content in the book. Think of it more as a forced intermission. And shit, I think the contrast of having a breather right now, aside from pro-viding a needed—(for me at least)—break from the emotional heaviness of the narrative there with Kelly, also gives more power to the tenor of the forthcoming narrative.

And listen, btw, as a whole separate issue, I'm aware that you may think this whole thing (the charts, the animation page, etc.) is a device [in the negative sense], that I'm just trying to do something quirky— [and, yes, *I know* this type of thing isn't at all "quirky," in the sense of it being new or inventive at this point in literary history; by "quirky" I just mean goofy]—as a cheap novelty for the sake of entertainment,[*] distrac-tion. But the point is: that is the point. I want a distraction here, a total separation, a new angle, an interlude, a comic relief, a palate-cleansing sorbet between courses, *something* that prose—in the medium-is-the-message sense, due to the fact that it's the vehicle we've been driving in, that prose is prose and can never be something else—simply cannot achieve.

---

[*] And yes, I'm aware this may not be entertaining at all.

Ok. So here are the arts and crafts animation pages:

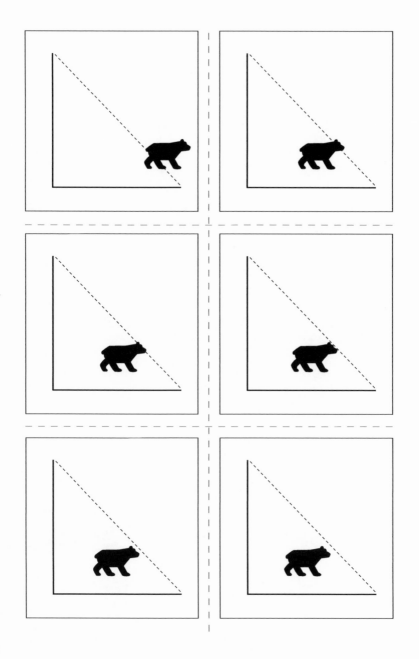

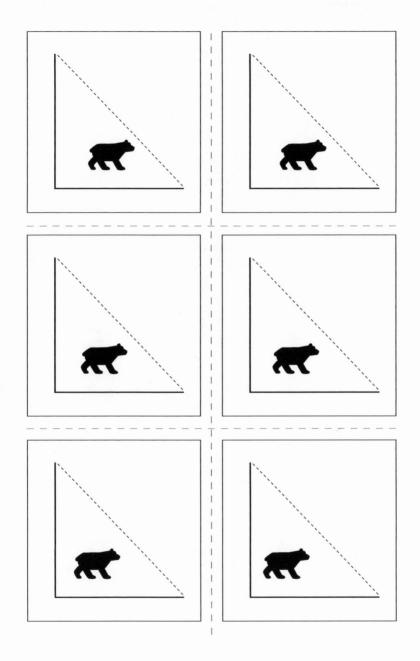

You know what? Forget the animation. That wasn't enough of a break. We need something more extreme, further away from the text, I don't even want you holding paper. Put the book down, go outside and jog a lap or two around your house or apt. or dorm or wherever it is you are right now; give me a good ten minutes or so and then come back. I really want to break this up for you. And listen, I know I'm asking a lot here. But I'm really not just saying this, it's not a joke. Put the book down. Go outside. Run a lap. (Btw, if you hate running, then just go outside and smoke a cigarette or go for a walk. The important thing is for you to *put the book down*, do something else for ten minutes then come back). I've thought this through. It's really the only way to get the true break, the distance I deem necessary before we start back in. Don't be a wimp and not do the activity, because for this—(this = what I'm trying to do over-all with this book; trying to get across what I'm trying to say)—to work I expect more from you than just to sit there on your ass with your eyes twitching from left to right. This book requires work. And by "work" I don't mean work in the intellectual sense like having to figure out what the fuck he's talking about in *Finnegans Wake*. I mean work as in physically *doing* things. It's gonna require more effort and if you don't want to put forth the effort, fine, obviously I can't force you, but, (and sorry for the teacher-ism), you're just cheating yourself. Because just reading (without these breaks from the text and activities you need to do) is simply not going to be sufficient for you to get, to embody, what it is I'm trying to get across. Ok, if it's two in the morning and you live in a bad neighborhood or it's raining right now, I understand, you don't have to go outside and run the laps. I probably should have given a warning at the beginning of the chapter like *you should only start reading this chapter if you will be able to go outside in about fifteen minutes from now* but that would have ruined the whole thing, you can't warn people of this stuff. If you *still* haven't gone—Go! Now!

This space indicates the ten minutes
you should be running.

**late june?**

Just so you know, I'm aware some of you might think any deviation from prose—(*especially* if that deviation is actually asking you to *do* something, not just a deviation like a chart or graph or font change that only requires mental [not physical] effort on the part of the reader)—for the purpose of trying to achieve whatever the desired effect is, is evidence of a deficiency in the prose, that a good enough writer should be able to communicate everything just through the text. But that is faulty reasoning, because words have their limits. Every medium—be it novels, film, talking, music, semaphore, whatever—has its limitations. There's only so much you can communicate in any one mode and why should I be held to just one mode? And all things considered, I didn't ask for much really. Because we both know there is so much more, it's endless actually, what could be asked of you, so believe me, the little extra I've asked of you—(jogging a lap? That's not so much!)—beyond the reading was nearly nothing, it was just the side dish, the crispy French fries, the steamed vegetables complementing the giant steak.

You see, because what I'm really dying to do is give you more commands, much more, than just arts and crafts and running laps. Break? Intermission? Hah. That was just a teaser. I want you not just reading but actually *doing* things for a far more important reason, that in a way is the opposite of me having wanted you to experience a *true*—in the medium-is-the-message sense—break: because that would be the only way you can truly get close to understanding, knowing, embodying what I'm trying to say. You can't just read about events and thoughts and feelings, you must *live* them. But once we go down that path of attempting replication, of wanting someone to live someone else's experience (rather than just read about it) the pursuit is near infinite because you can always get closer, there will always be something else you can do or think or feel to get closer to perfect replication and the whole endeavor would be futile and a mess. I suppose that's the rationale and advantage of having parameters in books (and other arts) because to try without parameters, without rules to get the audience closer is an exercise without end. I must either operate within parameters or demand that you fully live my life (or the life of whatever or whoever it is I or anyone else is trying to get across). (Either I'm given a canvas with defined borders to paint on or I won't stop until I cover every surface in the world). But how can I know you really understand unless you fully live it, inhabit it? (And by "live" it I don't just mean doing the same things but somehow ensuring that you will feel the same things that I felt as I did them. Because that's what this is all about anyway isn't it? Understanding exactly what someone else is going through in life. That's the point of—I was going to say *art* but it's not just art, it's really everything—to really inhabit someone else's experience, to really know what they're going through and learn from the differences and revel in the commonalities and universalities. I mean that is the only way to feel not alone.) I want you to go back and fuck Amy's friend and hug Koala and ride the Cyclone and make an album at The Watershed and really *see* the smile on Kelly's face then feel time drop into the frozen moment and sit there in a poorly-lit studio staring terrified at your guitar wondering why you can't pick it up and play, can't do the one thing that makes you feel whole in the world. I want you to think what I thought and feel what I felt, live what I lived. There is no substitute for this. I want you to do everything—see, feel, hear, *be* everything I did and am. I just so desperately want you to know, to *know* what it's been like to be me. Words, *telling* it, can't be enough—you have to live it. But in the end (of course) I have to draw the line somewhere because you can't live as me. 1) By all known laws of science it's impossible, and 2) (impossibilities aside), it is just outrageously selfish, narcissistic of me to ask that, to wish that of anyone. I know this, I know this! but: I just want *so badly*, am trying so hard, to make sure I'm not going through this alone. And I'm sorry for even just this, for you hearing my voice in your head right now, for reading my words, your time, your precious finite time!— what an obscene indulgence!—but I am (and have been for a long time)

**late june?**

so desperate to know that you *know* what I know. And but hey, don't we all owe each other this indulgence? But I know the answer is (of course/obviously metaphysically) we can never truly indulge each other in living each others' lives. And this makes me *so* sad because, shit, forget about me for a moment, I want to know *you*. I want to get inside your life, everyone's life. I want to live everyone's life. I want to know! I don't want to just guess what it's like, I don't want to just imagine it through reading words—that's not enough. I want to be inside you, to *be* you. I want to know! I want to know it all and I want everyone to know me.

But I know this can never happen and we're all just doing what we can to try to connect with each other. So before I say anything else—and I should have said this before I said anything to you, before the first letter on the first page—I want to thank you, most sincerely—[and it's a shame "sincerely" (and all its conjugations) is so overused as a closing in letters and misused—as a figure of speech or even worse, disingenuously—just about everywhere else that when you *really are* sincere you're stuck using the same word that now has so little impact. So, here,] I need to specify, amplify that when I said *sincerely* I mean it in a spiritual/energy/body-core/ultra-maximal/full-life-essence sense—for giving me your time, your *self*, to try to know (ahem, *know*) me. And I know all I have are these words because you can't be me and I can't be you and maybe we don't want/need that direct replication of experience anyway, maybe all we need are words or music or pictures; maybe art is enough. Or maybe the fact that art—no, fuck that—that **nothing**, will ever be enough is the point. It's the honest effort (in trying to connect), in all its glorious imperfection that is the point.

BUT . . . maybe this/that is all a sordid despicable lie. Because everyone's *doing the best they can* and what the fuck does that mean? Where the fuck has that gotten us? Because, oh God, I'm still floating here, we're all just still floating, alone. And BUT, no!—because every once in a while, every once in a great great while there's a cosmic fortuitousness, where somehow, in some way, whatever *it* is that makes each of us who we are overlaps. And it is a miracle, a most authentic embodied empathy, a true knowing of what someone else's life is, even if it is just for a moment or on just the thinnest of planes; and man, sometimes it is (or seems at least) to be so much more—the enveloping overlap, the near mirror redundancy of commonality, the overwhelming shock of fraternity—and somehow words, just words!, every once in a while, are enough to bring about this miracle of overlap, of something truly understood, truly shared. And so:

knowing you are there[*]
right now,
wherever I may be at this moment as you read this,
may be all that is keeping me—to say in perhaps what is the most banal yet succinct language—

ok.

. . .

It's sometime after 7:00 and I'm on the couch watching a Seinfeld rerun. I never laugh out-loud at Seinfeld episodes but I do have a sort of internal laugh, I'm likely not even flexing a smile but inside, I'm mildly amused. And that is all I want right now.

But something strange has happened to me. I'm watching this episode and George is freaking out about something then Jerry makes a crack about his behavior, and normally I'd have my usual sort-of-internal-laugh at their antics but this time there is nothing. And I'm not sad or angry or bored so it's not that my mood is affecting my enjoyment of Jerry and co. It's something stranger, almost like perceptual computation

---

[*] (i.e. here with me)

is off-kilter in my head. It's like everything is broken down into slow-motion but not in the cool, dreamy slow-motion way but fragmented, in that things are broken down almost in an arithmetic sense, like everything is A + B + C = X. I know this is a joke, I recognize the wordplay, the shtick, the contrived situation but it's not funny because it's not cohesive. I'm unable to take the jokes in their completed form. I'm stuck in this analysis mode and everyone knows that breaking-down why a joke is funny is not funny at all. I'm not analyzing on purpose, I don't want to do this but I'm frozen in this mode, dissecting. It's as if I *know* this is funny, but my brain is unable to connect all the parts. It's like an extreme version of when people say, "that's funny" rather than laughing (if something is truly funny, you laugh, you don't say "that's funny"). Everything is just fragments.

For days I have been walking around like this. The world so new and different from what I had ever seen before (but of course I know it's exactly the same, it's only me that has changed). And in a way this feels like a gift. I have an acute awareness, a hyper-analysis of all the data of the world. The world is in micro, in ultra-order, its basic components, all its parts neatly laid out; even when I recognize they are linked together I still see them singled out, floating, separate.

But life's meaning comes from the sum of parts and the ability, or rather, necessity of seeing them as a whole. When all you see are the parts nothing amounts to anything, there is no chemistry, no amalgam, no greater purpose. You taste the sugar, the flour, the butter, the salt, but you don't taste the cookie. And we all know ingredients like vanilla extract taste awful on their own, they only work when they're mixed with everything else. This is interesting, yes, but this is not good.

All I've wanted for so long is to be just a little smarter, to see just a little bit more of what I've been unable to see. If only I were a little smarter perhaps I could figure things out and not feel so confused, I thought. But now, maybe because I've wanted it so badly, my brain has shifted involuntarily into this new mode and now I'm overthinking, overanalyz-ing everything and it's not under my control and it hasn't led to learning anything or reaching any new conclusions. In fact, nothing has a con-clusion. It all feels pointless. And I've had enough. I don't want to see anymore detail, to know anymore unknowns. I want things laid out in front of me, finished, formed, ready to be consumed as whole entities. I'm wearing x-ray specs and seeing all the innards of the world and it was interesting for a spell but the world in little pieces is not fun anymore. *I'm ready to take them off now, please.* But I cannot. And I'm getting scared because I need the macro, I need the sum, I need the connectivity of it all. And I fear I'm getting further away from ever going back.

And what makes this all even stranger is that I'm totally aware of what's going on, I see what I am doing but I am unable to stop. I'm stuck in this warped perception mode and I know it and I know it's wrong. Maybe the homeless guys on the street muttering to themselves or screaming at no one know that no one is there but still are unable to stop. I always assumed they didn't know but maybe they do.

It was a terrifying beginning to this whole mess. One afternoon I was wandering the streets feeling anxious, (as is my routine), worrying about all the things that I wanted to do and should have been doing but I was not. I stopped in the St. Marks Bookstore. I thought maybe there'd be a cute girl in there and maybe I could figure out some way of talking to her and just maybe that would lead to something between us, some-thing grand. This scenario has never happened but I always hope it will. *Endtroducing* was playing on the stereo, its enigmatic sounds darkening the store. The place was pretty crowded, which didn't surprise me because it often is, but still fascinated me that there are so many people wander-ing around the neighborhood, futzing in a book-store, not working the nine-to-five. A cute girl with short brown hair and tortoise-frame glass-es, in flip-flops and one of those skirts that look like a slip (man, what a great trend that is) was skimming through a paperback off the front wall and drinking one of those teas with the tapioca balls in them. (This part of the hopeful scenario—that there was a cute girl in the store—usually panned out, it was the rest of the scenario—the whole talking to her and us falling in love, ok maybe just hooking up, ok maybe me buying her a drink—that never seemed to come to fruition.) For no reason in particular I was feeling pretty hot that day. (Sometimes I get this feeling like I have an extra power, like a fourth-dimension pheromone. [I'm convinced years from now they'll discover that we do in fact have some sort of magnetic pheromone field and periodically it packs an extra charge]). I stood next to her, not crowding her but close enough I imagined for my power-field to reach her. As I was waiting for my invisible waves to take effect I glanced over the new releases, turning my head in her direction a few too many times, giving her the eye, but she never looked up. If anything, I could feel her giving me the I-see-you-staring-at-me-and-I-want-you-to-stop-creep body language, so I moved on. Despite her rebuff I still was feeling the power (it doesn't work on everyone).

But suddenly I wasn't that into girls right then anyway. I think I was checking her out more out of habit, almost like an unconscious obligation than out of present desire. It was one of those shell days I have sometimes when the world takes on a distant feel, like nothing is close to me even if I touch it. I was there, in the day, as I had walked the streets I felt the pavement under my feet, I could see the yellow cabs and dirty white trucks race down Bowery past St. Marks, in the store I could hear the music and feel the wind from the fan and see the vaguely irritating strobe effect the blades of the fan made as they passed under the ceiling lights but the whole while a thin invisible shell coated me, keeping me removed, just a visitor. Reluctantly, though with a bit of a shrug, I fell deeper into myself, the only place there is left to go when the world is beyond reach. Not necessarily thinking, emoting, or dreaming. Just falling.

My heart was beating too quickly or at least it felt that way. I tried doing long, slow exhales, subtly, quietly through slightly opened lips. The music was loud. (How do they expect people to sample books with music blaring)? Pounding drums hidden behind a blanket from the depths of a cavernous sepulcher delivered themselves muted and echoed through static crackles. Mid-century voices from long-forgotten films or radio shows talked nonsense over the beats, piano notes trickled in the ether. I meandered unsteady through the aisles, lightly brushing the stacks with a listing shoulder, my eyes scanning all the spines. A woman in one of those super-short Twiggy haircuts with cat glasses looked at me indifferently from behind the rear counter. *Breathe, slowly.* My fingers started to tingle. I glided them across the covers of the discount books laid in uneven piles on the table in the back of the store. The books felt strange under my fingers. With the reduced sensitivity I had less control and had to watch my hand carefully so I wouldn't knock something over. Those fingers gliding across the different covers, following the different heights of the stacks as I bumped from one pile to the next, going up, then dropping, then back up again, it was like I was tracing the outline of a skyline. I stood there for a moment, then turned around and ran my other hand across the books walking in the opposite direction. I thought of the guide-wheel hanging down from the ceiling in a car-wash, rolling along the hood, then up the windshield, across the roof, then down the back window and trunk. The tingling in my fingers was dissolving into numbness. That could be someone else's hand there on the table. I can't feel the books at all. *Breathe, slower.* Maybe I need to breathe *faster*? Or hold my breath? This isn't working. I wish I had oxygen running into me like that time I was twelve and in the ER—(having been brought there by my mom because I was experiencing chest pains, tunnel vision, and dizziness and after an MRI, chest x-ray, and blood work was deemed a panic attack)—the thin tube with the end-piece like an elbow macaroni curling into each nostril giving me what I can only describe as a grounded high, a sort of uber-reality.

My head feels heavy and off-balance like an inflated ball one-quarter-filled with sand. God. This sound, the beats, the static. Vinyl from the past somehow reaching back from a bleak future. It feels so dark. DJ Shadow—fitting, I suppose. It's like hidden messages from the afterlife, or the underworld, or one of those purgatorial or supernatural dimensions. There's a fissure somewhere in our world and DJS is pulling it open with both hands, though it's tight and immovable, like he's one of those no-rope rock climbers, he has chalk on his hands and they're bent inside the crevice, every fiber, every knuckle straining under his body's full weight as he's dangling there off the edge of this rock-face, and we're peering into this crack that his hands are not so much trying to open because he knows the rock will not open but it still appears like he's trying to open it, focusing our eyes on whatever's deep inside that crack because it's some sort of portal leading to beyond what we know.

The aisles begin to collapse, the stacks of books closing in on me as if I'm standing between towers in midtown looking up and they're so tall they bend in toward each other like the inverted-V perspective of opposing shoulder lines narrowing on an infinite two-lane road in the desert. I start spinning, or maybe I'm standing still but it feels like I'm spinning. All those books, the spines, one after another, row after row, shelf after shelf, they're endless. There's a flash. I see all the notes on my walls, the yellow squares everywhere now, the unstuck bottoms on some of them slightly curled, like extra large square Fritos, the text filling in some of them so completely that from a distance they appear almost black or blue instead of yellow: [slightly magnified for clarity]

**late june?**

> the inexorable and bewildering internal struggle
> of **Observer vs. Participant!**. . . → seeking to
> behold the essence of life? consciousness? (is
> consciousness the essence of life?) avoidance of
> mortality?
> —Which side is the right path, what is the bal-
> ance?. . . it is in the nature of the introspector/
> creator to be an observer, therefore, this tendency
> must certainly be linked [i.e. just one step removed
> from (though quite dissimilar)] to the dissocia-
> tive state of consciousness, (i.e. out-of-bodiness);
> though, one may argue this "separated" state
> has widespread prevalence among the Western
> population regardless of one's level of introspec-
> tiveness (though complexly—too much to get into
> here—the non-introspectors are blissfully unaware
> they are in this dissociative state) due to the domi-
> nance of a fictionalized environment. . .

and there're the ones like the "Privatization of Public Space" and "A Condensed Treatise on Neoteny" (that I won't bother reprinting since they're borderline indecipherable, as they have more text crammed-in than the note above). Other notes have slightly less text though, the axioms:

> <u>Cell phone</u>: the tyranny of
> connectivity → elimination of
> being in the moment/ being
> present/ loss of reality
>
> (see also: <u>video</u> and <u>still
> cameras</u> for this phenom!) →
> so, paradoxically this is really:
>
> <u>Cell phone</u>: the illusion of
> connectivity! (see also: TV)

and others still even less, the XY charts, the J-Curve diagrams, or perhaps just one word or phrase or maxim or dots or lines or selectively extracted quotes from my own or sometimes other's vast texts:

**late june?**

> "the more the worker
> exerts himself in his work,
> the more powerful
> the alien, objective world
> becomes. . ."
> → YES!

> **Ambition = Anxiety**

Flash. I'm in the store. Books. More books. Endless rows, and inside, endless pages, endless words! What does this all mean? What they hell is everyone trying to say? None of this means anything! I keep trying harder and harder but the more I try the further away it [*The Answer*, answers, sanity, serenity, satisfaction, understanding] gets—my mind, or maybe it's the whole goddamned world, a Chinese finger trap. And I'm just so exhausted sometimes, and frightened about what I don't even know. It's all just too much, everything, all of it. I don't know what to do anymore, I just know that what I am doing doesn't seem to be working. Sometimes it seems that all I want, all I am really seeking is the same answer. There is only one thing I need to hear, so I can keep going. Just one thing. And I don't care what's written in them, every book is saying it, *needs* to be saying it, whether they intend it or not, that's what I will read, that's what I will hear. Please. And since it's all the same why do I need any of them? I only need one book. It is 330 pages, and every one of them is blank, and there is a blank cover and blank back, maybe there is a slight decorative border on the cover, maybe not, but inside there is nothing, you can turn each page slowly, a full second spent on each one of them, absorbing the blankness, after a while noticing little flecks and imperfections in the paper itself, or you can fan through the pages with a satisfying *fffft* as your thumb zips along the side, or perhaps you'll know where to go, and you'll jump right there, to page 273, the only page in the

**late june?**

whole book where there is anything written at all, where in a standard-sized font, in the middle of the page, there will be the words:

**Everything is going to be o.k.**

And this book will be on the shelf at home with all my other books. It'll fit in nicely. No one will know, their eyes will gloss right over it. But I'll know. And when I need it, when things have reached that point where I'm not sure if I am going to make it, I will walk over to the wall, reach my hand out, place my index finger on top of the binding, tilt the book back then grab it with my hand and pull it out. And whichever way I choose, I may go slowly, bringing my heart-rate down, reveling in each delicious blank page, the blankness, the nothingness itself soothing me, clearing my head, slowly, and then finally, I come to 273 and I can stare at those words, and I can close my eyes, and I can close the book and I can rest. And maybe sometimes I will need to go quickly, I'll need 273 like an epinephrine shot for anaphylactic shock, the page will be dog-eared and I can jump right to it, SHRRRRT, black ink letters alphabet words I know what they mean I do not need to read them there is no time I just need to see the shapes the black on white and they will transpose all of them the letters 23 abstract forms black molecules specs like a spritz explosion off the paper into the air into me.

Things are declining quickly. No matter how bad I felt, compared to now as the Seinfeld credits start to roll, it was just a mild confusion. I was like a dad trying to help his eighth-grade kid with his algebra homework. For years he hasn't done any math beyond figuring the tip on a bill, so the "solving for X" causes him to squint for a moment as he tries to figure out how to do this equation. Now though, as we go to commercial, I'm

**late june?**

in full-scale advanced calculus and utterly bewildered because I have no idea what the hell "the number *e* is irrational and transcendental" means other than it has something to do with going on forever (I think)—the parts of the world are more and more fragmented by the second, it's no longer A + B + C, everything whole is crumbling, it's just tiny particles swirling like dust caught in the light. Somehow after Seinfeld (and the absence of the internal-sort-of-laugh) and a restless ten minutes of flipping between the *News Hour* and *Jeopardy* and *Access Hollywood*, I manage to extricate myself from the couch and the grip of the TV. Once mine is shut off though I hear Dayna's set through the wall. All that TV she watches, it makes me sick! (*I know*—I hate her because I hate myself, etc. etc. but really I hate her more because at least I'm disgusted with myself, she doesn't even have the dignity of shame. [And yes, *I know*, we needn't all be ashamed for watching TV, we're allowed to unwind with mindlessness from time to time blah blah blah, but really, trust me, she watches *a lot* of junk and she should be ashamed]). I brush my teeth, put on flip-flops and head outside. In the stairwell I see Andrea walking down a half-flight below.

"Hey there!" I call out, my voice echoing.

She stops and looks up. Simultaneously I hear, "Dan. Hi," and "Da-an. H-i." *Oh God.*

Her voice sounds weary. (Or do I just think she sounds weary? She always seems like she's a little annoyed talking with me but I can't tell if she really is or if for some reason I'm only imagining that she is or maybe she's not annoyed or weary at all, this is just the way she sounds). It's strangely reassuring that even in my mildly psychotic, neurologically impaired state, my default feelings of paranoia and insecurity and neuroses regarding Andrea are still intact—this realization is depressing, but nevertheless, grounding.

"What's up? Where're you heading?" I say as I catch up to her.

It sounds like she says, "There's a book release party for a friend of mine." But it's so chopped up it's hard to understand, but I play along smoothly, not letting on that I am cracking up. I feel like a football player playing through the pain of a near-busted ankle, hiding my injury from the other team.

"Oh, that's cool," I say. I want to know, what friend, what book, but I don't dare continue the conversation anymore than I have to. I know what she's saying, I think I understand, it's not like a foreign language, but it's maddening to hear e-ver-y syllable in e-ver-y word. I survive a few more lines of dialogue before we both leave and part ways out the front door. I head up Second Avenue, avoiding eye-contact with everyone and try to avoid hearing anyone talk or any other noises. It strikes me that leaving the apartment in this state was a bad idea, but I couldn't stay inside either. Nowhere is safe, there is nowhere to go. Street signs, stores' names, freebie newspaper boxes on the sidewalk—7 t h S t r e e t, *S a n L o c o, V O I C E*, the words are breaking down to letters suspended, unaccompanied, each hovering in their own spaces like bits of fruit in jello. It's not dyslexia where the letters or words are jumbled; it's the opposite, everything is too ordered, too s-e-p-a-r-a-t-e. There is no culmination and there is no conclusion. I can see them, I know they're there right in front of me but I am unable to grasp.

I'm afraid it's becoming apparent that without the sum of the parts, that really, in effect, there is no point in anything. All these letters and words and people and trees and cars and blades of grass and everything everything everything is all alone in its separate parts. I can see them together, I can see the car, I can hear the conversation, I know this to be the truth, and seeing this *right here in front of me Goddamnit, FUCK* but I can't quite *get* it—(all they are are words; there is a bumper, windshield, four doors, and a trunk but they are not hinged together, they are not one thing—it's a *sentence* but not a sentence, it's a *car* but not a car)— can't quite *see* it all together, formed, unified, is a sublime torture. There is a different world, a better world, the proper world of connectivity. I

**late june?**

know it's there!—I can see it—but it's on the other side of this unbreakable glass.

And it's all quite clear to me now—(and I know this answer that I'm about to reveal is dramatic but in a time like this how can I not be dramatic?)—I realize that of course just like everything I am seeing *I too* am separate; yes, in some distant vague way that I am unable to access I know I am a piece inexorably tied within, inherently connected with everything of the world, yet still, nevertheless, right now, with wrenching immediacy, through this prism with which I am now forced to process the world, in the implacable present, I am forever floating, alone, separate.

. . .

Ohhhhhhhhhh. Ihavetogetoutofmyhead. Ihavetogetoutofmyhead. Shut up. Ok.

But the thing is: I can't. Or I don't want to. I mean, I *want* to but I also don't. Not because I'm enjoying this, (I'm not), but because I'm afraid. Because if I start to leave my head that means I'm less alive. Not alive in the sense of breathing, heart beating etc. but alive in the sense of consciousness, awareness. Because isn't an unexamined life a life not lived? Socrates, you got my back here, right? I have to know what's going on at all times. I need to observe then process, analyze, ruminate on, reflect back on then observe some more. That is the only way to truly be here. Because to be in-the-now, *in the moment*—(the time/state that it is considered one is *most* alive)—confusingly, paradoxically is actually not to be truly alive because that would make me more like an instinct-based creature, because *in the moment* I am not examining or reflecting, I am simply, purely *being*. And the more the balance tips to instinct/being and away from thoughtfulness, the less value we attach to a creature. The problem of course is, being in the moment is the only time I *feel* truly alive. So is that feeling an illusion? Or is the value of thoughtfulness an illusion? Which way am I supposed to go?

I mean because think about it: we view different levels of consciousness as different levels of being alive and the more you are alive the more you are worth. A human is more aware than a dog, a dog is more aware than a gerbil, a gerbil is more aware than an ant. This is why we'd have less guilt killing a dog than we would a human, killing a gerbil than we would a dog, and think nothing of stomping on an ant. (*I know*, there are the Hindus and Jains who sweep their path before they walk so they don't step on any bugs but generally, humans, cross-culturally, feel less guilt over killing ants than dogs, a gnat than a buffalo, a mouse than a whale [I know, there're whaling expeditions and slaughter of buffalo, etc. but still, even the men who did that, I bet they'd admit to feeling some sense of, if not guilt than at least gravity over their murder of these large, seemingly sentient {and I don't mean sentient specifically in a perceived ability to experience pain sense, I mean it in a consciousness, awareness of the world sense} creatures than if they swat a fly]). We can't know the exact level of consciousness for any creature but we have a general hierarchical sense. The more perceived awareness-capability we attach to a creature, the more existential value we attach to it. (Obviously, many people believe that everything has value in a religious sense because it's all part of God's world blah blah, and people know that everything has value in a scientific sense in that everything is needed for the function of the food-chain and ecosystem at large but you know what I mean, those attached values are different than the pure guttural hierarchical sense we have about worthiness). *Therefore*, the more conscious I am, i.e. the less in-the-now, i.e. the more in thought/reflection/awareness mode, the more "alive," (i.e. valuable) I am—because consciousness equals value, and the higher the level of consciousness, the higher the value. YET, to only think/observe/reflect is to be separated from the *Now* (or it could be argued "reality") and to be separate from that is to not fully be alive either. Because Action/the Now/being *present* means you're actually *in it*, you're feeling it, you're running down the street, you're singing a song, you're screwing some girl, you're laughing with your friends, you're ALIVE capital A motherfucker, precisely because you're *not* thinking about it, you're not reflecting on it. (Of course you could be doing any of those things and not be in the moment, you could be separated, watching, thinking, but I was talking about when you're doing those things and you *are* completely *in*, not watching or thinking, just *in* it. [You probably knew that—{that in giving those examples, the singing, screwing, laughing that I clearly was implicitly referring to the times you are doing those things and are in the moment, unaware, and of course I didn't mean that every time you're doing those things you are automatically in the moment, they were just examples of when you *can* be in the moment}—but I had to give that parenthetical defense just in case you're being difficult. *AND YES*, me doing *this* all the time, this hearing of your voice, your potential criticism, your questions, this dialogue with you that doesn't exist, that I create, that I hear, is taking me one step beyond the Reflection Mode {which someone generally is in while writing} {which is in itself as you know a step back from the Now} {b/c imagining and running through a hypothetical examination of what *you're* thinking is certainly further from the Now than examining what *I'm* thinking}. So, now I'm TWO LAYERS deep away from the Now. I know this, I'm aware of this. And actually, me knowing this, being aware of the internal-dialogue-hypothetical-examination-of-what-you're-thinking mode that happens when I'm in the writing reflective/thinking mode which is itself the flip-side to the Now mode means I'm now THREE LAYERS deep, away from the Now.

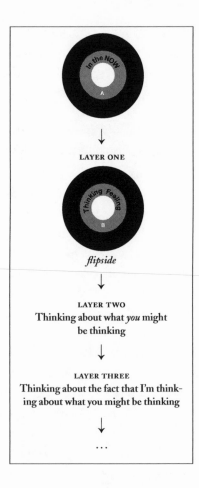

**LAYER ONE**

*flipside*

**LAYER TWO**
Thinking about what *you* might
be thinking

**LAYER THREE**
Thinking about the fact that I'm thinking about what you might be thinking

. . .

And I'm just gonna keep going further, layer upon layer, and you can hear my voice getting smaller and fainter getting lost in the distance, dissolving in the air, like I'm calling to you from the caboose of a fast moving train *Byyyyye byyyyye fohhhhlks!])*

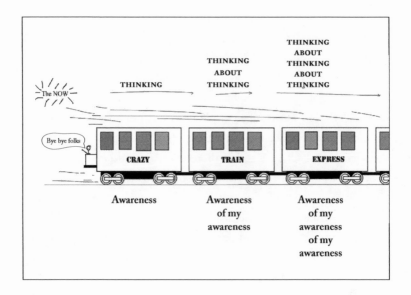

Anyway, so you can see the problem I face. Which is the real reality?— thinking or acting? I'm trapped in my head thinking but I'm afraid to leave and be in the moment because that isn't truly living, though those are the times I truly do feel alive but when I'm in those moments, in the Now, I sometimes involuntarily sabotage them by pulling myself out of the Now because (on some unconscious and to a degree conscious level) I'm afraid I'll get stuck in the Now and not be able to reflect ever again which would leave me basically just like an ant, not really alive in the way that reflection makes one alive. I'm stuck. (We're all stuck. I think. But since you don't worry about this crap the way I do and you're able to without much consideration slide effortlessly back and forth from the Now to Reflection and back again like a delicate and unconscious dance, your toes tapping on the surface of each world in artful syncopation, you're not really stuck—in a theoretical sense you have the same dilemma but since you don't worry about it then in a real sense you do not. The dilemma only matters if you let it matter).

I am so fucking afraid. I'm going to spend my whole life in my head, separate, removed, distant, watching the movie. I don't want to be stuck there. Please! I want to LIVE Goddamn It! (Stop smirking. I was saying "I want to live" in a joking voice. I'm not that dramatic. No! That is not true. I wasn't joking. *Look what you've done to me!* Is naked sincerity not allowed? Why do I fear that being earnest automatically makes me in your eyes a rube, a dork, a simpleton? I tell you I'm being sarcastic because then I'm protected; cynical, but protected. And it seems like the only time that I can take sincerity from people is when I know that they've gone through the stage of irony, that they've seen all the angles and layers, and now they have graduated back to sincerity. [Yes, Circle Theory again]. As if earnestness must be earned and elected. How do we tell the difference between the earnest originals and the born-agains? The only thing I know for certain is, is that I am jealous of anyone, regardless of how they got there, who is able to be earnest without worrying about the implications of how that comes across. Because I am swinging around the circle always landing in a different spot because while I know I want to be at the top of the circle resting in earnestness-land I can't seem to quiet this nagging voice telling me that I can only come across as sophisticated if I am not vulnerable, i.e. not earnest. I know this is not true. You know this is not true. Yet the voice persists. And let me tell you, I've been fighting that voice all the time and it's really scary and weird telling you so much, *being so earnest* and feeling so unprotected but there is no other choice because the other choice, to listen to that voice, will leave me utterly, utterly alone).

Can you believe this shit? I know this sounds crazy. I guess I am crazy. There's something very wrong with me. And by the way—this is fairly obvious but—if all I'm doing is reflecting and I'm never in Now Mode then what's the point of reflecting if I have nothing to reflect on? Sure, I'm still out there in the world doing things, buying a beer, walking down the street, chewing gum, whatever but I'm not really there, ever. I'm just watching myself do these things rather than really doing them. So, my reflections are really just reflections on reflections, rather than reflections on genuine moments that I would have been inside of, unconscious of at the time. And this problem of course speaks to the paradox of art and creating. Because when you're in the zone creating you're obviously not out there living. So, the more time you spend creating, making art, reflecting on life, the less time you actually are out there being *in* life. So, how can you accurately reflect on life when all or most of your time is spent not "out there" living, in Action, *in* life, but in your head?

I have no idea what I'm talking about. Or maybe I do. I don't know. I don't know. I don't know. I don't know anything. Yes I do. No I don't. Do doo doo. La dee dah. Drifting away . . . drifting away . . . There really is nothing left to do

# TV

**late june?**

This apartment is killing me. These fucking notes! Leave me alone! Shut up. They're all yelling at me, laughing at me. The yellow square army on full assault against its creator. How dare they! I MADE YOU! How dare you revolt against me! *We know, Dan; thank you for creating us* they're all saying, I can see them all flapping on the wall, the yellow squares like little mouths yapping as they talk to me.

*Guess what Dan? We are you.*

I have to get out. Get out of my head, get on the street, do something. STOP. Stop thinking. Shut Up Shut Up!

. . . I'm on the street. Wind. Air. People. Noise. Anything, anything. Bombard me, fill me up, take me away. I'm out I'm out I'm out I'm out! Adrenaline. Sweet sweet adrenaline, flowing through me. Flowing through me. Tight. Endorphins, baby. Dorphin. Dolphin! Porpoise. Purpose. What is my purpose? What is the purpose? My heart is thumping. My head is throbbing. The whole world is pulsing like I'm sitting inside John Bohnam's kick drum on the stage at MSG 1979. I'm ready to pop. I'm ready to smash someone in the face. Gimme a reason gimme a reason please someone. I want to smash you in the fucking face.

I explode into a run. A spastic dash of pure freedom. A frightened schnauzer taking a shit next to a tree barks ALARM as I gallop toward him. Without breaking stride I lean down to him, stare him in the eyes, and get so close to his face I can smell his doggie breath, "RAAAHHHH!" *Don't fuck with me pooch! This is primal!* The owner is yelling something at my back, though it just sounds like garbled noise. I want to run like this forever. I want to feel like this forever. Nothing can touch me. I cross Bowery. A car swerves and screeches to a halt, the driver leans on his horn and yells at me out his window. But I am already halfway down the next block. *Just try to catch me fucker!* I'm passing people right and left, making cuts like an all-star running back. Dead-ahead a family is holding hands three across. No time to—**BAM!**—I demolish the mom in the middle, knocking her out of my fucking way, the hands of her husband and kid torn out from hers as she stumbles forward and to the side; I hardly skip a beat and keep going. *This is easy! I'm in great shape! Those weaklings working out every day, sucking wind after a lame jog on a ten-thousand dollar treadmill at their bullshit gym. Ha!* **You people are all in my way!** I cut right heading north up Lafayette, planting my left foot, slamming it on the pavement so you can hear a *SLAP* as I turn on a dime. Here it is, a double-wide sidewalk straightaway. It's beautiful. I'm cruising now, like a skier in a deep-powder bowl, making gentle S-curves around pedestrians when I have to. *Am I breathing? I don't even know if my heart is beating at all.* I'm in a tunnel, all the people and buildings and sky and road and the plastic boxes with the freebie newspapers and screeching buses and stammering bums and the rotting garbage and the stinking shit, it's all melded together, smeared away off to the sides. There is no sound, there is no sight, there is no smell. I'm finally alone, all the world reduced to an amalgamated, gray, tubular streak around me as I zip through the tunnel. The world: what a pathetic joke. *This is all you got for me? Ha! You can't touch me!* I am alone. No senses, no thought, no intrusion. Just go. Run.

And then: for what seems like no reason at all, I stop running. I don't want to be walking but here I am, this is what I am doing. The obligatory fall. The inevitability of the letdown. My body, this physical shell cannot do what I want it to do. I feel heavy, my steps deliberate, my legs stiff and awkward. I hear my heart deep inside my ears. The tunnel starts to dissolve. I see Astor Place a few yards ahead. The sounds of the city fade back in and I see a vision of Tim floating in the sky with his hand sliding a master fader, the God Fader that controls the sound of the world. And even though I'm back again, the life-film rolling, the DP composing a great shot, the THX sound streaming through all the speakers, I can hear it, I can see it, I know I very much am here—but yet I am not fully here. *God, I wish it were two minutes ago.* I'd do anything to be alone again, free in my tunnel.

And yet now out of my ecstatic tunnel and in my state of being here yet not fully here I don't feel sad. Because the flipside to glory is not despair, (oh, if I could only feel despair), it's nothingness.

I've been here before, this familiar old haunt of numb unreality. The magic particles I felt, that swirled around and through me have all gone away, they're just a notion now, so vague and distant I'm not quite convinced they were ever there at all, this new state so starkly contrasted with where I was, like a prisoner after one day in the pen, already his life on the outside but a wispy dream like a film projected on a gossamer curtain blowing gently in front of an open window; what I once knew to be fact is now merely theory.

I cross Broadway in a mob of pedestrians, the thousandth of the day, the hundred-thousandth of the year, ordered by a traffic light in one-and-a-half minute cycles. I'd wish that I could feel sad if I had the energy to wish. This is not one of those rare times when the fear and anxiety have lifted and I am left at peace, bathing in a flood of serotonin (if only . . .); no, rather, the terror is still here, it's just delicately obscured under a thin veneer of blankness, like watery Wite-Out on top of black ink. Opaque. My body is coated, my senses filtering the world through a Vaseline sheen. Somehow I still feel fear while immersed in this nothingness yet my sense of it is oblique; in this state, even the purity, the beauty of fear is polluted, diluted, its fangs worn to mere suggestive nubs. The honor of true emotions, be they dark or bright, is sadly, sickeningly compromised. Desperately, somewhere in the recesses of my psyche I know I should feel terrified yet in this cloudy abyss I am in, terror, caring, wanting, *everything*, life itself is just a vague notion.

*Yet* somewhere, sprinkled in this void, in unseen particles of molecular dust, in the immeasurable distance of atomic minutia, is a message, a voice. And it says: *There is more.* We know you are afraid and we know you can't quite taste it but it's there waiting for you when you are ready to come back and take it. This numbness will not last forever. There is more

**late june?**

than this. You must hold on and remember, There is more than this.

And as I drift in this nothingness I must use all my strength gathered from depths I cannot know to reach for that voice. My mind's hand, outstretched trembling fingers, grasping for contact. The voice is a beacon; the sailor is so many miles offshore, in a moonless night, in a starless sky, seemingly lost in his blank nautical infinity, except for the faintest twinkle, it may not even be a twinkle, it may just be the reflection of a twinkle, but nevertheless(!) there is a flicker from a lighthouse on the shore. Hold on Dan. Hold on.

So I keep walking. I am not tired. I am not excited. I am not sad. And I wonder if I am not me, if I am anything at all. And the city is beginning to feel quiet. There's Tim again in the sky messing with the fader. But I can feel the subway grates under my feet; and I can see the cabs, feverish and yellow, lurching, surging down the avenue; and I can see all the girls walk on by but for once they are not magic, and they do not sparkle and shine and they do not sparkle and fade, they simply walk on by. And somehow, far away, I know this is wrong. And suddenly but subtly that distant notion of worry doesn't feel so far away. And now I am just the slightest bit nervous, oh yes, I can feel the tension coming on, and for that I am sad and glad. And inside I begin to churn, and I feel my fingers close in on themselves making fists on the end of my forearms like swinging mallets off my elbows. I look ahead and catch the sharp glint of late afternoon sun off an office-building window. My face is slapped with an ugly wince. And in that pin-prick of time I am gone, swooped up, lifted off the ground like some jerk attached to a recoiling bungee cord.

And there I am, the circus acrobat dangling from his practice safety cable, floating above, watching this guy Dan Green walk down the street. Seems like a nice fellow. Good looking guy as he walks down the street, I must say. This guy used to be me and sometimes I would watch me as him, him as me but I still knew I was me watching me. But now, that is no more. Now I just watch. And I'm not watching me. I'm watching this guy. Dan Green. Who *I* am is irrelevant or if not irrelevant, I must confess I am not thinking about it, I am not able to know. Dan is not on the screen though; he's in the 3D world and I'm just here, floating, omniscient watching him.

Poor Dan Green. He appears troubled, making strange faces, looking forlorn and agitated moving gingerly by himself down the street. A city bus, the mechanical, urban pachyderm cries out, its brakes squealing as it pulls up next to him at an M6 stop on lower Broadway. In that instant, the sound is back. Oh boy is it back! The God-Tim jolted his finger down, releasing a depressed *Mute* button on the mixing board in the sky: SCREEEEEEECH. To show you how piercing that sounds is, I wish I could make the letters jagged and angry, like a font from an 80s metal band. What the hell, I guess I can do that: **SCREEEEEEECH**. (One marvels at what angularity and gratuitous serifs can do!) They say that humans are attuned to certain frequencies more than others. As it seems it is with almost everything else—thinking certain women are hot, butterflies in your stomach when you're scared, etc. on and on—it's all rooted in survival. That's why when a baby is crying or little kids are screaming the sound slices through the air to us more than any other sound to the point sometimes that it hurts because nothing is more important than caring for that baby or that child. We must know if something is wrong, if they need us. The city bus screech must be near the same frequency as an infant's wail, only it's ten times louder. Dan has his fingers in his ears and is squatting and hunched over. The heavy flow of pedestrians just swerve around him as if he's an inanimate obstacle randomly left in the way. Two NYU students give passing glances at him as they walk by. Just another freak on the street. One of them turns around though for a double-take—aside from being hunched over in the middle of sidewalk traffic, he looks so normal, his clothes and whatnot, not like a disheveled, psychotic homeless person or something. For a moment it looks like she is going to walk back to see if he is hurt, if he needs help but she turns back around and keeps walking.

Why can't the world just Shut Up! He's sitting down now on the crowded sidewalk, his head buried between his knees. People are stepping over him, around him. After less than a minute a man leans down and asks if he's ok. Dan mumbles something, unsure, nodding his head. The man grabs his arm and pulls him up to his feet, looks him in the eye for some sort of certainty then walks away. Oh God, the noise of the city! The static. The noise of the world. They've done tests on rats, exposing them to constant noise. Within hours they all had high blood pressure. Within days they started to drop dead. It's true. They've done tests!

And worse than the breaks on those fucking buses and cabs is the metal on metal grind of a subway train pulling into the station. Every time you stand on the platform as a 6 Train pulls into the Astor Place station you shave one day off your life. I'm sure of it. Humans are not designed to take in this much Goddamned noise. And all these people. *They're* the real noise. *Look at them*. With their cell phones and their hair and their twitching hands and their bobbing heads and their moving mouths. And the girls with their absurd sunglasses the size of welders' shields. And the old, the poor, the pimple-faced teens, the jumpsuited street sweepers, the badass bike messengers, the too-hip, the not-hip-enough, they're all making waves. And it's not just the people, it's the shops. The bastard deli on Waverly charging forty-five cents for a fucking banana; it doesn't matter what their damn rent is, it's still a crime. And all these clothing stores lining the avenue selling wares with names and logos plastered all over them so idiots can show other idiots how rich or cool they are. And the fucking asphalt and the concrete and the light-killing too-tall towers. But oh! the beautiful women and the ugly girls and the hardened thugs and the homeless man and the German tourist studying his pocket map and that kid on a skateboard brazenly weaving amidst the cabs and the trucks and the swerving Jersey-plated SUV and the blown-up pop tart

**late june?**

looking at all of us with fake longing from her illuminated poster inside the window of Tower Records and in strobe light memories a violent slide flashing somewhere along the cerebral cortex Koala's smirking face. Everyone just needs to Shut The Fuck Up.

And we watch the character, Dan Green, walking around the streets for a long time, and we can sense his feeling of being surrounded by all of it. And then we see him sitting alone on his couch back home, staring at the wall. And then we watch him go into a hardware store on First Avenue where he buys a paint-mixing stick and a white piece of cardboard. Then we see him at home, laughing, cutting out the cardboard into a small octagonal-type shape and we see him with a black sharpie writing something on this shape. Then we see him take the paint-mixing stick and place it on the back of the cardboard and lay it down on the table. He then rifles through a box in his closet and comes out with a staple gun in his hand and staples the small cardboard cutout to the stick. We then see him on the street, and in what seems like arbitrary moments, pulling this thing from under his shirt and extending his arm out, stiff, to various people and objects of his choosing And we zoom in a bit and see the thing he's holding is a little sign, like one of those paddles that bidders use at an auction. And we swing around to the front and see that his little sign has large block letters that read:

**SHUT UP**

He is expressionless as he now walks with the sign at his side and remains deadpan as he lifts his arm and holds the sign in anyone's face he selects. SHUT UP. The East Village dude in his three-ringer T and permanent two-day stubble. Hey buddy: SHUT UP. Stupid JAP bitch whining on her cell phone: SHUT UP. Bushwick black kids with their nightgown basketball jerseys, and their swagger like they own the fucking sidewalk, blasting their shit-ass hip-hop distorting the speakers on their crapola boom-box. You guessed it: SHUT UP. And all those posters for the latest Macintosh or new Vodka or some banal indie-film hyped as some auteur's brilliant work that line all the boarded construction sites, yes, even you, because your presence makes more noise than people: SHUT UP.

Dan is looking a little crazy, folks, roaming the streets holding his sign at all objects animate and not. As I watch him descend the stairs to the Second Avenue F, I'm entertained but uneasy with worry at what's happening to him. The Brooklyn-bound F pulls in and he gets on and I'm no longer floating watching him. I'm now at home on the couch watching the screen and there's this cool shot of him sitting alone at the end of a subway car and they must be using a funky lens of some sort because the shot makes it look like the car is a mile long, and the symbolism, it's totally artsy and not in a pretentious or clichéd way but in a very powerful, moving way, lets you really feel, meditate on, how lonely he is/feels. And the DP (or is it done in editing?) has the shot in these washed-out pale blue tones where it all looks sickly and bleak under the subway car's fluorescent lights. And then I see this montage of shots where Dan is getting off one train, sitting on a platform, getting on another train, riding the train, getting off again, then switching to a different line and while riding that train the montage halts for a scene where we see him sitting in the middle of a half-empty car and there's an Asian man picking his nose sitting alone in the corner and Dan slowly, still with no expression holds up his sign to the man's face: SHUT UP. Then the montage continues of Dan riding more trains and sitting or standing at various platforms and then the montage fades to black indicating the film equivalent of an ellipsis, letting me know that this continues for some indeterminate amount of time.

And then the film fades back in and we see Dan sitting alone again in some unknown subway car and it's not clear to me how much time has gone by but I assume it's been several hours at least judging by the length and what I think was the intended effect of the preceding montage. Then I see three black teenagers in their ghetto-garb of sports jerseys

**late june?**

and shorts that are so long that they're really just cropped pants also sitting in the car. And the four of them are the only ones in the car, so now I assume it's late at night. And I see Dan lift up his sign at them and I see them laughing, startled and amused by this quirk of the New York City night. Then there's a shot of just them laughing and then one of the three abruptly stops laughing and says, "Hey man, why don't *you* shut the fuck up!" And his two friends are cackling away and the one kid gets up and walks toward Dan and now is visibly angry. Dan is just sitting there, with no expression and not saying a word, still holding the sign, pointing it right at the kid as he walks closer. And I can feel impending doom and I'm so angry with Dan for doing this and I want to shout at the screen at him What the fuck are you doing? But I know he's so far gone at this point that he's unable to help himself, that he's just completely detached from anything resembling sanity at this stage, and it's not clear whether he doesn't even know that he's holding this stupid sign anymore, doesn't even know that he is sitting in a subway car in New York City, doesn't even know his name or anything else, Or that maybe he does know exactly where he is and who he is and what is going to happen, it's just that he simply doesn't care. And I'm a little annoyed that this has to be the cliché of having minority teenagers be the ones who are going to bring the reckoning to our main character, (hero, if you will), rather than some white guy but so it goes and I tell myself to try not to be too PC about it and get too distracted by this element of the plot development. And I know exactly what's going to happen and I'm really tense watching this, I don't want to see it but I of course am riveted. And the sound drops out and I see the black teenager say something else to Dan and Dan just sitting there catatonic, and the kid grabs the sign out of his hand and throws it across the car and the longer Dan sits there not reacting the angrier the kid gets, then the kid takes his open hand and slaps Dan across the face and Dan is still just sitting there and the kid gets even angrier, Dan's defiance some sort of affront to him, a challenge, then he takes his

**late june?**

closed fist and whacks him on the side of his face and this knocks Dan's head to the side but he's still sitting there, and then there's a shot of the other two kids still uproariously laughing as if nothing in the scene had changed from two minutes before their friend started beating the shit out of this guy, and then, not in any sort of poetic or beautifying slow-motion shot but in an ugly, wide-angle, long-shot of the car in real-time we see the kid holding his fist at his side for a second, then in a sloppy, almost side-arm motion, swing his arm around and punch Dan square on the temple. And the camera stays still, holding the long shot of the car, the director opting for harsh real-time, stripping the scene of any-thing "cinematic" opting for an almost low-tech, documentary style as the most brutal way to show this scene. And in this long shot from seem-ingly the other end of the car we see the kid is just standing there looking down on Dan who is now flopped on his side, knocked unconscious. And then, after excruciating seconds of this image, s l o w w w w w l y, tick by tick the scene finally fades to black.

There are a few moments of black which may infer seconds or hours, there's no way to know. Then as the next scene starts to fade in I realize I am now in the theater in my reserved seat, a few in from the right side aisle in the back of the middle section. The screen is huge and it takes a moment for me to adjust after having been sitting on my couch previ-ously watching this all on a TV screen, just as it took me a moment to ad-just to the TV screen after I had been floating in space. And as I'm sitting here in the theater and watching this, I start to analyze it and I think: I don't know how believable all this is, this guy running around with a sign. *Who's the screenwriter for this?* I guess if the guy, this lead character, really "lost it" he might do something like this. But I don't know. If he's gonna lose it, how 'bout something more extreme—maybe some sort of psychedelic montage depicting his insanity, culminating with him jump-ing off a roof or something like that. But I accept that this is what's hap-pening and despite or perhaps because it's not the cliché "crazy"/acid trip montage thing (the abstract sequences, the exaggerated lead character POV shots with a hand-held camera, the kooky zooms and distorted images etc.), I'm totally zoned in on the screen now. You know, when you're in the theater but you don't even know you're in a theater anymore, you don't even know you're you anymore; the whole world, the only thing you're conscious of is this movie, and you only realize you were in that zone when the film ends or someone coughs or the girl sitting next to you grabs your hand and all of a sudden you're tugged out of the zone, your camera lens pulls back and you see the perimeters of the screen, and you see all the heads in front of you and you feel the air-conditioning and you see the exit signs at the bottom left and right corners of the theater.

I'm so totally in the zone that I'm *inside* the film now. And there's blood running down my face. I'm surprised that it feels just like water but I can taste that sick salty taste in my mouth and I touch my hand to my face and look down and see blood all over my hand and fingers. I look up and the car is empty and I see that I'm on the A Train. *How did I get on the A? I never ride the A.* The train pulls in to the 14th Street station and I hope I'm going downtown but I can't tell so rather than risk traveling another stop uptown I get out and figure I'll just walk home from there. I'm glad I got off because I look at the sign across the platform and realize the train *was* going uptown. *Where the hell was I coming from?*

Avoiding the gross thoroughfare that is 14th, I walk down 13th heading east. The street is deserted. Everything on my face hurts and my head is pounding and woozy. Strangely though, in this most extreme of nights, for what feels like the first time in my life, I'm not worried about whatever has happened to me, whatever is wrong with me. I start laughing for what feels like no reason at all and it feels good despite my head pulsing with a surge of pain with each bursting guffaw.

The walk seems to go on and on and on as I pass one townhouse after another and expensive apartment buildings I can't afford on the quiet blocks of 13th Street. I'm so utterly exhausted that I'm finding it hard to believe that

I am actually walking. I look at my feet moving one in front of the other and I feel separate from what they're doing, as if they're on auto-pilot. I chide myself for not switching to the L which I could have at least ridden cross-town to Third or First Ave cutting my walk by a good measure. Left. Right. Left. Right.

I remember back to when I got an endoscopy, the days when my stomach felt like it was on fire all the time, the burning so bad that almost nightly, I was getting woken up out of deep sleep to the taste of bile, thinking someone had cracked open a D battery and poured the acid in my mouth and I would look down at my stomach and plead with it to *please calm down*. And I would visualize my stomach coated in icy blue, just focus on that image until I fell back asleep sometimes not until hours later. And so I had this endoscopy done which means they stick a scope down your throat to look into your stomach and they give you a general anesthetic through an I.V., I think they call it "twilight" anesthesia. (After it was done is when they started me on those purple pills btw). But the whole reason I'm telling you this is because on the walk home from the doctor's office, there must have still been a lot anesthetic left in my system because I felt just like I do now. I was trying to walk at my normal pace but I was unable to move my legs any faster than a sort of slow-motion. I wasn't like an old man taking little steps, I was fully walking with nice big strides; I just couldn't do it at the normal speed. Perhaps I didn't look too different from an actor playing a zombie or from a mental patient from the fifties who had gotten a lobotomy. And I was pretty nervous because it was a disconcerting feeling to say the least and I thought maybe the anesthesiologist fucked up and gave me too much juice, he probably miscalculated my weight, I'm lighter than I look, and now I'm loaded with this stuff, and maybe it's not just flowing through my veins but I have some sort of neurological damage because he gave me too much juice and I'm going to have to walk like this, in this bizarre full-stride slow-motion forever. And then it occurs to me that maybe I'm walking completely normal but I'm just *perceiving* myself to be walking in slow-motion. But that's just as bad, I decide.

So, ANYWAY, here I am walking (or perceiving myself to be walking) just like that afternoon after the endoscopy. Right . . . Left . . . Right . . . Left . . . But this time I'm not nervous and for the second time on the walk I laugh but now it's a small chuckle, almost under my breath. I look up and see a twenty-something year-old guy approaching me going west. He stares at me long, turning around and slowing down as he passes me. I think this is the first person to pass me since I got out of the subway, five, or is it fifty? minutes ago.

*God, the streets really are empty; it must be very late.*

As I keep walking, the streetlamps and car headlights and lit-up store windows and glaring florescence leaking from the corner delis all fade; somehow the black of the sky—not the city sky but the real sky somewhere beyond the city sky—takes over and the world feels dark. Dark as it should be before man started with all these lights. And there in the darkness—not the sole visual in front of me as if I've lost perception of the physical world but an open-eyed vision seen at that same time as I see the real world, maybe something like a hologram but not the way they're depicted in movies, not a diaphanous hallucination but one that was solid and covering my full field of vision just like the real world—in front of me I see floating in the black space a triangle. Each point has a ball or dot on it like one of those three dimensional models of molecules in science class. And the three points on the triangle represent an album, a book, and a film; the words are written next to each point.

Even though I have not made a film or written a book, and I recorded an album but almost no one has heard it, I somehow understand that these three things together, floating here in space in front of me, *are* me, my statement. They are my pure soul, my way of communicating who I Truly am to others without the façades and filters of everyday life. No phony chit-chat, no nervous smiles, no explanations necessary. And although everything is dark, I feel warm and I don't feel nervous. And for the first time in my life I feel a tremendous pride in myself. This vision is so real, so intense, powerful, consuming, that it feels as though I actually *have* made an album, a book, and a film and this pride I feel is a pride of accomplishment. And with this newly proud me I realize that all I've been trying to do for so long is communicate. And all the nervousness and pain that I've been feeling is the struggle to communicate. And it's not that I'm saying I need to communicate because I have something so earth shatteringly important or consequential to the world to say, I guess maybe it's just that it's earth shatteringly important and consequential *to me* to say it. And the thing is, I don't even know what it is I've been trying to say, I just know now, that even if I never reach it, striving for the beauty of the triangle is enough for me to feel whole, for me to feel that I am alive. It's not about having the triangle finished, perhaps it's never finished, it's about the honest journey toward the triangle.*

After this initial wave of seeing my triangle and understanding all I just described above, I then shift and imagine—and not imagine as in just thinking about it but *deeply* imagine, completely embodying the notion, so much so that the duality of seeing the real world and the triangle world at the same time ends and now I only see, only live what I am imagining—that everyone on earth has this triangular representation of themselves, this not unfiltered but at least *less*-filtered way of communicating what they really are about, who they truly are (compared to how we communicate in regular life). And I say "less-filtered" knowing it's in contrast to having said earlier that the triangle was this Truly Pure way of

---

* Note: All this stuff was not broken down into this detail in my head at the time. I wasn't running through this step by step in my head—I can only do this now looking back—this all simply was *understood* in that moment.

**late june?**

communicating because the nuance of what I'm trying to say is that the purity isn't the triangle itself, it's in the honest process of everyone's striving to make their triangle. And then I realize that somehow we all have a magic power to absorb each other's triangles in their complete states *even if they aren't complete* because simply by a person striving to make his or her triangle in the most honest way, everyone else becomes enabled with this magic power to see the end result, the fully formed triangle anyway. The earnestness in the effort from someone somehow unlocks the truth for everyone else to see what it is they are trying to say even though they themselves most likely can't see it.

It's an actualization, a literal rendering of the cliché the journey is the destination: in this triangles-floating-in-the-darkness world, simply by attempting the journey (of making one's triangle) with sincerity, the destination (of communicating one's true self) is reached. All that's needed is the honest intent.[*] And with each one of these points on the triangle there wouldn't be any businessmen or marketing people or focus groups to alter the product, it would be pure, it would be art, solely the creation of the individual, no filters, no add-ons, no outside hand directing its creation.

And it doesn't matter if you can't sing, or if you can't write, everyone would find their voice in some medium one way or another. Everyone can have their own three things on their triangle. Maybe one person would have: dance, book, painting; another person would have: album, photograph, black pen design; another person: avant performance piece, sculpture, multi-media painting type thing. People would have artistic

---

[*] A weird side note for those interested in an academic deconstruction of the Triangle Vision: it strikes me that there's something vaguely Marxist—*each according to his ability*—about this. Not in the sense of capital distribution obviously but in the sense that in this vision honest effort alone (i.e. working to one's ability) is sufficient to reward oneself and society; in this case the reward being communication of who we really are, our souls/essences/etc. to each other. And as long as I'm getting scholastically tangential here, doesn't the biblical "to every thing there is a season and a time to every purpose" have some sort of link to this Marxist sentiment?

creations in media I can't even fathom on one or all of their three points. It doesn't matter. Three things to cover all bases. And but maybe even some people would just have two things and that would be ok too, those two things would cover everything they needed to say. And maybe some would just have one point. And maybe their point isn't "art" but the most perfect blade of grass. And somehow when we see that person's one point representation and we see that that one point is the blade of grass we would just *know*, we would understand what that means and it somehow would explain everything.

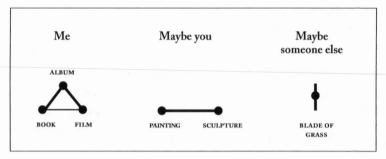

And unlike the art we have in real life, it can't be judged and it can't be clichéd or lame or too weird or too difficult or anything bad. So no one has to be afraid of people putting it down. It is simply everyone's Truth. And since it's everyone's Truth, these artistic things wouldn't even be representations of people; they *are* the people. And here's something I need to impress upon you: it's as if there only is this other world; people and the normal world as we know it don't exist anymore. There are no trees, no buildings, no sky, no physical beings moving around. Nothing except darkness and these triangles floating. Billions of them. Or maybe we still all do exist here on earth in this dimension but there is this other dimension, the triangle dimension, happening right now at the same time. Either way, I can see, feel, *know* it's there, that it exists. We're all floating around in dark space as these triangles and we don't even have

**late june?**

to read the books or watch the dance routines or see the films; simply by seeing each other's triangle, we would just *know* the full contents and meaning of it. Who we all are would be unsaid, any explanations and interpretations unnecessary. Each of us a floating triangle in the darkness, pure; experiencing a connection that supersedes talk or any other communication. And I'm just bursting with love and excitement and peace in imagining showing who I truly am to everyone. Finally! And everyone is showing who they really are to each other. Everything would simply be the truth and we would understand everything as it's meant to be understood. And knowing all these billions of separate, different truths would in fact make us all connected. Separate but one.

Then this vision of the universal triangle world dissolves and I am back in the duality of the two worlds of the nighttime city street and of looking at my lone floating-triangle-in-dark. And I continue back in this dual world for some time. And then at some point, on some street, I realize that I'm suddenly quite nervous. Because now even the lone triangle world is starting to dissolve and I am coming closer and closer to only being on the city street. And as I come closer to the normal world again, I begin to gain the wherewithal that what I was just experiencing was borderline, if not downright, psychotic. And I'm relieved to be returning to sanity but also sad to be leaving my triangle-floating-in-the-darkness world, and also increasingly scared that I was there. I start to wonder how this possibly could have happened. What exactly is going on with my brain? I decide that maybe the part of the brain that handles thoughts and imagination—(and I don't mean the part that handles just wishing for something really hard, I'm talking deep unconscious abstract thought processes)—for some reason became so powerfully charged that whatever was in there transcended out of my head into the realm of the world in front of me. That if something in your mind is truly powerful, transcendentally so, and if the right ingredients of circumstance are present, then it can break through, combining the thought world with the real world.

Granted this new world is all just in one's head but at the time it feels as real as regular old reality. Coming up with this explanation though offers no consolation to the growing terror I am experiencing as I further acclimate to the street. Yet strangely, in my growing terror I retain a residue of serenity lingering from the TFITD*world, that even though I'm back in the harshness of ROR**, the way you can sometimes sense someone's former presence in a room, the other world remains.

I look up and see that at some point I had turned off of 13th and onto Fourth Avenue and am now outside Jason's place. Finding myself in front of Jay's now is kind of like when you are driving and you space-out and all of a sudden shake your head and realize that you totally weren't paying attention at all to the highway for the past ten minutes; you weren't completely gone, you weren't asleep, if someone pulled in front of you, you probably would have seen them and slammed on the breaks or swerved into the other lane but still, you weren't totally there either. I think on a certain subconscious level during all this I knew that I did not want to be alone and my body steered itself on auto-pilot to Jay's.

I buzz him and wait a minute but there's no answer.

*Fuck. Jen! He already moved in with her. I am the last man in Manhattan.*

I buzz again, this time holding it down for a solid ten seconds.

"Hello?" comes crackling out of the intercom.

"Jay, it's Dan. Can I come up?"

"Dude, it's three o'clock in the morning."

*Shit.*

There's silence just for a moment, then the door buzzes letting me in.

I push on his apartment door and it's unlocked, as always. Jay is behind his turntables with headphones around his neck.

He mouths "Oh my God," drops the headphones on the table and walks toward me. "Dan, what the fuck happened to you?"

---

* Triangle(s) Floating In The Darkness
** regular old reality

**late june?**

"What?! What?!" I'm more startled than frightened, the triangle episode having left me with a slight protective haze. I scurry to the bathroom and look in the mirror. My face, beaten like an outclassed boxer's, a golf-ball inside my cheek, my right eye swollen, the puffed skin a dirty red and there is dried blood in a trail from my nose down my face and neck onto and all over my shirt. I am the NBA star's abused wife, the car-crashed toddler without a baby-seat. *My face*—I had completely forgotten.

"What happened!" Jay repeats as he follows me into the bathroom, both of us looking at me in the mirror now.

"I, I . . . I don't know." My voice comes out shakier than I expected.

"What do you mean? What are you talking about?" Each question incrementally sped up and louder. "Whatthehellhappened?"

"I'm not sure." My jaw is clicking with each syllable, all movement accompanied by searing pain along the whole left side of my mandible. "Something—. I was on the subway . . . And—" He can see I'm trying to piece it together but nothing is coming. Mercifully he doesn't press me on it. He leaves the bathroom, walks across the apartment then tosses me a clean t-shirt. I gingerly pull mine off over my head and run his under the tap and wipe my face and neck. He brings me some ice and we sit down on the couch.

"The shirt was for you to put on not to use as a rag," he says smiling.

"I thought you were moving." I delicately rub my jaw and moan. My bite feels off, my teeth unaligned.

"Next week."

"I don't know what's happening to me."

"You're going to be ok. I'm here," he says, even though I sense we both know that's just one of those things people say even if they're not sure it's true.

I feel my face pulsing from the inside. I pull the ice away and touch my cheekbone but the skin is numb. I put the ice back.

"I just don't know what's going on anymore," I say, the words warbling through an LLQ like a chanteuse on an old 78. "With anything."

**late june?**

I'm shaking like I have fever chills. I think I'm about to cry but I can't. It feels stuck. "I think there's something wrong with me. I mean that I don't remember anything . . . I was outside this afternoon and then . . . I don't know. It's just sort of fuzz after that."

"It's ok, man. Just relax."

I try to talk but I can't seem to formulate words. Nothing is coming out. My jaw is moving (and clicking unfortunately) but my vocal chords are clipped. The room starts to distort like one of those little, rounded rear-view mirrors that truckers stick on top of the large rectangular one. A thousand butterflies flutter on my naked torso and arms and it feels like grease is swirling in my stomach and up into my head. Jay is talking to me but there's all this static like he's on a distant AM radio station. I can barely make out what he's saying. I'm squinting with my ears to hear him through all the crackle and fuzz. I'm desperate to hear him but the signal is too weak, the air flooded with static. But, and here's the really strange part during this—I am not scared. In fact, I'm almost relaxed. *What is this? This is not a panic attack. I know what panic attacks feel like. It's something else. But what? What's happening to me?*

My brain is on its way, somewhere. I'm here but I'm not here. I know exactly what's going on yet, I don't. I'm right fucking here but, I'm not.

*So, this is what it's like to be insane. It's not so bad.*

And now I'm starting to feel a little afraid and also a little happy, excited even. *Do do doo, la de dah.*

Goodbye cruel world; don't know where I'm going but I'm on my way; this is Major Tom to ground control, I'm stepping through the door.

Aaaaand, but look at this, the room is coming back now. The contour of the little, round side-mirror is flattening out. The static is dissolving into the ether like dispersing mist from a can of hairspray. I see Jay in front of me. The triangle! I start telling him all about the TFITD. And talking about it brings back the feeling I had on the street, the peace, the oneness. It feels, I feel, beautiful. Then: while I'm talking I feel myself start to shift. Somehow, and for some reason, while talking about the triangle, I slip from being in a past tense Memory Mode into a present tense Thinking Mode and like a submarine bursting through the ocean's surface, a realization dramatically materializes in my mind:

*I have felt the pressure, the anguish over what people have thought about me my whole life. I've been* **So Fucking Worried** *about what people think about me my whole life.*

I'm not sure what this has to do with the triangle, if anything, all I know is this is what has come to me. And I know this seems like some incredibly naïve realization. In fact I've been under the impression for quite some time that I *didn't* really care what people thought about me, that I outgrew that. I mean, sure, I cared a little bit, and I know by watching me all this time it might seem perhaps that I cared a whole lot, but really, essentially, I've always thought I was pretty much above all that, that even if I did consciously care it was just surface level, my core was solid, indifferent to others, resolute. I had really believed this on the deepest level that I was aware of. I knew this to be true. But somehow, on some even deeper level that I didn't know exists, apparently it was not. And I'm terrified now because I can't believe that I've been so Goddamned self-conscious all along, and that what I thought, what I *believed* to be true about myself is not so; that I don't even know myself; that the truth has suddenly been revealed to me and it is ugly. I've been walking around some cocktail party with a tiny sprig of parsley stuck between my front teeth that must have gotten there from some foofy hors d' oeuvre I ate two hours ago and I only notice it now when I'm in the bathroom giving myself the obligatory glance-of-reassurance-before-walking-back-out and instead of a quick head-nod-of-approval to myself and I'm out the door, I see this jackass in the mirror grinning with a green shrub between his teeth. I had this crap between my teeth all along and I didn't even know it! Ok, not the best analogy. Take that feeling times, like, a thousand.

And what's extraordinary is that I feel a tremendous positive rush because I am suddenly seeing something in myself that until this moment I had been unable to see—the truth!—yet at the same time I'm horrified and immensely saddened at what the truth really is. And this overwhelming notion takes me under like a wave, my body upside down, my head being ground into the sand.

*So fucking self-conscious. My whole life. And I never knew.*

Then, in one moment, I am at once in the past tense Memory Mode, my mind inside the triangle zone *and at the same time* I'm also in the present tense Thinking Mode, my mind processing the Realization. And the feelings of the MM (TFITD)—a profound sense of piece, oneness, and beauty—COLLIDE with the feelings of the TM (the Realization)—a dark shame not only from knowing that the truth has remained hidden from me for so long, but also that once I finally have found out the truth about myself, I see it is ugly, and weak.[*]

And so these two super-deluxe max-level diametrically opposed feelings of beauty/terror, serenity/horror, pride/shame converge in me at the same time.

I would love to insert some sort of onomatopoeia right here—a *flash*, a *bam*, a *whoosh*, *zam*, *zing*, whatever, *something*, to try to give some sense

---

[*] I don't mean caring what other people think, specifically or exclusively means you are ugly and weak—I recognize that not only is it totally "ok," it's even essential, on a certain level or in a certain way or at certain times to "care" what others think about us if we want to be "good" people—being good to others and even yourself sometimes *requires* caring about and knowing what other people think of you.

What I mean is that the notion, "I don't care what anyone thinks about me," in the sense that you're comfortable with who you are, that you aren't an overtly phony person who excessively tries to please others or tremendously insecure person whose every move is thought out in regard to how others might perceive it, is now suddenly something I'm not so sure I can say or feel, and *that's* what feels ugly and weak.

**late june?**

of the weight of the initial moment, to give the impression of the wave, the wall, the force, the *raw power* of the cerebral and psychic overload of two diametrically opposed states on top of each other, within each other, colliding, converging, combusting, but there is no sound, there is no flash of light, it's too large for any sense, and so for the briefest of moments, there is a state of utter complete blankness, the information overload too awesome to process, the calm before the storm, the *rest* in the score before the full orchestra erupts, the sharp intake of breath before the scream, the electrical second before the first kiss. And then:

I am inside myself, in the Now, in *it*. I am outside myself, separate, watching. I'm here. I'm not here. I'm everywhere. Nowhere. My eyes are shut tightly. I think they are. Or maybe they're open. I don't know. My head is bobbing, shaking, trembling though it is utterly still. Everything Everything Everything! churning in a blur like the inside of a blender, torrential force pushing on the outer walls trying to burst free but not a tear, not a sound. Every synapse firing, electric currents sparking madly like glorious roman candles. Dendrites burning like spinning pinwheels shooting bottle rockets into the night sky. And all those chemicals, the serotonins, the dopamines, adrenalins simultaneously erupting, release valves pumping like Formula 1 pistons, the neural cocktail surging with the rage of Poseidon around my brain and throughout my system. The generator is shaking and getting ready to blow. The lid on the cauldron is rattling and about to bubble over. I am a Mack Truck engine roaring inside a VW Beetle. I am not built for this. I do not want this. I have no control. I just might literally combust or explode. My body, the skin, the blood, the bones, it's nothing, just a shell, as delicate as a fly's wing to be shredded into particles carried like dust in the breeze, a Baccarat crystal vase to be shattered, blown apart, dissipated, decimated, annihilated. Physicality, morphology, tangibility is nothing. Nothing! Everything I truly am is impalpable, celestial, from the ether. I'm untouchable, baby.

Invincible! I'm pure energy. I'm nothing and everything. The most horrific terror is upon me, imprisonment in the throes of imminent death and never-ending confusion. The most sublime bliss is engulfing me, a thousand times cumming, answers, The Answer, finally within me. Truth, beauty, God, spirit, energy, vibes, purity, magic waves. It's all the same shit. It's all just about tapping into that special place that is more than ourselves. Or no!, it is *exactly* ourselves. You reach a certain point where everything converges, at their peaks they are all the same they just got there from different directions. Because here it is, the pendulum has swung all the way around, there is no arc, there is only a circle and every single emotion there ever was is topped off, maxed out, at its peak, piled on top of each other, within each other, on the same mark on the far far end of the circle, a thousand hands of the clock merged together at 12. Because at their peak, in their purest essence, they are either on or they are not. And mother fucker, They Are ON. And everything is bright. And I am ON, more on than I have ever been. I am *Ultra*-Alive. And a message arrives riding a lightning bolt fired into my head from a void: I DON'T CARE WHAT ANYONE FUCKING THINKS ABOUT ME! I don't *think* that I don't care. For the first time, **I *know*** that I don't care. Fuck *thinking*, this is *knowing*. This message, the words, flashing over and over, faster than a strobe light, teetering in a realm of speed that's as fast as it can get before it is solid, it's but one flicker, one frame away. There is only knowing these words in my head, the flashing light: I don't care what anyone thinks about me. There is nothing else. I am stronger than I have ever been. I can wrestle a wild boar into submission. I am brilliant, glowing energy. I see myself lifting up his coffee table and hurling it across the room smashing into his TV and his bookshelves and stereo. I have no control. I am on internal-chemical-spiritual-induced auto-pilot. I am terrified. But! What is this?! To my surprise, to my relief the table is still here. Somehow, on some unknown level beyond the chaos I must have had just enough of a grip on reality, this room, this world as we know it, that I actually *am still here*; it was only my ghost I saw, a crazed doppelganger from another dimension throwing the table. All right! I'm not totally gone! The giant ship is far out to sea but there is a thin, weathered rope still tethered to the pier. But now, no! that rope is unseen, perhaps it's burst free; I do not know for I am on the top deck, two hundred feet above the vast rippling ocean surface and I am nowhere near land. Perhaps I *am* gone now for sure. And this whole time the room has been bathed in orange. YELLOW BLAST. I see my head and my bare torso. And I see Jason's head in the room except the room I see us in has small, lead-paned, rectangular windows (like nineteenth century brownstones have in the West Village) and the room is filled with sun. Not sunlight. SUN. Itself. It's like I have just stepped outside into the brightest day you can ever imagine and you can only make out vague shapes and colors, like we are inside overexposed film. But the brightness isn't washed out. Everything is blazing yellow and red and orange and white and everything, the world, our world, is viscous, as if we are in a new atmosphere where you can feel it, like being underwater except it isn't like water because it isn't cool or dark or blue, it is orange orange ORANGE! All the laws have changed, the properties realigned, there is no air, there are no elements, just orange flow all around us, within us, and we are within it. So much orange! so much Light! that light itself is present, tangible, physical, Real, everywhere, to be held, touched, surrounding us, surrounding everything. We are swimming inside the sun. And everything is warm and good and I am relaxed and happy.

· · ·

At the risk of belaboring the explanation for the sake of clarity (and because, clearly, I just really dig them), here's a diagram:

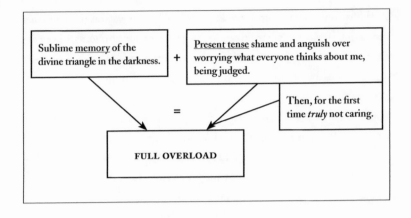

Listen, I know what you're thinking: *This is it? This is the big epiphany? The great insight?—that you reach nirvana, oneness, an ecstatic peace— (whatever-the-hell you want to call it)—when you don't care what anyone thinks of you?* I know; I'm with you. To be honest, I feel kind of disappointed too. *This* was my moment of zen? My revelation? Not caring what people think? Yeesh. I didn't realize that self-consciousness was causing me so much inner turmoil. And I don't want to get into the whole *knowing* versus *thinking* thing again but really, to one degree or another over the years, I truly thought I was above caring. But I was wrong. It's almost embarrassing. I always figured inner-peace would come from something grander, a loftier realization. Something I'd be overwhelmed with while atop a mountain. But maybe I'm not to take the words literally, maybe it wasn't specifically the relief from worrying about what others think but more simply, a relief from self-consciousness, a liberation from worrying about what *I* think of myself, how I view myself. I'm so fucking nervous about everything all the time, I finally, if only for a long moment, didn't care about anything. Not in some nihilistic way. I just knew that everything was right, that I was right, that my heart was right, that I was ok. Nothing I had ever done was wrong, I was on the right path, nothing mattered. I was me and whatever that was/is is ok. I was released from everything, all of it. Emancipation.

**late june?**

I'm on Jay's couch under a blanket. He's snoozing away, probably dreaming of Jen and their loft in Williamsburg. Strangely, it didn't take long for me to come back to earth. The light meter fixed, the tint adjusted, my mind recalibrated to ROR. I've got some *major* residual jitters but still, as I lie here on Jay's couch, I am back.

"I don't know what's happening, man," I say out loud even though I know Jay is asleep. I think I'm just testing myself and I needed to hear my voice to confirm that I am in fact here. My jaw is still sore but my voice comes out pretty solid and this feels good, like gaining your bearing after stepping off a boat onto the dock. It's so dark in here. What a luxury compared to my place with that damn alleyway light bleeding though my window. I had forgotten the pleasure, the normalcy of going to sleep in total darkness. Though of course I cannot sleep. My mind is scrolling over all that has happened. For once though it's not racing, I'm too drained for that, but still I'm not quite able yet to turn it off.

I keep getting hung up on the notion that this all happened to me without being on drugs. I find this to be the most frightening aspect of all of this. If I had dropped acid and this happened, it would still be heavy but at least I'd know what caused it. What worries me is I'm not only contending with what happened but that it occurred without any artificial trigger, without a deliberate outside inducement. I keep thinking that *that*, whatever it was, shouldn't happen to someone without drugs—acid, shrooms, peyote, salvia, whatever. Leaving earth should be voluntary. I have no control. And even though it was the highest bliss, it also was the worst terror. I guess maybe there is such a thing as feeling too much. I don't want this again. (Ok, eighty-percent of me doesn't want this again. How can I not have a small part of me that wants to know such power again? But stil—twenty-percent—no more.) How do I know this won't happen again! I have no control. I'm so tired. Why can't I stop thinking? Is it possible someone slipped me acid and I didn't know? When I was in junior high kids used to talk about how some psycho or maybe just a real asshole had put acid on the back of stamps and on those strips of paper that had those little candies glued on them that looked like solid pastel ladybug shells that you bit off. I've always suspected that I got one of the paper strips with acid on it and that that sort of explained everything weird that my mind has ever taken me through. So maybe this was just one of the flashbacks—like the panic attacks and those times when I don't understand anything at all, only this time of course it was much much more, a spike on the graph—that I'm going to be plagued with the rest of my life. If this is the case, it's still no consolation but at least it explains things. Maybe I'm—

– *Here we go again. Do you really have to start in with the worrying now? After all this? Can't you just wait until tomorrow?*

– I know. I'm sorry. I can't stop myself.

– *Just stop.*

– Besides, I think worrying about this is totally warranted. I mean, something really heavy just happened here. I mean, I was really gone, in some other dimension.

– *Like Jay told you before ordering you to sleep over on the couch—it's a gift. People search for this type of experience their whole lives, taking crazy drugs, going on retreats, zenning-out with OM. It was beautiful. You're lucky.*

– I'm scared.

– *I know. It's ok.*

– It's so dark in here. I'm really tired.

– *It's ok.*

– I think there's something really wrong with me. Come on! Let's face it, there's something really wrong with me. My brain was malfunctioning. I was losing my mind.

– *Maybe it wasn't malfunctioning; maybe it was mega-functioning, using sections previously untapped. You were transcending beyond the normal ten percent or whatever miniscule amount it is that people use.*

– Malfunction, mega-function—is there really a difference? This **isn't** supposed to happen without drugs. I mean, I know it can happen on its own but I'm not sure I want it to happen. To me. I mean—

– *I thought you were tired?*

– I *am* tired but I can't stop.

– *Stop.*

– Until tonight I thought I understood things about myself. I thought I knew before but I didn't and I didn't realize how far off I was until I went through it. Intellectual versus the experiential. The difference between knowing and *knowing*. I had never truly *understood* it until it was happening to me.

– *I thought you were tired? Just stop.*

– I'm trying.

– *Shhhhh.*

As I lay here drifting, finally, drifting off to sleep, I realize that somehow this all let me know that I am on the right path. That I don't know what the fuck is going to happen with me. I don't know what this all means. I don't know what all those notes mean. And it doesn't even matter anymore. All that matters is that I am on the path.

# IV

# JULY

I rolled my head to the side to steal another look. She was thin but well-built with a strong, athletic tone to her, like a professional beach volleyball player. She was lying on her back, yellow string bikini, body glistening with sweat. I locked in on her waist. Her hips jutted out, just beyond the surface of her stomach, so the top front of her suit-bottom ran across from hip to hip not touching the skin in between, making a little bridge. *Maybe* it was just grazing in the middle. In the blaring sunlight with squinted eyes I stared into the space below the bikini bridge trying feebly to see something in the dark of the little tented area.

I rolled my head back facing the sky, closed my eyes, and saw shapes and designs floating in the colors of the sun on the underside of my eyelids. My back was itchy even though I was on a towel. Central Park. There was so much grass surrounding me on the meadow, the power of suggestion made me feel it on my back anyway. *Don't. Look. Again.* I rolled my head to the side again pretending to keep my eyes closed, trying to open them just a slit and without squinting, peering through an out-of-focus mesh of eyelashes. Ohh that smooth, lean body, that slinky bikini bottom, taut as a snare drum. If I could just crawl into that little tent under the bikini bridge. It's why we like skirts (and why women wear them and men don't [excluding Scotsmen])—they represent, symbolize, allude to that space to be entered. Yes, it makes perfect sense: the skirt is the extension of the vagina. Girls have always asked, "what's it like to have sex as a man?" It's like the satisfaction you had when you were a little kid building a fort with pillows and blankets and then crawling inside. Everything is warm and dark and you're protected and cozy. I want to be inside every skirt I see. It's not specifically that she's thin— (in fact, I do prefer a bit more meat)—it's the bridge made by those outstanding hips. With its ten-fold symbolic power of a skirt, I want to be inside that bikini tent.

"How long are you going to keep ogling that woman?" A voice from behind me whispered to the back of my head. I twisted around my head first then my body following, flipping onto my stomach. Lying on her stomach, her head propped up with her chin in her hands, a beautiful, older, maybe late thirties, otherwise-fair-skinned face colored by converging freckles, framed by straight red hair hanging, kissing the tips of the blades of grass met me with a broad grinning gaze.

"I . . ."

"Oh, I'm just teasing you, Silly," she said, her smile expanding now, revealing a wide set of perfect teeth.

"How long have you been here right behind me?" I was less embarrassed than I thought I would be. Her good cheer softened the blow.

"Oh, I don't know. Ten minutes. Twenty minutes."

"Twenty minutes?"

She laughed, her wide mouth opening wide and her head tilting back just a bit so I could see the underside of that wall of ivory blocks. Somehow with her laugh, any concerns I had were dismissed. Beautiful women, they can get away with anything. "Besides staring at girls, what are you doing in the park in the middle of the day? *Dreaming* of your book?" She said "dreaming" in a voice that was both sexy and funny, dragging out the eee.

"How did you know I was writing a book? I mean I'm not writing a book. But, I mean I'm not a banker or anything. I just mean I don't have a regular job." I don't know how to talk.

"Yeah, I figured investment bankers aren't lounging in the meadow on a Tuesday afternoon. You look too sad, a little too weathered to be a student. And the shaggy hair, something about your demeanor. I figured either some angry young guy working on a book or a musician. You seem too determined, too angry or is it sad?—Why are you sad baby?— to just be some dude chillin in the park. I could tell—you're working on something."

"Wow. I'm . . ."

"You big dork" she said, breaking up laughing in mid sentence—this time more of an exhale burst through her lips rather than the head-tilt open-mouth laugh from before—grabbing my notebook that was lying on the grass next to arm and smacked my shoulder with it. "What's this!"

"How'd you know it wasn't for, I mean how do you know it *isn't* for something else? Like a journal or, or maybe I'm an artist and it's for my sketches. It's not automatically a book."

"If you were an artist you'd be more aware of your surroundings and you would have known there was a smoking hot red-head lying on the grass watching you."

"Well, I'm not writing a book." Was I writing a book? When she initially said so it seemed right but I didn't know what I was doing. Recently, actually today was the first day, I decided to try writing my notes in a small book rather than post-its. I was running out of room in my apartment. "Don't confuse deduction with intuition."

"Whew!" In a swift move of gymnastic prowess she sprung from her prone position to her feet. She reached her hand down to me, "Come on big shot, on your feet."

She pulled me up then let go of my right hand and grabbed my left and started walking, tugging me along for the first step until I realized she was walking. A distant voice questioned what was happening but she moved fast and projected such authority that one had to be swept in her wake.

"I'm Ambrosia," she said turning to me as we walked through the mostly empty meadow. "You can call me Amber or Rose. Pick one."

"Which do you prefer?"

"Neither actually. I prefer Sandy . . . it's from my mom, when I was a kid and never wanted to leave the beach."

"Then why didn't you just tell me to call you Sandy?"

"Because I wanted to see which one you'd pick. It's a test. Rose is an old woman's name. And Amber is for a girl who's probably hot but the name's still a little cheesy. Whichever one you'd pick says something about your personality or what you think of me. But asking me which one *I* prefer says something too."

"What does it say?"

"I have no idea." Head-tilt mouth-wide, underside of gleaming choppers.

"You've got a great set of teeth."

"I know! Thank you."

We exited the meadow and strolled through the park holding hands like young lovers. I was glad that in the past few days the last remnants of my shiner had finally faded away. The clicking of my TMJ and the half-a-golf-ball on my temple repaired themselves mostly within a week but that damn shiner took a lot longer, changing colors and shape daily until settling in for a very long final stretch as a smear of dark mustard under my eye. I never looked tough with the bruises, just ugly.

She was in New York for two weeks for the launch of an exhibit of her art at Dia: Chelsea, the abstract art museum.

"What type of art do you do?" I asked as the sound of the organ from the carousel floated over the trees from somewhere nearby.

"The short answer is mixed-media collage."

"Like paintings but you use other materials on the canvas besides just paint?"

"Yeah . . . but I work in sculpture too. And video, computers, installation."

"So basically, you do whatever you want." What am I doing holding this woman's hand walking through the park?

"Yes, that's the trick," she said. "I can do whatever I want!" She gave a swing with her arm, pulling mine with it.

"So, if you're visiting New York, where do you live?"

"Good ol' Mississippi. The Ol' Miss."

"Mississippi?"

"I'm a professor of art at Mississippi State."

"Oh . . . But still, Mississippi?" I wondered out-loud.

"I travel to New York and other major cities often enough, sometimes as much as ten times a year for shows of my work or to do research or just visit people. I like having a home-base separate from the art world, a place where I can essentially be by myself and not be bothered. I go around out into the world, I absorb, then I go home and reflect and create."

"That makes sense," I said. "But why college? I mean, why not just make your art."

"Well, for one, I get health insurance. But mainly I'm there just lending them my name. I teach one class a semester and that little bit of interaction with the students is fun. I like exposing people to new things. Plus, they were the only people to offer me a job fourteen years ago when every other art program told me to take a hike. So now that I'm a success," she jangled her arms in the air when she said "success" which I took to be the opposite of ironic air-quotes; it was a sincere and matter-of-fact declaration, "I feel like I owe them."

My palm was beginning to sweat. Or I feared it was beginning to sweat. The colors of the park, the green of the leaves and the grass was near-phosphorescent, her strawberry hair glinting, her blue eyes shining reflecting the sun, the magenta and white hydrangea popping, everything vivid, saturated, like an ultra-high-def film, where the tint is so rich it seems fake.

"That makes sense," I said again, feeling dumb for repeating myself but I didn't know what else to say.

"What a beautiful day!" She said and breathed in deep through her nose. An exquisite feature, compact and almost chiseled but its tip was softened and its sides blended down into wells before the swell of her cheekbones, as if her face was first sculpted with tools then smoothed over by the artisan's fingers.

"It is. I was just thinking how everything, the colors, the smell, it all seems almost hyperreal."

"I don't believe in hyperreal. This is what it is. That's what makes it so special."

"But you know, Central Park, this is all man-made, the simula—"

"Hah! Are you trying to bust Baudrillard on me?" she shook her head, incredulous, amused. "Let's go grab an ice cream." She squeezed my hand and grinned, then she let go and smacked my ass and ran ahead. I paused a beat, unsure of everything for a moment, then took off after her.

---

Ok. Listen:

before I get to the part where we go back to her hotel room and fuck in the middle of the day I need to apologize for and/or at least explain this narrative development. I owe it to you. Because I have Plot Guilt. Because let me warn you now, from here on out it's all straight-ahead Action/plot/highlights/drama. And how can I do this to you in light of the Fiction/Action-Falseness Dilemma? How could I lament that all the A/p/h/d* in all the fiction that surrounds us is making me sad, angry, confused and basically driving me crazy and then perpetuate the problem? *Betrayal!* you cry. **BUT** the problem is—the following happened. Real life after all does have its highlight-packed times. And so to not rev up the action for the rest of the story just because I'm worried that you'll think it's a cheap plot enhancer and that I'm hypocritically perpetuating the F/A-FD**, wouldn't be right. It has to be in. So, consider this my explanatory mea culpa, my apologia for what is about to happen for the rest of the story. You know I'm fighting the good fight here, I'm trying.

---

* Action/plot/highlights/drama
** Fiction/Action-Falseness Dilemma

Just remember, for the vast majority of time *nothing happened at all*, internalize it, remind yourself so you don't fall into the F/A-FD that's been killing me for so long.

(Btw, I recognize that for many of you, perhaps you've never felt any repercussions of the F/A-FD, that unlike me you're completely fine with your life and are neither obsessed nor even just slightly singed from time to time by the grass is greener/I-need-to-be-doing-more-with-my-life/ my-life-feels-repetitive-and-dull/etc. mindset [that I propose is at the very least indirectly related to the F/A-FD] and this whole apologia/ explanation for the forthcoming action is totally unnecessary. But, if you fall into this camp, maybe you just *think* that you haven't been/are not affected by the F/A-FD but in truth you are, it's just on some level you're unaware of or won't or can't acknowledge).

- *Are you done now? You keep talking about this imminent plot yet we still can't get out of your head.*
- I'm sorry. I can't stop myself.
- *Try.*
- It's just that I need to know that you know what I'm going through. I need to be sure you know *exactly* what I'm talking about.
- *We know* exactly *what you're talking about.*
- I know, I know. It's just . . . it's a disease. I'm very nervous. I'm so afraid you won't know, that no one ever knows, really knows what I'm talking about, what I'm going through.
- *Get over it. Do your best and move on. No one really knows what the hell anyone else is going through. We think we do, we approximate it sometimes but that's the best we can hope for and that's ok.*
- So we all really *are* alone?
- *Yes.*
-
- *Gosh, don't take it so hard. Sure, some people believe that there are cosmic connections, soul-mates and all that crap but most of us know that isn't*

*true or if it is true it probably won't happen for us. But that's ok. We still can be close, we can still be connected, just not in that way. And like good ol' Fromm might've said, that's probably a good thing.*

Sandy has on a snug skirt, just above the knee, with a million little flowers on it. Here in the hotel room is the first time I'm really noticing it. (I saw it in my periphery when we were walking around but you can't spend too much time looking at a woman's skirt when you're walking with her). Her legs are athletic and taut and covered in the same converging freckles that tan her face. She has the sexy and youthful body belying her age like that of a wealthy, pampered, suburban housewife. I imagine her in a tennis outfit, the white ultra mini-skirt falling just a few inches below the little bump of her ass, exposing the full length of her legs down to her KSwiss sneakers and the ankle socks with the little pom-pom at the back. *This is what I need. I need an older woman.*

During our walk, after she asked my age but before I could answer, Sandy volunteered that she's forty-one. It made me think of the way little kids talk, "how old are you I'm seven," all in one breath. She's one of those women that people would say, "she looks five or ten years younger than her age." But I don't think that's quite accurate. Frustratingly, it's seems the only way people compliment an attractive woman is to tell her that she looks young. Sure, she could pass for someone in her thirties but what makes her look good isn't specifically that she looks young. And if you study her, there are subtle hints, clues on the body, faint crow's feet, perhaps something about her hands that I can't quite place, but mainly it's an air about her—a confidence, experience, wisdom combined with a sort of fearless insouciance—that a thirty-year-old doesn't possess. Her body is still young and healthy enough looking to maintain that primal fertility appeal but I wonder if her features are even more devastating now than they were when she was younger, if age has given them a little edge that a too-sweet youthful face lacks. A really hot forty-one year-old need not look like she's thirty.

The tennis-mom-at-the-club image is eradicated when the shirt and bra come off and both her nipples, red and stout like fresh cranberries have silver rings dangling from them. It's a wonderful juxtaposition: fair-skinned, fresh faced, red-head, the hot middle-aged babe in a floral skirt, white baby-T and fashionable expensive sling-back sandals, looking like she stepped out of a fancy catalogue yet underneath it all are two nipple rings, dangling like glinting secrets. There is something sexy about private adornment and private actions that are not betrayed by the outer appearance or disposition.

So, here it is, another woman, another naked body and I'm waiting for it to hit me as it always does in this situation—the distance, the loneliness, the curious and sad nostalgia for something that has never happened that I must fight through, that I must ignore so I can focus, focus on the task at hand, on the moment. But—I'm not hit. I'm waiting, bracing myself. But it doesn't come. And so I'm left startled, here with this woman, each second that passes drifting me further into unfamiliar territory, the seconds dissolving, time melting away and I am no longer waiting, my moments of quiet dread, of being braced in anticipation for the sorry inevitable are now supplanted by a nervous, callow excitement.

Hah.

Just like that, one woman, one moment can take a hundred moments of uniformity, of resigned acceptance to dim monotony and throw them all away. Patterns that would seem to go on forever can be broken unexpectedly. So many of those times for so many years, all those girls, it's all an indiscernible wash now, a dripping water-color painting in my mind, the colors murky and bleeding together. And that sodden canvas is flung to the bin of Vague Memory with a flick of Sandy's delicate and strong wrist. Oh these wonderful wrists that I grip in my hands now as I lay on top of her; the thin bones of women, an eternal source of loving fascination for me. I'm brought back a long way, past the monotony of these many years to something I thought I had forgotten, something I did forget until now. A moment filled with pure wonder and joy, the I-can't-believe-this-is-my-life moment I had when I screwed Jennifer Adler in her bedroom—(in *her* bedroom, the place where she talked on the phone, painted her toenails, listened to The Pixies; the place where she changed every morning before school and was momentarily naked (naked!), the place where she slept softly for thousands of hours)—the summer after senior year when her parents were out of town. It's a moment of grave thanks to whatever it is that controls all that we don't know and understand. A solemn rejoice.

We roll across the king size bed without separating and now she's on top. Staying connected, she shifts onto her knees and arches her back. Her breasts are smooth, buoyant, and white and I want to hook my fingers in the rings and tug, gently. So I do. Her vagina is sopping wet, almost unnaturally so, perhaps to the point of embarrassment but of course embarrassment is not part of Sandy's being and therefore there's nothing embarrassing about it at all. Her unbridled, almost virulent enthusiasm and confidence feeds her reality. Because she *believes*. Because of who she *is*, the world around her is what she wants it to be.

• • •

Wednesday night. Dia: Chelsea. It's the launch night of Sandy's exhibit. Invitation only, wine and cheese thing. But before I get to that, let me go back:

On Tuesday, after the hotel romp, Sandy said that she would call me the next day to let me know the details, the where and when of the show. But by four o'clock I hadn't heard from her and was in agony holding myself back from calling her. I felt like a dog dutifully waiting for his owner to come home to take him out so he could pee, knowing that the consequence of a temporarily joyful release in the house would be outweighed by the punishment when the owner came home. I wanted to call Sandy. Desperately. But I could not. Why hadn't she called me yet? The hot coals in my stomach flared like they were being stoked by an aborigine dragging a rake on a ceremonial fire pit. *Relax Dan. She's busy. She has a show tonight at a museum; she has a lot going on. She'll call.* Who knew what she was off doing during the day—talking to curators, making deals with gallery owners in Germany, perhaps picking up another young guy in the park? I of course, was doing nothing, unless you count waiting for someone to call you as an activity. I had already popped one of my purple pills this morning but my stomach still was aflame. Things really must have been churning because the PPs had always helped in the past. According to the "literature" (I love how they call it that), these pills are totally on the pharmaceutical vanguard. They're in this new class of acid reflux pills called proton pump inhibitors, that actually shut down the pumps in your stomach that make acid, (as opposed to just neutralizing the acid that's already there, which is what regular antacids do). If these don't work I'm really in trouble. Come on proton pumps—Inhibit! Inhibit! I imagined a thousand tiny pumps like pistons, firing up and down cranking out acid in my gut. I tried to do a mind-over-matter exercise, visualizing the pumps being coated with a halting purple goo, sticking their gears, slowing the pumps down to a lethargic grind until the rhythm stopped completely like the wheels on an old train pulling into the station. *Relaaax.* I could not call Sandy. She already had the upper-hand; there was no ambiguity about that. The imbalance was known and accepted by the partners from the beginning—but even an imbalance has its balance, a stability, and if I called her it would make the implicit *ex*plicit, the unsaid would be said, and for that the arrangement too exposed. It's only fun if we pretend. I could not appear too eager for she already knew I was too eager. To keep things alive I had to feign, for her, for us, that things weren't really what they were. If I could just play along, if I could just hold on a little longer I knew she'd come through with her end of the bargain for me. (At least, this is what I constructed in my head).

And at 5:30 she did. My phone rang, her voice ebullient—or maybe it was just me; it's hard to tell—saying she couldn't wait to see me at her show tonight. When we hung up I danced around the apartment and did a series of quiet triumphant fist pumps.

When I arrive at the museum my name is on a list and despite my typical unease at all things social, this slight bone, (that everyone else here has gotten), propels me to walk in defiantly like I belong. And fuck, I do; the star of the show invited me. The standard art fart crowd is here: men in tight fitting, smart suits without ties; beautiful women in little dresses mixing with guys in dirty jeans and three hundred dollar sneakers; reassuringly, I spot at least two guys with the obligatory thick, black-rimmed glasses that I expect to see at a thing like this (sometimes there's a certain comfort in seeing a cliché); and a smattering of women in extreme outfits—feather boas, extra-large safety pins hooked in random spots on a shredded silk dress, I think one even has a shirt with a dangling third sleeve out the back—the type of style that says in a whiney scream, "Look at me! I'm different! I'm an *artist*!"—mingle through the crowd. I never did "get" this extreme end of fashion and I waver between being irritated at these people for their pretension and their palpable need for attention, and being filled with gratitude and mirth that people like this exist to keep things interesting in the world.

"There you are!" Sandy saunters toward me through the crowd. She has on a slinky, black strapless dress with an asymmetrical hemline, the low end dropping just below her left knee. Her face is done-up with that makeup that has sparkles in it yet the colors are smoky, making her at once dark and shimmering. Hair—silk. Eyes—glowing blue. Legs—still Tennis Wife taut. Feet—perched on two-inch heels, contained by thin black straps crisscrossing the tops of her feet like Zorro slashes. She has the appearance of an actress staring in a "serious" studio film as the famous surgeon's wife in a scene at a thousand-dollar-a-plate charity event. She's the sensitive, book lover's idea of gorgeous—older, sexy, urbane, commanding. I instantly can see myself in my jeans, my trendy tight-fitting untucked dress shirt, and dirty Rod Laver sneakers and am certain that I am sweating through the back of my shirt. I feel hopelessly mismatched with her, with everyone here; I do an immediate scroll in my mind of all the clothes in my closet, though come up with nothing that would have worked for this. She takes my hand and walks me around the museum leading me just like she did in the park. I'm aware that I'm being tugged around like a toy and am embarrassed but at the same time feel proud that I'm attached with her. She knows it's demeaning but knows she can get away with it.

As we wander through the museum Sandy introduces me to countless people and to my surprise, at least a few of them—Jonathan: dark, smart suit, gallery owner; Jane: artist and an old friend of Sandy's from "like, a million years ago, back in, what? '84? '85?—God, I'm really dating us," brown hair done in the International Symbol for Woman style; Terrence: black pants, black sweater, black horn rims!, collector; there may have been a balding Victor or Vincent—seem genuine and are actually glad to see Sandy and meet me. After yet another well-wisher approaches us (err, her), Sandy turns to me and puts her lips in my ear and whispers, "You look *very* foxy tonight," gives a quick bite to my earlobe and abruptly excuses herself from me. Is she going to the bathroom or does she just need a break from me? As she struts away, I want to call to her back, "You've had enough of me haven't you? It's all over. This was it, right?" But I restrain myself, grab another glass of shitty white wine while patting the pill-box in my pocket reassuring myself that the Pepcids and Pepto pellets are in there should things get ugly, and stroll around taking a look at the art for the first time.

There's a film projected on a wall in a two-minute loop of a man walking on his hands on a lawn while three cats wander around him; I pass several people staring at a painting that appears to just be a black canvas; and there's a pile of rope and broken glass in the corner. Again: irritation—mirth. Just beyond the handstand-cat-man and the other crap that I feared would be here, on the far wall is something that catches me. A film triptych with three, large LCD screens, each tilted at slightly different angle is flashing. Varying scenes play on each of the screens: people eating and laughing at a large dinner table, bucolic National Geographic type footage of the great plains, a boxing match, a sit-com, a football game, and other seemingly unrelated footage. The only apparent connection between the screens and the different scenes is its vividness on the large modern screens. Periodically, for spans of several minutes at a time, other film appears superimposed on top of these scenes, as if two films were being projected onto the same screen. It's disjointing and confusing but after concentrating on one screen for a few minutes my brain somehow seems to be able to separate the overlapped images and the effect is mesmerizing, as if I had figured out some sort of key, some new way of viewing things, of being able to process things. When the screens aren't showing the overlapped superimposed footage, the differing scenes on each of the three screens every once in a while seem to intertwine in some way, to work together. I can't discern if this is all in my head at this point or if they actually are unified in some way. Then all three screens do unify, showing the one scene of the dinner party spanning across the three of them as if they were one long screen. A part of me feels that I should just think this all is annoyingly abstract but somehow instead it's compelling. The screens then split again, and images of the boxing match appear on one screen and I recognize that this is the sequence that was playing when I first walked up to the wall and that the full piece has started over again. I do a quick dog-like head-shake, breaking the trance as I turn away and glance at my watch and am startled when I see that I've been standing here for twenty-five minutes.

I walk toward a large open doorway leading to another room. On the wall to the side of the opening is a sign **Sandy Mason Exhibit**. Walking around the museum with Sandy we never made our way into the room housing her work. I don't know if she purposely steered us away from there or we just didn't reach the room in the back because of all the schmoozing. Maybe she was keeping me from her work, she didn't want to have to explain it to me. Maybe she didn't want to explain it to anyone and was avoiding the room all together. Of course I was curious about her work but while we were socializing I was too coy to ask her if we could head directly there. Shit, but now I'm wondering if maybe it was rude that I didn't ask her right away, that I didn't show enough enthusiasm. Please. I'm an afterthought in this whole thing. Asking; not asking—there's no impact either way.

It's a massive, empty, white room, what real estate agents call "raw space." There is nothing on the walls. The only thing in here is a giant iron boulder that must be near ten or twelve feet tall, in the center of the room. People are milling about. A few are looking at the boulder, studying it with a practiced aloofness. As in the rest of the museum, most though are standing in little groups of two, three, or four chatting, indifferent to the boulder, indifferent to any of the art in the other rooms as well, as if the museum were just another venue to socialize. I decide that's not necessarily a bad thing. Maybe art is best when it surrounds us, hovering just below our radar as we go about our business. Nah, I don't believe that.

I walk closer to the boulder. The surface is pitted with large divots and bumps like a cartoon drawing of an asteroid. I walk around it and run my left hand along its surface. The metal feels more smooth and cooler than I expected. As I reach the far side of the boulder, there's a small hatch that two women are climbing out of, one after the other. Adjusting their hair and fixing their clothes from their exit one says, "Looks like she's going through her Richard Serra phase now." They both start laughing. The other says, "I know. I'm getting a bit tired of giant clunk art" as they wander away. I suddenly feel like I want to go home. I turn around and start to walk away but in a jolted impulse, like when you just remember that you forgot to buy some item as you're about to walk out of the grocery store, I turn around again and climb into Sandy's boulder.

The low rumble of conversation disappears and is replaced by the sound of air and my own breathing. There isn't anywhere really to walk or move inside since the bottom is round. I get nervous for a moment wondering if it is going to start rolling but reason that it hasn't happened yet so it must be bolted to the ground somehow or maybe it's too heavy to move. I like the quiet and hearing my breath and do some exaggerated inhales and exhales for fun, my wind filling up the sphere, swirling around, echoing off the walls. I think of an illustration of Poseidon I saw in a book when I was little, enormous and drawn in the clouds blowing fierce winds on the vast sea, sailors and ships mere specks being tossed around in the violent swells. I smile to myself at the randomness and goofiness of the memory and do a few owl "hoo hoo hoo"s just to hear the echo. I sense something and turn around and see the top of a red head peaking its way in.

"Someone's having fun," Sandy says as she necessarily hikes up her dress to mid-thigh as she climbs in. **SEX**. It hits me like the word is written on a canoe paddle swung right into my face. Sssssmack. **SEX**. The Muslims, the Hasids, the Puritans, the Quakers, they all really were on to something enforcing modest dress. When they drew up their rules they knew it was the only way men could be free to think of something, *anything* else. I feel ashamed for being reduced to this base instinct, she deserves more from me but I am quickly saved from guilt because Sandy's presence is so magical that it, whatever *it* is that she has, overpowers the rawness of my lust and it fades after a moment. It doesn't disappear, it just melds into the overall mix, the power that she exudes.

"This is great Sandy. I love it in here."

"Ahh, but you haven't done the best part." She reaches her arm through the hatch and pulls the door closed. She whispers, "come lie down," the words filling the dark silent sphere.

We lie down, our bodies arched to the curve of the boulder. The pull of gravity and the arc of the sphere slopes us toward the center, pressing our bodies' weight into each other as we contort and shift, eventually settling on our backs with our legs straight, feet planted on the wall. Sandy kicks off her shoes and they drop to the bottom with two clunks.

"Makes you wish you do yoga regularly, huh?" Sandy chortles. My eyes still adjusting, I can just make out the block of white teeth of her wide-open mid-laugh mouth. You can't tell from the outside, and inside with the door open there was too much light but with the hatch closed, now visible are a thousand pin-holes in the boulder allowing in just enough light to see specks but not enough for it to stream in. It looks almost like the night sky.


Ash, that fucking bastard. They stole my album. They stole my life. What am I supposed to do now? The only one who fought for me was Tim but no one listened to him either. What am I supposed to do now?


My whole left side is starting to tingle from being pressed so hard into Sandy. But I say nothing and don't even allow myself to shift just a little. I should be more nervous around Sandy but she's so cool, her presence so sweeping, enveloping that it's that micro-step beyond the peak of cool. Again, the circle diagram! Anytime I'm around someone else so beautiful, someone else so hip, so inspiring, so . . . I'd feel the obligatory stomach burn but Sandy, she is so much of everything, so far on the other side of the circle that in the times when I allow myself to just be with her, to not watch myself, to not think, to not observe, when I am there, when I am in it, when I *am* it, I am made calm.

"So, what do you think?" she asks.

"I could stay here forever."

"I'm glad." She wraps her leg around mine, hooking her bare foot under my blue-jeaned calf. "Were you having fun before? What do you think of all the art here?"

"I really liked some of it. But a lot, I don't know. I just don't think I *got* it, I guess."

"Oh, that's bullshit! There's nothing to *get*. If you don't get it, then it sucks. Either you like it or you don't. And if you don't just move on."

"I'm sure the art history professors at Miss State would love to hear you telling your students that."

"You can always learn more about art. And you learn and change throughout your life and some things you used to hate or find boring now you love. But I'm a firm believer in the school of the best art, the best of anything really, should work on many levels. If you have to take a course to enjoy something then it's not doing its job. Maybe a course will help you appreciate it more but there should always be something there on the surface too. Art should have a million layers."

"Like The Beatles. Little kids love their music and so do the most obsessive music dorks who analyze every cough by Paul McCartney on a B side outtake. Everyone loves The Beatles because they work on every level."

"Yeah, sweetie. Like The Beatles."

*Dan: Sandy = Kelly: Dan.*
*Oh God, I'm going down.*

. . .

I didn't want to bring her over. The notes. Things had progressed with them over the past several months. I should have taken them down the day I met her. Now I'm stuck. We're walking up the stairs and it's too late. She's going to burst into laughter. No; I'll be lucky if all she does is laugh. She's going to walk in, freeze wearing a painted-on, nervous smile that poorly conceals her horror, and slowly step backwards out the door and give me a, "don't call me, I'll call you."

Burning. *Relaaax*. My stomach is burning. Inside, those aborigines are raking coals again, little tufts of ash poofing in the air. They're getting ready to dance around the ambers glowing in the clear dark night. Then the procession will begin. Run! Run across the burning coals you bastards. What kind of tradition is this? I don't want to be ethnocentric but come on—What's wrong with you people?

And what the fuck—why are the coals burning in me now anyway? This shouldn't matter, I shouldn't care. I've already had my big revelatory episode. My epiphanic moment. Shouldn't I be beyond caring about this stuff now? Beyond worrying about what Sandy—or anyone—thinks about my apartment or any other extension of me?

And listen, I know, you're probably pissed too: You're wondering—We're past the peak now, aren't we? Hasn't he gotten over this shit? By now we should be coasting on our asses down the back-end of Aristotle's arc like we're on a giant slide at a water park. Our hero was supposed to have grown, have learned, transformed. Isn't that the hallmark of literature—*the guy has to grow!*

But the thing is: I *have* grown. And the thing is: it's not that I don't care anymore what anyone thinks about me. It's that I don't care *as much* anymore. And that feels like a start. And if not a start then maybe even a goal. We *should* care to some degree. That's why I hate the damn bed-headed thrift store-clothed dudes projecting their indifference like a badge of honor. Ok, fine, so *I* own a carefully selected thrift store jacket and my shaggy hair just might be viewed by some as as much of a conscious attempt at appearing cool as the bed-head. All right, so maybe the look isn't that important! I'm over that; a look doesn't indicate everything. See?—I have grown. The point is what I was really referring to is action, interaction. If there's one goddamn thing I'd like to change it'd be to make it so the mumblers, the flat-affecters, the strivers masquerading as idlers are not cool. I'd make it so *indifference* will never be perceived as cool again.

Maybe it's not about growing. Fuck change. Fuck growth. Maybe it's just about experiencing that one pristine moment. And as long as I can remember that moment then that's enough. After that moment I need not act differently, perhaps I don't even need to feel all that different. Because the way an Oscar winner will always be an Oscar winner even if every subsequent film she does sucks, the way a band who was once great and now is merely ok but still gets revered, the glow of past glory is seemingly eternal. One great moment when I was better than I'll ever be, when I was more alive than I may ever be again, can be revisited forever. Maybe that one moment is enough.


We pass the landing between the first and second floor. I fumble in my pocket for a Pepcid. My pits are damp. Is there a bead of sweat on my temple? Shit. Today was an off-day for my real deodorant, the kind with aluminum in it. You know all anti-perspirants all have aluminum as their main ingredient? It's in dandruff shampoo too. It must seal your pores or something. That can't be good for you. Preventing sweat is just completely unnatural. Your body needs to sweat. (By the way, where does all the sweat go when it can't seep out of the pores in your pits?) Also, they say aluminum can give you Alzheimer's or brain damage or something. Seriously. There's a movement underway of people who won't use aluminum foil. And that's just the foil touching your food! Rubbing aluminum into your *skin* every day must be far worse than some foil wrapped around that pizza slice in your freezer. I know this. So, unwilling to go completely *au natural* for fear of never being able to get laid again, I've decided that cutting my aluminum exposure in half may be just enough to keep its ill effects at bay. Every other day I've been putting up with stinkpits because instead of the real (i.e. aluminum) stuff, I use this holistic, no aluminum "deodorant" by *Toms of Maine*. Nothing but good ol' propylene glycol (totally natural!), something called flower water and other ineffective ingredients in their potion marketed to schmucks like me as a healthy alternative. (And who am I kidding, it's probably made in an industrial park in Jersey. Maine?—please.) So here I go. My pits are dripping. Why did today have to be the off day? I need aluminum!

Days ago, just after we first met, I allowed myself the fantasy that she might actually come over. I thought about her seeing the notes yet I did not take them down. At the time I didn't care at all. I was at the peak of the arc, baby! But now look at me, I'm sweating and I've got coal-walkers in my stomach. But [Warning: Trite Pronouncement Alert]: there comes a time in one's life when he must accept who he is and must be willing to show someone else who he is. There. I'm feeling better.

And what am I worried about anyway—Sandy is an artist, *artiste*, and an "out there" one at that. She appreciates strangeness, uniqueness. No, not just appreciates it but is drawn to it. I need to be interesting like her. I need to shift the balance in our relationship.[*] I have to show her I'm not just some dilettante. Although, it occurs to me now that being weird doesn't make someone not a dilettante, it just makes him a freak. But it's a good diversion anyway. Weirdness gets mistaken for brilliance all the time. I want to be weird! The stranger the better. And lot's of notes on the walls = WEIRD.

   – *But she took a shine to you when all she knew of you was some cute, lost, artsy guy that she could lead around. Now you're changing everything. You're going to shift the dynamic once she walks in.*
   – But that's what I want to do. I want her respect. I can't remain in awe of her. Or at least not if she doesn't have some sort of reverence for me. Too much imbalance.
   – *Hah!—You're killin me here. Are you joking? You think by her seeing your shit apartment with your freak-ass notes all over the place that that*

---

[*] Little r relationship, not capital R. I'm not getting *that* ahead of myself.

*will somehow make her think you're more interesting, more her equal?*

– No. I mean, maybe. I don't know. Leave me alone!

– *I'm just saying . . .*

– This is the exact type of shit, this internal dialogue, which I have to stop. I thought we moved beyond this? I mean, come on—that night at Jay's and now everything with Sandy. It's a different life now. Things are different. It's like I'm alive. Not that I wasn't alive before but you know what I mean.

– *ye-*

– Actually, no, wait; shut up. That is exactly what I mean. I really do feel alive now. I am . . . things are different. I'm different.

– *Nah, you can't let me go. You're too afraid. This is what you do.* Of course *I'm here now that you're "alive" with Sandy. That's the whole point! I'm here to stop it. Because if you're too "alive" in* this *way then you aren't alive in the other way. I'm here to put you back in your head, to make sure you don't forget the other side, to preserve the balance because that's where you're safe.*

– I need to stop thinking. Stop. Thinking. Stop.

– *I'm still here.*

– No. No No No No! This is the problem. You need to shut up. I need to let you go.

– *You can't. Without me, life is gonna go by so fast you won't even know it happened until it's all too late. I'm here to slow you down, to take you out of the action for a spell so you can preserve it all.*

– Ok, ok. I agree. I know, I'm afraid not to preserve it. But enough right now. Stop it! You're upsetting me. I have a lump in my throat like I'm gonna cry. Is that what you want now? I know I'm afraid to leave you. I know I so desperately don't want it all to slip by and you're the only way I know how to preserve it. But maybe you could just let me be in the moment and not worry so much. Because you know the painful irony—that stepping back to preserve a moment by default ruins the actual moment I'm trying to preserve. You know, maybe you could take it easy on me, please. Help me tip the balance just a wee bit.

– *Ok.*

– Really? You've never been so, so nice, so, cool about it before.

– *I'm getting tired too.*

– Hah! Attrition. Good. So we're in agreement: If you can't leave me alone—wait, that's not a fair way to put it—if *I* can't leave *you*, then at least you can be a little easier on me. Let's not make this so hard.

– [singing] *You shouldn't take it so hard . . .*

– Is that that annoyingly lame Stones song from the 80s?

– *Actually, Keith Richards solo stuff. But, yeah, sorry. It just popped in my head.*

– Thanks for the levity at least.


"Ok, so I have to warn you about something," I say. We're standing in front of my door and I'm hesitating with the keys in my hand.

"Dan, I don't care what your place looks like."

"It's not that. I mean I think this is a little beyond just having the tub in the kitchen type of thing, if that's what you're thinking."

"Ohh kay," she sings through a nervous chuckle. She's annoyed. Or is it freaked-out? Freaked-out is good. It's better than bored.

"Look, I've been working on this project for a while. Well, it's not necessarily a project, it's just, well, I have all these notes all over the place and I just didn't want you to think I was crazy or something."

"Too late!" Head tilt, mouth open. "Open the door already!" She attacks me, squeezing and tickling my sides and grabs the keys out of my hand. "Ok, which one is it?" She asks holding the keys up in her left hand, her right arm pinning me against the door-jam.

"The rounded one," I say sheepishly, "that goes in the top lock."

We walk in and she halts a few feet in from the door. I'm not sure if she lets out a gasp or if I just hear it in my head, my mind filling in the fearful blank of the moment as she stands in one spot slowly turning around scanning the room. The apartment is covered—all the walls in their entirety, (the few posters and framed photographs long since taken down when I ran out of space); the coffee table; the side of my bureau; the refrigerator door, around the edge of the TV; even an undulating line of yellow creeping a foot or so in from the perimeter (these notes held with tape for reinforcement) threaten to take over the whole ceiling, the center of which is the only remaining clear surface—a paper fungus engulfing the apartment. With the notes covering all the walls and beyond, I had long since stopped bothering hanging the bed sheets.

"I love it! You're a total nut-job!" She's still slowly spinning with the dazed pivot of a tourist in mid-town Manhattan. Without looking at me, she continues, "This is great in here. How long have you been working on this?"

"Umm. I haven't really been working on it. It just sort of happened."

"So organic of you," she says with a genuineness of tone distant from both sarcasm on one end and art-speak pretension on the other. She walks to the far wall, her eyes wide and lightly runs her hand along the curled bottoms of the post-its. I feel naked. Wedged between the back of the couch and the wall she turns around to finally look at me but is startled when she bumps into the couch as if it shouldn't have been right there. She climbs over the back, one short-skirted bare leg after the other and plops down on the cushions. Laying on her back she looks up to the ceiling and sighs. "Come lay down on top of me" she calls out.

It's a small couch, more of a love-seat than a sofa, and her legs are bent at the knees. As I walk toward her she reaches her arms out to me like a mom welcoming a running child. She drops one leg to the floor making room as I clumsily try to climb on top of her, her inside leg pressed against the back cushions. Lying on top of her, my legs are bent at ninety degrees, my feet in the air, an untied shoelace dangling. I put my head down and bury it in her neck and her hair. She smells wonderful. Not of perfume but of that fresh, ill-defined natural scent—girl aroma. I conjure up the image of one of those douche commercials where flaxen haired, fair skinned women walk in white lace dresses in a field of grass holding daisies. But what makes this smell magical, rather than just a floral springtime breeze, is that it's weighted by a subtle undertone of estrogen-fueled feminine musk, a switch-triggering vaginal pungency. I've been lucky to be in the presence of this *essence de femme* bouquet before. Times when I'm feeling cynical, I dejectedly assume this scent comes from some chemist contrived deodorant or shampoo or some product that women use—after-shower lotion? body wash?—that men don't know about. But when things are good, and I am happy, like right now, I don't worry or think about those sorts of things. I allow myself to simply soak it in and believe that this charged and bright air, this opiate of the olfactory, the scent equivalent of a girl tucking her hair behind an ear, says despite it all, despite everything wrong with my life, with the world, not only that everything is going to be ok, but that everything *is* ok. Now. Here. In the permanent present. I kiss her neck and that space behind her ear, the smooth, hard, rounded bone of her head before her hairline begins. That majestic spot you only get to see when a woman's hair is held in a ponytail or a bun, or when you're with one of them and you tenderly sweep the hair back with a soft hand or better, in one motion you gently but forcefully comb it away with your fingers then nestle your hand deep inside her hair cupping the back of her head. In the end, the world is good. This is enough. The world is good.

We lay on the couch for a serene spell saying nothing as I kissed her neck and drunk in her aroma.

"So, what do they mean? What are these all about?" Sandy finally though softly broke the silence. She was staring at the ceiling and her hand was up my shirt lightly scratching my back.

"I don't know. I just started writing things down a while back."

"What's a while back?"

"I guess around the time I stopped playing music."

"Of course. Of course. You need to create. Eliminate one avenue and the creative mind will blaze another."

"I never thought of this as creating." I tried to shift my weight for fear I was crushing her but there was no where to go. "Not in the sense of . . . not like making music. They're just notes, about everything. About nothing . . . I just have so much stuff, so much noise, static, chaos running through me. You know?" I suddenly felt self-conscious. I wasn't sure if I was going off on some embarrassing tangent or maybe this was the exact right way to be, myself, honest.

"I do," she said and I felt better.

"What happens if your gift is to feel but you don't have the means to express yourself? I mean, what do you do if you're an artist but you can't create anything? Although I guess if you can't create anything then you're not an artist." Sandy's expression slid from warmth to pity for me, slightly frowning as if I were a little boy whose dog was just run over. She looked beautiful. I knew we were talking about the notes but I realized then that I was probably referring to music too. Regardless, maybe she was right, the notes did seem to mean something even if it wasn't as clear and definitive to me as writing a song. "I mean, I don't know what to turn them into, what to do with them. Maybe I'm not supposed to do anything."

"Well I think it's terrific. It's a little strange my boy, but that's good" she said, giving a hard jagged scratch on "but that's good" for emphasis. "Don't worry about what it's supposed to be. Everything speaks for itself. Everything stands on its own, or at least it should."

"I don't—"

"You're so tense!" She said cheerfully not letting whatever lament I was about to start continue. "Such a nervous young man. Don't be afraid of chance or abstraction. It doesn't all need to be worked out and defined, set in parameters."

"I know, I know. Improvise, take it as it comes, accidents often times yield the best results, the moment, serendipity, jazz. But that doesn't work for me. When I create something I need to know exactly what's happening. I need plans, structure."

"You don't. There's a meaning behind it, I know there is."

"But these are just ideas. Ideas aren't art."

"Everything is art. Art is anything you say it is."

"But I need to make something, *do* something. "

"You already have, you just don't realize it. Now tear my clothes off and throw me on your bed."

Under the sheets, naked, kissing, groping, to my chagrin I was overcome more with nerves than elation. Plus, I was being gripped by immediate nostalgia. Even though it happened only minutes before, I kept replaying in my head, as if I was reminiscing some poignant moment from years ago, the image and the feeling of tossing Sandy onto the bed. From the couch, I had rolled off of her and fell to the floor as if it were a controlled stunt. On my knees I leaned over her and in two swift motions, up, then down, like I was a crazed fan doing a wave in sped-up motion, I tore her shirt and skirt off. I sprung to my feet and hooked my arms under her, one behind her neck, the other in the space underneath her bent legs. Despite her size, carrying her off the couch and trying to run with her to the bed, though, was a clumsy romp. I wasn't sure if I'd be able to toss her so much as shove or maybe just drop her. But after stumbling with her, as I reached the bed, I heaved her out of my arms with surprising ease, as if I were a burly man-cheerleader throwing one of the pigtailed pixies on the squad in the air for a flip, Sandy's body suddenly and with perfect timing lithe and light as she was launched effortlessly onto the bed. When she landed, she bounced slightly before sinking into the thin layer of down on the mattress pad. Her hair flew outward as she fell and after she hit was splayed on the pillows, extravagantly topping the compact body in a white wonder-bra and tiny satin and lace g-string that was laid out before me. Looking at her in that moment, laying there on her back, smiling and laughing, her form athletic yet still delicate, her manner at once commanding and submissive, her hair the color of her lips, as if that was the only color hair could logically be coming from someone so vibrant, I knew the moment was captured, to be placed in the permanent slideshow highlight reel in my memory bank. The moment was so fresh, so powerful that the slide was still in the center of my head, behind my eyes, as if it were superimposed on the image before me—present reality—as it rolled on. I didn't want to lose her. I wanted this all preserved and to go on forever. I could live in Mississippi, I could leave New York. I could go anywhere.

"What's wrong baby?" Sandy asked sweetly after feeling my equipment suddenly small, as if it were frightened.

I breathed through a smile. "I, I don't know. I think I'm nervous for some reason." I wanted to tell her everything. Everything about me, everything about the world, about how her presence was kinetic, that a field of energy vibrated around her like the buzz off of high-tension wires. And I wanted her to tell me everything. And to share everything of herself with me. I needed more time with her. A lifetime may not even be enough. I felt a strange desperation.

"Relaaax," she said softly.

My mind started churning. I don't even know what I was thinking. Things were garbled together, as if all the notes from the walls were being shuffled in my head. I no longer was concentrated on her. I had things to think, things to worry about, things to say. None of this was relevant to her right then, to this moment, and I knew it but I couldn't stop. Perhaps all these notes shuffling in my head was *supposed* to not have anything to do with the moment. Unconsciously, almost surreptitiously, my mind was doing this trying to remove myself from there. The moment was too much, it was all too much. I rolled off of her and onto my back. Then, staring at the ceiling, I found myself talking:

"Is New York really the place to be? I can't shake the feeling that not only is New York *not* the place to be but that there is no *place to be* right now—no San Francisco of the sixties, Paris of the twenties, fifteenth-century Italy," I was speeding up, "China of the Ming dynasty, ancient Greece, Jerusalem—whatever. We're in one of those lulls in history, a no-man's-land, no-man's-time. Even on a recent level in New York, the fifties and sixties in the Village, the seventies at Studio 54 and downtown at Max's, the eighties with Keith Haring and the start of Hip Hop. And the nineties—pfft. That skipped New York and went to Seattle. And what now? Am I supposed to believe that some fake-ass Russian-themed bar with fourteen-dollar martinis is it? That Williamsburg, a vinyl-sided, post-collegiate wasteland of Oberlin grads wearing suspenders or leg warmers or Capezios or whatever-the-fuck ironic, or post-ironic clothes are hip this week dancing to electroclash or some bullshit is it? Where should I go? Tell me where to go to feel alive, to feel like I am part of something. I'll go anywhere! Is it Brazil? Tibet? Silicon Valley writing code for some VC-primed soon-to-be world-altering tech-corp juggernaut who'll have paid me with a million options that are about to explode after its imminent IPO? Why doesn't anywhere sound right? And don't give me some pat answer like, 'everything is happening wherever you are' or 'only boring people get bored.'"

Sandy laughed in her usual way. Then she swung her lean leg over me and straddled me. Like a psycho mom Christmas shopping on Black Friday snatching the last "it"-doll of the season off the shelf, she grabbed my dick with urgency and vehemence. With five violent jerks she got it hard and straight like the neck of a guitar and slid on top. She bounced and thrust and ground into me. Her ivory skin dusted with freckles, flushed and taut over her ribcage, light twinkling off the rings dangling from her small, hard nipples. She tossed her head wildly about, her red hair flying like a blaze, every strand whipping its vitality to the corners of the world. She kept at it savagely for minutes. I'm not sure if I was breathing. I didn't know what to do. I put my hands on her ass. The crack was hot and moist with sweat. For a time she seemed to keep speeding up but then suddenly she slowed down almost to a stop, moving but in a slow even pace a bit like those oil pumpjacks in the fields out West. She stared into my eyes then with both her hands grabbed my hair and started grinding again. In synch with the thrusts of her body she smashed my head into the pillow vigorously and rhythmically like she was a prairie wife washing clothes on a board. "Stop thinking! I can tell you're still thinking!" She yelled. After the initial frenetic pace, the pounding continued, her body, my head, all in unison, but now getting slower and harder like a triumphant retard in a classical coda, the bed was cricking, I thought it would break, then in synch with the decelerating thrusts of her hips and my head slamming down she panted

"Stop! Fucking! Thinking!"

each word aligned with each pelvic-thrust-head-slam. I couldn't feel anything, vertigo overtook me. I was afraid but unable to say stop, and I didn't want to. But we had already reached the final thrust and grunt. Rendered numb and nauseous I lay immobile as she climbed off of me. She knew I had come even though I didn't until I saw my cock, now out in the open, still sputtering and convulsing, glistening. She knelt over and licked it up and down like a cat cleaning its paw. Then she titled her head back and spewed it all in the air like a geyser and it rained down on us. "Woo!" She screamed. "Yeah, honey baby! You're alive mother fucker!" She whipped her head about, her breasts jiggled. Then she was still, sitting back on her heels. "Woo!" She cheered again, like an exclamation point.

. . .

"Greenie, are you listening to me? Are you there?" Fades in through the receiver.

"What? Yeah, yeah," I answer defensively, realizing I haven't heard anything until that moment. I don't even remember picking up the phone.

"Dude, you're still asleep! Rise and shine Final Green!"

I stare at the digital clock on my nightstand. The green numbers come into focus: 9:32 a.m.

"Why are you calling? You're never awake this early." The oscillating fan in the window is halfheartedly blowing tepid air from the alleyway on my head in tired gusts. As I climb one step further from sleep an awareness that my apartment is stiflingly hot materializes in my brain.

"I can't tell you now. Just promise you'll come over today as soon as possible."

"What's going on? . . . Jen's not—"

"Nothing to do with Jen. Just promise you'll come over today."

"Yeah, yeah," I croak and hang up still in a morning fog. The word *hot* is all that my brain registers for a moment. I study the numbers on the clock—9:34—each digit comprised of multiple thin strips with beveled ends meeting at the corners.

Sandy! I whip my head to the side reflexively, having forgotten she was here. But her half of the bed is empty. On her pillow lays a small paper cutout of a girl meticulously cut in the customary arms and legs-splayed skirted silhouette, the kind where they're all connected in a chain. On its head she has colored in red hair and on the bottom right corner of the skirt drawn in a little, fancy *S* like an embroidered letter on a skirt in the 1950s. Sweating under just a sheet, I tear it off and lay on my back, naked and exposed, holding the Paper Sandy tenderly in my palm as I slowly acclimate to consciousness.

By twelve I'm walking to the Union Square station. Sandy is leaving in a few days. I want to call her but I know she's busy. I should just call her, this is ridiculous. I'm ridiculous—I'm carrying Paper Sandy in my pocket.

"Hey, it's Dan. Just wanted to say . . . hey. I, uh, got your little present you left me on the pillow. Not quite the same as having you with me when I wake up but thanks. Very sweet. Did you make that while I was asleep or do you carry a stash of those around with you to leave on guys' pillows?" I'm so lame. "I'm just kidding. Obviously. Ok, I better shut up now. I'm heading over to my friends Jay's. Gimme a call. See you later." Sandpaper.* Worst message ever.

I slam the payphone down transferring all the disgust in myself into the receiver. If I had a cell phone I couldn't do that. When you're upset, carefully pressing a little button on a keypad doesn't quite offer the same satisfaction. I stand for a moment looking down 14th Street as an endless stream of people brush by. A kid on a skateboard nearly clips me, which I'm sure he did on purpose. I watch him as he trucks down the sidewalk, twice in half-a-block pulling his saggy jeans up at the waist.

Waiting on the platform to hop the L to Williamsburg a large black guy and a younger, smaller white guy play bucket drums in unison. They are deep into a sophisticated, syncopated rhythm, their feet tipping the buckets up on their sides on the down beat to bring in the bass then dropping them back down flat while they hit the top and rims for the tight counter beats, and the black guy has a metal pan on the side as a kind of ride symbol/high-hat, the whole effect a rough equivalent of the basic kick, snare, high-hat set-up. The sounds echo throughout the station, flowing down the tunnels and up the stairwells. On the far end of the platform when I came down the stairs, the sounds were distant and muddy, the different hits having bled into each other. But up close now I can feel the bass through me and the sharp top hits clap my ears, the perfect and rich subway reverb not so much carrying the sound but pushing it in waves of thick air. High-speed fills like Tommy Guns clacking cut on top of long decaying bass hits. The white guy gets up and starts in on the side of a garbage can, then a steel girder, then the floor, then drags

---

* As in: smooth as

his sticks along the metal poles of the stairwell railing, all the while staying on the beat with his partner. Jaded hipsters look on with practiced disinterest, though a few breaking role manage to nod approvingly. Old, hunched-over Polish women in babushkas, their backs hard and curved down like weathered turtle shells stare at the tracks immune to the noise and all their surroundings. The drums are so loud I worry about my hearing. I'm always sticking my fingers in my ears when the trains screech in or when yet another police car or fire truck screams by me on the street. Subways in other cities don't sound like this. In D.C. they're near silent as they glide in to the stations. I don't know what's wrong with New York trains. All this screeching and the sparks feel like an anachronism from the industrial era. We have microchips and cell phones and palm pilots, surely we can figure out how to have a train run (and stop) smoothly on its rails without the bombast. I used to feel embarrassed but I'm noticing more and more people wearing earplugs walking around these days. Now I look at people standing stoic or fakely oblivious when a fire engine's 110 decibel, earth-ending horn blares and I feel secure in that they're the ones who look silly not me with my fingers in my ears. Nevertheless, like any New Yorker, over all these years I'm sure I've done damage. But here I stand, ear canals naked to the rapid-fire crack and boom of the bucket drums. It's such a wonder to hear sound not from a speaker, not electronically reproduced but straight from the source, all the spectacular original dynamics bursting, uncontained. No matter how advanced we get with recording and stereos and speakers, *nothing* competes with pure, raw sound from the source. I am so grateful for this moment, for this city. I want the noise. In fact I want it louder.

Black guy: *BOOM BOOM Clack! B BOOM BOOM Clack!*
White guy: Tap t t tap tap tap tap tap t t tap tap t t tap

What glorious sound! The native Lenni Lenape would be proud. The need for drums, the community, the human connection they command will never go away. I'm still worried about the potential hearing-loss damage but covering my ears in front of these two would be sacrilege. I focus on the sound, letting it flow through me.

Black guy and White guy in unison: *K K K K K K K K K K K K K K K K BOOM BOOM Clack! B BOOM BOOM Clack!**

I stare down, zoning in on the gritty platform, like the floors of the whole subway system, leopard-spotted with old gum.

I wish I was at The Watershed hitting a power-chord, standing with Alex and Jay in the Live Room as we track a new song, the mix loud and heavy pouring from the studio cans into my head. *How could I not be playing anymore? This is wrong. Something has gone horribly wrong.* A gleaming new L train pulls in and I debate for a moment whether I should let it pass so I can stay with my modern tribalists but the electronic door-closing tone rings and I jump in at the last moment, the back of my heel getting bit by the closing doors as I yank it in. Their sound now muffled, through the closed doors' windows I watch the drummers recede as we pull out of the station, which strikes me as a sad metaphor for watching my own music life disappear into memory.

Sandy • I am going to play music again. This is what I should be doing. This is what I am meant to do. • I've already tried that and it didn't work out. • I must never stop. • Ever. • But how am I going to live? How am I going to pay the bills? • I'll figure something out. I'll suck it up. I'll work at dumb jobs forever just so I can make music. Fuck it. • Sandy. I

---

* For those of you tapping along at home.

Black guy:

White guy:

Drum fill in unison:

don't like this. I don't like thinking about you so much. • What do I have to offer you? Why are you with me? I don't even make music anymore. • Sandy. I am excited. I am guarded. But I am excited.

Too quickly the train is in the tunnel, my drummers gone, the recorded voice that all the new trains use instead of a conductor comes on letting us know that Third Avenue is next. I could listen to those drums, any drums for hours. No melody, no tune necessary. Just give me the pounding beat, over and over, a mad rush of syncopated whacks, thumps, clacks and dings. Tim used to take the opening drums of *When the Levee Breaks*, loop them, smoke salvia then sit back in the captain's chair and drift away with the towering studio monitors pulsing the raw beat at full volume. Sound. Human beings, some more than others, but all of us in some way, transformed, trans-ported, -planted, -posed to some*where* else, into some*one* else. I want to feel the swell, the shockwave, the surge of air pressure ripple through me. I want to stand behind a cannon blast. I want my hair and jeans to flap in the sonic boom of TNT. I close my eyes. Sound.

The cliché is true: Life does come in waves. Waves of inspiration. Waves of depression and bad luck and dark times. And yes, waves of jubilation and of mirth, cascading down, nearly crippling you with good fortune so overwhelming, so invigorating and life-affirming that you are left uneasy and unsteady. Things shouldn't be this good, you fear. You sense this not out of a foolish religiosity or superstition but out of knowing there is balance in the world and sooner or later things even out. Or maybe you are simply chary or paranoid and need to learn to enjoy good fortune as it comes your way. There is not some inevitable equilibrium that must be met in your life. Or if there is equilibrium, your good fortune will just balance out with someone else's misfortune. But ultimately perhaps you don't believe any of this. There is no karmic internal balance, no system of just punishment and reward, no external yin-yang of complimentary and opposing forces. Life simply is what it is. Fuck it.

Standing in Jay's new loft on North 2nd Street—complete with views of the Williamsburg Bridge and a decrepit tenement half-shrouded in scaffolding under renovation across the street, a polyurethane-sealed cement floor, obligatory sheetrock pressure-walls carving the open space, twelve-foot ceilings with the rough concrete finish you see in parking garages, and although I haven't seen it, no doubt a bathroom closet fallen prey to a woman's accouterments—he handed me a check for twenty-one thousand dollars. He had licensed one of his songs to BMW for a national ad campaign for their new convertible. And in that song was a guitar riff that I wrote. He used it without telling me, without okaying it with me.

"I knew you'd say no. But this is for your own good," he said. "It's half my commission. Without your riff I wouldn't have had the song." I stood with what I'm fairly certain was what is commonly referred to as "a blank stare." It was a lot to take in. He paused then added, "This is for both our goods."

He clicked through a few windows on his Mac, then with a final dramatic tap of his index finger he took a step back and the spot ran, the audio track booming, the spritelike, black Bavarian beauty racing across his vast flat-screen monitor. Thing is, you couldn't even hear the riff. It was so manipulated with effects and buried in the mix that you'd never recognize it. He didn't owe me anything. But there it was, a check for twenty-one thousand dollars in my hot hand. I folded it in half and slid it into my pocket on top of Paper Sandy. It was a very good day for that pocket.

"It just started running about a week ago but I'm surprised you haven't seen the commercial," he says in a raised voice over the music, "it's all over the place."

"I've been out with Sandy every day and every night, and for the first time in a long time, I haven't turned on my TV in days." I feel a little rush realizing what I just said.

"Well, this was just the up-front fee," Jay says, clearly enjoying going over the details. "Usually they don't pay this kind of money to an unknown but the ad agency had money in the budget for a name-brand act, which is like a few hundred grand, but they wanted my track, and so even at forty-two K, this was a huge discount for them. And check this out: royalties are on the way in a few months. I don't even know how much more that'll be. If this is a big campaign, with spots running nationally all the time, we're set for the next year."

"Jesus Jay."

"It's crazy money. Bout time. Hey, like my new monitor?" He says with a grin. "Thanks BMW."

"You deserve this, man. It's a lot of money. I can't keep the check. You can't even hear the riff."

"It's in there. I know it's buried but I built the track around it. I wasn't planning on using the riff, I was just fucking around with it for fun but somehow the whole thing just came together around it."

"I'm not EMI or The Rolling Stones or whatever. You don't have to pay me for the sample. This is insane."

"I do. I want to. I wouldn't have landed this without the riff. End of story. Maybe legally I could get away with it, maybe not, but it would be bad karma for me not to give you your due."

He drops into his desk chair, one of those expensive Herman Miller style Aeron mesh chairs. I sit in his old, not-yet-discarded swivel chair that seems prehistoric by comparison. I glance over his shoulder and marvel at the monitor.

"I know what you're thinking," he says.

"Look, it's just—"

Jay cuts me off, "You're not a sell-out. You're being an idiot. You're flat broke. Use the money to live so you can make music."

"I didn't say I was—"

"I know how your mind works. You're running through all the different angles in your head. 'Am I a sell-out? But what does being a sell-out *mean* anyway?'" he says in a mocking voice. "Yeah, yeah, yeah. You have to grow up and get over this shit. If you had tons of money and fame and then sold one of your songs—and one that was recognizable at that—to a commercial that'd be one thing. That's pretty lame. BUT YOU'RE BROKE! This money can enable you to make art! You're not even making music anymore. You sit in your apartment all day watching TV and writing your crazy notes. You're beginning to scare me. I'm really worried about you."

"Jay, I'm keeping the money. I'm tired of being poor. I want to be able to buy rice milk and not have to look at the price. I want to pay my rent, pay off my credit cards."

"Wait. Who am I talking to? Are you Dan Green?"

"Hah hah. Listen, you're right. Everything you are saying is right. I don't give a fuck about selling out or whatever. Or any of the stupid shit I'm always worried about. Life is good. I don't know why I'm feeling this way but I've just been feeling different recently. Things are coming together. I feel . . . I don't know . . . I guess maybe I feel happy."

Jay lets out an uproarious laugh. "Are you joking?"

"What?"

"You don't know why you've been feeling happy?"

"What?"

"It's because of that girl. That's why you're happy. As soon as you met her you've been acting different."

Hearing him say this scares me. I hadn't thought of this.

"You think this is all because of Sandy?"

"Yes. It's very obvious." My face feels hot.

"I don't think so," I say through a cracked smile. "I'm sure it's part of it but, you know . . ."

"Dan, it's ok. You need to chill and know when to enjoy yourself."

Shit. Is this true? Shit. I don't want anyone to have that much power over my happiness. I'm not one of those people. But . . . "Ok, ok." This is good. This is good. Life is good. I'm really fucking happy, actually. This is better than good. "This is fucking great. I'm really fucking excited," I say feeling surprised. This is how people feel. This is what's supposed to happen.

"Hey," I say remembering. "You have to come to this party this weekend so you can meet Sandy."

"Yes. Yes. The almighty Sandy. I do want to meet her."

"I think I . . . I don't want to say I love her but, I don't know. There's something there. I've never met anyone like her."

"Whoa, loverboy!" He says, nudging me with his foot, sending my chair coasting back on the hard floor.

"You know what it is?" I plant my feet stopping the roll. "It's not that I know what's going to happen. It's not one of those trite 'I knew it was love at first sight, I knew it would last forever' bullshit things. It's more that, for the first time in my life there's potential.

"Every other girl I've ever been with, almost from the moment I met them, I knew it would never last. There was always some sort of tbd expiration date in my head. I knew there was something about them, their look, or their vibe, or . . . *something*, it doesn't matter what. Something was off. And no matter how great things were with them, that *something* was always in the back of my head, the wretched feeling that every time I smiled or laughed or looked them in the eyes that it was duplicitous, disingenuous, that even if the moment was sincere—which so many were— I was rarely ever able to enjoy it, to bask in it as we all should, as is our right, our duty, because rather than being fully there, instead, I was beset and punished by guilt over my ambivalence, that to not feel a hundred percent toward someone—and by a hundred percent I don't mean thinking they're perfect or even being convinced of a future with them, I just mean knowing that there is *potential*, an open road—to know or even just suspect that ultimately there was an expiration approaching and to not tell them so or end things immediately once I sensed this but to keep going, even if it was with good intentions, even if I was genuinely trying to figure things out, give things a chance, prove my hunch wrong, still made me feel like a fiend, a wicked liar, a charlatan. That sickening 'this is fun, *but* . . .' feeling mercilessly, relentlessly nagging me, pulling at me, separating me from them. Separating me from . . .

"But with her, with this woman—hah, it feels weird saying 'woman.' I always say 'girl' but I guess I have to say woman—with her I don't have that niggling thing—"

"Niggling? What the hell does that mean? It sounds vaguely racist." Jay you are a riot sometimes, I tell ya. I'm in the middle of a soliloquy here and you're breaking my flow.

"It means nagging, or irritating. I'm just saying with her I don't have that *niggling* feeling, ever-present, lurking in the background, coating everything bittersweet. I'm not saying I know what our future will be. I'm not naïve. I'm not infatuated with her or anything. It's just that there's this potential. That fucking bittersweet feeling I've always had is gone. Now it's only sweet, it's pure. And I don't mean 'sweet' in some light-weight, fey kind of way. I mean for the first time it's not complex, there's no duality, no ambivalence. It's not that I'm convinced of my future with her. I don't need certainty. I don't need that security. I'm not even thinking about the future." Not too much, at least. "God, just having potential, not knowing the future, not knowing there's an expiration date looming at some point down the road, that's what I'm talking about . . . it's just amazing having a blank slate. Anything can happen."

"Not to bring you down or anything but isn't she leaving like next week or something?"

"Yeah, I think late Tuesday."

"So like what are you going to do? Isn't that sort of the end?"

"I don't know." Screw you Jay. You're so boring and normal sometimes. That's the difference between us: I'm not afraid to chase the magic; I'm afraid not to. I may be a dreamer and off in space half the time and miserable most of the time but at least I'm going for it. "I haven't really thought about it," I lie. "I mean, well, I don't know. I don't think it matters. Maybe I'll go out to Mississippi for a while. I never thought I would do something like that but maybe I would. I fucking hate New York sometimes. I don't *need* to be here anymore. For the first time I'm not consumed by the feeling that I'm going to miss something if I'm gone. Maybe it would be good for me to get out of here for a while . . . Not that I would definitely do this; you know, I mean, I'm just saying it's an option. I feel like I have a million options. We'll work something out. The details don't matter . . . We'll work something out."

· · ·

Sandy and I are walking into the lobby of the Chelsea Hotel. We had spent the first half of yesterday in my apartment sleeping in — (I had wanted to stay in her posh hotel room and not my shitty apartment but she said she always prefers the "comforts of someone's home—even yours, Dan" and she didn't mind wasting the money on the room because the gallery was picking up the tab)—then we bummed around the East Village, sharing a mid-afternoon brunch on a sidewalk table at 7A, wandering into second-hand shops and boutiques on 9th Street, and ending up sunning ourselves on the steps in Union Square while watching the skaters, hacky sackers, painters, protestors, and itinerant hordes. Today, we were supposed to hang more—I had the whole thing planned—genteel stroll in the West Village ending with a picnic of Malumpo sandwiches in the garden behind St. Luke's Church—but she said she had gallery people to meet with, old friends to catch up with, you know, "obligations" which was a shade too vague for my comfort but was perfectly reasonable so I didn't press. And when we parted ways early this morning it occurred to me that whenever we make plans Sandy never asks me if I am free, if I want to meet her for this or that. She just assumes, *knows* that I will go with her and so she doesn't bother to ask, she just lets me know what's next on the agenda. The funny thing is, there's nothing rude about it. In fact there's a respect for me in her candor over the situation, that ironically I think would make the politeness of going through the motions of asking rather than telling, itself a rude act because of it's phoniness.

She mentioned that maybe we'd have dinner together tonight (which I was very excited for because for the first time in a year I actually could afford to go out to dinner) but sometime in the afternoon she called and said she was running late and would pick me up in her cab on the way to the party tonight instead. I'm mildly resentful about any time that I can't spend with her but I know that's irrational, she's only here a short while and she has stuff to do, and who am I anyway, to take up all her time. Besides, the very reason I like her is because of who she is, and I know that that includes being a whirlwind when she's in town schmoozing up all her art-world people. Even so, I do want her all to myself.

"Have you been here before?" Sandy asks as we walk toward the front desk.

Shamefully I have never been to the Chelsea Hotel before and am embarrassed to admit as such to Sandy. Any bohemian, wanna-be-Bohemian, or just curious or remotely about-town/in-the-know/ok-just-plain-*cool* New Yorker must have been here but I decide there's no way I can pull off pretending I'd been here before. I'm a horrible liar and a worse actor.[*] It's the same shame I experienced when I was with Kelly at The Cyclone—yet again being at a place I self-consciously feel I already should have been—with Kelly because I wanted to impress her with my

---

[*] Yes, I'm aware of the irony of the fact that I'm a bad actor yet stricken with the whole depersonalization thing, wherein essentially I am an actor all the time anyway.

New York savvy and wished I was more of someone she already thought I was, and with Sandy it's not out of trying to impress—I wouldn't bother with a fruitless pursuit—but more out of simply trying to keep up, to not un-impress.

I'm bursting to tell her how psyched I am to be here but settle on a nonchalant, "No—a couple of my friends were at a party here last year," not true. "They said it was really cool."

There's an air of history in the lobby of all the alt. culture celebrities who've stayed here. I think of Dylan Thomas, Bob Dylan, William Burroughs, Johnny Ramone—did he live here?, Leonard Cohen and his song. I want to take in whatever aura there is, whatever ghosts of brilliance that have been left behind lingering for me to absorb, like walking into a cloud of cologne that you spritzed in the air rather than directly on yourself. But despite the overwhelming history, I get a sense that The Chelsea's time hasn't fully passed it by, it's not just a relic. Or, perhaps . . . I wonder if on some level I'm trying to convince myself that things are still happening here just so I don't feel like I've missed all the glory years. And it strikes me that this uncertainty I'm having here is a microcosm of the same debate I continually have about New York in general and my place in it.

Sandy glances at the artwork on the walls. The hotel has the exact right mix of grandeur, of history, of elegance yet at the same time is wholly not pretentious or stuffy, like being at a rich friend's house filled with impressive furniture yet his parents are totally cool and you're allowed to put your feet on the table and there're scuff marks on the walls from their dog. Somehow my mind lets go of the is-this-still-cool-now? debate and I have one of those moments when I think, "this is it, I'm finally experiencing the *real* New York."

I think I've figured it out: I suppose the Chelsea can weather debates at this point because the people here are beyond worrying about such stupid shit. It's not the place du jour and that very fact means that it has some sort of longevity, that it won't be reduced to some spot that's hip for five minutes, which inevitably would render it unhip in the sixth minute. There's a certain type of cool that only comes with time I suppose.

Sandy presses the button for the 10th floor (the top) in the elevator.

"Are you going to know a bunch of people here?"

"I don't know. The hosts are friends of this guy Victor I know. You met Victor at the Dia show. Tall guy, black shirt, painter."

"Yeah, umm . . ." We both laugh, realizing she just described about thirty guys who were at the Dia that night. She doesn't do the head-tilt laugh but more of a large grin trying to conceal a laugh, noise coming out in quick little bursts, the air exiting in delicate puffs from her nose. Her eyes squint under the influence of her grin and in the strange elevator light her crow's feet appear magnified in a way I hadn't noticed until now. A new laugh! I feel triumphant in my growing closeness to her. Such ease we have around each other! These creases around her eyes give me a new feeling of power I hadn't had. She's less invincible, more approachable. I will take care of you in old age. I will never tire of you. I see your flaws, your age, you will not last forever, and if you let me I will see you embarrass yourself, I will see you when you have a cold and are congested, I will laugh at your farts, I will console you when you are down. I can see the future and I am not afraid.

As we ascend in the elevator I wish Jay were here. He would see I've really made it, not that I need to impress him but it still would feel good. But I want him here more for him, he would think this is so cool, a party on the top floor of The Chelsea Hotel. I want to be able to share this with him, not experience this alone. Jay had warned me earlier today that he probably couldn't come and gave me his standard annoyed spiel about how I need to get a cell phone because "this is a perfect example Green. I'm meeting with people on the Lower East Side and I don't know how late I'll be with them and I want to be able to call you to see if your party is still going on before I trek all the way over to West 23rd." Nevertheless, I cling to the idea that Jay may take a chance and show up anyway.

The hosts of the party are fairly big in the art world, Sandy says. They were at her show and told Victor that they'd be "delighted" for her to come to their party while she was in town. It hasn't occurred to me until this moment in the elevator that people actually live in the Chelsea Hotel not just rent rooms here. I keep this revelation to myself.

We enter their apartment, which is decorated in a wild and worldly hodge-podge of African masks, Middle Eastern tchotchkes, Asian screens, oddball modern pieces, and Occidental prints, making the overall effect overwhelming, yet strangely warm and unintimidating. One gets the sense that the people who live here are genuine art lovers and while abroad just pick items up that catch their eye. I think of Andrea and her intercontinental travels that I've always been jealous of and she seems utterly pedestrian compared to them. Somehow being here makes me feel as though I finally have one up on her, even though I've done none of the traveling myself.

Sandy and I are introduced to the hosts, Stella and Bruce, maybe early sixties, who look relaxed and unpretentious in their not hip yet still funky duds. She's in an animal print, flowing cotton dress and wood beaded necklaces, he's in old corduroys and a (toned-down) Hawaiian shirt. Almost like art-world hippies. Someone calls out to Sandy and she looks at me for a moment, giving a panicked expression of "I have to go run over to this person, sorry to leave you but you understand" and excuses herself from us, leaving me alone with the hosts. I spy her as she saunters away. Again, legs exposed, this time she's in a silky, tight fitting lavender skirt with flowers embroidered on the side—both prim and sexy—that drops just at her knees. It seems cruel for her to show her calves but not to show any of her thighs. It's almost worse than her not showing anything at all. I imagine her in winter wearing a pair of jeans, or a long skirt with high boots. God, what relief that would be! Summer is just so exhausting. I'm always stewing in my vulgarity.

There's an awkward silence for a moment as Stella and Bruce smile at me.

"You have a fantastic apartment."

"Thanks," Stella says.

"How long have you been here?"

"Sixteen?" Stella asks turning to Bruce.

"Yeah, sixteen years," he confirms.

"But we've been in New York pretty much since seventy-two," she says.

"No, since sixty-eight."

"I wasn't counting that since we were in San Francisco for close to three years before we came back."

"What about the six months in Kenya, and, huh, cumulatively it must be over two or three years in Paris?"

Their banter is lighthearted the way healthy married couples are together. They're the type of old-guard art people (not that I know any but what I imagine is a type) who've seen it all, who've led lives that if I were to learn about them, would seem mythical, unapproachable. They probably hung with Warhol, danced with Jagger at Studio 54, knew Basquiat when no one else did. I want to ask them about all of this. I want to ask them if they think New York has changed, has it lost whatever specialness I think it once had or have people always been romanticizing its past? But after just a few minutes, most of which are spent by them recalling various travels, to my surprise and a little bit disappointment, they don't seem all that interested in talking with me.

"What do you do?" Bruce asks but it comes across more as an obligation rather than something he or Stella really care to hear the answer to. I scroll through a list of responses I could give but for everyone's sake I just say, "I'm a musician." I feel a sharp pain when I say this. I wonder for how long I'll be able to keep telling people (telling myself?) that I'm a musician without being a liar. Maybe I already am.

"Do you play out often?" Stella asks with the same disinterested obligatory tone as Bruce's.

"I do but I'm taking a bit of a break for a while," I say and feel another stab of pain as the words leave my mouth. I consider for a moment that their disinterest is all in my head but then Bruce like a talkshow host wrapping things up leading into the commercial break, hastily but politely tells me to enjoy myself at their home as an obvious conversation ender, and I take the cue, say thanks, and turn away.

I wander around the living room alone trying to look occupied, comfortable, as if I am meeting someone on the other side of the room, a routine I've been doing at parties since high school. There should be a word for this charade that people left alone at parties must perform. How 'bout a French phrase: *Faux Occupé.* (1. *When his date temporarily left him alone at the affair, Daniel's faux occupé fooled no one.* 2. *Stacy was a natural at parties, even when left alone she adeptly performed a faux occupé until another suitor approached her).* I remember once in college standing alone on a crowded Thursday night at P.J.'s Pub, one of those meat market college bars, when in a maniacal fit of insecurity, I actually gave a head-nod and finger-point to a nonexistent person across the room in case anyone was watching me. Not knowing what else to do, I then walked across the crowded bar toward this imaginary friend, actually pushing people out of my way and making an annoyed face of exacerbation at them for hindering the path to my awaiting pal. I assumed if someone had been watching me they would have lost me in the crush of people at some point before I ducked into the bathroom at the far end of the bar and turned away none the wiser to my profound loser-ish existence.

In the far corner of the main room there is a spiral staircase. I wonder for a moment if we're allowed up there, as you never know at parties if other floors are off-limits or not, but decide the hell with it, no one's interested in me here anyway and climb up the stairs. I pop out into a small room like a home office with a desk and some other crap pushed to the walls. There's a guy facing the wall, slightly hunched over who I think just snorted something. Coke? Meth? What the hell do I know? There is a sliding glass door that opens out to the roof. I move by him and slide the door before he turns around, glad not to infringe on his business. Partly to my relief and partly to my disappointment I quickly see I'm not alone as I step out the door into a smattering of guests. There are fancier roofs and tops of buildings with better views but the roof at The Chelsea surpasses them all. The whole roof is a massive multi-tiered deck covered with wooden floorboards connected via various paths, stairs, and catwalks. In addition to this elaborate system of decks, what makes the roof so cool is the overwhelming amount of foliage up here. Not just shrubs and plants but fully-grown trees, all of which help to isolate and privatize each section of the roof. Several other roof-appendage rooms like the one built above Stella and Bruce's place are sprouted about. As I walk along a pathway beyond the main deck area I pass a ten-foot-high pyramid cupola capping someone's apartment. I glance in the window as I walk by and see a middle-aged man in colorful, blousy pantaloons of the M.C. Hammer ilk with his shirt off revealing a wiry, tan, and weathered torso smoking a hookah with a large, gilded-framed Mark Ryden leaning against one of the slanted walls. My instinct of course is to stop and gawk in the window but in a surprising flash of restraint I keep walking, my instant change of mind evidenced only as a stutter-step. Somewhere up here there is a barbeque, the smell of charcoal and grilling meat wafting over to me.

Loosing my sense of place for a moment alone on a pathway, separated from everyone, I look down and spot what seems to be a randomly placed large tin bucket of iced beers. I grab one and walk toward the edge, gazing at the panoramic city view and savoring the mild breeze that has just kicked up. Whether it's out of stubbornness and immaturity at feeling like I was ditched or out of being laid back and coolly letting her do her thing, I'm resigned to stay up here in this spot until Sandy finds me. Rooftop lights on distant buildings glisten out of focus and I find myself on a third beer. I turn away from the edge and try to make out the people on the other side of the roof through the flora. Sandy is talking to some guy. Who is it? Is it Victor? Is it some other guy? I can't tell. Does she even remember that she came here with me? She looks so happy and involved talking with this guy. I can see her Goddamn perfect teeth as her laugh drifts toward me with cruel provocation.

"Hey stranger," a sweet voice, both girlish and husky snaps me.

"Hi. It's Jane, right? From the Dia?" I am about to vomit. Please don't talk to me.

"Are you having fun at the party?" She knows. She sees my eyes darting back and forth from her to Sandy across the way.

"Yeah. It's great up here. It's the coolest roof I've ever been on." You need to leave. This is a private pain I must inflict on myself.

"Dan—" she looks at me with a little too much pity.

Eyes dart: Sandy. Jane. Sandy. Jane.

I want to bust a faux occupé and dash to some other side of the roof and avoid whatever is happening here.

"Jane, should I know something?"

Her face is revealing more than I want it to. I turn quickly toward Sandy again then back to Jane. Finally she says, "Dan, she really likes you. I really like you. But you have to understand Sandy. I don't think you know her that well. I mean, she does her own thing. You know that, right?"

"What are you saying? Is she gonna, like, hook up with that guy or something?" I say this with an embarrassing amount of terror in my voice.

"No," she says unconvincingly. "She's with you. She knows that. It's just that . . . she's a free spirit; I mean she has her own reality. She collects wonderful boys like you."

"What?"

"That didn't come out right. I just mean she operates in her own morality . . . She really cares about you. I know she does."

"So, wait. Am I being dumped or something?"

"No. No. I'm just trying to warn you."

I take another swig of my beer and hurl it over the edge of the roof, instantly worrying that the bottle might hit someone below. I walk across the roof and stand next to Sandy not sure what else to do. "Hey!" Her face lights up as she says it and she lays a big kiss on me. "Victor, this is Dan. I think you guys met at the Dia exhibit the other night." I'm rushed with warmth, joy. Endorphins flush through me leaving me hot, light, tingly. Weeee! As I stand here and small talk it with them I'm doing a private dance. It's a mix of an Irish jig with an 80s dork, freak-out, my fists together, arms moving in and out from my stomach in a jerky circle like I'm churning a giant crock of butter.

· · ·

Look at me, Mr. Bigshot riding in a cab and not even worrying about the fare. At 2a.m. the traffic's light and we're flying down 7th Avenue. The windows in the back seat are open all the way and our hair is chaos. The driver is prattling incessantly in—what is that? Farsi? Arabic? God, I don't know anything about the world—into his dangling cellphone earpiece.

*Potential.* Anything can happen. Tonight. Any night. Any day, the rest of my life. My hand is on her thigh, tucked under her skirt. We're looking at each other, smiling. Her blue eyes, flashing strobes in-between flying tangles of red hair, wild like unmanned firehoses.

We hang a left onto Bleecker and in an instant there is no wind, the roar silenced, as we hit a line of taillights. The radio is playing timidly—I hadn't realized it was on until now—something staticy with sitars. With no wind, it's hot, instantly. I don't mind. I'm on vacation, a tourist absorbing the city anew. We're on a trip, we've left the resort hotel for a night on the town in some equatorial city, San Juan, Mexico City, Rio. There's a hint and thrill of Third World danger in the air. This is all new. This cab, the people outside, this city. The sweltering late-night air. This woman looking at me. But of course, I'm right here in New York. I've finally made it. I'm here. I did it. So this is the next chapter? This is how it goes.

"So, I was thinking about maybe coming out to see you. Maybe, I don't know, in a couple weeks, a week or something." There. I threw it out there. That wasn't such a big deal. In fact, why don't I just leave with you on Tuesday! This is ridiculous. We should be spending time together. Now. This. Us. This is happening . . .

Answer me answer me answer me say something. *Say something.* "You know, I mean, I . . . I. We don't want . . ."

"Dan . . ."

No.

"Sweetie." She places her hand on my hand that's on her leg.

It's a thousand degrees. The trip is a disaster. We were mugged by dirty, teenage thugs. One of us was clunked on the head during the incident. We have no money. Why didn't we get traveler's insurance? Do we go to the hotel first for our passports or straight to the hospital? I need to call the embassy. Or is it the consulate? Who helps us, how does this work?

"I don't think that's a good idea."

"Oh." I pull my hand back, embarrassed. I'm inside a toaster oven. "So, so this is nothing?"

"No, sweetie." She has tears. Wow. Stop pitying me, you're making it worse. "This is real. My love for you is real. Don't ever question that. But I fall in love all the time. There are so many beautiful people. Spread out sweet boy, try them all!"

"I just . . . I'm not saying I wanted to be with you forever. It's just that you were the first person I ever felt that maybe something could happen. I know, it sounds dumb now. I just felt like there was potential, for something. It was open. Things were open."

"Oh Dan, that's not how I am. I'm not . . . Listen to me. It doesn't have to end like this. Let's enjoy our time together. Let's enjoy this for what it is. Live in the moment."

I know she's right.

"I'm sure I'll regret this later but I don't think I can do this right now. I don't think I can see you."

"Maybe you will come visit me one day. But this is what it is. My life is very complicated, all over the place. I need time for my art. I don't share. This is how I am."

"I'm ok," I say out-loud, a non sequitur to her perhaps but it was a response to the looming question floating around my head. This feels strange but I think I'm ok. "I think I need to go though."

"I don't think you should go."

The cab's not moving. It's too hot. The cabbie hasn't stopped yammering the whole ride: Ashkintokati. Shtekoo? Stekolomiezxcfvasdfasdpf. Pejfafsdontoch. Wheashkontofskas.

The light down the block has changed. The cab two ahead of us is beeping at the car who didn't jump on the green. What the hell does she want from me? I'm a small person. I wish I could do this. We're rolling a little now, idling forward. I want to be like her. I thought I was that kind of person. "I have to go," I say and pull on the handle and throw the door open and step out. I almost fall as my right foot hits the moving pavement. He jams the break, the car jerks and the open door hits into me as my left foot securely hits the road. He's yelling at me, wringing his fists. "What the fuck you doing! Bark Bark Bark! . . ." I slam it shut. Cars are beeping. I walk away from the back of the cab as it sits there. I take a few steps further and as I turn around it starts rolling forward, the car in front of the cab and the rest of the traffic now nearly a block down the street. Here it is, one last glimpse. Sandy is turned around looking at me through the rear window of the cab as it pulls away, accelerating down Bleecker. With the pain and immediacy of a brand searing the wet meat of my brain, the image is seared into my mind. And I know where the scene will end up: a 70s tint, the colors somehow both garish and faded, catalogued in the slideshow of my memory. Sandy. Her tousled red hair and a face aglow with life even when framed in a dirty taxicab window, looking back to me with an awkward, crooked, sad smile that is distant so quickly as the cab races her away. I want you. I want you more now than I ever did. And this is a betrayal that I am leaving you. I know I am weak. I'm sorry.

## LATE JULY, THROUGH AUGUST

Most days I just stay in. Jay has called a few times saying hello, just "checking in" on me but I can't seem to get the energy to pick up the phone. I saved one message from him that he left the day after the party. "Hey man, sorry I couldn't make it out last night. Jen wasn't feeling well so we headed home kind of early. Chelsea Hotel, man—very cool. Well, I'm sure you had a blast . . . Oh! You're probably hanging with Sandy right now. If you guys are there listening, Hello Sandy! Heh heh heh. All right. Later." I listen to it once a day, which depending on my mood either depresses me or simply amuses me. Even feeling sad often comes as a relief when your prevailing emotional state is detachment.

People think that because winter is the bleakest season it is also the darkest time for the soul. Literature, movies, TV all push this notion, commonly portraying those among us who are susceptible to our darker selves succumbing to our inner woes in that time of the year. But there's a heaviness, a fetid poignancy that comes with being alone (and lonely) in the poor, urban summer, sweating in your boxers on a dirty couch for hours on end, the putrid air of cooking garbage outside your window leaching its way in. Oh the insidious guilt one feels for rotting away inside! The inherent vulgarity, the sacrilege of it, when just beyond your walls is the glaring sun, *life* is calling you! waiting for you out there, how can you be inside when it's sunny *out there*. Rainy December blues are easy, but feeling down in summer, it's as if you're not only at odds with yourself but with nature, with God.

Oh sure, I tried to get out. I went for long walks, usually at night, but as is such an ancient affliction in the city, being around all the people just made me feel more alone. Down on Attorney Street I saw my wife one night. She had just stepped out of Sin-é but there was no crush of people so she must have left in the middle of some sorry band's set. She had long, wavy dark hair and her face had a peculiar sadness in it. I almost approached her. I really was going to do it this time. But as I got closer she answered her phone and I had no chance. I followed her down Stanton for a block cursing whoever was on the other end of that phone fucking with my destiny. By Clinton Street I had already lost my resolve and turned north, veering off her path.

Slipping back into my familiar slump was like an old shoe, worn-out and kind of sad yet comfortable and easy. It wasn't so much, or exclusively that Sandy was gone (and how things ended) that led me back to my slump. I mean that sincerely (unless of course the Sandy breakup[*] was impacting me on a subconscious level but we won't get into that). It was more that I was simply falling back into this natural state I seemed to conform to when I was alone. I was back in the same situation as I had always been in, the only difference was that now I was a little older. I had yet another girl who came and went, and maybe I learned a little something new but the knowledge didn't seem to change anything. I was quietly sure my role in life as a failure was one step closer to calcification.

And yet again, money was saving me from facing inevitable external forces, yet not saving me from myself. First the advance from the label and now the check from Jason; there seemed to be a financial safety-net tossed out for me when I needed it at the last moment yet ironically that same net trapped me. The weave of mesh that at first seemed a divine life-saving gift slowly revealed itself as an entangling web. Is it worth being caught from your fall in a net if you can never seem to climb out of it? Perhaps if I hadn't paid up my past-due rent and the landlord served me with the eviction notice he had been threatening I would have hit some sort of rock bottom, forcing me into action. It would have led to me doing *something*, temping, waiting tables, (anything more than scribbling these notes), and then everything else would start to fall into place, and once again my head would be filled with music and I could start—… But

---

[*] I know, perhaps the term "breakup" is stretching it a little. How long do you have to have been together to call it a "breakup"?

**late july, through august**

alas there was no kick to the stalled wagon. Inertia continued its reign.

I knew to all appearances I was a shameful loser, an ungrateful fool squandering good fortune, and not even on clichéd but jubilantly debauched vices like women, drugs, and fancy toys, instead I let the money quietly trickle away like air slowly leaking from the tire of a parked car that never left the lot. But I knew no other way.

And so, as they had for so many years—(excluding the occasional tryst and the rare, glorious, shining frozen moments—neither of which had occurred recently)—the days wore on.

EMAIL I

Sandy, I'm a little drunk right now. It's 2am. You know me, I'm not a big drinker, so it didn't take much. Being depressed and getting drunk alone at home —Hah, I'm such a cliché! I never do this sort of thing though, so I guess it's not a cliché for me, so then it's ok. Does that make sense? I have no idea what I'm writing right now. My fingers are just flying over the keys. WEEEEEEEEEEEE This feels good!!! I'm typing so fast!!!

So anyway, I'm just spitting this out, or er uh, pecking it out. Plunk plunk plunk. What can I say? God, this feels really strange to be writing to you . . . Look, I'm sorry what happened, how things ended back in the cab. Anyway, I totally respect and understand where you are coming from, how you live your life, etc. I think I'm like that myself. But despite that . . . look, I just don't want to lose touch with you.

This is a disaster. What am I doing?

I really *would* like to come out and see you. I didn't mean to scare you off or anything that night. I totally don't have any master plan or any illusions for us. Unless I'm crazy, (which is possible), I know you like me. I *know* there was something there. So, I'd assume you would want to see me and spend time with me again. No? I just don't fully get it. I mean, I get

**late july, through august**

where you are coming from but I just don't, well, get it. Maybe we could just see how things go. I don't know. Maybe I was just a fun thing for you, or not even just fun, something more important than that but nevertheless, still something temporary. I know, there is a beauty in the temporary, in the once-in-a-lifetime thing. But still . . . I don't know, I feel like I want more. I feel like you do too. Can you just sever yourself from people that easily? (That was sort of rhetorical. And if the answer's yes, then that's a neat trick you can pull off. [I don't mean trick as in "tricking" me—although that is sort of what happened. Ok, maybe not really b/c there wasn't any sort of explicit agreement as to what we were doing buuut OTOH perhaps in this day and age, when two people get together the way we did there is always some sort of implicit agreement—I mean trick you can pull off as in a skill—that you can spend that kind of time with someone and just end things and move on to the next.])

Ok, so anyway, despite all that stuff, I do believe (or hope—not sure which one it is; I'm trying to stay level-headed here) that there is something deep inside you that may want more (w me) but perhaps for various complex psychological reasons you are unable (consciously or un-) to acknowledge those feelings. Ok, this is getting weird and mushy and I'm certainly not going to do some sort of armchair analysis of you or grovel to you either. That's totally pathetic. But what I am doing—and what I believe is valiant—is acknowledging my feelings and what I think is there between us. And if you want to bite, if you feel the same, and maybe this note will somehow unearth that sentiment, then cool. If not, that's ok too. At least I did what I had to do.

So—I'm thinking maybe we could just hang out, as friends, whatever, and if you (or I guess, we) are feelin some warm and fuzzy and tingly vibes inside once I'm there then we could feel it out from there and maybe fall in love and I could live out there, you know I could just stay out there and I'll work on my next album or maybe I'll write a book staying in a cabin we rent in the countryside while you teach your class at the college and we could have this big detached garage or a barn (I could build a barn!, we could bring some of your students out or something to help) where you could do your work, like Pollack out in East Hampton, and you'd drive bucolic back-roads commuting to and from school and then you'd come home to our totally rustic yet contemporary cabin after class in the evening and I'd play you some guitar and cook us dinner and then we'd have mint juleps (and I don't even know what the hell mint juleps are I just know I want to sip them with you) on the porch on a sweaty August night and you know, I'd bounce back and forth to New York for a while as we take it slow, test things out and I'd pick up mucho frequent flyer miles but after just a couple trips we'd decide I should just stay out there through the Fall and although I'd miss the city and definitely go back a lot and maybe even keep an apartment there somehow—we could keep it together, we could have a place together in New York, split the rent, whatever, so we'd both have a place to stay, our pied-a-terre, as it were—but mainly we'd just stay together out in our super-cool cabin, you know, the kind of place with beautiful exposed wooden beams in the ceiling and we'll go for long walks through the forest under steely Autumn skies surrounded by the changing leaves and the whole thing would be wonderful and dreamy and bathed in warm light and super-8 nostalgia.

Ok, I know I'm going on and on here. You thought I had too much running through my head when I was sober—hah!—this is worse. I've said too much. But whatever, I have to be me. I have to let you know. Ok. I've said too much! Arrgghh.

– Dan

EMAIL 2, SEVERAL DAYS LATER

Sandy,

Ok. I totally regret sending that last email. I was alone, it was late at night . . . God, it's too easy to just hit that Send button, huh? Not the same buffer for being able to take words back as having to walk to the post office. Fucking email.

I was feeling . . . strange. You know how it is. Look I didn't mean to freak you out or anything. But, you know, it's pretty lame for you to not even write me back. If you don't want to see me again, that's cool. I can handle it. I'm a big boy. But give me the respect of at least writing back.

EMAIL 3, THAT NIGHT

Ok. I realize that maybe you're traveling somewhere and you haven't gotten any of these emails yet. So, if that's the case, sorry. Oops, little overreaction. If not, then refer to the last email.

– Dan

• • •

And sometimes you're standing in the shower, alone once again like you've been thousands of times before and it's late and it's dark outside and because it's a strangely mild night for summer for the first time in months you turn the handle just slightly to the left welcoming water warmer than your standard summer-cool-down temp. Or maybe it's a winter Sunday afternoon or just another morning, any morning, it doesn't matter: the hot water is streaming on your head and the back of your neck and you tilt your head back and let it wash over your face and slick your hair back and then you're looking forward at the slightly mildewed tiled wall, and you blink a few times because your eyelids are heavy with water and the droplets are dripping off your lashes and you feel like you sometimes do on a solitary walk on a brisk gray November day and you're standing there, your bare feet looking strange, your skin getting pruny and it's not that the world is silent but more of a blur, an auditory swirl, a smear. And I feel a layer of me, a presence of me is lighter somehow, drifting away and yet also humming around me like a vibrating field, and I'm tingling yet I somehow feel nothing, and I feel heavy, heavier than a thousand, magnetic stones being pulled into the metal core of the earth, and I think the force should surely melt me into the ground, and yet I feel numb, and in a way I feel sad and wonderful, blissed-out, and in all its Goddamned divine rarity, calm, exquisitely calm, and music's playing, *Loveless* is radiating from the speakers, filling the apartment, filling the air, melding with the steam pouring from the bathroom, the air, some sort of the supernatural hydro-sonic amalgam, the infinitely textured wash of noise is Autumn lived inside a celestial prism from Neptune and it's scary and sweet and seductively Delphic and dark, and so much like home, home of me, of my soul and warm and—(I know or fear this is going to sound trite or adolescent, like bad prog rock lyrics, but I don't care)—I feel the magic of me and the magic of the world. And why am I so lonely and why am I not *here* and why is there a magic when I am alone and thinking and creating and in my head that I never quite feel when I am with anyone else? And drops are beading on the ceiling above my head. And I keep feeling this way and whenever I get to this place, when I am so alone, so distanced I'm not even here, I barely exist, I am just a whisper, but that whisper is trembling energy, more real than anything I know, when I am here I remember back to all the other times I've felt this way and I feel connected with all my other selves as if the me from different times could be separated into different people and we're all together, we have each other, we're in this club and we all know each other and we all know exactly how it feels to be me because we all are me; it's as if I split my soul into a million pieces and we are all together. I am we, and we are my own club, family.

And the strange thing is, the kicker is, I keep wondering, thinking, suspecting that there is more, that there is more to all this (life) than I can see. And I'm so desolate and I'm shouting from inside my chest and my stomach and violent, sharp rays like jagged lasers, green blue red yellow and white lightning firing out of me but I'm just standing here with my mouth closed, inside my shell, the water coming down. I have so much to say and I want to feel you. I know I am not alone and I want our energy to form a union. And it will be awesome and wonderful. Yet

I suspect, even then, that in the end, maybe not at that moment, but ultimately—(and here we go again, with the adolescent angst, the angry, teenage journal pronouncement, and damn you for putting it down and for making me do this)—I am alone, floating on earth, floating in space all alone as we all are.

. . .

I'm on the F train. We've just come out of the tunnel and I think the rest of the ride now is above ground. We're at Seventh Avenue. Over-A.C.'d, the train is cool and sickly as I watch a golden Brooklyn unfold outside the car . . .

I walk toward the Cyclone. I didn't plan this out, coming here. It's not that I felt myself pulled here but it also wasn't a totally conscious decision either. It just happened. It's clear what I am doing, what I'm trying to do. But this whole thing feels fake. I'm back outside myself again. I'm not sad. I'm not anything.

*Uggh. I've already heard this before.*

I know, I'm sorry. But I guess things haven't changed all that much.

*I just don't want to have to listen to a whole other schpiel about how you're watching yourself etc. etc.*

But this time it's a little different. This time I feel like I don't even care. I'm no longer pounding on the screen. I'm just sitting here in the theater watching, half-bored, popping Jujyfruits. I think I've accepted this is it. This is going to be my life from now on. I will never really be in it anymore. It sucks. I'm sad. But what can I do?

*Ok, I guess that is, if not an important, then at least somewhat interesting difference. But spare me the scene. We don't need it.*

Ok, fair enough.

. . .

*You're dying right now, aren't you? You can't stop yourself. You want to do the scene don't you?*

No, no, it's ok. I don't need to. I don't even want to, frankly. I just needed you to know that this is where I am. Again, I am defying the arc. No growth. Uggh!! And if you think *you* feel let down, how do you think I feel?

*So tell me quickly what happened.*

It's obvious. I was trying to capture something. I was trying to get back that feeling I had on the coaster with Kelly but of course that is the type of thing that can only happen once. It's all about the moment.

As I step up to the Cyclone, two girls, probably around sixteen are on line ahead of me. They both could understatedly be described as nubile but one of them is particularly attractive. The distraction is enormous and unnerving. Girl: short jean-skirt, arrow straight, long auburn hair, and plump breasts, probably 34 Cs, healthy and firm, suspended under a white tank-top. She has green eyes, the nose of a sylph, and the tan unblemished skin of the young. A comet of lust surges through me with the requisite melancholy riding its tail. To behold any attractive woman who is not mine can never elicit pure joy, the titillation is always saddled with a sadness that she is not mine.

Lisa was always shopping, buying new outfits or bags or shoes every other week.

"Can't you just admire the sweater without wanting it, without feeling some sort of loss for not having it?" I asked her.

"No, I can't," she said annoyed. "I can afford it and it makes me feel good to get it. Why is it good for me not to buy something that makes me happy?"

And then an argument ensued about environmental destruction, the vague generalized anxiety Americans feel (aka the twentieth-century blues) caused by ceaseless desire, commodification of emotions, exploitation of third-world workers, and the pleasure principle, versus the necessity of commerce as the engine that provides jobs at home and for third-world workers who would be even worse off without them, and "I still don't see what's so wrong with buying something that makes me happy." But now, it dawns on me, reluctantly, I feel what Koala must feel seeing the latest frock on a hanger in Barneys—I can't solely appreciate it just by seeing it. I must have it too for that appreciation to be complete. (Though, she is much more equipped to satisfy her desire by putting down the plastic, whereas alas, I will never be able to have every beautiful woman I see).

And beyond this sadness there is a disquieting sense of guilt and shame for objectifying this girl, which right now is even more pronounced because she is clearly too young. Having a conscience really is a drag sometimes.

"Hey," I stammer to their backs, "how you guys doing?"

The girls turn around and smile. I feel sickened and nervous. I smile back uneasily and after an awkward pause of eye contact choose not to say anything else and they turn back around. I feel a sliver of relief from disgust with myself; my moral compass is still in tune.

But hey, only actions are immoral, right? Thoughts, no matter how prurient (or sadistic or violent or of whatever nature) are still merely thoughts. And can this feeling about women even be defined as "thoughts"? It's more of a genetic trigger, DNA, survival of the species. Enthrallment surely is not in the same vein as thought. To be enthralled is to *not* think but to be mesmerized, enslaved, transported to another realm. But if all this is true, why do I still feel guilty?

Despite all this maddening duality, despite this exhausting ambivalence I must go through, ultimately, seeing this girl, seeing any of them is, in the end, always a good thing, a gift. I may even feel worse off than I did two minutes before, but in a deep sense it's always still worth it.

I ride the coaster numb. You can see it, very clichéd, cinematic: poignant music in the background, something classic, stark but warm—maybe a lone acoustic guitar; blank expression on my face juxtaposed against the amplified liveliness of everything else around me—the speed, the rattling car, the screaming, smiling faces of the other riders; perhaps the obligatory slow-motion shot as the coaster whips around a turn or goes down a huge drop, my hair blowing crazily in the wind, though seen in slow-mo waving hypnotically like it is underwater. With Kelly I was separated from the coaster and her and the world but I suspect it was some sort of response to a too-powerful, overly emotional, hyper-real type of moment. Now I'm separated but out of a lack of emotion, lack of humanity, lack of life. (The circle diagrams surface again!) The two states seem so far away from each other, so polar, if you will, yet it is the poles that are such dependable triggers for the separation. And the scary part to me now is that the south pole, the one of dispassion/depression/ nothingness is so hard to break out of, stranding me here for longer and longer spells, which in turn means that I am stuck watching for longer and longer spells. Even the episode of ogling and lusting after that girl on line was not enough to break me out of my south pole.

But maybe I'm getting better at this. Maybe I can break out. It is no longer as scary as it once was. Memories of that night of white triangles in the black sky, memories of the sun haunt me, return to me like surfacing whales, unpredictable yet inevitable and evocative. They let me know that I've been through more, I've been further than this, my mind has felt lost and untethered in a way that mere dispassion cannot approach and I still made it back. I close my eyes and think of the sun. I know I can make it back.

My lids down, the bright world on the other side darkened and dissolving to silence, my mind falls in on itself, electric currents spark at atomic levels, iridescent beams streak throughout like lines in *Missile Command*, doors upon doors upon doors open, neurons at lightning speed traverse infinite tunnels a micron wide, cascading catwalks of intraconnection crisscross from synapse to synapse like caramel wisps in a lattice-domed dessert—memories are found.

I remember, I think I was ten at the time, I was with my dad at Bristol Falls. My parents weren't separated yet but they were on their way. My dad had taken me on a trip to Vermont while Jen and Laura stayed home with mom. My parents must have worked it out ahead of time that this was how they'd tell us. Dividing among gender lines, how orthodox of them.

I had started feeling nervous and sick a lot back then. Although at the time I didn't know it was nerves, I just knew I felt strange, indefinably *off* all the time. I told them repeatedly that something didn't feel right but I was never able to explain it beyond that.

"Little D, you have to tell us what's wrong," my mom said one night as I crawled into bed between them after waking up with a pounding heart at three a.m.

"Was it a nightmare, did you have a nightmare?" my dad asked leadingly. But I couldn't remember any nightmare. I just woke up feeling *bad*.

On the drive up my dad didn't have to say anything. There weren't even any furtive glances. We talked as if everything was fine, but we didn't talk too much as if to cover up. We laughed at silly jokes my dad told and sang along to Springsteen songs but didn't laugh or sing too much. We sat in silence but not for too long. There was a balance we seemed to achieve to avoid veering too far into any territory lest it lead to an awkward moment of acknowledgement of the unsaid. It just hung in the air in the cabin of my dad's burgundy 240 DL like humidity, invisible but present. I knew that they were breaking up and he knew that I knew. He ended up never giving "the speech" I'm sure he had prepared.

I had never been with my dad, just the two of us, this long. Trips were always with the whole family of course. We were supposed to go camping for a few days but we ended up staying at a motel, which felt conspiratorial and fine with both of us considering I had never camped before and as far as I knew, my father never had either. We were destined to spend the whole trip like fugitives, holed-up in our room, eating junk food and watching movies. We only ended up at the falls because perhaps out of pity, the bearded young man in cut-off jean-shorts behind the desk at the motel told us about it, calling over to us when he saw us in mid-afternoon stop down to the coke machine for the third time in less than two days. "Aww, it's just down route 116," he said when my dad asked a second time for directions, as he tended to do because he rarely paid attention when people talked.

We parked the car off the side of the road and made our way through a short trail in the woods. Neither of us had suits so we just took off our shirts and shoes and went in in shorts. "Those look like a bathing suit anyway," my dad said pointing at my navy blue Adidas shorts with white stripes down the sides that I had been wearing as part of a set that matched my shirt. The waterfall was at the far end of a pool and we walked in the shallow water toward it. The bottom was covered with small smooth rocks that shifted under my feat. Once we were in front of the falls and couldn't walk any closer because the water was too deep and the current against us too strong, we stopped. Next to where we were standing there was a path that ran along side the water and curved back into the water between the falls and the cliff. My dad seemed content standing where we were but I wanted to go further. I wasn't sure if it was because I wanted to get away from him or because I wanted to explore. He never would have let me do something like this before but maybe he was too preoccupied with thinking about his failed marriage or maybe he wanted to come across as cool or maybe it was because the falls, in retrospect probably no more than ten or fifteen feet high, really weren't so imposing and dangerous, they just seemed that way to a ten-year-old. "Go ahead Daniel. I'll watch from here," he said.

I got out of the water and walked along the path, my feet having been numbed by the frigid water, barely registering the dirt underneath them. When I reached the falls and where the path curved back to the water,

I climbed down and shimmied my way on a ledge with my back against the cliff, facing the wall of water just a couple feet from me. The falling water roared as it arced in front of me and the sound reflected and amplified off the wall behind me pinning me in a furious echo-chamber. I stood there for a moment taking in all the sound and the protective solitude of the walls, both water and rock, surrounding me. Then, without really thinking about it, I leaned forward and stuck my head into the rush of falling water. Only with all my might was I able to maintain my balance on the ledge. The sound doubled, so deafening it was like miniature sold-out Giants stadiums cheering in my ear canals. The force of the water pummeled my head and neck as if I had stuck my head out the bottom of a screaming cigarette boat. And it was colder than anything I had ever experienced, so frigid it shocked me near breathless.

Leaning forward, my head engulfed, I felt alive and calm at the same time. I hadn't known I had been feeling bad, feeling bad all the time, until that moment submerged in the falls when the feeling stopped, like when you only realize you had been listening to the refrigerator motor once it shuts off. You were not aware of the low-grade noise. If you had been asked if you were in silence, you surely would have said yes. If the noise has been there long enough and is constant enough, it becomes all you ever know, it disappears. But when that disappearance eventually is revealed as an illusion, there's always a queasy relief—I'm glad to know the truth but unsettled that I hadn't known it until that moment.

Beyond the biblical (or is it Freudian?) notions of rebirth, renewal, and cleansing associated with water, what has made that moment with my head plunged in the falls seminal, what has made it the ultimate and the original FM, was the sensory overload. It took the opposite of peace in order to bring peace. (Circle diagram, yet again!) All the girls, the guitars, the roller coasters, the Maxell stereo-blasting-man-in-chair listening sessions on couches and beds in so many living rooms and bedrooms over the years, those errant nights from long ago before my stomach gave way when I drank until I couldn't talk or move, that time I was walking down the beach in Montauk when I pet a baby shark dangling from a fisherman's rod and its skin, wet, cold, and somehow both smooth and rough felt like nothing I had ever touched, this wonderful creature, its majesty, its life-force channeled into me through the pads of my fingers, but mainly the music, playing, listening, writing, thinking of it, the countless thousands of hours, and mainly the girls, faces inches from mine in the serenity of sleep, eyes looking into mine while in a slow dance, or closed just before a kiss, a beaming grin as she turns to me, an arresting new face from across a room—a feeling beyond feeling, a notion of capturing time—maybe they've all just been an attempt to get back to Bristol Falls.

When I got off the Cyclone, I was sweaty, overheated and hungry. For a minute I thought about hitting Nathan's but quickly reconsidered, not feeling confident in the outcome of my stomach versus nitrate-infused ground-up hooves and tails. I rode the forty minutes back to the city on the D train quiet and starved with the sickly feeling on my face, neck, and torso of sweat drying in air-conditioning.

Maybe so much info passes thru us in certain moments that the only way we can perceive them is as frozen or slowed-down b/c we can't process all that data in that short frame of time. (Like how filmmakers create slow-mo by filming at twice normal speed; when the mind works at twice *its* normal speed, reality, i.e. the scene before you, is in slow-mo.)

Maybe during FM there's a part of the mind that knows on some level something important is happening, something big, and the slo-mo is more than just 2X mind-churn but a hyper-time-perception gear b/c of an intuitive acknowledgment of the importance of the moment. Your subconscious forcing you to make it last.

"Is this Daniel Green?"

"Yeah. Who's this?"

"Oh, hi Daniel!" He's thrilled. "My name is Peter Gerstein. I own a gallery here in the city," his voice is at once friendly and crisp, and vaguely gay in the way so many of these art people speak, "in Chelsea, and I'm a curatorial consultant for the Dia museums. Sandy Mason had left me a message when she was in town . . . I guess it was a week or two back. Unfortunately, I was away in Berlin and just got back Thursday so I think I missed her by a few days. Anyway, on her message she mentioned that you are quite an artist. In fact, she insisted that I contact you about your work."

"Umm, I . . ."

"She said, you'd be coy . . . I'd like to come by and see this installation piece that you've done." His tone is forceful yet still friendly, kind of a tempered arrogance. "She said it was wonderful and powerful. What did she call it?" he said thinking out loud, "'Notes From An Autodidact,' yes, that was it. I'm always searching for new artists; this is very exciting. Sandy has magnificent taste so I'm inclined to follow a lead like this."

"I, I think she . . ." Installation piece. Installation piece. Oh my God. "I, guess, you can stop on by."

*Next Day*

I wake up late. It's one of those days when the transition from sleep to wakefulness doesn't seem to click. I wander around groggy and slightly dizzy for hours, trying to adjust. It's all in the sinuses, I'm convinced. Lying down all night, all those hours with gravity tilting everything the wrong way, it just throws the equilibrium out of whack. I make a mental note to sleep sitting-up tonight. Maybe it's not sinuses. Maybe I just slept too long and woke up in the middle of a sleep cycle or something. My apartment is a mess. Stacks of highlighted and underlined printouts from websites with dissertations on and dissections of countless thinkers and theories line the walls, clothes are thrown all over, dirty dishes are rotting in the sink. This place is a cancer. This apartment. This city. New York has won. I need to get out. Now. Even after paying my back rent and my credit cards I still have around ten grand left. I'll buy a car! A cheap, used one, a piece of shit. I don't care. No, that'll take too long. Title, registration, insurance, the DMV. Plus, I don't want to worry about it breaking down. Rental. Maybe there's a weekly rate? Monthly rate? Ah, who cares. I have plenty of money. Rental, yes.

I stuff my back-pack hastily with a few pairs of boxers and t-shirts, toothbrush and toothpaste. I feel like I'm in a movie and I'm running from the law or the mob, trying to skip town. Flip flops, shorts and t-shirt are on. As I sling the bag over my shoulder, I realize that my morning fog had lifted at some point during all this activity. I didn't even realize! A flash of relief blushes over my agitation and determination, the little wave of good news fueling my state, as if the new clarity is a divine reinforcement of whatever it is I am doing. I am indignant.

Phone rings.

"Is this Daniel?"

"Yes." Oh shit. Peter.

"Are we still on for three o'clock?"

"Um. No, actually. I'm sorry." My finger is picking at the strap on my shoulder.

"Oh, that's a shame. I was very much looking forward to coming by."

Oh man. Sandy, what the hell . . .

"Listen. Tell you what. I'm leaving town. I'm actually headed out the door right this second. Where are you located? You're in Chelsea, right?"

"Yes. On West 24th. 562."

"I'll drop off a set of keys for you in a half hour. You can take pictures, come and go as you please. Do whatever you want." Fuck it, why not. Maybe I'll make some money from some rich, idiot collector who'll buy pictures of my freak lair.

Peter Gerstein is short and trim. He's wearing wire-rim glasses, gray buzz-cut hair, black pants of the type that people of a certain era would call "slacks," and a stylish off-white, button-down shirt, just subtly left-of-Brooks-Brothers, that looks casual yet expensive. I wonder how much his shirt costs. I have to get out of New York.

"Thank you Daniel. This is wonderful. So tell—"

"Listen, I don't have time to talk. The car's running outside. Take the keys, do what you want." I drop them into his hand and run out to the car idling at the curb. I muscle through traffic down 24th then cut onto Seventh Avenue and down Varick and on through the Holland Tunnel.

. . .

As I cruise down the Jersey Turnpike, my Ford Focus is filled with the constant whir and rumble of road-noise that is the bane of economy cars, all of which lack decent sound insulation. It's one of those generic cars, so nondescript and utilitarian that it should just be called *car;* the kind bought by people who value price and pretty much nothing else. In my haste I didn't pack any CDs. But I'm enjoying the non-silence silence and so haven't even bothered turning on the radio. It's a perfect mid-level noise, too loud for me to think but consistent and level enough that it's not grating or provoking. I've melded with my Ford Focus, the white noise[*] surrounding me now feels as if it's inside my head itself, no longer just being absorbed from the car but somehow tied into my being, as if I'm producing the noise myself in concert, or maybe even competition with what's around me. All is drowned-out as the gray wash of static whirs inside my head, like when your neighbor's stereo is too loud, and rather than asking her to turn it down, you just turn yours up. Even if it's illusory, sometimes the only way to reach silence is through an arms race of noise. I stare forward, hands firm yet at ease at 10-and-2 as the black-top forever dissolves under my front bumper.

---

[*] Yes, not technical "white noise" but colloquially speaking.

It's been a long time since I've driven a car. College? No—the van! Of course, the van, the tour. This car, it felt awkward at first, getting inside, driving down the city streets, seeing things, for once from the perspective of the maligned driver rather than the pedestrian. I felt guilty at first, like a traitor. I wanted to call out to the people on the street, "Don't worry, I'm one of you! It's just a rental," but once I made it out of the tunnel and accelerated up the ramp toward the Turnpike, the F.F. and I were in accord like a disabled man and his electric wheelchair. Cars. Freedom! America! Yes—Pollution! Isolation! But still—Freedom!

Somewhere in Virginia on I-95 it's dusk and I'm wired and over-tired at the same time. I have a vague sense of where Mississippi is and figure I'm around half-way there. At some point I think I need to head west but I'm not sure when. I pull into a rest-stop and reluctantly order a sub, a coke and chips from Subway that although is a notch up from a mystery-meat McDonalds burger is still mass produced Frankenfood, slimy turkey and all. Guiltily, I savor the meal but I know this is only because I am starving. I haven't had a coke in at least a year and as I take a long sip, the rush of that blissful, sugary *coke* flavor is instantly familiar, setting off all sorts of dormant *coca cola* signifiers in my brain with endorphic sparks of recognition. I smack my lips and feel the chalky, corrosive film on my teeth.

Everyone here is fat. When I walked from the car to the building, a young couple waddled in front of me, the woman's ass barely contained in her low-cut jeans, a large roll of pudge overhanging the waistline like cake batter swollen over the edge of the tin after it rises in the oven. Entering the building, a black family of four walked past me on their way out, all of them obese, the kids' guts, even in ridiculously oversized shirts, still pushing out firmly on the fabric, leaving the shirt bottoms dangling in mid-air an inch from their bodies like maternity wear. At the table across from me a white woman and man, maybe in their forties, with flabby jowls and meaty arms, have just sat down. They are biting into twelve inch subs, while tubs of soda and bags of potato chips and cookies await them on their trays. I take another sip of my coke and now wish it was a water.

At the store, running my tongue across my teeth, I pick up a pack of Trident and look for the maps. I unfold one and see that I am *very* far from Mississippi. Fuck. I think I've gone *maybe* a third of the way. It seems like I-95 was a decent choice so far but I've got to start curving west. Ok, it looks like I can hop on 85 and that'll take me all the way through Georgia into Alabama. And no, I don't know where exactly she lives but I remember she said Miss State was in Starkville. When I get there, I'll find her. I'll go to the school, take it from there. I'll figure it out.

For some reason I thought I could do this in one drive. I don't know my geography very well. Sometime after midnight I make it to Gastonia, North Carolina experiencing the kind of exhaustion where you have to slap yourself in the face to stay awake (which I've been doing off and on for the past fifty miles) and pull into a Super 8 just off the highway. The room has two Queens and it occurs to me that I hope they're not charging me more than a room with just one. The last time I've been in a motel room was two years ago with the band on our lone tour, a glorious and horrible three-and-a-half weeks. Most of the time we crashed in people's basements, dorm-rooms, and living room floors or futons but we had five or six nights in motels, the four of us sharing two beds, no one wanting to sleep with Jay because he's so damn tall. Bass players, they're always tall.

Maybe these places only have rooms with two beds? I can't remember. The room has the obligatory chain-motel funk of old smoke masked by air conditioning and Lysol. I take the pillow shams and the bedspread off one of the beds and chuck them on the floor, then stack the two white pillows and punch the top one and get an expected though still dispiriting bounce off the spongy fill. I strip and ease into the cool, cheap sheets. They're so coarse and pilly that I fear full-body exfoliation if I move around too much. My head propped up at an awkward forty-five degree sponge-induced angle, I pull the bottom pillow out and shove it to the empty side of the bed. As I do this I notice a small yellowish stain of dubious origin on the pillowcase. I reach over and turn off the bedside lamp. The notion that maybe I should have at least left my boxers on sprouts foggily into my head but as if an over-eager anesthesiologist cranked the juice on me, I'm unconscious before the thought breaks the surface.

The next morning I wake up at 6:52. I had forgotten to close the blinds and the room is lit like a flare. For the first time in I don't know how long, I'm alert and alive from the moment I opened my eyes. My apartment in the city is so dark that I'm not used to waking up with the sun. This is what people should be doing! How many months, *years* of my life have been lost from the cumulative morning hours I've spent groggily trying to wake up in my dim apartment? Rent stabilization be damned, I'm getting out of that place. I've been reborn! I am now a man of the earth, the sun, in tune with the planet's circadian rhythms and I cannot go back.

I'm zooming down 85. Frankly, aside from the obvious aesthetic shortcomings, and sure, maybe the seat isn't so ergonomic, and it doesn't quite handle like a Beemer—I like this car. Ford Focus, baby. Anything more is a shameful, Veblenesque waste. Utility rules. I love this car. I look over to the other lane at the fake blond in her luxury supertanker, its crisp white metallic paint, chrome grills and rails twinkling in the sun. The Fugazi refrain *You are not what you own!* churns righteously in my head. I imagine that I turned on the radio and this was playing on some high-wattage FM station. Perfect. I remember when I was in high school in Greg Sowarsky's Malibu blasting this tape as we drove around town aimlessly on Saturday nights, cursing the A-crowd, cursing our parents, cursing the world. "All I fucking care about is music," I declared, shouting over Ian MacKaye. And in the pure way that only a teenager can, I meant it. "Fuck yeah," Greg agreed and we slapped and clasped hands

**late july, through august**

as we sped down Arklanding Turnpike on our way to the 7-11 parking lot or Chesterfield Park downtown or some other non-place to kill another night. Perhaps it's preposterous but even now, sometimes I think my only goal is to do the seventeen-year-old me proud, to never let go of whatever it was that I felt back then, the drive, the certainty that guided my existence. However immature and naïve and destructive my limited and myopic tenets may have been, they connected me with myself, connected me with simply feeling alive more than I ever could in an adult life filled with its inevitable and endless, demeaning capitulations and compromises.

As the F.F. and I vroom down the interstate, in my head the guitars are tearing through the speakers. Go! Go! I head-bang (in a punk, not metal, way [yes, there is a differentiation to be made]) and make a I'm-in-terrible-pain face that comes from the ferocious joy that only loud, raw, chugging, electric guitars, tight drums, and a passionate, skinny, shouting, white man can elicit from me. I come to a town called Boiling Springs—(not that the names of any of these towns mean anything; they're all the same from the highway. [And who am I kidding, I suspect they're pretty similar, if not indistinguishable, off the highway too.])—having done fifty miles in forty minutes and pull over at a trucker rest step. A gangly man in jeans and a t-shirt and judging from the back, sporting what might be a mullet walks ahead of me to the building. His long-legged gait reminds me of Jay. Unlike the grand stops with fast food emporiums, gift shops and infrared sensored sinks and urinals, this is a no-nonsense structure, what I imagine most rest stops off the highway looked like twenty, thirty years ago, consisting of two bathrooms and a small lobby area between them with vending machines and a map on the wall. Maybe Jay was right, maybe love isn't like the magic we feel making music. Eyeing my options in the candy machine, casually debating between the three major food groups—little sugary drops, chocolate bars, salty crunchy things—I feel around in my pocket for change. I wonder what Greg Sowarsky is doing now. Last I heard he was in Colorado working for PIRG, one of those "fighting the good fight" lefty non-profits, but that was years ago. I pause for a moment, not looking at anything, just sort of mindlessly feeling the coins in my pocket. I can't get the image out of my head of seventeen-year-old me looking out the windshield of the speeding Malibu as I meditated on the trueness my pronouncement. I feel a fierce responsibility to that kid. "Music is everything," I whisper to myself. I hold off on the candy and study the map a few paces over from the machine.

I pull back onto 85, go about a mile, then get on 26. I think I'll be on this for about an hour. Then: 40, 75, 64, 65, the highways will clip by me like a quarterback's count. 65 and just keep going. Fuck Mississippi. It's ten hours to Chicago.

. . .

Again, I've underestimated my driving time. When I really want to be somewhere I think that anticipation infects my cerebral processing, and an unrealistic optimism takes over my sense of reason. But this time I'm only off by an hour or so. As I drive down Damon, the neighborhood eerily looks both familiar and new. I barely left the studio the last time I was here, so even though it was for six weeks I didn't see all that much of the neighborhood. Also, what I did see looked different in the winter. Now, even with the sun setting, there's a different, brighter energy in the August air.

As I head further west crossing Division coming up on Chicago Ave., the old vibe of the area comes back stronger. I pass an angry barking dog in an abandoned lot, the billboards are in Spanish, and the row houses have detailed frontage to the street featuring the standard early-century curlicues, moldings, and finials comically juxtaposed with sides left blunt and unfinished looking, just flat walls of ugly brick, as if the builders only had enough money to splurge for aesthetics on the front. Further west still, as I get closer to The Watershed fading light industry and old warehouses are dotted within the residential area. This end of the neighborhood is what's known in real estateeze as "up and coming" and you can tell that a smattering of adventuresome hipsters are creeping out here from Wicker Park. Every major city in the country seems to have neighborhoods like this where the funky coffee shop with four-dollar lattes is next to a boarded up house that's next to the dive bar that's next to the Thai restaurant that's next to a rubble-strewn lot. The urban landscape in perpetual transition; I remember Tim telling me that his building had already doubled in value in the four years since he bought it.

I ring the doorbell (which actually has no bell but flashes the lights upstairs) and wait. I hear the thudding of footsteps coming closer down the stairs. Dalia opens the door.

"Oh my God! Dan. What are you doing here?" She leans over and hugs me, not with a huge warmth but still with sincerity.

"Uh, I don't know, to be honest. I was driving around the country a bit and figured I'd swing by and say hello."

"Wow," she says though without seeming particularly rattled. "Well, come on in."

"Great, great. Thanks," I say as I follow her inside. "So, is Tim around? Is this a bad time? Is he in the middle of recording anyone?"

"Tim's not here, Dan," she says as I'm following her up the stairs to the main living room area. Two steps behind her, her ass is right at my face level and it looks great, a little meaty but still compact in her army shorts. I hadn't noticed it before. I remember that she was almost a nonentity during my recording and I suddenly feel a little weird knowing it's just me and her here right now.

Now that I'm inside The Watershed the familiarity of everything is vivid. The green velvet couch, the Christmas lights dangling from the tops of the walls, the kitchen table with the chess set, the musky and floral scent of all those leaves mixed with a hint of alcohol from distillation processes in the air. Mr. Bones gallops toward us from the kitchen and launches himself on me, his paws resting on my chest. But after a few zealous licks from him and pats on his head he abruptly loses interest, drops back to all fours and nonchalantly scampers away, like an actor instantly dropping out of character right after the director yells cut. Dalia plops on the couch putting her feet up on the coffee table. Her calves suspended between the couch and the table are thick but strong looking, like muscles had been built up from years of athletics in her youth combined with a layer of fat on top from recent years of sedentary living. I quickly look up from her legs not sure if I was staring.

"Tim's been in Oaxaca for the past three months. He went down there to be with the Mazatec, the native users of salvia." She pauses for a moment then confirms, "You remember that we were involved in all that stuff?"

"Yeah."

"He wanted to study with the shamans, learn the ancient practices with salvia and learn how to cultivate the plants himself so maybe he could grow it back here in the states. In the meantime, he's been sending me shipments directly every two weeks or so of harvested leaves. Our old contact down there . . ." She cuts herself off for reasons unclear whether out of doing a syntax realigning we all do in mid-speech or whether there's some illegal or just plain secret elements to the whole business that she either didn't want to reveal or were too involved to bother getting into. She drops back in to her explanation, "Tim felt our shipments weren't consistent in quality and so now he can oversee everything that gets sent back. He could grow it here at home but he insists that the Mexican soil makes it different. But I don't think he really cares about the business element, that's not why he went down there. He's there to be with the shamans and to learn about their culture. The whole thing is a spiritual quest for him."

"Wow. That's . . . amazing," I say soaking it all in. "So, are you running

**late july, through august**

the business here?"

"Yeah. He sends me the raw materials and I'm handling all the shipping stuff. He taught me how to do the distillation and extraction process before he left, so I process all the leaves and stuff too."

"Wow," I say again. "Cool."

"Yeah."

"But wait—how long is he going to be down there? Is he still recording?"

"It's kinda weird. After your album got, well, you know, after all that stuff with your label and the album being basically stolen by those dicks—which is such fucking bullshit by the way," I'm a little surprised that she seems to know the all the details, "—I think that really took a lot out of him. You know how much he loves music but I think he's become really disillusioned. The industry's just worn him down. He recorded some small projects here and there after yours for maybe, like, six months or so but then he started getting heavier into our business and also getting deeper into the culture." This is the most I've ever heard Dalia speak. Was I so in my own world recording here that I didn't see her as a person, that maybe she was talking or wanted to talk but my (and Tim's?) focus on the music rendered her near invisible. Or maybe it's just that she's alone so much now, kind of like that solo backpacker you run into when you're in a foreign country and he can't stop talking to you because he hasn't said a word to anyone for twelve hours. "It's really beautiful, what they do, their history and stuff. You know Tim, he's so passionate and brilliant and you know, he just kinda really latched onto the whole thing, the spirituality, the people. Before he left, he was getting active in some NGOs and other groups and forums dealing with indigenous cultures all over South America and other places, trying to preserve their ways of life, stuff like that. You know what our government does, basically trying to make all entheogens illegal, it's so wrong it's so against our basic freedoms."

"Entheogen? Is that like, hallucinogen?"

"Yeah. It's basically, like, any drug that can transport you to a mystical state."

"Oh. Yeah, the government is against anything that encourages people to think on their own, to not be a mindless consumer and producer. You know the drill." As much as I'm fascinated with the content of our conversation I can't help but continue to be just as fascinated by the fact that Dalia is so talkative. And I feel an undercurrent of guilt over this, as if it's a betrayal to Tim or the purity of my admiration for him for me not to be solely transfixed on his story. "So wait, is he just down there indefinitely? Is it rude for me to ask: is that tough on you, you know, on you guys, on your relationship?" It feels funny asking about their relationship, I never much considered it before. But I guess with us having a sort of rapport now, I've become inadvertently interested.

"Well, I'll tell you, when he left he said he thought it would be for a month, maybe two. It's now been close to three and a half months. And Dan, it's kind of scaring me a little. I haven't gotten a new shipment of leaves in a while and he used to be pretty consistent with that. And his emails to me have been less and less frequent over the past couple weeks. He used to email me at least once a week. He would make a day-long trek out of this far-flung area in the mountains where he's staying into the port at Veracruz to get supplies and used the internet cafes there. But he hasn't emailed in over two weeks now." She looks at me pleadingly. "I'm just starting to get worried."

"Things are crazy down there, I'm sure. They operate on a different schedule." I'm not sure what else to say.

"I know but this is just . . . I'm just afraid something's happened to him. There's so much corrupt shit that's going on with the DEA and the Mexican government . . . and the Mazatec, they're like nothing to them. I don't want to get all conspiracy theory about it but . . ." She shrugs and lowers her eyes.

**late july, through august**

Tim. He always has to be five steps ahead of me. Just when I thought I was getting closer to some sort of enlightenment, empowerment, bravado, getting closer to what I thought of as the way Tim lives his life, he goes off to study with shamans in an obscure tribe in a remote Third World village. Fuck. I can't compete with that. I guess that's the way it should be though. There should always be someone at least one step beyond you so you have something to work toward, and someone to look up to. I'm kind of glad I guess. No matter what I do, no matter how cool I become, I'll never be as cool as Tim. He's like the cool guys you knew growing up in high school who were a year ahead of you. Even if you run into them now, all these years later, there's still some vague, untouchable element to them that will forever be above you.

Dalia asked more about what I was up to and I gave her a rundown, touching on the money woes, then the recent check for the commercial track, that I haven't been able to bring myself to play music, and that's killing me, and that I don't know what I'm doing now, as in, "I don't know exactly what I'm doing here at The Watershed but I also just mean in general—I don't know what I'm doing." I left out all the Sandy crap. Surprising myself, I kept it all pretty succinct (which you know is rare for me). Attempting the summation of the last year or so of my life, it dawned on me that I think I've now simply lost interest in thinking or talking about anything having to do with my life. I've reached my burnout point. And losing (even if it's just a touch of) my self-absorption feels welcomingly refreshing and relieving. My spontaneous road trip suddenly makes a bit more sense to me. It's not so much an avoidance of dealing with my life, it's more that in order to deal with my life I need to get away from it. Dalia offered for me to stay at The Watershed for a while. And I think it was an open secret between us that it was as much for her as it was for me.

I stayed in Chicago for three days. I left Dalia alone at the studio a good deal of the time, knowing as good as our new rapport was, a few hours a day in each other's company was probably all that either of us wanted. She's attractive—her full figure with the meaty butt and strong thighs; the cheerfully fake magenta-brown hair—but refreshingly, (yes, there's that word again), our vibe was starkly platonic. (In her company I did entertain some semblance of sexual fantasy but only in the most abstract sense—[a baseline level I deem as an almost obligatory, biological directive of male DNA when alone with a woman]—as opposed to actively visualizing any salacious act.)

I took Tim's bike on long rides around the city each day, going all the way downtown, cruising around Wicker Park, and one afternoon over to Humbolt Park where things still seemed depressed and a little scary. Tim's a good three inches taller than me and I had been riding the bike basically with my tiptoes on the pedals and with my arms straight, elbows locked just barely able to grip the handlebars. As I rode down a side street lined with vinyl-sided row houses, two Hispanic guys were working on an old car parked on the street.

"Aw man, look at dat!" The mustachioed one said pointing, at me, laughing as I clumsily made my way down the street toward them.

"Comere, son! Wha choo ridin that too-big bike for?" I braked in front of them bracing myself to be beaten with a tire iron, too afraid to even feel guilt over my unintended racism.

I hopped off the seat, uncomfortably resting my crotch on the crossbar, my tip toes pressing hard against the pavement. "It's my friend's bike. He's out of town."

"Hop off, man," the mustachioed one commanded, giving an encouraging tilt of his head while he said it. He went into his tool box, grabbed a wrench and went to work on the nut while his companion with pockmarked skin and a wife-beater held the bike and I stood aside watching the two of them. With a few cranks the seat dropped down, the chrome pipe disappearing into the metal shaft of the frame. He pulled

**late july, through august**

it up an inch and tightened it and then did the same for the handlebars. He stepped back, "All right, man," which he pronounced like 'Maine' in a clipped way, "check it out." With his partner still holding the bike, I climbed on.

Mustachio: "Maine, a couple years ago you never woulda seen a little white guy like you riding your bike around here."

Pockmark: "Yeah, man, things are changing, I guess."

"Not that much," he countered. "You better not stay out here too late," he said turning to me.

I thanked them for adjusting the bike and shook their hands and patted their backs like we were old friends. And I wished we were. I never could do anything with tools and I always felt emasculated by that. And even though I didn't do any of the work, perhaps absurdly, I felt like I was a part of the process anyway with the bike. I felt some sort of male camaraderie, or maybe just human camaraderie, humanity, something. I wanted to thank them for being nice to a stranger, for being here. For being alive. But instead I pedaled away, down the hot, poor, Chicago street, newly stable with my feet secure on the pedals and I raised my right arm and shook my fist in triumph hoping that they were watching, hoping that that would suffice in saying everything I was feeling.

With Tim gone, all the equipment downstairs, the drums, the guitars, the mic stands, the amps, all of it, and every piece of gear in the control room were covered in cloths. I desperately wanted to run from one piece to the next throwing the cloths off with triumphant flair, like a magician unveiling his scantily-clad assistant revealing her as unscathed after having been cut in half a few moments before. But in a way, it was ok seeing everything covered up, it seemed almost more as a sign of respect for Tim while he wasn't here rather than as sensible protection for the equipment.

Dalia had given up her apartment and was living at the studio full-time, having made one of the musician rooms her de facto bedroom. Although there were several other empty bedrooms, I slept on the couch in the control room. By the third night it felt like it was time to go. I wasn't sure where I was going but in a very determined yet pleasant way, I felt ready to move on. It reminded me of the feeling at the end of eating a great meal, the kind when you're full but not over-full, and you wouldn't mind having another few bites of dessert but you know it's time to stop and happily, it's easy to do so.

Despite our somewhat distanced vibe, (in that while I was there we unspokenly knew to give each other our space), Dalia seemed sad the next morning when I told her I was taking off. I felt bad leaving her, wondering if she was lonely, and knowing that she was anxious about Tim. Yet, there also was a bit of Schadenfreude guiltily energizing me. After all, Dalia got to be connected with Tim in a way I never could be—(spare me the psychoanalytical homoerotic angle; it's not that)—I always wanted more from him, more assurance that he respected me, or even liked me. Maybe my reverence of Tim was unnaturally pure, and that much passion can never be linked with equanimity, that there always must be jealousy or even resentment of having to share.

(And I understand this is not only petty but irrational) but I felt almost annoyed that she would be anxious over where Tim was or what was happening with him. This comes with the territory of being with someone like Tim: if you marry a rock star, you have to deal with the fact that he's going to be on the road. If you're partnered with Tim, you have to know that a soul like his doesn't lend itself to adhering to convention or even courtesy emails. She never struck me as being of a kind with Tim, in his world the way I viewed him. She didn't earn the right to be worried about him. In some way, her worrying was evidence that she just didn't "get it" the way I did about Tim. I had always badly wanted confirmation that he viewed me on a par with himself (even though I didn't believe it myself) and being around Dalia made me feel (or fear) I was more like how I viewed her, an admirer, a protégé, a hanger-on to Tim, rather than a compatriot. Being down there in Oaxaca was a perfect confirmation to me of much that I valued and envied in his personality, his carefree, non-neurotic yet still intense nature, his wanderlust, his joie de vive, his willingness to sink himself without a second thought into whatever captured the imagination of his brilliant mind. It was an essence I knew I could never posses. There's that small piece of me, maybe five percent, that would absolutely love to try salvia divinorum, (that would love to do all sorts of things), but the ninety-five percent of me that is afraid of what could go wrong prevents me from doing so.

I gave Dalia my number and told her that I wanted to keep in touch with her, that I wanted her to let me know what was going on with Tim. I mainly said it to comfort her, letting her know that I was there for her if she was feeling scared or abandoned, but—despite all my foolishness with the jealousy, Schadenfreude, and (probably false) assumptions about her connection or lack thereof with Tim, etc.—I too was a little concerned about Tim and I wanted her to comfort me too and ease my fears once she heard from him. I was angry with Tim for possibly being in danger, I was angry with myself for knowing I didn't have the guts to ever be in a position like the one he was in, I was angry with myself for being distracted with jealousy of Dalia when I only should have been feeling admiration and concern for him, I was angry for the twinge of Schadenfreude I felt to Dalia, for she did not deserve any malice, and, bringing back my old-school, meta capper to the whole thing, I was angry that I was dealing with all these layers in my head. And this anger over my anger was an unwelcome jolt after days and days of internal silence. However briefly I had escaped who I really am, this surge of reverberant noise, the cacophony of internal dialogue shocked me out of what was only an ephemeral reprieve. *How dare you forget!* my soul chided me, because until this moment the quiet did feel like me, so much so that I wasn't even aware that it was a new state, it simply *was*, *I* simply was.

It was then, in what should have been harrowing dismay but was more a tired and not-quite-grudging acquiescence, that I welcomed back my old nemesis like a Wild West sheriff in a weathered tone saying, "Ah, we meet again" to the bandit who had swung back into town. After all, without the bandits the sheriff wouldn't have a job; I could not escape myself, the noise in my head would forever return.

I found the roads quickly leading me east, and not as a capitulation but as a calm acceptance of fate, as if the car was on auto-pilot. Within an hour I knew I was going back to New York.

$$\bullet \quad \bullet \quad \bullet$$

I drop off the car and walk back toward my apartment, the dazed buzz of twelve hours in the car leaving me just shy of full coherence, like being up at five a.m. or at high altitude. I come up on the-ever-changing-bar. The universal *workmen inside* indicator, the thin sound of music coming from a portable radio, flows out the open door. I peek my head in. Putting in night-time hours; they must be nearing completion now. Drop-clothes are over everything and small Hispanic men in splattered jeans and t-shirts are painting the walls a deep red and the ceiling black. *Right*. I had forgotten: *Hammer and Sickle*. Good to see they're staying true to the motif. Maybe he'll open a spin-off restaurant and make everyone wait on a bread line for seven hours.

There's a gaggle of smartly dressed people outside my building. Thin women in knee-high boots, handsome guys alternately in jeans or sharp, tightly-tailored suits. Who the hell are these people waiting for? I don't understand why they're here, chatting on phones, looking cool and occupied leaning against our crumbly cement steps. I hate them for making me aware of my image, something I hadn't been since I left town. It's not that I feel bad in my road clothes, my two-days-on stinky white undershirt and fraying and food-stained khaki shorts, (in fact, I feel good, weathered, worn-in,) but next to these fashionistas I feel as though I don't belong. I'm back in New York for ten minutes and I already feel out of place. Spillover from Jeollado next door. That's why they're loitering here. The reign of sushi will be long-lived.

I don't know what I'm doing here. In New York. In anywhere. I knew it was time to go from Tim's. There was no point in going to Sandy. So the pull back to Gotham was inevitable. Yet, when I'm in New York all I can think about doing is leaving. And when I'm gone, it's not that I want to come back so much as it just doesn't feel right anywhere else. Are you getting tired of this? I'm tired of this.

I brush by them into the building, then head upstairs to my place. Walking down the hall I hear muffled chatter. Dayna's having a party. Unbelievable. I just want to crash and now I have to deal with a party next door. I get closer to my. door. and

Twenty people are crammed into my apartment. They're all mingling, walking around, looking at the walls, my walls. My notes. There are champagne bottles and plastic flutes, and a cheese and cracker spread on the coffee table. A fiercely attractive woman with impossibly beautiful, one-thousand-strokes-of-the-brush long, brown hair and delicate arms like limbs of a fawn is leaning over the table pouring herself a glass. A pair of my boxers and a t-shirt are jumbled on the couch, old magazines and papers are in a mess on the floor under and around the coffee table. Someone is walking out of the bathroom. The party chatter sounds like chaos, I can hear everybody's voice, every single one of them. Peter Gerstein is in the corner holding court over a small group, motioning with his arm to the wall, his voice lofty, authoritative.

"A room is someone's sanctuary and so of course there is a standard intimacy with that but this is an amplification of that intimacy. We are inside his head. Everything, all his thoughts, emotions, ideas, an almost computer hard-drive cataloguing of his mind's workings is on view. A journal to end all journals."

"Peter," I call out, my voice somewhere between a bark and a plead.

His eyes open just a trace wider. Without skipping a beat, "Ladies and gentlemen," he beams to the room, "Daniel Green." The chatter silences like it was sucked down a drain. All eyes are on the circus freak. Or is it the star? Everyone starts applauding. I step up to Peter and grab his arm.

"What the hell is going on?"

"It's wonderful, I know!"

"What are you talking about? Who are all these people?"

"Daniel, this has worked out fantastically!" Am I on Mars? String theory is proven, I've slipped into another dimension. Does he not see that I am fast becoming overwrought! "We'll have to figure out how to re-create the installation so I can set this up at the gallery. And I've already had calls from my partner in Germany, we'll bring it over there too." He knows people are watching us, *that's why*. What a bastard. It doesn't matter if the conversation is a non sequitur as long as they see him smiling. "I'm hoping to set up more shows here next week. It's very underground, invitation only. Columnists from the *Times*, *Paper*, *Art Forum* are all coming by tonight. You're going to be a star."

"What the fuck are you talking about? What the hell is happening? I thought you were coming here to take some pictures or something. You're throwing a party."

"Daniel," he says softly and forcefully, leaning toward me. "This is not a party. This is a showing. *This* is art."

"This is my apartment."

Strangely, his demeanor shifts. He seems sincerely surprised, even empathetic at my distress but he's indignant. "No, no, no. Sandy told me this was an installation piece. You left it this way on purpose, for me to use. You gave me your keys."

I don't know why I thought he was going to take pictures. At the time—I was leaving town, I wasn't thinking. I didn't . . .

I am spinning. No, the room is spinning.

Everyone in the apartment is back to schmoozing, respectfully letting "the star" disappear into the crowd. There is a man across the room holding a pair of reading glasses up to his face tilting forward, intently studying the wall. Peter's back is now turned to me, he's glad-handing his small group which now includes my champagne reverie. I grab the flute out of her hand and down it like a shot. I don't know why I do this. Then I turn around and break for the door.

I'm in the lobby heading for some air when Andrea enters through the vestibule.

"Dan! I've been trying to reach you for days. Where have you been?" Her face is animated yet I'm having trouble hearing her, her voice reaching me muffled like there's a cloth in front of her mouth. I think my mind's a bit overloaded.

"I was away . . . I was out in Chicago," I stammer, "at a recording studio." *Oh*, I get it. She knows about this ridiculous art installation thing. Now I'm cool enough for her. Before she was always in a rush. Hi Dan. Bye Dan. *Now* she wants to talk with me. The cloth over my ears lifts, agitation bringing her and the room into focus. Remarkably though, I'm still nervous talking with her. "I know. My apartment . . . It's not what you think. I didn't kn—"

"What are you talking about?" She cuts in, flustered, angry. "What about your apartment? I've been calling you about Lisa."

"What?"

"*Lisa*," she says exasperated. "She was calling you for days and then she called me looking for you because you weren't returning her messages. Why don't you have a cell phone!"

"What, the hell, are you talking about?" I say slowly, each section on a beat.

"She's . . . it's a long story. I can't believe I'm telling you this, here, in the lobby. Maybe we should go into my apartment or something."

"Andrea, what the hell is going on?" Where's the cloth? I want the cloth back.

"Dan. Lisa's pregnant . . . More than pregnant. She's due any day now."

She meets my stare, waits a beat and raises her eyebrows.

"It's your kid, Dan. She told me."

I'm still staring.

"She wasn't going to tell you . . . I don't know. I don't know all the details . . . It's crazy. But I guess at the last moment she couldn't keep it from you . . . But WHERE HAVE YOU BEEN? God, get a fucking cell phone already. She couldn't get a hold of you and then she called me looking for you."

"I was in Chicago," I say unnecessarily.

Andrea ignores me and continues, "She's in Spain at her grandmother's or cousin's or something. You need to call her. You should see her. Maybe you can get there before . . ."

"Spain?!"

"Yeah, that's where her family's from. Or at least part of it. She doesn't talk with her mom in the states. You should know this. Didn't you know that?" My head quickly scans its memory banks like a finger running across the spines of a thousand books. Did she ever tell me she had family in Spain? I'm in the library of my brain, I'm running down hundred-yard aisles, one stack after another, millions of books streaming by me. I can't find it. "They're taking care of her there. She didn't want to be here alone."

"Wait. I don't understand! Did she move there? Is she coming back?"

"I'm sure . . . I don't know . . . I'm sure she is. Just call her. I have her number there upstairs."

I'm so nervous all the time. I'm so overwhelmed with anxiety . . .

Everything . . . there are too many layers. I've been drifting above. I've been shoved aside. Watching. I've been locked away in the corners of my mind. And yet, now, at a time when any sane person would have already slipped away into dissociation—perhaps it's all the practice, the relentless anxiety that for once, rather than leaving me worn down has left me tolerant to the most extreme of stimuli—I am very *here*. I've been in a cordoned-off world for so long, numbed to Action, and but now, finally, the reality-confirming proverbial pinch is not just pinching, but squeezing, clamping me with the force of a thousand twisting vice grips with jutting steel teeth, CRUNCHING, CRUNCHING down on me, grinding through skin, cartilage, and bone, it's disgusting, the intransigent lucidity of it, the blunt reality, ACTION, it is unavoidable, on top of me, on top of everything, it is everything. And you, you all would crumble, you would be pulverized under this weight. But in this incandescent moment, I am here, in Action. And more than that, I am strangely calm. Weary, buzzing, vertiginous, yet calm.

As Andrea commands me to come upstairs I open the outer door. Stepping outside her voice is still going. As the door slowly closes, the peoples' voices on the stoop smoothly lap on the tail of hers like a radio station cross-fade.

I'm on the street now, the thick, night, late summer, city air mucilaginous like tar. A serene daze surrounds my head insulating it like an astronaut's bubble. Voices that were clear and harsh when I had come outside, strangely, as the door clinked shut, abruptly morphed to muffled tones as if someone threw the cloth over my head again. And now as I walk down the street, their voices, everyone's voices slip even further away, almost snuffed out completely, just feeble whimpers from geriatrics' faces smothered under pillows. Then silence. I'm nauseous. My body has been dunked in a vat of Vaseline, every pore, every orifice sealed. The street is so hot. Droplets and globules of goo are dripping off of me. But now, cutting through the paste, a raw, discordant screech of a city bus breaking to a halt shrieks in my ears. There are no buses on East 4th. A stinging, sibilant, metallic *tsss* reverberates in my head, the highest band on an EQ jacked, ants bashing symbols on miniature drum-kits in my ears. The sustained *tsss* is punctuated with *zzzt*'s of digital distortion, like an electrified bee pricking through a membrane covering my ears. My head is wrapped in cellophane. I'm chewing tinfoil. I am besieged by metallic sizzle. Every nerve, all five billion of them, exposed wires sparking like a blazing sea anemone. The cellophane begins to tear open, the world leaking back in. I'm in front of *Hammer and Sickle*. I wish *Crimson and Clover* were coming out of the radio. Or *Needles and Pins*—do you know that song? Something jangley and old, but sadly, transistor radios only play A.M. music from the sixties in movies. Instead it's Latin pop. There's an electronic dance beat and repetitive vocal track. I have a rapid yet incremental shift back to lucidity, like I'm quickly ascending steps out of a pool. I feel a wave of wakefulness, a brightening. I'm under control now, folks. Don't worry. I'm back. I duck in *H&S*. The workmen are not there but their brushes and rollers and paint buckets are all out. On break? I grab a bucket of black and head out of the bar.

I'm bouncing now, not in my step but in my head as I race back to 132 East 4th Street. The preening sartorial militia are still out front. Or maybe it's a different crew from before, it's too hard to tell. Doesn't matter, the interchangeable dudes, dudettes, and that Goddamned, obligatory and ubiquitous cell phone prattler are here. The yammering, the incessant yammering! of a girl's voice into a cell phone. Shrill. Ceaseless. Zooming in, her jaw is mechanical, robotic in its relentless movement. And even closer, lips shifting and mutating with dazzling choreography into an unpredictable series of shapes and poses at an impossible speed. And that voice! In one clean, arcing motion, I swipe the phone out of her hand and hurl it at the side of my building and watch it burst against the brick wall. I bound past her and through the front door, then run up to my floor, taking the stairs two at a time, paint splashing on my bare forearm, my hand red from gripping the bucket wire, my pit-stained

**late july, through august**

t-shirt, sweat-soaked through the back and chest. I can barely contain myself. I run down the hall then shoulder open the door.

"THIS ISN'T ART!" I proclaim, silencing the room. There is a pregnant moment of icy stillness

"NO! *I* AM NOT ART!" Peter, a cappella, begins clapping. A tentative applause then starts to build from around the room. The approbation swelling, a man turns to his friend's ear, "Oh, this is brilliant. Brilliant."

"THIS ISN'T A PERFORMANCE!" I cry out while I heave the black paint onto one of the walls, dousing several guests in the way. They stand soaked, aghast. I am exposed, ripped open, and they are inside. My heart, my dreams, my soul on view, to be judged, or worse, only to entertain. All these faces, everyone fixed on me, strangers. I shove the doused people out of my way and run back and forth along the wall frantically smearing my hands in the paint, spastically tearing notes off the wall in the process. Behind my back the room erupts. The fervent clapping is punctuated by a "Bravo!" And . . . timidly my hands lower to my sides. Ever so slowly, I turn around. Standing there, my hands dripping black, I scan my studio apartment. My notes, thousands of them are enveloping us. All these faces, everyone fixed on me, strangers. The fury inside me is crumbling like slow-motion footage of an imploding building. The red-lined needle drops. Slowly, an anxious smile grows on my face.

Despite how tired I feel my eyes are not bloodshot. I'm half disappointed I must admit. Sometimes you want to look good when you feel bad but other times, like now, fresh-faced and standing straight, it feels like my visage is betraying me, like I'm being a phony. I remind myself it's not my fault. Look at them: surrounding the dark corneas, smooth white spheres, like porcelain knobs, a little glassy perhaps, but still, too clear, too white. Betrayal. I pull the skin down below them, tilt my head down and look up. An index finger tugging below each eye, I see crawling up from the normally-hidden bottom of the orbs a few jagged, and a couple intricate and squiggley lines like an angry child's doodles with a red pen. Yes! Finally, some veins. (Wait, those aren't veins. They're capillaries. Or is it blood vessels? Are blood vessels capillaries?) Bloodshot indeed, I just had to look a little harder, cheat a little. At least this is something. I feel better now. I pull my hands from my face, lift my head back to facing straight and blink flutteringly, my eyes desperately trying to remoisten.

Surprisingly, it doesn't smell in here. I expected it to, like a port-o-john, but all there is is a faint antiseptic smell. Maybe airplane bathrooms always smell ok, I just continually forget. Or maybe I'm just lucky this time. Note to self: check out bathroom on the way back for a more conclusive idea. It's a strange relief being in here. I don't get cabin fever, at least not more than the average person, I don't think. But I'm finding I like this break from being amid everyone. It's bad energy, being crammed in like that. All those people, *sitting there*, reading, eating, breathing. Sometimes privacy is welcome even if you have nothing to hide.

Ever since my early twenties, when it first came on my radar via other college kids doing semesters abroad, I developed the notion that my first time in Europe should be while on tour with a band. It seemed like the only right way to do it. And I'm not talking about a triumphant arena tour. Dingy clubs would have been fine. Better than fine. Perfect. I imagined four of us would cram into cheap hotel rooms or if we got lucky certain nights we'd crash in fans' apartments. I'd do some interviews and warn the journalists not to misquote me. After hard nights of partying, we'd wander around a few obligatory sights hung-over during the day before heading off to the venue for a late-afternoon rehearsal for that night's show. I've held onto this fantasy so tightly that I even turned down a basically-free* trip there my junior year. At the time, the thought of being a generic student-traveler as my first experience across the pond seemed like a gross failure. Since then the opportunity to go to Europe hasn't come up. The Warner deal never materialized domestically let alone with their foreign counterparts; (even though once things were collapsing in the U.S. I tried like hell to get the label, the managers, anyone, to try that route for the band. Beyond touring, I was ready to *move* to England or anywhere else if some sort of deal came through). If it weren't for this I may never have come; not because I would have continued eternally to wait for the European tour fantasy to come true but out of obstinate deference to the part of myself that wanted it that way. If I couldn't go there on tour, then it didn't seem right going there at all. The lure of that fantasy was so powerful that I was willing to sacrifice my reality just so I could hold onto the way thinking about that fantasy made me feel. Does that make sense? When reality lets you down, the only thing you have left is to hold onto fantasy, even if you know it will always remain fantasy. But, here I am, at thirty-plus-thousand feet, standing still, studying my eyes in a bathroom mirror while going five hundred—(is it five hundred? I'm guessing)—miles an hour across the Atlantic.

I know what you're thinking.

Listen, I did the math. I sat down, looked at a calendar. It's possible. It's not possible, it's definite. The timing. The pill really is only 99% effective. Maybe she wasn't even on the pill. But . . . unless . . . no! . . . *Jeff.* That fucking bastard. I never trusted her with that guy. How can you even talk to a guy with a goatee? It's possible it was him, oh it's fucking

---

* Subsidized student exchange thing; not worth getting into.

possible. Maybe he's flying out too. Maybe he's on the plane! She's going to have a paternity test showdown. Camera crews will be waiting outside the jetway. Reality TV. Or . . . maybe it is me.

Koala. I can't believe this.

•  •  •

My martyred tour fantasy is essentially still intact. Don't expect a travelogue. Airport, long (expensive) cab ride, Aunt Christine's house. Then reverse. I saw nothing. How could I?

I tried to keep my mind clear as much as I could but of course that was not a possibility. Despite it all, I had hoped that I would have some time to, well. . . . not relax per se, but at least experience the Spanish countryside. On the flight over, I pictured myself staying in a villa, distraught, overwhelmed but nevertheless eating good food and napping during siesta. There was something poetic about it all. I did figure, however ridiculously, that I would travel around a bit, try some of the food, go to the beach (I didn't realize at first that Madrid wasn't near any beaches). I know it sounds crazy to be thinking about such things but I couldn't turn my imagination off. Sometimes we think of the stupidest shit just to avoid focusing on what's important.

Mostly though, my mind *was* focused. The country, the food, the ruining of my European tour fantasy, my newfound stardom from my installation art triumph (or farce, depending how you view such things), even Koala, were at most, brief distractions. I was only thinking about my child to be. I didn't even know the gender. Lisa may have known but I didn't ask her on the phone before I left. Our conversation was awkward and brief.

"It's Dan. I just got your messages. I was out of New York. Long story."

"I don't know what to say." Her voice was shaky, unsure. "I guess

Andrea filled you in?"

"Yes. I . . . there's so much . . . Listen. I'm coming out right away. Tomorrow. As soon as I can get a flight. Is that ok?"

"Yeah," she said quietly. "I think you should come out."

"Give me all the info."

And that was basically that.

That night, and on the plane, and when I was in the cab, and when I was lying on the couch in the guest room I slept in staring at the ceiling late every night, I thought about my son. I didn't know it would be a boy but somehow I just felt it. I didn't prefer it, (it's not like I was setting up a grand patriarchy), the notion just intoned in me. A dreamy montage kept playing itself out in my head: I imagined him growing up at various stages of his life, as a little boy wobbling around the way nursery school kids do on their little legs; as a teenager asking ala *Cats in the Cradle*, "what I'd really like, dad, is to borrow the car keys, see you later can I have them please" (without all the negative connotations of the song—I was just picturing the scene); as a young man about my age now, living in some big city somewhere, doing good, being confused, seeking advice from his, by then, noble and wise pop. None of it was logical: some mythic suburban scene where I actually live in suburbia and own a car? And why would he be with me anyway, his parents aren't even married, never were? But there it was, this hazy chronology of vignettes of someone I didn't know, informed less by my own life than by a pop song and too many books, too many shows, too many movies.

And I kept ending with the beginning. I'm in the hospital with Lisa—(the hospital has some non-specific European flair to it, maybe the staff have smarter uniforms, maybe it's a touch less corporate or sterile inside than American hospitals)—and the nurse is holding the new baby, so new there's still blood and other guck on him, and he's screaming, and everyone, the doctor, the nurses, me, Lisa, her family (whoever they are) are all smiling, beaming through exhaustion. And I think . . . No, not think, *know*, embody, feel, live the knowledge that there is my son. Light emanating from him. There's this glow around him like a corona. And now I understand why they call a son, *son*. He was the sun! And I don't know the etymology of the word but the homonymic pun seemed fitting enough for me that there must be some connection. SUN! The world, life itself is that boy! Not just my genes, my DNA, but the species as a whole will continue!

Swell of nausea. Waves of fuzzy, vibrating energy were trembling through me. Soft afternoon rays streamed through white, gossamer curtains shrouding Koala in seraphic light. She was propped up, her big belly's silhouette visible under the white sheet covering her. She was just staring into space—not a contemplative stare out the window, just a blank look into the middle-ground—before she noticed me in the room. *Who is this person?* I wondered. We spent a few months together, there was a spark once between us but no love. There was no history, no real meaning or connection beyond being a shared chapter in each others' own stories. Look at that woman, at that belly. That's my child in there. Made with this woman I don't know and don't love and she doesn't love me. I don't know, maybe this is okay. Maybe this is what happens these days. How could she not tell me until now? Because she'd known what I would have said, what I would have wanted. Women have the right to end a pregnancy but I rarely thought of it the other way around. I should have known, dating a girl who was a "lapsed" Catholic. Lapsed, my ass. Religion, dogma, family, ancestry; that stuff doesn't just disappear from your psyche after a few women's lib classes at Dartmouth and mingling with urbane friends in New York. And who am I kidding, it's about none of those things, it's about what she wants. She's running the show. Feminism in extremis.

"Listen I don't expect—"

"I know," I said.

"I don't know what I was thinking not telling you."

What, that you lied to me about being on the pill? You did this. You did this on purpose. I *am* flattered that I was picked, that my genes were suitable for you, but still . . .

"This wasn't something I planned on . . . I mean the pregnancy, obviously. But also I mean not telling you. I just thought I could . . . I wanted to do it on my own. I didn't want to burden you—"

"That's not your decision."

"Well, it is technically," God, I hate her. "But I know, I should have told you. I'm so sorry." She let out an exhale in a short burst. "Well, anyway, now I did."

"What happens now?"

"I don't know. I'm coming back to New York in a couple weeks after the baby is born. We can go over more stuff then."

"Should I be calling a lawyer or something? I have no idea what's going on, what to do. This is my son . . . This is my son."

"We're going to work something out."

"This is my son."

"Too. This is your son too. And we don't know if it's a son."

"Do you already have names picked out? I'm allowed in on that, right?"

"We'll name him, or her, together." I hate you Lisa. "Dan, you are not prepared to raise a child—financially, emotionally . . . I am . . . My firm has great maternity leave and then, in a couple months I'll be back at work. I have enough money . . ." *Without you*, she wanted to say.

"I'm sure you have enough money. But who's going to take care—"

"My cousin is going to move in with me for a while."

"Wow, you've really figured this all out, haven't you? What about me! Where the fuck do I fit in to all this?"

"We'll figure something out." She keeps saying this. Does it mean *you're fucked, fuck you*? Or genuinely, *let's talk about this later, in depth. I recognize your role in all this?* "Let's talk about it back in New York." She looked exhausted, or was it exasperated?, and turned away from me toward the window.

Over the days in Spain and shortly afterwards I couldn't shake the thought that maybe she got pregnant on purpose. And maybe it wasn't even mine. Should I demand a DNA test? I don't think she cheated on me, but . . .

Women always get custody in situations like this. Do I even want custody? She's probably right—I'm not prepared to raise a kid. But I'm not going to be blocked from being a part of this child's life.

I wanted to say something. I was about to say something. This conversation did nothing for me. I wanted answers! I wanted beseeching apologies! I wanted her to seethe with remorse for not telling me, for not including me, for not giving me a say. I wanted us to like each other. I wanted everything to be different. This was madness. I opened my mouth but nothing came out. Diffuse pain exploded in my head and down my neck. My back was on fire from within, the underside of my flesh searing like it was on an oiled griddle. My mouth tasted metallic and I felt something dripping off my chin. Surprised yet unstirred, I realized I was crying. Koala turned toward me.

"Dan? It's Dalia."

"Hi!" I'm surprised at how good it feels to hear her voice. With everything that'd been going on, I had forgotten about her and Tim. "I'd been meaning to call you. But I've had a lot of crazy stuff happen . . . too much to get into."

"That's ok," she says, her voice sounding strange.

Crumpled and torn notes still litter the paint-spattered floor. I haven't cleaned the apartment since that night weeks ago. The swash of black on the wall now a Rorschach test that I often stare at for hours trying to cull some sort of meaning from everything; the splattered and smeared paint taking on different forms, providing different answers each time.

"It's so good to hear from you," I say cheerily, masking my concern over her tone.

She takes a deep breath into the phone and I feel a dyspeptic surge. Tim.

"Tim's not coming back . . ." Then after a beat she blurts, "*He's ok.* God, sorry for starting that way."

"Wait. I don't understand," I say, tasting acid in the back of my throat.

"A week or so after you left I finally heard from Tim. He said he felt alive in a way he can't explain and that he decided he was going to stay with the Mazatec indefinitely." Her voice has a hint of shakiness, hurt, but there's also an indignance to it. I can see her shaking her head. "Not forever, probably, but he doesn't know when he's coming back. He said he hadn't gotten in touch with me because he was mulling it over and didn't want to say anything to me until he was certain."

"Whoa," I say absently, trying to absorb it all.

"There I was, worrying that something had happened to him," she laughs. It's hard to tell if it's a bitter laugh or genuine. Dalia seemed to be so at ease with what Tim was about, maybe she was taking this all in stride. Though even for her this would be a lot to swallow.

"Man. Tim."

"I know." There's a pause for a moment. "He loves them, or his quest, more than he loves me," she says with a heavy sigh.

"Maybe it's not more, it's just different."

"Maybe."

Another, longer pause.

"I've thought about going down there to meet up with him, we had talked about it, but that was a long while back. You can't chase someone who still needs to run; that's what my mom says at least. When he called me this last time neither of us even mentioned it. In fact, he told me I could stay in the studio, or entrust Marty or some other engineer to run the place, or I could do nothing. He didn't seem to care." She takes a breath. "I don't know what to do."

In a starburst moment, with no contemplation, or even awareness, without any of the normal processes that occur, a notion rockets through me:

"I can do it."

"Do what?"

"I can run the studio."


We talked a long time. At first, I think simply because she was taken aback by the idea, Dalia barraged me with questions and proclaimed all-but-certain pitfalls. And as we talked I had a running debate circling in my head with all my own reservations and impossibilities. Between the real dialogue and the one in my head, I had a notion a second, and each one felt like the definitive, final answer until the next one came right after. Her voice, my voice, the voices in my head—it was all a jumble of broken pieces but there was an order to it, a sequence, like a path laid with irregular stones.

I can't leave New York. My son.

No, I *can* do this. I'll come back every two weeks for a weekend, that's all the time I'll get anyway.

Fucking lawyers.

Fucking Koala.

Yes, *fucking* Koala. That was the problem.

"But you're not an engineer."

I can do this.

"So what. I know a little bit and I'll bring in Marty to work the board when I have to."

I can't live there. It's Chicago. I'm a New Yorker.

New York doesn't need me anymore. And the New York I need doesn't exist anymore, maybe it never did.

You don't believe that.

"I guess you don't need to record anyone anyway. It's not like the place is being used now."

"I don't even know what I meant by 'run the studio.' I think I just meant I could *be* at the studio. I can see myself there."

I've got to follow my life; this city is a damn prison . . . Besides, I'll never leave the studio anyway. It doesn't matter what city it's in, that's the whole point. I won't be in Chicago or anywhere; I'll just be in The Watershed.

Is that the kind of life you want?

"It'd be nice to have you around."

"*Shit.* I'm sorry! I hadn't even thought about if you were . . ."

My apartment. The Notes. Peter.

Get out! Get out of the apartment.

"It's ok, I wasn't exactly clear . . . I don't even know if I'm going to stay. Who knows if he's still going to ship stuff back here; we didn't talk about it."

I can do it. I'll come back every other weekend. I'll figure something out. I'll save money, I won't fly. I'll make the drive. I'll buy a cheap car, a small one. A hybrid—good gas mileage, no guilt.

"I know you and Tim had a special bond, different than most of the bands he worked with. He really respected you."

He did?!

"You should come out here. I'm glad you want to do this. You really should come."

You can't stay out there. Your son! Once every two weeks is not enough. You have to continue to fight her on this.

This is what the mediator had us agree to. I can't afford more legal fees to keep fighting her, especially with her war-chest. And the courts, unless the mother is a meth addict, they always side with her. Besides, maybe she's right. I can't do anymore than that anyway.

What kind of a person are you?

I have to be realistic.

What does that mean?

I don't know.

• • •

I catch a morning flight on an econo, no-name airline with an absurd two-and-a-half-hour layover in Detroit but the flight was dirt cheap. I debate taking the L from the airport out to The Watershed but decide to spring for a rental car. I've already burned through so much of the BMW money I might as well keep going. For a moment, I think about renting a Beemer for the karmic humor of it but reason gets the better of me and I find myself at the Thrifty counter requesting a subcompact. Driving from O'Hare I keep replaying what Dalia had said about how Tim had really felt a connection with me. Part of me wants badly to believe it, just the idea is triumphant. But when I start to believe it, I feel strange. Until she said so, the possibility never even occurred to me. No matter how tantalizing the thought is, I don't ever want to see Tim as anything less than a hero, let alone an equal. We all need somewhere to go.

I pull the rental to the curb. Walking to the door, the air is heavy. I have to take deep breaths. I don't think I'm nervous; the air simply feels *heavy*. Just before I'm about to ring the bell I see an envelope heavily taped to the door. *Dan* is written on it. I tear it off the door and open it.

Gone to my folks in Wisconsin.
Key's are w/Marty 773-871-2260
More info inside.
– Dalia

I go to a payphone at the gas station down the street and call Marty's. His roommate Jim picks up.

"Marty's in LA, man."

"You're kidding. I was supposed to pick up . . ."

"Dude, I got it. You're Dan, right?"

"Yeah."

"There's an envelope here for you with the keys."

I get lost driving over to Marty's, turning what I had guessed would be a ten-minute drive into a half-hour. When I get there Jim tells me that Dalia had stopped by yesterday looking for Marty. (He had left the week before and wasn't coming back for another month. He had landed a gig assisting some hot producer on a bubblegum pop project at a studio in LA). Standing in the doorway as Jim goes to get the envelope a slight funk of stale beer hangs in the air, a video game is paused on the TV, and the standard US Male Bachelor detritus is littered about—pizza box, plate of bones leftover from an order of wings, Graphix paraphernalia on the table. I spot a gig-bag leaning against the wall.

"What's going on with your band?" I say as he walks toward me with the envelope. "You do solo stuff too, right? You still playing?"

"Yeah, sort of."

"I remember Marty telling me you were thinking of hanging it up; that was a long while back though."

"I'm still sticking it out, trying to figure out what to do next."

"Yeah," I say with a trace of a smile.

"It takes a long time."

"It takes a long time."


I make the return trip to The Watershed, and with the aid of Jim's revised directions—"no, you have to keep going down Ashland . . ."—it takes no more than five minutes.

I get in and walk up the long flight of stairs to the main living area. The heaviness in the air I felt before outside strangely dissipates as I clump up each step. The main room is bright and clean, opaque light filtering in through the frosted double-paned windows. On the dining table is another note from Dalia.


Dan,

Sorry to surprise you like this and not be here. I just couldn't stay another day. I'm a bit of a mess right now and decided this would be a good time to rekindle a damaged relationship with my parents and spend some time there. I might try to start the salvia sales again sometime, maybe even out at my parents—yeah, they would love that—but for now that's that. I can't be in the studio.

So—sorry to leave you alone, or on the other hand, maybe you want the place to yourself for a while anyway. Tim thought you were such a great producer and a kindred soul, he always respected how much you cared about music and really cared about making everything perfect (or at least trying to get there—God, I remember the two of you fighting!). This is a good thing. You belong here more than I do. I know you will do an amazing job with anyone who comes in. And for God's sake, start making some of your own music again.

My contact info is on the bottom. Give me a call when you're settled.
Love, Dalia

P.S. Mr. Bones is with me. It's weird, he doesn't seem the same ever since I got the call, like he can sense it. And sadly, I'm sure he can. Dogs know these things.

I stare at the note. There is dust on the table left over from dried salvia leaves, the faint scent of the plant and their distillery is still in the air. I turn around and absently start walking, my steps feeling mechanical yet soft and slow like after my endoscopy when remnants of twilight anesthetic were still trickling through me.

I come to the stairs and hesitate for a moment, not contemplating or thinking, just blankly pausing, then lightly take the first step.

Downstairs, the front live room is black save for the slivers of light where the edges of the drawn shades don't meet the window frames. Protectively waving my arm in front of me I pass gingerly from the near-dark of the front room into the total darkness and hermetic silence of the carpeted and sound-proofed back room. My footsteps disappear into the carpet and the sound of every breath is present then abruptly snipped, its decay sucked into the void of the thick foam walls like a vacuum on a puff of cigarette smoke. The unearthly lack of echo is like a gated black hole, taking everything, even the ambient noise of air itself. Standing here in this sensorial absence, I have an ephemeral sort of metaphysical crisis, wondering if I am really here. Have I graduated to the next level of dissociative insanity? Not only am I not here, am I no longer even able to watch myself, the other me? Am I not *me*? Perhaps I'm somewhere else, some void of existence, divorced from all of me-s, the *Action* me, the *Watching* me, the *FM* me, from all realities. But no, I must be here. I can still think, and if I can hear my voice in my head then I am here. In fact, the only thing I know to be true is that I am here (and I'm not even certain of the *here* just of the *I*). There is no more Chicago. There is no New York. There is no child. There is no woman. There are no notes. There is nothing. The world is beyond my back now. The noise, the light, the chaos—a distant cacophony, fascinating, even beautiful, yet impotent to harm, like a tiny, dying star in the night sky. In the black silence I feel along the wall, my hand gliding slowly over foam ridges until I find a switch. A dim red light glows in the corner. As my eyes adjust I see all the equipment covered in white sheets, the different drums and speakers and instruments and stands obscured yet still identifiable, soft-focus cartoon versions of themselves like fire hydrants and mailboxes after a giant snowstorm. I walk to the far corner and lift a sheet revealing a Martin acoustic on a stand.

I pick up the guitar.

There are the moments, sweat dripping off my brow, a trickle of blood on my index finger as my arm mechanically, maniacally chugs over and over across the strings, when time and the world and all of you and I don't exist, when I am utterly alone yet divinely connected to everyone and everything. And those small, errant and spectacular moments are like scattered flecks of mica sparkling amid the vast stretching sidewalk that is the timeline of my life.

But: there is more than those moments. So much more. And I need to tell you but I don't know how to tell you—

Shhhh. Slowww down. Breeeeathe slowly. Listen to your heart beat. Listen to your breath. Quiet.

Listen.

I want the words to melt into this page. I want them to unfurl in a single-file line and wrap themselves around you spiraling from toe to head. I want them to soar off the paper and dance in the air and punch you in the face. I want you to please read this slowly because you can see this is just about over. I want you to squeeze the book hard right now, and maybe, just maybe, you can feel what it is I am trying to say. Keep squeezing. Harder. Because I am lonely and I need you. And maybe, just maybe, there is someone who needs this/me.

3636969